THE SEAMSTRESS OF WARSAW

REBECCA MASCULL

First published in 2021 by SpellBound Books

Print ISBN:978-1-8384252-8-9

This book is dedicated to Susie White: inspirational teacher, superlative reader, wonderful mother and dear friend.

ALSO BY REBECCA MASCULL

As Rebecca Mascull:

The Visitors

Song of the Sea Maid

The Wild Air

With Vanessa Lafaye:

Miss Marley

As Mollie Walton:

The Daughters of Ironbridge

The Secrets of Ironbridge

The Orphan of Ironbridge

PRAISE FOR REBECCA MASCULL

"Just loved it! Wonderful and inspiring" – **Jill Mansell on *The Wild Air***

"I loved this book, riveting and compelling" – **Rowan Coleman on *The Wild Air***

"showcase her talent for writing intelligent, impeccably researched, absorbing historical fiction" – **Louise Walters on *Song of the Sea Maid***

"Wonderful stuff...poignant and highly memorable" – **The Bookseller on *The Visitors***

"she writes with the fluency and dexterity of a born writer" – **The Sydney Morning Herald on *The Visitors***

"A fine achievement" – **Culture Street on *The Visitors***

"Movingly told" – **Australian Woman's Weekly on *The Visitors***

"a wonderful, inspiring read...stunningly beautiful...immensely powerful and moving" **LoveReading on *The Visitors***

"Haunting" – **Irish Tatler on *The Visitors***

"Powerful" – **No.1 magazine on *The Visitors***

"an inspiring read" – **The Lady magazine on *Song of the Sea Maid***

I am not yet born; O fill me
    with strength against those who would freeze my
    humanity, would dragoon me into a lethal automaton,
    would make me a cog in a machine, a thing with
    one face, a thing, and against all those
    who would dissipate my entirety, would
    blow me like thistledown hither and
    thither or hither and thither
    like water held in the
    hands would spill me.

Let them not make me a stone and let them not spill me.
Otherwise kill me.

Louis MacNeice
From 'Prayer Before Birth'.

PROLOGUE

FEBRUARY 1920

He said to wear her best dress, the one with the poppies. Whatever could it be for? Perhaps they were going for lunch. That would be a miracle in the midst of these dark days, when he came home from his long walks with empty pockets and the scent of hard drink, without a word or even a smile. But she hoped for the miracle all the same. He waited by the door, shifting from foot to foot.

"Come on! Come on!" he laughed and took her hand. It was the first time he'd laughed in weeks.

They walked arm in arm down their street, slowly, on dense snow. They turned one corner, crossed the road and stopped. There was a shop. In the window, there were photographs of a baby, a young couple and a soldier.

"Darling, I‘ve decided to enlist."

"No," she said. "No!"

"I'm going away tomorrow."

"Don't leavc me," she said.

"Here. I want a photograph of you to take with me."

He opened the shop door to an anteroom. The owner came through and she watched as they made arrangements. Her lover turned his back to her and kissed her cheek, his touch like paper. She was led through to a small studio, shrouded in heavy curtains, a chair centrally placed. The photographer had a kindly face. He asked her to sit down. Her lover stood behind the camera, grinning.

"My Helena is a beauty, isn't she? I want a close-up, just her face. Those eyes. One day, I will write a sonnet about them."

She might be able to stop the tears coming, if she pressed her nails hard into her palms. Harder.

The photographer said, "A little smile, my dear?"

She was thinking of their room, how tiny it was, cluttered and dirty. How vast it would be tomorrow, when he had gone. His stories, his dreams, his plans for them: only now could she see them clearly for what they were. A handful of thistledown.

She heard them talking of the photograph, ready next week. She was to pick it up and pay. With what? Where would she find the money for milk, for bread?

At the door, he hugged her roughly.

"When the Russians are gone, I'll come home to you. And one day, I will write an epic poem about it."

They stepped out and stood a moment in the cold.

He said, "You must send the photograph on to me."

He kissed her. Warm against the icy air. A taste of vodka.

"Where will you be?"

"I don't know yet. As soon as I'm settled, I'll write to you."

They walked on through the snow. The east wind wailed through Warsaw.

CHAPTER ONE
SEPTEMBER 1940

It was a beautiful Saturday, hot sun and pure sky. At three o'clock, Daniel was cycling back from the library when the air-raid siren sounded. Most in the street ignored it. Then came the heavy hum of bombers. He saw a couple of plane spotters on the roof of the nearest building, pointing into the air and blasting on their whistles. The drone became a roar and the air itself trembled.

He heard voices call to each other and the mad barking of dogs. The planes came. Leaping dots of light thickened to black spots. Dark rows filled the sky, flying in straight lines. People in the street were saying, are they British? No, they're German, someone said. Our boys fly in Vs. How did they get through, some asked? What's happened to the RAF, the ack-ack guns? People were shaking their fists at them, one man brandished a penknife. People were just standing and staring, hardly anyone was running. There were over a hundred planes.

Bombs began to fall. Daniel actually saw them drop. People ran and scrambled for cover, behind or beneath or beside anything they could find – a milk cart, a doorway, a policeman - more for comfort than safety. Daniel threw his bike against a wall and bolted to a shelter, filled with men and women and kids and the hot, rank smell of sweat and panic. The children whimpered and wept and everyone flinched at the explosions and clanging fire bells. Once the walls shook, the children screamed and Daniel saw huge black spiders crawl out of the cracks. People talked about the terror of the shelter getting bombed and of being buried alive. One man said, "If I get it, I hope I cop a nice clean hit and go out like a light." This made the children cry more and the mothers scolded him. A man appeared at the door and sat down. He wiped his brow and covered his face with shaking hands. A woman tried to soothe him, others ignored him, turned away even, as if he would infect them with fear. He spoke: "This is it! No more Phoney War! The big attack. They're saying it'll be every night from now on." The mothers shushed him. A girl cried and two boys whispered. They were in there for two hours. Silently Daniel swore he'd never to go into a shelter again.

When the All Clear sounded, it was curious how quickly they all returned to normal. Filing out of the shelter, some argued about politics and some about what was for tea. In the street, there were masses of people going to and fro. It felt hot to breathe. Daniel's nose filled with the tang of cordite. The streets were a mess of soot, brick and broken glass. The sky was tinged with red, with billowing smoke blotting out the sun. The air was alive with sparks and everyone patted them out on their clothes. There were families with cars loading up offspring and bags and driving off at speed, and people were saying, "The docks are on fire!" One man said, "Why did the poor have to get it in the neck? Why didn't they bomb bloody Mayfair?" Daniel watched young people running about to see the fires, rushing towards the docks. He found his bike and dashed down there. A terrible inferno – the great dock warehouses consumed by flames flaring high in the sky, furious black and orange. Dozens of firemen were working their legs off.

Finally, he thought of home. He raced back to see if Dad and Magda were all right. He left his bike at the front and pelted up the communal staircase. Doors were open. Neighbours on the landing were swapping stories.

"Daniel!" called old Mr Cardew. "Your father! He's been desperately worried!"

Dad was at the door and said, "Thank Heavens you're safe!"

Magda was putting her coat on. "They're coming again tonight!"

"How do you know that?"

His father said, "They said on the wireless they've bombed the docks to use as a beacon at night, to guide them in for another raid."

"I'm not going back to any stinking shelter."

Dad paused then said, "Me neither!"

Magda threw her hands up and said, "You two are the crazy men!" in her funny Polish way. "You, Mr Summerskill should know better. And you Daniel, I didn't nurse you as babe in my arms to be bombed on the head!"

"Listen, my dear," said Dad. "It seems London is due for many a night of bombing. Most of those street shelters were simply not built for long raids, some without lavatories or water or even seating. And they're probably unable to withstand nearby bomb blasts. I can't imagine anything forcing me to leave the comfort of our home and go down to one of those filthy dugouts."

"Then go to church," said Magda. "God will protect you."

Daniel laughed, "What's the point of that? Tons of stone to crush you and a great big spire sticking up into the sky just begging to be bombed."

Magda crossed herself and said, "You are a wicked young man!"

So she could not persuade them. She left shaking her head. Daniel knew she would go down to the shelter with a bunch of local Poles and have a fine time.

Daniel and his father sat in the flat and got the chess board out. They had bread and cheese with Magda's chutney. Dad had a little whiskey. About seven o'clock the sirens sounded again and they looked at each other, then carried on their game. The ack-ack guns were doing nothing – why had they been so useless? After an hour, they couldn't bear being cooped up any longer and went up the stairs to the roof of their building. They gazed out over London towards the docks. Fires upon fires upon fires. Searchlights criss-crossed the dark skies to the north, but a heavy layer of smoke had settled over the Thames to the south and the lights couldn't get past it. Crowded layers of noise: the crackling and roaring of flames, the crash of falling masonry, the screams of women and children, the shouts of firemen and wardens, a few voices singing to ease the panic. "My Eyes are Dim, I Cannot See", someone sang out.

They went back inside and sat out the night. They tried to sleep, Daniel on the leather chesterfield, Dad in his armchair. But they couldn't manage it. At first they talked of harmless things. Chess moves and cricket. He realised he hadn't spent this much time with his father for ages, years probably. Despite the bombing, it was a nice night in that way. Once, an explosion came quite near and the window frames rattled like billy-o.

After an hour or so, Dad asked, "You're still set on the RAF then?"

"Yes."

"Almost a year till you're eighteen. They might not take you even then. Eighteen is… still very young."

"I'd enlist tomorrow if I could."3‹

To be a pilot. To be in the Royal Air Force. To dwell in the air.

To escape this earthbound life. Last month, he had gone down to Dover with Jim Mackay to watch the dog fights. The *Chronicle* had an editorial team at the Grand Hotel day and night waiting for air battles. The editor told Jim to "take the lad down there and see what's what in the Channel." Jim was an old hand, louche in his crumpled grey suit, speaking little to Daniel on the train. The only advice he gave, "Write sideways on your jotter, not lengthwise," though he didn't explain why. In the hotel foyer, a man shouted, "Here they come!" and they all ran up to the roof. The sky, was a perfect cornflower blue and scored by bright vapour trails. Daniel watched a Spitfire chasing a Messerschmitt 109, spotting the flare of machine-guns. He saw the Spitfire take a twist past the German fighter and shoot the bastard down in flames, its white trail turn black as it plunged into the Channel. Everybody cheered. Jim shook his hand and said, "The fate of civilization is being decided fifteen thousand feet above our heads, laddie!"

Daniel and his father listened to the raid, more distant now.

Dad went on, "You should be glad you're in the newspaper business. A journalist in wartime, now that's a marvellous thing to be. A war correspondent is a brave and necessary job and if you stick at it, it could take you far. A warco can be given a foreign assignment one minute and, within a day, be literally thousands of miles away. If you want adventure, you should stick with it at the *Chronicle*. Within a year or two, I'm sure they'll give you your apprenticeship. You'd be an invaluable foreign correspondent, with your talent for languages."

Daniel had Magda to thank for raising him in English and Polish. From his earliest memories, she had spoken both languages to him, side by side, strange cousins. When he was a little boy, Dad would perform an English song for him from time to time, about black sheep, curds and whey, a mulberry bush. Yet Magda would only sing in Polish, curious nursery rhymes about a magpie making porridge; a wooden boy and a waxen girl; an old hag in a house made of butter; a train to Warsaw that came from far away and never stopped. Daniel wanted to ride that train. There was a lullaby he still hummed to himself at night sometimes, about two grey-brown kittens, and the moon yawning, and Magda would promise to give him a star from the sky. Her round face looking down tenderly upon him as he lay in bed one December night long ago, telling him that Saint Nicholas would bring him a biscuit if he were a good boy, a sharp slap if not.

Dad had also taught him French and German, and even a little Russian. He had been schooled at home. A lot of writing, reading and thinking. The odd cricket match in the park. Little chance of making friends, though Dad's colleagues sometimes brought their sons to talk to, kick about a ball and compare collections with. There was a lot of history, geography, politics and just about every war through the ages. Novels and poems, a little maths and science. A look through the newspapers every breakfast time: this man is called… he is the prime minister of … we don't like him because... There were daily lessons in the morning, then he wouldn't see Dad till bedtime. He was shut up in his study. Tall people came and went, mostly lean men, smokers. Papers in their pockets and pretty ladies on their arms. Famous people too, Magda said. A man called Auden. A woman called Woolf. Laughing in Dad's room, the whiff of whisky. Journalists, writers, there till dawn on occasion. Magda would tut and mutter disapproval in Polish. Daniel would shake his head. But he badly wanted to be behind that closed door.

He did want to be a journalist like his father. But not until after the war, after he'd served his country - in the skies or on the sea or the field of battle - not with a pen. He was seventeen years old and sick of waiting. When would the editor make him a cub reporter? And what if the war didn't last that long?

"Oh, it will," Dad said, and he looked very old and tired and wiped his face with his handkerchief.

Daniel asked, "If being a foreign correspondent is so marvellous, why'd you give it up all those years ago? Why set up your own literary journal, stuck at home, when you could have been back in Russia or Poland? It can't have been that great a life, if you gave it up."

"I had you. And you know how sick your mother was. What kind of father would I have been to have gone off gallivanting around the world? As wonderful as Magda is, she is not your mother. And I never would have left you. Without family."

Daniel stared at the floor. They sat quietly for a time.

"Dad. Tell me about Mum."

He cleared his throat. "What is it you want to know?"

"Anything really. I don't remember her."

"I know…I know. Well, let me see. She was beautiful. And very talented. A marvellous pianist. Didn't quite have the nerve for it though, performing, I mean. So she taught pupils. Enjoyed that, I think."

"I know all that. What about me? I mean, what was she like with me?"

"We named you after her father. And you had her smile."

"For God's sake, Dad! I know all that. I want to imagine her, as a real person, how she felt about things, how she felt about me."

Dad stood up and went to the window.

"It was a very difficult time. Your mother was ill. She had a… she was a nervous person. Not very good with babies. But she loved you. She did her best, but babies are hard work. Then she became really ill. The influenza. Terrible. You were less than a year old. And Magda was always very good at it all, babies, you know. And Magda adored you. Always adored you. You two were as thick as thieves. You would scream your head off when Magda put you down. Your mother died soon after. I'm sorry, Daniel." There were other questions to answer, but Daniel was drained. It was nearly dawn. The All Clear came. Magda returned soon after, her face grimy, her eyes white. When she saw they were all right, she took hold of Daniel and hugged him. She took her employer's hand and held it between her own.

"You two give me weak heart being brave."

But Dad said, "Not bravery, my dear, just snobbery."

Magda scrubbed her face and immediately set to making breakfast. Toast and plum jam. Daniel took his up to the roof and gaped at the view. A new world had been created overnight. Buildings he had seen hours before were gone, completely gone, transformed into a heap of smoking rubble. He watched London wake up and stretch. ARP men strode along and shouted out, "Anybody hurt?" Crowds of scarecrows dragged themselves home from shelters, past ruins of buildings with belongings spread out across the road, the docks still glowing beyond. Children ran around brandishing shrapnel and larking about in the thin sunshine. The children of London - those who were never evacuated or had returned soon enough – had a new appearance, feral, grubby and vital. A bunch of ATS girls were helping old people and mothers with babies along the streets. One fellow loped along, his face all black with smoke, patting people on the back as he passed them. Daniel heard him say in a cheerful shout, "We won't let the Nasties get us down, will we, eh!"

Daniel decided he couldn't stay at home. He had to get out there and see it all. He was off out to have a nose around, he told Dad, who said to take his notebook. "Write what you see. The boss might print it!"

Magda said, "Stay away from buildings falling over."

He grabbed his bike and left Tavistock Square, pedalled through Bloomsbury, down towards the river. He had to negotiate hosepipes, dozens of them strewn across every road, with firemen still fighting flames. Other streets were roped off. There were houses further on which had simply been demolished by the bombs, the insides scattered everywhere. There was the smell of scorched beams and drenched plaster. People were sitting on bundles and WVS women were bringing them cups of tea from a mobile canteen and trying to console them. Daniel saw an old man weeping and weeping, a dog staring up at him, its tail giving a half-hearted thump every now and again. He got off his bike and was pushing it over to talk to the man but a Warden stopped him and said, "You'd better not, lad, just let him cry." Apparently, he had popped out for tobacco and got caught in a raid, and when he came back his house was destroyed with his wife in it.

He cycled on, passing women pushing prams along the pavement. It was curious to see all those babies together, but he saw the prams were filled with belongings and heard a woman complaining to nobody in particular that the gas main and the water main had been hit and nobody could even make a cup of tea, and "When is the ruddy van coming anyway?" she said, as she squelched along. Her shoes were wet through from the water in the streets from fire hoses. He stopped and told her there was one just around the corner and she hurried off. A cup of hot tea was very important.

Further along, fire engines were parked next to a vast smoking building which looked as if it had just about been put out, and the firemen were lying outside all over the place, in the gutter and on the bonnets of cars and vans. He thought they were dead, until he saw they were just dead tired. They must have been fighting the fires all night and only now could grab a few minutes' kip. He'd never seen such abandoned sleep. And there they slept, fully dressed in their tin helmets and oilskins, lying in the street, with people stepping round them and everyone talking and the noise of traffic nearby and the smoking building still creaking, and those exhausted firemen spread out fast asleep, sleeping the sleep of the dead. And to think that only last month, the papers had been complaining about what a dreadful waste of public money the AFS was and how they were earning money for nothing. Look at them now, he thought. They were magnificent.

Daniel went around the corner and stopped.

There was a corpse, amidst the ruins of an ARP post. He couldn't see the face, there was ash and dirt covering it, but could see its right leg bent unnaturally, and the hands resting by its sides. A man. An ARP warden – there was the familiar insignia on a sleeve and a helmet lay upside down inches from his head. Daniel couldn't move. He just stood there, and stared and stared. He knew the man was dead. It was the stiff leg. He knew nothing alive could be that crooked.

Another ARP man walked past.

Daniel said, "I'm awfully sorry."

"What for, son?" he said, and Daniel pointed to the dead man. "Oh, right," he said grimly. "You'd better move along. Not something you want to see." And Daniel felt ghoulish for having stood there and stared, not even tried to help. But what could he do? A man lay dead in a pile of rubble and all he'd done was stare. He hated himself. He hated himself for being there and seeing a man twisted and dead like that. He hated the boy inside, the one he'd still been until that morning, the boy who'd raced around looking for dogfights to watch and pilots to worship. He hated himself for only being seventeen and not being a pilot, up there in the blue skies away from all this grey death.

On Monday morning Daniel left early. He waited outside the Drill Hall until the door opened. Inside, there was a series of booths, with various doctors who asked questions. He lied about his age without blushing. He was ushered on to have physical examinations. One doctor asked about any childhood conditions. A bit of asthma as a little boy, but not had an attack since he was ten. The doctor made a face. He was sent over to another doctor who did rigorous breathing tests. Then a booth where a man told him: "You will not be needed at present," and gave him a form which read, *Grade – III (three)*. He had tried to enlist and failed his medical.

He arrived late at work. He told them he'd had a doctor's appointment. The water was off and he was told to fetch buckets from a standpipe around the corner. Another stupid errand. On the way he saw a pile of dead pigeons in the gutter, all bloody around their mouths. A man in the street said that the poor devils pick up fine glass thinking it's food and this makes them bleed inside. He stared at the dead birds. Nothing he could do. He took the water back and the boss told him to get over to Elephant and Castle and deliver papers to an office. He tried without luck to hitch a lift and the bus he needed wasn't running. He had to take the blasted Tube.

The Underground had become a cess pit. It was only ever supposed to be the old and sick who were to shelter there, but hundreds of families camped out all day and night. It was a city beneath the city, but without space and sanitation. It stank down there. People like sardines, packed top-to-toe along the passages and platforms surrounded by all their kit and caboodle. Travellers had to step over them. As Daniel did, he brushed against so many he swore he could feel himself catch scabies. It took him a quarter of an hour to get from the platform to the station entrance. People were eating dinners wrapped in greasy paper, some were singing, some even playing chess. He saw babies plonked in carpet bags, a cat sleeping in a lap and dogs clambering about amongst the rubbish. Ragged little children were ranging around in laughing packs, begging ha'pennies to buy chocolate bars from the machines, or queuing up to weigh themselves. And when he returned to ride the train back to the office, he saw these same children jumping on the train and pointing at all the people at the different stations in between, as if it were all a fairground ride. The Tube had become a lawless place. Daniel had even heard that people had sex down there, though he hadn't managed to see this himself.

That night he went home in a blue funk. Dad was in his study, rifling through old paperwork from dusty boxes. He didn't notice his son come in.

"All right, Dad?"

His father pushed things aside and looked up strangely, his head tilted, as if distracted by a distant sound. He had done that a lot lately. In his sixties, after all. Not getting any younger. Daniel considered telling him about his failure. But suspected Dad would crow about it.

He found Magda in the kitchen putting on her coat and hat. She was always out lately. She did keep up all her usual domestic responsibilities and worked marvels with their food rations. But most evenings she was busy and rather secretive about what she was up to. When asked, she would say, "Out with the Poles".

She looked up.

"What is wrong? Ill?"

"Nothing."

"Something to tell me?"

"I tried to enlist."

"Oh, I know this."

"How?"

"I followed you."

"What?"

"You put your best suit on and left early. Not likely a girl that time of morning. Probably join army. I wanted see for myself."

"Magda, you're terrible."

"They say yes?"

"No. Childhood asthma."

"Why you tell them that?"

"I didn't think. I'm a fool."

"Yes, a fool." She placed her hands on his cheeks and smiled. "A safe one."

"Don't look so pleased."

She pulled on her gloves. "Come out with me, Daniel. I think pilot coming tonight."

Daniel had wanted to meet a Polish pilot. He knew she was acquainted with some, that she met them at the Polish club. He had asked her and asked her. He was desperate to talk to them. Feel closer to the RAF, to the war. Maybe the Poles in London would make a good story for the paper. If he did a super write-up and presented it to the Editor, maybe he'd get a proper job.

"What, really?"

"Yes, yes. Lovely young man, my good old friend's son back in Poland. He escape last year, at beginning. He in RAF now. Come and meet him. Cheer you up."

The meeting was going to be an informal affair, Magda told him. Just a few friends, tea and biscuits in a church hall nearby. They set out at six-thirty and on the way she said in Polish, "Let's speak no more English tonight. You are an honorary Pole now, my boy!"

and kissed him on the cheek. There were dozens of people there in loud and laughing knots. The lively hubbub of the Polish language bubbled. It was a thrill to hear it. Daniel worried that his Polish wouldn't be up to scratch, even though he'd spoken it all his life. Perhaps real Poles wouldn't humour him like Magda did. He might sound a half-wit.

They were served tea in chipped cups with mismatched saucers, then she spotted the pilot. A dark man in his late twenties dressed in RAF uniform with a Polish flash on his arm, gulping down tea and talking to an attractive blonde woman. When the pilot saw Magda, he stood up and threw his arms around her, kissing her on both cheeks. They all spoke in Polish. The man said, "This is my substitute mother, old Magda here. My English-Polish mother!"

"This is Daniel Summerskill, the son of my employer," she said, and the man gave her another hug, saying quietly to Daniel, "And I understand she is the same for you? Your Polish-English mother!" She laughed and told him to sit down and behave himself. The blonde woman gave a guarded smile and left.

"So Daniel, this is my good friend, Tomasz Dabrowski, a Polish pilot of some renown, who the Great British Royal Air Force has allowed to wear its precious uniform!"

The pilot shook his hand and said, "It is a pleasure to meet you, Daniel. Magda never stops talking of you. She is very proud of your job as a reporter."

"Oh, not yet. I'm not a proper journalist. I was only doing it until I get called-up." A wave of hot shame recalled that morning's humiliation. He knew he could not bear to tell this pilot the truth of his failure. He wondered if Magda would.

She said, "I have people to see." And gave Tomasz a pointed stare. "Look after my boy."

Daniel watched her go and thought about what he might say

next. Think in Polish. What did he want to know from this man, this Pole in exile, this pilot in the RAF?

"Was that blonde your girlfriend?"

Tomasz guffawed and shook his head. "No, no. We were getting to know each other."

"I'm sorry I interrupted you."

Tomasz shook his head, took from his inside pocket a silver flask and sloshed something into his tea, and then Daniel's.

"I'll see the blonde later," he grinned and downed his drink. Daniel tried his. It still tasted of stewed tea, but with an extra heat behind it.

Daniel told himself, think like a journalist. He asked, "How did you escape from Poland?"

Tomasz refilled his cup, this time with neat vodka, splashed into Daniel's again too. "After the fall of Warsaw, I went on foot with other pilots to Romania and we eventually got to France. We all stayed there for a time, under the useless command of the French army. We were kept grounded. Then our leader Sikorski flew to London and, if you remember, met with Churchill in June this year. And the very next day Sikorski gave notice over the BBC that Polish forces should not surrender but make their way to ports in the south of France, where British and Polish ships would pick them up. Did you know, the French even sabotaged Polish aircraft?"

"Well, the French are spineless, aren't they?"

"Not at all! Nothing is that simple, Daniel. It's easy to paint a whole nation one colour. French, English, Polish. When we got here, we were shocked how little you knew about us. Most of the English think that Poland is at least a hundred years behind England. Do you have trams in Poland? Do you have cinemas? But I realised we knew very little of your country. We had of course heard of Shakespeare, and Sherlock Holmes, and the London fog. We thought all Englishmen were like cold fish and English girls were ugly."

Daniel glanced around the room at several good-looking Polish women. He wondered how they compared.

Tomasz added: "And on this last point in particular, I have been delightfully mistaken!" He grabbed his arm. "Listen, Daniel. Let's get out of here. I know a great pub for meeting girls. Are you with me?"

"But Magda..." he said, half-heartedly.

"Oh, she'll understand. A young man like you, not made for drinking tea, eh!"

They left quickly. No time to tell Magda.

Once outside, Daniel tripped over a sandbag.

"Watch out!" laughed Tomasz. "Is it the drink or the blackout?"

Daniel pulled his torch from his pocket and used it to guide their way. He thought how the blackout made you more aware of moonlight, the romance of it. But also the ideal setting for trouble. Accidents and crime. He said, "You know villains have been making money selling dud batteries for torches?"

"War brings out the bastards."

They reached the Wheatsheaf in Rathbone Place. As they went in, Tomasz said, "Poets come to this pub. Look." At each of the tables sat a couple of foppish types wearing flamboyant neck-ties and romantic hairdos, surrounded by a weird bunch of brown-nosers all poring over poetry books they had splayed out on the wet tables. The women were very pretty.

"The so-called artists," Tomasz scoffed, as they pushed their way to the bar. "Writing little verses for the war effort. Not like you, Daniel. A writer but a fighter too, eh, one day?"

Daniel said, "Their girls are lovely."

"Ah, we can get better than that. I'm a pilot and I'm a Pole. English girls love me!"

Tomasz was shouting in Polish now and a few local blokes were watching, knocking back pints like water. Tomasz handed Daniel a beer.

"And the English men hate me!" he added, pointing and laughing.

"That's not true. Is it?"

"Where do I begin? Even the RAF doesn't trust us. Like the French, they think we gave in to the Nazis. They really believe that Polish airmen aren't skilful, or that we'd lost our nerve with the Luftwaffe. They had no idea how hard we fought those German bastards. Did you know that weeks after the invasion of Warsaw, Polish pilots were still attacking German ground troops with hand grenades thrown from their cockpits?"

"I didn't know that." He felt he did not know anything and took a long draught of his beer.

"You and most of England. Our problems in Poland had been a lack of modern aircraft. I tell you, I couldn't wait to get my hands on a Spitfire or at least a Hawker Hurricane. Did you know that most Polish airmen have been flying at air clubs since we were youngsters, and many of us are proud graduates of Deblin, one of the most difficult and demanding air force training academies in the world? In fact, Sikorski wanted us Poles in separate units within the RAF under Polish command, but the British refused. To begin with, the RAF wanted to assign us to Bomber Command, not allowing us to be fighter pilots at all, even though that's what we were trained for. The CO said we should stop going on about the 'Jerries' and being damned egotistical, show some decent British team spirit and learn better English. The sods just wouldn't let us in the air. Even when the Germans started bombing sector stations, they still kept us grounded. Only once they were desperate did they let us fly. We were so frustrated, so angry, so worried about all our family and friends trapped back home."

"What's happened to your family? Do you know?"

"My parents and my sister moved from Warsaw just before the invasion. They went to live in the south with my mother's sister and her husband's relations. Most of them work the land. I can only hope a few Polish farmers living in the middle of nowhere don't interest the Nazis."

"My father and I listen to the news several times a day. There's never anything about Poland."

Tomasz looked down. "Poland has become the black heart of the Nazi hell. All news we receive is bad news."

What had Magda told Daniel of Poland? As a boy, he'd asked her, "Why did you come to England? Why did you leave Poland?"

"To meet you," she had said and never explained further. She spoke of Poland now and again, a country of ancient forests and beautiful cities, haunting songs and comforting food. A proud country, often invaded, never beaten.

"You must miss it terribly, Poland."

"Yes, yes. But there are worse places to be than here, eh? Wonderful London, the girls, the nightlife, the dreadful beer! And to fly, with your comrades. To shoot down those fucking Germans. Avenge Poland, our friends and families."

Tomasz's eyes flared, his fist on the bar.

Daniel asked, "Do you ever feel fear when you're flying, when you're in battle?"

"Sometimes I do. The first time I engaged the Germans, back in Poland, I did taste fear. It's sour and metallic at the same time, and you can't make it go away, and your arse tingles. But you're too busy concentrating on your equipment and your controls. There's no time to be afraid. And I hate the enemy. Hate is stronger than fear. And we Poles really hate the Germans, you know. We *hate* them."

Daniel ached to be a pilot. And now something else. He ached to be Polish.

"What is it like to kill a German?"

Tomasz frowned and finished his pint, grimaced. They got

more beers in, then Tomasz went on, "You are just a boy, Daniel. You don't know the world. You don't know yourself. I'll forgive you for asking me that question. What you need to know is that it is wonderful to be alive. But it is not wonderful to kill. To risk your own life. Watch a friend die, burn to death in a plane below you, and you can do nothing, nothing. See a Nazi floating down from his ruined plane, holding on to his parachute straps, and though it's against every rule, picking that man off, seeing his face turn inside out from gunfire. Not very wonderful."

Daniel's face was hot, his hands sticky. "Sorry. I've offended you."

Someone tapped him on the back. It was Bobby Cardew, a cub reporter from the *Chronicle*. His uncle lived in Daniel's building, a retired civil servant from the Home Office who was matey with Daniel's boss, and got his nephew the job. Only two years older and already writing copy for the paper.

"What's this then, Danny?" he said. "A Pole out and about in Fitzrovia?"

"Good evening," said Tomasz in English, unsmiling.

Daniel had seen Cardew around at work, forever smoothing back his oiled yellow hair. Watched him chat up the prettiest typist who often came to sit on his desk. Heard him call the older lads out for a drink after work. Wondered when he would be one of them. "Robert Cardew of the *News Chronicle*, this is Tomasz Dabrowski. As you can see, an RAF pilot."

"Jolly nice to meet you, sir," said Bobby and shook hands. "Marvellous what you Polish boys are doing for our chaps. Really marvellous. Danny here has kept you quiet. But then, Danny here doesn't say anything to anyone, do you, Danny boy? Why didn't you tell us you had the toast of London as a drinking buddy, eh, Danny? A real life Polish pilot. Want to get pissed?"

Tomasz glanced at Daniel. "Actually, *old chap*, Daniel is doing talk with me for newspaper. Front page, I think, Daniel?"

Cardew threw his head back and laughed. "This one, writing

for the front page? He's having a joke with you, I'm afraid. This one makes a good cup of tea, that's about it."

Tomasz put his beer glass down on the bar and took a step forwards. He was taller than Cardew. "My English is no good, but I'm not idiot. Daniel is a good kid. And you are a shit who talks too much. Pissing away war writing silly stories. Where is your uniform? Why not fighting for England?"

Cardew's broad cheeks were flushed dark pink. His bow tie seemed to strangle him. "Now, steady on, my friend."

"Perhaps we should go," said Daniel to Tomasz. "Sorry, Cardew."

"What?" shouted Tomasz in Polish. "Why are you apologising to this arsehole?" His voice boomed, Polish anger streaming across the English room.

A voice in the bar yelled, "Bloody Poles!"

A fist thumped into Tomasz's cheek. A man grabbed Daniel and tried to punch him in the face, but knocked a girl standing beside him. He heard Tomasz's reckless laugh, blood on his forehead, people hitting each other everywhere. He still had hold of his pint glass and a bloke grabbed it and he wouldn't let go and the next thing someone kicked his legs and down he went. He really ought to stand up. There was a wallop on his ear and he was gone.

He came to in the street. Tomasz was sitting beside him, shaking him and sniggering and swearing in Polish.

"Daniel, wake up, wake up. Magda will kill me if you're dead."

"I'm not dead," he said. Tomasz hauled him up, using his cuff to wipe the blood from Daniel's face.

"You're a mess but you'll live. I'd better get you home."

When they reached the flat, Daniel invited Tomasz up.

"No, no. Magda will beat me and I deserve it."

Daniel watched him go and he turned one last time and waved a hand, shouting, "I'm off to find that blonde!" He stood very straight, raised his right arm and touched his index and middle fingers to his forehead. A Polish military salute, but it made him look like a boy scout. He staggered off down the street.

Daniel made it up the stairs, slowly. The key in the lock was a puzzle. He lurched across the hall. Magda was there to catch him.

"Where's Dad?" he blurted.

"Ssh! Asleep in his chair. Lucky for you."

She got him into the bathroom and closed the door, producing cotton wool and Dettol.

"Tomasz is a very bad boy," she muttered in Polish.

"He's marvellous," Daniel replied in kind.

Magda gave him a scolding look, which soon dissolved. "Yes, he's marvellous. And so are you, my boy. Did you have a good night with your Pole?"

"Oh, Magda," he sighed, as she patched him up. They were both talking in Polish now, as if it were the most natural thing in the world. "I can't explain it. There's something strange about it all. The best moment tonight was when someone in the fight shouted, 'Bloody Poles!' and I thought to myself, they think I'm Polish! And I was proud! I was happy to be Polish! How ridiculous it is. How stupid."

She stopped. "I don't think it is stupid."

He was gazing at the white tiles on the bathroom wall, sketching a picture-book Poland of woodland and mountains.

"I would love to go to Poland one day."

"Would you? Why is that? Why do you think that is?"

He thought about it. "Well, speaking Polish since I was little. Being with you, always, as long as I can remember. Your Polish lullaby."

"You know, Daniel. Deep inside. You know something."

"What?" When he looked at her, he saw her eyes were glistening.

"Are you blotto, Magda?" He was still drunk himself and thought this a great joke. She turned away and tidied up, sniffing.

"I'm sorry. Do you miss Poland, is that it?" She shook her head, wiped her eyes and ushered him onto the landing.

He felt coldly awake. "What on earth is it?"

She answered in English. "You are very drunk, Daniel. And you are making up things in your head. Go to bed now. Tomorrow, you will forget all of this."

The air-raid siren sounded. Dad came out onto the landing, blinking away sleep. He saw his son's face.

"What the hell's going on here?"

Magda grabbed Daniel's winter coat from the peg and her own. "Just a bit of drink and silliness."

"Drink? And who beat him up, one of your beloved Poles?"

"No, Dad!"

"Come, Mr Summerskill. We must go to the shelter. All tonight. All of us. Come on."

"He's in no fit state to go anywhere. And we're not going down to that death-trap."

Magda's colour was up. She stopped herself, clasped her hands and stared her employer in the face. She chose her English words with care. "I am sorry, Mr Summerskill, but I put my foot down this time. If not for you, think of your son. Think of Daniel. Keep him safe. Your son, Mr Summerskill."

"I will decide what's best for my son, thank you, Magda. He was under your care tonight, and look what happened to him."

They went into the sitting room. Daniel heard the front door slam. He peered behind the blackout curtain and saw three bombers perfectly silhouetted against the silver mass of a barrage balloon. A second after they had passed, the balloon exploded, a monstrous cigar ablaze, and dropped from view.

"Bloody hell! They're close."

A kind of heat in the air, a kind of secret. The clamour of planes was closing in on them. Louder, louder.

A colossal crash came very close and the whole building shuddered.

Dad yelled, "Get under my desk!" and thrust his son through to the study.

Another crash, another. He scrambled into the desk's kneehole.

"Come under here!"

"Not enough room." His father was crouching under the dining table in the sitting room. They listened to the explosions, far away – crump crump – then close, too close. The building shook again. A new sound – plink plink plink on the roof – incendiaries. Then silence.

Dad said, "I should've sent you to the shelter. I've been a damn fool."

He could see his father through the open door. He looked very small. Daniel got up and ran to him.

"Get back in there!" He pushed Daniel away. "Do as I say! Now!"

He relented and went back under the desk, shoved in all knees and elbows in the tiny space.

Dad shouted something to him.

"What?"

"Son, listen to me."

A terrible gust ripped through the flat. Daniel felt an almighty force lift him from the floor and drop him down again. When he opened his eyes, all the lights had gone out. He felt the desk was on its side behind him. He looked into the other room, draped in silver light. He saw the dining table was gone and the floor strewn with glass and rubble. The windows were blown to pieces and there was a gaping hole in the wall. Dad was lying on the floor on the other side of the sitting room, his legs covered in lumps of wall, shreds of wallpaper still clinging to them. He was awake, his eyes screwed tight shut. He was spitting dust.

"Are you all right?" He lunged over to him. "Dad, are you all right?"

He opened his eyes but did not speak.

"I'm off to get First Aid."

But his father muttered, "No. Raid still on. Too dangerous."

He fetched blankets to put over Dad and wrap round himself.

"Daniel?" His voice was so small. Daniel looked down at him. Was it only the Bomber's Moon that made his face so white?

"I'm going to get help." He jumped up.

"Daniel, Daniel." Dad lifted his hand and beckoned his son closer. He leaned down and held his hand. He was frightened that Dad knew these were going to be his last words.

"Daniel, before it's too late. I have to tell you. I loved you. I do love you."

"I love you too, Dad."

"You have to know something. Listen to me. I adopted you. I found you in an orphanage in Poland. In Warsaw. You were a baby. I took you home. I don't know who your real parents are. But you are my son. You are my son, Daniel and I love you." He squeezed his son's hand. "I'm sorry, so sorry." He closed his eyes. His face changed. He was dead. Daniel knew that. He was dead.

Daniel drew the blanket over Dad's face. He sat beside him for hours. The raid came and went in waves. Never so close again, but near enough to make him recoil at times. He never once looked down at the body. Quiet crept in stealthily. The moonlight caught sharp edges across the ruins of his home.

When he heard the All Clear, he found his torch and used it to negotiate the stairs. There wasn't a soul around. They must all be in the shelters. He went out into Tavistock Square. Theirs was one of the few houses still intact. One side of the square had been flattened. Fierce heat billowed from the burning houses. He stumbled across debris, then saw a little boy appear, all alone, his hair sticking up a hundred ways. He was rifling through the rubble and holding on to a large chunk of metal. He saw Daniel and said, "Look! A bit of an oil-bomb!"

Daniel spotted two ARP men on the far side of the square and ran over to them.

"What is it?" one said.

He could not speak. They followed him. Three torch beams bobbed up the staircase. When they got in there, he showed them the body. One of them peeled back the blanket. A torch lit up Dad's face. Daniel looked away. He said, "I know he's dead."

One warden patted him on the back. "I'll go get a van."

The other ARP man placed his torch on a shelf, illuminating his notepad and pen.

"What's your name, son?"

Daniel thought about this.

"You in shock?" the ARP man said gently. "What's your name, eh?"

"Daniel Summerskill."

The man wrote it down. "And your Dad. It is your Dad, isn't it?"

Daniel sat on the floor with the body for a long time. Someone touched his hair. He looked up and saw Magda's face, round and pale.

CHAPTER TWO

I have not written like this for years. But now I must. Today we learned it is true. The walls that have been going up are indeed the boundaries of a ghetto. Of course, the Germans are not calling it that. It is to be known as the Jewish Quarter. But we know what this means. There have been rumours over the past weeks, when walls appeared closing off streets in the Old Town, on Marszalkowska St., at Sienna, Swietokrzyska and Prozna, and Dluga St. People have been asking themselves, "What are they for?" Notices went up at the entrances of streets saying they were infected by typhus. Many of these streets had suffered bad damage during the German bombardments. Then a couple of days ago Isak brought home that German newspaper they write in Polish and it explained about this new Jewish area, saying here we could enjoy our own freedom and practices. It is to be walled, it is said, to prevent the spread of Jewish diseases. And what exactly are Jewish diseases, may I ask?

Isak predicts chaos, as of course Jews are scattered all over the city. Some will be lucky and find themselves already inside the ghetto margins. But no walls have been built near to our apartment. As yet, we have not been informed of the exact limits of the ghetto. I think we ought to start looking for a new place soon, perhaps near to where the walls are, as I suspect these boundaries will not change.

Over the past couple of days, everyone has been talking of nothing else but the ghetto. Pan Wilner reminded us that the creation of a ghetto in itself does not necessarily mean a threat. After all, ghettos have existed before in Europe. They are nothing new in history. He also says there is a kind of comfort in it, as we will be surrounded only by Jews. You can be yourself. Better to be in the ghetto than have to deal with Polish Jew-haters. Pani Lewartow agreed, saying "As long as that lot can't come in." Being in a ghetto, at least you don't have to deal with the embarrassment of walking down the road with your armband on, surrounded by your fellow Poles without them. I know Jews who are so frightened of walking in the streets of Warsaw now, that they have made a prison of their own home. It is not only the shame. Since the Germans arrived, Jews get attacked or spat at in the street by Aryan Poles. This is a daily occurrence. Of course, there was Jew-hating before the war, but the German control has meant that all this is now actively encouraged.

We could have escaped perhaps, back in '39. But many tried and did not manage it. A few days after the Germans invaded, Josef, Chaim and Ryszard all left on a coal wagon heading east, leaving their wives and children behind. They were agreed that within two or three days they would be conscripted into the Polish army anyway and did not want their families to be on the road when their men were called up, as the women and children would be left all alone in a strange new place. Our friends did not get far before they had to turn back. It took them ten hours to travel a two-hour journey from Warsaw and there were dozens of air raids that day on the road. Their horses ran away into the forest with the cart and they decided to turn back. Of course, those who did manage to get to Russia fared little better. Once the Russians invaded Poland, they say around a million Poles – Aryan and Jewish alike – were transported to Siberia and other frozen wastelands.

But none of us foresaw this back then. Our friends had tried to persuade Isak to go with them, and I wanted us all to go. Yes, I've lived in Warsaw for twenty years, but I have no particular loyalty to it. My childhood taught me to be beholden only to myself. I lost count of the number of times our little town of Novogrodek changed hands from empire to empire, once Russian, or Polish, or Byelorussian. We remained static, as governments altered around us. Even the notion of any kind of national feeling was alien to me. Not like Isak, a born and bred Varsovian and a fiercely loyal Pole and proud of his Jewish heritage. He said, "Helena, I will never be routed from my home like a rat." I fear I disappoint him. But there are things he does not know about my past, things I will never tell him, that have moulded me, that have produced this woman without allegiances. At times, he thinks I am hard. But there is much he does not know.

So we did not escape. We stayed in Isak's beloved Warsaw and Isak tailored his suits and I made my dresses for the Varsovians as before. But the official sanctions began almost as soon as the Germans arrived. Within a month, the synagogues were closed and even gathering for prayer in private houses was forbidden. Of course, this did not mean anything to us, as we observe only a few Holy Days, yet it was an early sign of what was coming. Then Jewish bank accounts were blocked and we were not allowed to have more than 2000 zlotys in cash. This made running the business tricky, but we hung on. Soon after, we had to get the white armbands with the blue Star of David, and then our shop was marked as Jewish (this was quickly followed by the windows being smashed in every few weeks). After that, I cannot remember the exact order of things, but new restrictions came swiftly. It seemed as if every day a new edict was announced. The primary schools for Jewish children were closed. Ilsa was only four then, but now she is five I have responsibility for her education. I'm doing my best. She can certainly sew and she reads all the time, just like her mother at her age. Then Jewish property had to be registered. And we couldn't travel by rail or even walk along the 'better' streets. As of last month we have been forced into a 'Jews only' space on trams. Now it's the ghetto.

We have put up with the sanctions. They are humiliating and inconvenient and unfair, but it is the lynching that terrifies us. The Germans began this in a haphazard, rather clumsy way, in cars, spotting Jews in the street and dragging them in. Soon the German imagination was engaged in thinking up more creative tortures, such as the Rabbi dragged from a restaurant and forced to shit himself in front of everybody. I did not believe it was true, but heard it on the same day from three separate people. Groups of Jews made to clear snow or clean toilets with their own hands, or thrown out of moving tramcars, or simply beaten over the head. None of these people had done anything to invite this. It was enough to be a Jew or look like a Jew. There was even a rumour going round that the Germans were hiring people with Semitic features to act badly around the city, in order to justify the general hatred.

And then we had the Nazi officer who came into the shop again and again to 'buy' dresses for his mistress, and he made us write statements each time that they were gifts that we made to him. A curious need to put a respectable face on his theft, when all around there are Germans beating the brains out of Jews with no provocation. Doctor Stagel has told us that cases of insanity are multiplying in the Jewish community, partly as a result of the large number of head injuries. And there are other sinister effects of these repressive measures. I see it in people all around me, every day. It is a new kind of thinking, of feeling, of being. A kind of mental slavery. Germans can beat you, humiliate you and you can make no reply at all. You retreat inside your own mind, but even there you begin to doubt the freedom of your thoughts. You can scream and shout at the Germans in your head, but no-one can hear you. And you are even afraid of this voice, because if you were to lose control for a moment and speak your anger out loud, you could be beaten or even shot in an instant. It begins to feel like you cannot even hear yourself. That is why I have begun to write this diary now. I need to hear my own voice.

Every spare moment we have had has been taken up with trying to find a new place to live within the ghetto. The newspapers are full of adverts for exchanges of apartments. Those like us whose homes are not in the area of the ghetto have had four weeks to find a flat, agree the terms of a possible exchange, decide what things to take with them, and sell the rest or find people who would agree to store them. In every home, the only thing people discuss is finding a new flat, if not for themselves, for family or friends. In the doorways of houses there are notices describing flats 'for exchange' and near the boundary of the ghetto, whole walls are covered with little cards offering or looking for flats.

Those who have the good luck of already living within ghetto boundaries do not have to pack their whole lives into suitcases. On the other hand, there are large numbers of close or distant relatives moved in with most, if not all, of them. And for some, the 'privilege' of staying in their own home has proven short-lived, since the boundaries of the ghetto have changed at least twice in the last week. Those who had at first been in a better position have found that they have to move again, and now with less opportunity to exchange flats, since nobody is moving out of the ghetto. There are few empty flats, and you have to find room in an area that is already crowded. We hear that Jews have found they have exchanged their fine apartment in Aryan Warsaw for a hole in rubble. Pani Lewartow says, "The Poles thank the Germans for locking up the Jews. Now they can be rid of us." Isak says she is being unfair to the majority of Aryan Poles, that most of them are not rabid Jew-haters. There are more good Poles than bad, he says. He asks what pani Lewartow would do in their place. "Would you risk your life defending a Catholic?" he said to her. She just clucks her tongue at Isak. I think they are both right.

Some have chosen not to move into the ghetto, going 'underground' as it were, but how can I live like that with a husband and a daughter? It would mean relying on an Aryan friend to hide us in their apartment and feed us, without any opportunity for us to go out or make a living. It is simply impossible. I couldn't live like that. Perhaps a single man or woman might manage it. Good luck to them. Others are trying to escape from Warsaw. But it is very dangerous. If you get caught on the road without proper identification, you are sent to Pawiak Prison, or worse. I have heard there are people you can contact to get yourself false papers, but I do not know who these people are. And I don't think I could bear to live a lie.

After days of searching, negotiating and wrangling, we have found ourselves a place on Sliska Street. I know how lucky we are. I mean, we are parallel with Sienna Street, which is probably the nicest street in the ghetto. Poor souls have had to move from nice areas in Aryan Warsaw to the hovels of Gesia, Smocza and Zamenhof Streets. Living there doesn't bear thinking about. The overcrowding, the filth, the lice, the overwhelming smell of misery and poverty. It was pretty bad before the war, and now thousands have moved into that tiny space, I hear it is like a waking nightmare. I have not dared to walk up there myself. I pity those people with all my heart.

I am glad we have found a place on Sliska, as we are in the same neighbourhood as my good friend, Vladka. Yes, Vladka and Samuel still have their one-room apartment on Sienna. All I have to do is slip across the road and I can be drinking coffee with her within two minutes (until the coffee runs out). She used to complain about their tiny flat, how the wages of a painter and a chef could afford little more, and she would make the trip over to my place for coffee as she was glad to sit in more space for a while. But now her flat is more valuable than gold, as it is self-contained and within the ghetto boundaries, and therefore beyond value. Most people have had to move into shared accommodation, as we have ourselves, shared with strangers. Vladka's little room seems like heaven to me now. I never thought I'd be envious of it.

I am very relieved too, as having a close friend nearby in the ghetto will no doubt prove invaluable. Already, Vladka has been a great help to us. On the day of the move, yesterday, she and Samuel came to see us at home, and helped us pile our stuff onto the pushcarts we had hired. We have had to give most of our books and furniture to an Aryan friend, pan Bradecki, the owner of the button factory, whom we have done business with for years. We trust him. He has always leaned to the political left and has no time for anti-Semitism. He has the space in his warehouses to keep people's belongings. He is doing the same favour for quite a few other Jews, we have heard. It's good to know that when this madness has passed, as it surely will, once the Russians arrive, or the West beats the Germans back into their own country, that we can simply replenish our lives. It would have broken my heart to sell our lovely things.

Samuel and Isak took the items over to pan Bradecki's place yesterday morning, making several trips. Meanwhile, Vladka and I packed the remainder - largely clothes, kitchen equipment, a few books and toys for Ilsa and our bath items - into suitcases and boxes. We waited for the men to bring back the pushcarts and then we carried everything down the three flights of stairs, which was not easy. Ilsa did her best, holding two books at a time, or a small bag or I'd give her spoons to take. She was keen to be involved. It almost broke my heart to see how excited she was by the whole affair. "Are we going on a journey, Mama?" she asked again and again. I have told her only that we have to move into a different house, because the soldiers need our building. That is how she understands the German occupation; that is what I have told her, that there are soldiers from a foreign land who have come to live here for a while, that they are important people and we must do as they say for our own good. She latched onto it in a cheerful kind of way, because she has a smart set of Prussian toy soldiers, and she associates the Germans with these. She plays battles with them, and then marries them off to peg dolls and starts families with beans wrapped in cotton wool for their babies. I hate to lie to her, yet what is the point of terrifying a five year-old with the horrible truth?

But yesterday, I could protect her from the world's malice no more, not once we went outside to begin our move. The worst of the Jew-hating Poles were out in force on the streets of Warsaw, joined by clusters of German soldiers who laughed and shouted and cheered them on. I was glad we only had a few blocks to travel, as there were scores of Polish hooligans jeering at Jews moving into the ghetto, pulling beards, and pushing people and kicking their handcarts, their carefully packed possessions scattering in the wet road. Isak and Samuel are tall men and managed to look fierce enough that we were not approached. But Ilsa saw the kickings, though I tried to shield her eyes, and she cried and couldn't understand why these people were being cruel. I told her they were mad people who would be gone soon. They wouldn't be where we were going. That is true, as pani Lewartow said, at least no Aryan Poles will be in the ghetto with us. Isak was very quiet about this later. He said no more about the good Poles.

We tramped on, the streets swarming with Jews, pushcarts stacked with junk, despite the German rule of hand luggage only. Everyone has ignored that, as it is bad enough that we have to give up our homes; we cannot bear to take with us only what we could carry. As we walked, whenever we saw a German gendarme in the street everyone would look away and go very quiet. We were all terrified the gendarmes might confiscate our belongings, which Isak had seen happening several times that morning already. Once we approached the boundary of the ghetto there were sentry posts on certain exits, manned by German gendarmes and accompanied by the newly formed Jewish police force. Most other Jews are finding these Jewish police highly suspicious. It is understandable that some people, especially intellectuals whose work has been taken away from them, might need to find suitable employment, and the police force seems like a good position to have. But they are beginning to be associated too closely with the German police and soldiers, and we have seen several of them trying to endear themselves to the Germans in unflattering ways. I have also heard that the Jewish police have even taken part in rounding up so-called 'suspect' Jews. Jews rounding up Jews. What is happening in the world?

As we entered the ghetto, we saw the true extent of the walls for the first time. Apparently, there are about ten miles of walls altogether, along a seemingly random zigzag boundary, kindly built by Jewish labour and paid for by the Jewish community. Seeing the walls had a peculiar effect on all of us. A hush descended in the streets as Jews passed into the walled area, an incredible stillness despite the thousands of people filling the pavements. The stony fact of those walls subdued us all. Whatever we may say about all being in it together, and won't it be fine to be away from the Jew-haters and such like, the truth is we are in prison now.

Our new home is an apartment we exchanged for our own with an acquaintance, actually a friend of pan Bradecki, an old bachelor called pan Kaczmarek, who had lived here alone. He moved his belongings by horse and cart to a halfway house, and today is moving into our old home. As you go in to the apartment, there are two small rooms on either side of a short corridor, with a kitchen at the end. It is part of a large building of four storeys constructed around a central courtyard, with shops on the ground level along the street and living spaces above and in the rear wings of the building. An alleyway leads from the street into the courtyard, where entrances provide access to separate stairwells.

Toilets are communal, and we are lucky that we have one bath for all the residents of the building, as many buildings in the ghetto have no bath at all and everyone there has to use the public facilities. Before we arrived, we had been led to believe that another family was moving into the same apartment with us. Isak, Ilsa and myself would sleep in one room, and the other family would be in the other room, and we would all take turns to share the kitchen. But when we arrived yesterday afternoon, there was no-one else here, and tonight they have still not arrived. We are concerned for them, of course, as they were supposed to have moved in before us. Secretly we are very pleased, because the thought of sharing a small space with strangers is an unsettling thought to us all.

We wait for our cohabitants to arrive, and we have begun to sort our things around this new 'home'. At least it is clean, and there is space. There is room enough for Isak to cut cloth and for me to sew and that is all we need. And thank heavens for the toilet and bath on the next floor down. And what I like most about this place is that it is on the top floor. When we look out of our windows we can just see the very tops of the roofs of Warsaw beyond the walls, stretching away from us here in the ghetto. I know we could have escaped last year, or tried. We could have lived secretly in the Aryan sector, or tried. But despite the worry we all have of what this ghetto life will mean, there is something to be said for staying with your own kind, to share their fate as an act of defiance. We are here, us Jews. We remain. We survive.

The ghetto closed a few days ago, on November 15th, 1940. A day to remember, when we Jews officially ceased to be citizens of Warsaw. All the exits have been blocked, guarded by German gendarmes, the Jewish police or the Blue (Polish) police. We weren't certain that this would happen, but now it is a fact. No way in or out. No official ways, anyhow.

Food prices have risen incredibly in the past few weeks, and supplies are running low. Our daily meals consist mostly of soup and vegetables. There is no or very little meat to be found. I give most of the potatoes to Ilsa. However hungry I feel, I know that what we do have to eat is luxury to many. The worst off are the thousands of last-minute refugees from other parts of Poland who have been sent to the ghetto, such as farmers uprooted from their land, with no trades or money or belongings. They are desperate people. The day the ghetto closed, we saw them everywhere in the streets, perched on mounds of bedding which were quickly growing more and more soiled from the wet dirt on the ground. All around there are women and children crying in fear. They have nowhere to go, nothing to sell or eat. Five days later and most of them are still in the same spots, calling out weakly to passers-by. Some stop to try and help, but they are mobbed by the frantic ones. Isak has tried, but Ilsa and I hurry by. I cannot subject her to the terror of grasping beggars. It may sound heartless, but I just want to protect my child.

Here in the closed ghetto we are cut off from the world. Radios are not permitted (though people hide them, at great danger to themselves), there are no newspapers and few working telephones, and these are only available in official buildings. Some around us are optimistic; they say, "When America finds out, all this will end". Others are already in despair; they say, "We have been put in here to die." Isak is in-between these two extremes. He says, "The future of the Jews is unclear." I don't know where I am.

One of the first casualties of ghetto life has been a sense of community. Put thousands of Jews in one tiny space and see how long it takes them to hate each other. The truth is there is more to divide us than unite us. A Jew from Nalewki St. and a Jew from Krolewska St. are from two completely different worlds. Before the war, Jews lived all over Warsaw. Now people of all social classes and backgrounds are shoved together in a hole, and we happen to be Jews. There are Poles of Jewish origin who don't think they should be here, who don't think of themselves first as

Jews. They have found themselves condemned to share with those they found alien. Nothing connects them with the Orthodox Jews, while everything links them with the Polish intellectuals who live beyond the walls in Aryan Warsaw, and may as well be a million miles from here. For others, the ghetto has become the first time they have felt part of the Jewish community and they have embraced this completely.

How do I feel? I feel like a Jew. I feel like one because I am one. I wear a symbol on my arm which tells me and everyone else that I am one. I live in a prison with thousands of other Jews. We all wear the symbols. Do I feel Jewish? I am not sure what this means. I was brought up by liberal Jews, who worshipped intermittently. My husband has a similar attitude, though he is more devout than I tend to be. Do I look Jewish? I am not sure. Do I speak like a Jew? I speak Polish most of the time. I speak Yiddish sometimes. A little Russian. A little Hebrew I remember from my childhood. Some here speak nothing but Yiddish, some nothing but Polish. Some speak only German. Some speak and write in modern Hebrew, as a kind of badge of Jewish honour. Polish is the official language of the ghetto. It is used in contacts with the Judenrat (the Jewish Council), with the supply organisations, in the street. Though the place is full of Jews, Yiddish is not the official language. What does that say about us? Who am I now? We do not know who we are.

We are trying to settle in to our new 'home'. The family who was supposed to be coming to share our apartment has still not arrived. We do not expect them now. This is good news for us, of course, yet the fact of it makes me uneasy. They have joined the growing ranks of disappeared Jews. Who can tell what happened to them? Now we will never know. I have expected them for days now, I almost wish for them. Our little family makes for a melancholy trio. I even find myself missing the company of our fussy old neighbours, pani Lewartow and pan Wilner, who used to annoy me with their elderly griping. We don't know where they are now. I think in the bad area. I am ashamed to say I could not bear to walk up there to see them. News from there gets worse by the moment.

Isak talks less and less since we have come here. He used to have an opinion for everything. Now he seems less sure. He stays in the apartment most of the time. But at least Ilsa and I have the company of our new neighbours. I cannot name any of them yet, as there are double the usual number of building inhabitants, due to the overcrowding. Isak warned me to keep quiet about our good fortune with the missing family. He says if we let out that we have a spare bedroom, we will find a hundred Jews there by evening. I have not been too forthcoming with our new neighbours, but I do go out into the courtyard in the evenings and listen to their gossip. Ilsa sits on my lap and sucks her thumb as I sew, watching the other boys and girls of the building in their little games of war, pretending to shoot Germans with their pointed fingers. I ask her if she'd like to bring out her toy soldiers and join the fun. She shakes her head silently. She is still shy and bookish. I see my own childhood in her watchful eyes. We sit quietly, surrounded by conversation. I think about how there are new spaces opening up in the ghetto, created by the ghetto itself. Though we used to talk with our immediate neighbours in our old place, we did not give the rest of our building more than a nod or a polite greeting on the stairs. We kept ourselves to ourselves. Here, there are areas where fledgling communities are beginning to develop. I notice this most in the domestic spaces. After curfew, the courtyards of residential buildings like ours have become places where a social life is taking shape, where information is exchanged, the day's events unfolded, even meagre rations shared at times, a sip of alcohol or a puff of tobacco. There is a kind of siege spirit.

As time moves on and we become accustomed to our prison, new allegiances form and groups begin to clump together. There are ghettos within ghettos, as each street tends to house the same kind of Jew. What I mean is that those like ourselves, who were independent merchants of the middle class before the war, we had the contacts in the better streets, like Sienna or Sliska, with whom we could swap apartments. The poorer Jews, often those less assimilated into the Polish way of life, only had contacts in the poorer areas, or - like the refugees - they had no contacts at all. Everyone ends up where their pre-war allegiances put them. Like clings to like. We do not speak each other's language, we do not look alike, we do not worship in the same ways, we do not know each other. Yet we are all condemned alike.

I grow maudlin. At least we have been able to make a decent living. Our pre-war tailoring and dressmaking business has been transformed into a two-person factory for producing and repairing the Star of David armbands. One would not imagine there could be business in these small items, but they are crucial. The punishment for not wearing one is at least three months in gaol. Some people have no shoes in the cold streets, but no armband can mean imprisonment or even death. It is the only essential piece of clothing for the Jew.

And there are now so many types of armband – one for all occasions – that we must work overtime to keep up with demand. Altogether, there are about twenty different ones in addition to the compulsory white band with the blue star. The Jewish police wear extra ones in yellow with red writing; the doctors and ambulance crew have white ones with a charming red star; Judenrat officials wear a sombre dark blue; undertakers sport an appropriately black band with a white border. Because the ghetto is squalid, the armbands get filthy, crumpled and torn very quickly. The specialist ones in particular cannot be washed and deteriorate within days. The ordinary ones can be laundered or you can buy a new one from street sellers. We sell them at a higher price, but ours are new and clean. Even in this mad world, people like to keep up appearances; the middle classes will pay extra for a smart armband. We spend our time repairing the official armbands, by a kind of book-binding. Cardboard is put underneath the band and we back it with canvas. The front is covered in cellophane and the whole thing fitted with a strap and a clip. We do good work and have had no complaints. We continue to repair clothes, and richer Jews, who still have money, continue to come for dresses and suits adjusted or mended. The most common adjustment is taking clothes in. Everyone is getting thinner nowadays.

Oh, before the war our business was so different! The dresses I made! My fingers enjoyed embroidering frivolous and lovely things: flowers and butterflies in six colours on the collars of evening wear. I would hang my creations in the window of our shop, alongside the smart men's suits made by Isak's skilful hands. We were proud of our business, and how it thrived! We had customers from the finest homes of Warsaw, elegant ladies and gentlemen who came across the city for fittings and conversation, Catholic and Jewish Poles alike.

I must not complain. We are extremely fortunate to have work. And it is an easier transition for us because we are doing a similar job to before we moved into the ghetto. Those in other professions, which have no use in ghetto life, are having to adapt hugely. For example, lawyers have become policemen or janitors (the latter is a very decent job, as it has good social standing and provides a place to live); an engineer can become a door-to-door salesman; a professor of music graduates to a street musician, but the tailor and street trader stays in his old job. Teachers, doctors, pharmacists – these people also keep their profession, though teaching carries its own dangers as education of Jews is banned, but people insist on their children not becoming imbeciles. I know there are Jewish children secretly being taught subjects, including languages both alive and dead. Children are speaking Latin, right here in the ghetto! It sounds ridiculous, I know. But I understand it. If you want to kill a people, cut off their heads: take away their ability to think. Education becomes a form of quiet resistance. And this is uniquely Jewish, I feel. The Jews have been known for millennia as 'the people of the Book'. Knowledge and learning are highly valued. Jews will not give that up to the ignorant Nazis.

There are still books to be had, which are sold in the street or from hand to hand of friends. A few were bought at the beginning of the war on the Aryan side, when books were collected from bombed-out houses. The joy of burying your nose in a book, when all around you is chaos, is indescribable. I am reading a poetry book by Mickiewicz at the moment, lent to me by Vladka. It reminds me of my adolescence, it reminds me of my first lover.

I read it to Ilsa. She does not understand most of it, and Isak does not like poetry. I read aloud but feel I am the only one listening. But it carries the fragrance of my youth into the foul air of the ghetto and I love it for that. Those days of my girlhood, of passion and disappointment, the sour-sweet taste of love. I wonder if Ilsa will learn to love in a place like this. I try to teach her about 'normal' life, about friendship and siblings, about schools and farms and flowers and trees. She does not know exactly what these things are. She is forgetting. She asked me yesterday, "Mama, what is grass like?" After only a few weeks in the ghetto she has forgotten the look of grass, how it feels under bare feet, even its colour. Here in the ghetto, there is no greenery, no trees, no grass. All parks and open spaces are outside the ghetto. You can only see them from the bridge over Chlodna Street or from the upper storeys of houses standing beside the ghetto walls. I told her that in the spring we may be able to smell the blossom from the trees beyond the walls. I am hoping this is true, that it will mask the stink in the streets, that my daughter's nostrils will be filled with the scent of creation and not only that of slow dying. How will she learn to be, to think, to love, in this place? What kind of life can grow on barren ground?

CHAPTER THREE

Magda touched Daniel's head, chest, arms and legs. He let her do it. She was feeling for injuries.

"I can't see you," she said, fetched an oil-lamp and placed it on a pot-stand. The other warden arrived and beckoned her to the hall for a talk.

She came back. Daniel was still on the floor. She knelt down beside him and spoke quietly. "They take your father now."

"I want to go with Dad," he said.

"We stay here. The looters will be waiting. And we have a lot of cleaning up. Stay here, with me."

After they'd gone, he wished he'd helped to carry Dad. But he'd turned away. He didn't want to feel the dead weight of his father's shoulders in his hands.

They cleared up what they could by lamplight. One sitting-room window was completely blown in, just a jagged hole where it had once been, but the other one had the remnants of a frame and a few rags hanging which were once the blackout curtain. She brought in two blankets and he nailed them over the window, to keep the night out. She used the broom from the kitchen to sweep up the glass and remnants of window frame and broken curtain poles into a pile in one corner of the living room. The chesterfield looked as if it had been dragged through a gravel pit. The books had been blown from the shelves, but hardly any were damaged. He put them back. Plaster dust covered everything. He found all the pieces of the dining table.

In the study, he put his torch down while he righted the desk. Hardly a dent. Next to the torch he found the telephone upturned on the floor in a pool of blue-black ink. When he replaced the receiver it rang. He picked it up but it was dead. A ghost on the line. He held the receiver and stared at it. Wet ink shone on his hand. He began to shake and sob.

Magda appeared with a candle in a jam jar and placed it on the desk. She put her arm around his shoulder and carefully removed the receiver from his hand.

He pulled away from her. "Magda," he said and looked her in the eye. "Dad told me I was adopted. He said he got me from an orphanage in Poland, in Warsaw, when I was a baby. He said it just before he went. I don't know if it's true. I don't know if it was just nonsense, because he was dying. Maybe he was just mixing everything up in his head. Maybe his mind was confused. What do you think?"

She looked away from him.

"You knew, didn't you? You knew. Tonight in the bathroom. You were trying to tell me, weren't you?"

She spoke to him in Polish: "I always wanted you to know where you really came from. But your father forbade it. He wanted you to grow up with all the luck of a well-off, well-educated English boy. And he loved you as his son, Daniel. He loved you so much. He thought it all for the best. But I always said you should know the truth."

A breeze swelled the blankets at the window. Daniel shivered. He looked at Magda. He spoke in Polish too.

"Are you my mother?"

Her eyes widened. "Oh no, darling. No, I'm not your mother. Oh, Daniel."

"Then who is? Dad said he didn't know. But I was born in Poland. And you're Polish. When did you come to England? Did you come with me? Did you know my parents? Did you?"

She was shaking her head and crying. She stepped towards him, but he would not be touched. He stood alone in the middle of the room, white dust on his shoes and his clothes and all through his dark hair.

"So many questions, Daniel. I think we need to sit down and have a hot drink. Then I will tell you everything I know."

"Everything?"

"Everything. I promise."

The electricity and gas had gone off, but there was water. Magda lit the Primus stove and made Bovril. They closed the door to the sitting room to keep the rest of the flat warm. They went to his bedroom, Magda carrying two mugs and Daniel the lamp. They sat beside each other on his bed, as they had done before, when he needed to talk, needed her to listen. The soft light cast their wavering shadows behind them.

"The year you were born, I was working as a nanny to a good Varsovian family. Yet I spent one day every weekend helping out at an orphanage. My mother was good friends with the woman who ran it. It was mostly babies there and I always loved babies. One morning in June 1923, I went to sweep the front step and when I was done I left my broom outside by mistake. I went back out to fetch it and I found a baby there. A tiny, tiny baby. Newborn. All wrapped up in a nice clean blanket, fast asleep in the sunshine. I looked around for someone, but nobody was there. The street was empty. I took the baby in my arms and asked, "Who are you, my darling? Where is your Mama?"

"I walked to the top of the street and back. But everyone was going about their business. This had happened before, babies left on the doorstep of the orphanage. But never when I was there. It was my first one. It was you, Daniel. I took you inside and we put you into a spare crib. We unwrapped your blanket to check you over, to see if your little body was all right, not bruised or anything terrible. You were fine, a little thin, but healthy. We found something inside your blanket. A photograph of a young girl, a very young girl. Beautiful, with great dark eyes. Your eyes, Daniel. A name was scribbled on the back. *Helena,* it said."

"*Helena,*" he whispered.

"Yes. Then you woke up, eyes all wide and searching for your Mama. Great, dark eyes, just like the girl in the picture. Then we knew. She must have been your mother."

"Where is the photograph now?"

"I don't know. Your father took it."

"Who? My real father?"

"No, no, darling. Listen. Let me tell you the story and then you can ask questions. You were only a few days old, we thought, maybe a week but nobody can know for sure. You cried out and I gave you a bottle of milk. You took it all down in one go and slept for six hours. I held you all that time. I fell in love with you from the moment I found you. I had to work for that family during the day, but every night I came to the orphanage and sat with you. Fed you when you woke and rocked you back to sleep. Every night for weeks. And all weekend. One Saturday, when you were around six months old, a man came to the orphanage. He was a journalist, English."

"*Dad,*" he said.

"Yes, your father. He said he was reporting on poverty in Warsaw and wanted to ask questions about the orphanage. He spoke excellent Polish. I sent him to my mother's friend, the manager. He seemed a very nice man, a gentleman. After he had interviewed her and taken lots of notes, he asked to have a walk around and see the babies. He looked carefully at each one. He tried to shush the crying ones. He was so gentle. He seemed very sad. There were so many unwanted babies. I should have tended to them all much more than I did. But I only wanted to be with you. He saw me and came over. The moment he looked at you and you at him, you smiled. You beamed! It made him laugh. He said, "He has my wife's smile." He asked if he could hold you. Sometimes you cried when others took you, but you stared at him very curiously and then pulled at his tie. He couldn't stop chuckling. He stayed for an hour or more, playing with you and asking me things about you.

"He came back the next day. He had another man with him, a lawyer. They spoke with the manager privately. He came to play with you again, held you and talked to you. Then he told me, he was going to adopt you and take you back to England. It was probably the best thing that could have happened to you. A good man like that and a new life abroad. But the moment he said it, I burst into tears. You know me, I cannot hide my feelings. The manager came over and told me off, but your father was very kind and spoke with me a while. He could see how I adored you. Then he asked me, would I come with him to England, as your nurse? He said his wife had been ill and she would need help with the baby. Would I come and live with them? Well, I took less than a second to agree. I was in my thirties then, a spinster, living with my mother, in a job I tolerated, teaching other people's children to behave. Then I found you and I was about to lose you. The Virgin Mary smiled on me. She brought me Henry Summerskill and a boat ticket to England. We left within the week. And came to live here, Daniel. In your home. And I have not spent a night away from you since then, my darling, in all those years."

Daniel felt as though he hadn't taken a breath for the whole of Magda's story. He inhaled and felt light-headed. Outside, the birds of London were chirping. It was dawn.

"Why did he want me?" he said.

"Because you were beautiful. And lovely. So sweet-tempered."

"No, I mean, why adopt a baby? Why didn't he have one with my mother? I mean, with her, his wife? With Elizabeth?"

"I was never told all the facts, but I eavesdropped enough on doctors' visits to piece it together. His wife couldn't get pregnant. Tests were mentioned. She had a breakdown. When I met her, I could see the panic in her eyes, and the shock of a baby in her house. It was all a terrible mistake, from her point of view. I think they argued about it. But don't blame her, Daniel. She was a broken woman. She got the influenza and died. It was awful for your father. But he had you. He wanted you and he loved you and he raised you as his son."

"You said my father had the photograph. Where is it now?"

"Oh, I don't know that, Daniel. It's probably lost now."

She turned off the lamp, opened the curtains and went to the kitchen.

He followed her. "But he wouldn't have lost it, surely? It was precious. The only link with my mother. My real mother."

Magda took out oats for porridge, filled a pan with water and put it on the Primus. "I don't know, Daniel. He told me once he would never tell you about it. He was determined. He wanted you to be an English boy. Perhaps he destroyed it." She stirred the oats into the warming water then yawned and rubbed her eyes. "Time to eat now," she said in English.

Daniel went to the study and yanked up the blackout blind. He winced at the sunlight. The cupboard in the wall was still intact. Inside were cardboard boxes piled up, full of papers. Dad had been sorting them in the weeks before his death. As if he knew. As if he were putting his life in order. Daniel pulled them out and their contents splayed across the dusty carpet.

She found him there, a bowl of porridge on a tray.

"Do it later, Daniel. Come and eat."

Daniel did not answer. He had looked through three boxes, packed with bills and receipts and notes and lists and every kind of pointless paperwork. His tired eyes blurred and his fingers shook.

"Come, Daniel. Eat, then sleep. We look later."

"No," he said and upturned another box. More papers. Drawings in a child's hand, his own. Certificates for music and elocution exams; essays on historical topics marked A+ in red; birthday and Christmas cards. A pair of knitted booties. Below all these, a small, plain wooden box, closed with a clasp. Daniel opened it. Inside were two sealed envelopes.

"These are your father's private things, Daniel. His solicitor will look. Here, give them to me."

Daniel ignored her. He opened the largest envelope first. Inside were three documents. One, a yellowed, crumpled piece of paper. He smoothed it out on the floor. It was written in a scratchy pen in Polish and was a birth certificate. In the box titled child's name were the Polish words for 'baby boy'. The date of birth was recorded as 'approximately June 1923'. No birthday. How strange it was all of a sudden to not know the day you were born. There was a section for the parents' names. Nothing for father. For mother was written one word: *Helena*.

The next paper was similar, scruffy and written in Polish, this one about the adoption. It had the address of the orphanage and Henry's name.

The third was superior paper, cream-coloured with a watermark. It was written in English. A legal document about the adoption of a child from Poland and details of the new parents. On this page alone did Daniel Summerskill see his name written. This was the moment he had become himself.

"What did you call me, Magda? When I was a baby, before Dad came. Did you have a name for me? Did you give me a name?"

"Yes. I called you Feliks. It means lucky, happy. That is what I wished for you. That is what I still wish for you." Magda wiped her eyes and covered her face with her hands.

He opened the other envelope. Two objects inside. A photograph and a little piece of embroidery. The black and white photograph was of a young woman, a girl really, with black shoulder-length hair and large dark eyes, wearing a flowered dress. She looked shyly at the camera. You could only see her head and shoulders. He turned the photograph over and written on the back in faded pencil was her name: *Helena*. The details of the Warsaw photographer were stamped in one corner.

Daniel looked at the embroidery. It was a red ribbon, with stitching all the way along it in purple and green threads. The tiny stitches all described the same shape, over and over, the length of the crimson ribbon. The shapes were stars. A special star. The Star of David.

It was too bright for a funeral. There should have been grey clouds and cold drizzle. But instead, it was sunny and pleasant. Dozens of people came in their black clothes. Daniel shook many hands. The Woolfs were there, their friends. Daniel's boss and even grumpy Jim Mackay, a few more from the *Chronicle* and other newspapers Henry had worked for. Dad's only brother was in New Zealand and there to stay. He had gone over decades before, a Plymouth Brother with new world ambitions. He had sent a card. There were family friends and neighbours from their building. A life collected in others.

When he stood at his father's grave, Daniel thought about his mother. Or the woman he had thought was his mother. Henry's wife, Elizabeth. He did not truly remember her at all. He had tried to imagine gazing at her from the crib, but he thought he may have invented a memory of it, from photographs. He wondered if, stored within, there was an image of his real mother. His real father even. He thought of that baby who had looked upon its parents and he envied it. His earliest memory was not even of Henry. It was of Magda.

The wake took place at the flat. The sitting-room had been cleaned and tidied. But the carpet breathed white dust with every footfall. And the boarded-up window was a blank, hard reminder of the reason they all stood there in black suits. Magda had the catering and drinks to keep her busy. As Daniel watched her, bottle of wine or plate of sandwiches in hand, he thought how good she was at buttering people up, making them feel special. How bad he was at this. He ended up in the kitchen. Magda said, "This is my place. Shoo!" But he wouldn't move. He had tried his best to make small talk, but in every look he saw pity and every shake of the head meant disappointment. In him. That he was not half the man his father was. Just a dogsbody at the *Chronicle* with no signs of promotion. Rejected for enlistment. No chance of the RAF. And did you know, the boy wasn't even Henry's? Adopted. A Pole. A Jewish Pole. Daniel had shown the Star of David embroidery to Magda and she had confirmed it. She'd worked at a Jewish orphanage. So, he was a Jew.

Perhaps Old Cardew had told someone, told everyone. Two days after the bombing, he'd knocked on Cardew's door, asked him for help regarding a Home Office issue. Came straight out with it; mother a Polish Jew. What can be done to get her out of there?

"Hopeless, I'm afraid," Old Cardew had said. "Firstly, with no surname or address, how on earth could the authorities locate her? If by a miracle she was found, she may not qualify as a refugee. Once war was declared here, all visas were cancelled and most refugees had to reach neutral territory before they were let in. Many were only accepted if they were children joining their parents or could contribute to the war effort. Does she have a skill?"

"I don't know."

"No, of course. You don't know anything about her, do you? Not a diamond worker, is she? We need those. A few came from Poland recently. We need manpower, you see. And I'm sorry to say this, Daniel, but Jews are the last on the Government's list. We let in far too many at the turn of the century, with all the trouble in Russia. They took over the East End. Then another load in the thirties, with Hitler looming. Another pile from Czechoslovakia last year. Don't want to be the dumping ground of Europe, do we? You understand my meaning, Daniel. No offence."

Daniel nodded. Nobody wants Jews. Shylock and Fagin. There was the internment of Germans a few months back, many of whom were Jewish. He remembered seeing Star of David armbands and synagogues on fire in newsreels about Austria. But Dad came breathlessly home from Cable Street four years ago, where the Jews and the Communists had barricaded the roads to stop Mosley's gang marching through, and Dad had said they stood shoulder to shoulder behind parked trams and piles of furniture and saw off the Fascists. When the police came, they threw marbles under the hooves of police horses and volleys of bricks met each baton charge. Proud Jews, defending their territory. Daniel Deronda heading off to Palestine. It was a complicated thing, the Jews. The Jewish problem.

I am a Jew, thought Daniel. *I am a Jew.*

"Only thing you could do now is smuggle yourself into occupied Warsaw and walk the streets looking for her yourself. Ridiculous, of course."

A shadow in the doorway. It was Tomasz. Daniel held out his hand, yet Tomasz embraced him and said in Polish, "We are two Poles now."

"Magda told you?"

"Yes."

"Did she tell you everything? The Jewish part?"

"Yes."

"She didn't tell me. I found out myself. Like she was ashamed of it."

"Don't be too hard on her, Daniel. She wanted to protect you. Being adopted and a foreigner was enough for you to take in. Being Jewish too? And a Polish Jew. It carries a heavy load. Magda is no anti-Semite. And neither am I. Yet the Nazis aren't the only Europeans to hate Jews. There's a lot of it in Poland. It's a fiercely Catholic country, you know. Maybe she meant to tell you later. Maybe never. But whatever Magda does for you, Daniel, it is because she loves you. You must know that."

He thought of how she'd been this week. While he avoided her, spoke little to her, would not sit for long with her, went out a lot and stayed at work late, he always found her there with a proper meal kept warm in the stove, whatever the hour. He was still angry she had hidden the truth, not once but twice. But she'd done everything right: organised the house, cooked and cleaned and ironed, arranged repairs to the sitting-room, sorted Dad's clothes and boxed his knick-knacks, a constant wet hankie balled in her sleeve. At first she might have been fearful for her future, her position in this, her employer's house, herself a housemaid on paper. The solicitor came the day before and showed them the will, assured them both they were well looked after, for Daniel a trust fund and Magda an annuity and residence at the flat for the term of her life. He realised with a prickle of guilt that she'd lost a friend, that kind man she'd left Poland for and shared her life with for nearly twenty years. Those past few nights, Daniel had woken a couple of times from nightmares to hear her crying in the next room. Yet he had not tried to comfort her once.

"Yes. I do know that."

Both men looked at their shoes.

"Daniel, I feel terrible about...this. Magda told me your father said he wouldn't take you to the shelter that night because you were drunk and beaten up. It is all my fault. If I hadn't got you into trouble, perhaps your father..."

"No. That's not true. Dad hated shelters. He wouldn't have gone anyway."

"All right. But I still feel responsible. I want to help you. I'm on leave now, but may be called away north, to help defend the east coast. Before I go, if there is anything you need..."

"I didn't tell you something. The day we met last week, the day Dad... That morning I'd tried to enlist. I failed my medical. Just childhood asthma, but they failed me anyway."

"That is ridiculous."

"I know. But I was wondering if you could put a word in for me, with the RAF?"

"Jesus, Mary! Are you joking? You know how the RAF hates us. Any recommendation from me would put you straight on the blacklist."

"Oh, I see."

"I can try, but it might make it worse for you."

"Thanks."

"But listen. I've been thinking about your mother. I mean, your real mother in Poland."

Daniel turned to him. "Tomasz, what can I do about her? All I know is she's called Helena and she's a Polish Jew, probably in Warsaw. Well, she was twenty years ago. But she might still be there. People don't always move, do they? She'll be in terrible danger, won't she? I've spoken to the Home Office and it's useless, they won't do anything. We don't have her last name or where she lives. How can I find it out? Can we contact anyone in Poland, someone to help us? Someone to look for her. But it's all cut off over there, isn't it? It's madness, isn't it? It is madness."

He smashed clenched fists together. Tears surged down his face.

Tomasz said, "Listen, Daniel."

"If I could only go there. I have her photo. I'd walk the streets, I'd look for her myself. Ask around. The ribbon she made. Magda said it was excellent work and she might have been a seamstress. Maybe I could start at places you find seamstresses. What are those, Tomasz? Where would you find a seamstress in Warsaw? But it's all crazy, isn't it? How can I get into occupied Poland? How could I walk the streets of Warsaw? It's all impossible."

"Not impossible, no."

"What?"

He saw Magda's face through a lens of tears. Magda had stopped in the doorway, tray in hand.

She said, "Did Tomasz upset you?"

"I'm all right." He rubbed his eyes, shoved his hands in his pockets.

She hovered, put her tray down and pointed at Tomasz.

"Be a good friend to him," she said in Polish and left the room.

"Sorry about that," Daniel said.

"Don't be. We're lucky she didn't pull my ear."

"What did you mean, Tomasz? What's not impossible?"

"Did you mean it, about finding your mother?"

"Yes."

"If you're serious, absolutely serious about this...?"

"I am."

"I know someone who may be able to help you."

"Who?"

"It's complicated. He won't come here. You'll have to go and meet him. How about tonight? I'll wait in the square. At six? Come and find me. Don't tell Magda anything about it."

"Why not? She'll ask me. She'll want to know."

"Your father is dead, Daniel. You are the man now."

The next day, Daniel helped Magda clear everything away. He hugged her and she held on tight and thanked him in a croaky voice. When the time came for him to go out, he said, "Just popping out for a drink. See you later."

"Who with?" she said, half smiling, her eyes narrowed.

"A friend from work. No one you know."

He found Tomasz on a bench in the square's garden, smoking and staring up into the trees. They walked briskly towards Camden through the darkness. They saw three women dressed in their finery, luminous blackout flowers pinned to their lapels. They looked up and smiled as they passed, and Daniel said, "It's a bit risky for them, walking home. You hear of all these assaults on women on the blacked-out streets."

"They're not going home, they're going to work."

"What do you mean?"

"They're tarts, of course! When a shop girl earns a lot less than an English pound a week, who can blame them? Lovely girls like those three can charge a pound a time. But there are ugly ones around Trafalgar Square who'll do it for a few pennies, or even a cup of tea."

He didn't ask Tomasz how he knew this. Tomasz went on about recent female conquests. Daniel wanted to ask him about tonight. But Tomasz avoided it.

They stopped before a block of flats not far from King's Cross. Tomasz looked behind him then up the street, rang one of the buzzers and waited.

A hand on Daniel's shoulder. He jerked around to see Magda.

"Come home with me, Daniel."

"Will you just stop following me around, for God's sake? I'm not a child."

"Go home, Magda," said Tomasz. "This is none of your concern."

"Don't you dare, Tomasz Dabrowski! I know who lives here and what he does. And I don't want Daniel mixed up in any of it."

Daniel could hear someone coming down the stairs of the building. Across the street, a couple strolling arm-in-arm was watching the three of them. Two young men and a middle-aged woman shouting at each other in Polish.

"Magda, this is men's business," said Tomasz. "Go home."

"Ha! Men? You are little boys playing at war."

The door opened. A blond man glanced at the two he expected, blanched as he saw Magda. He said, "What's she doing here?"

Magda spoke with a venom Daniel had never seen in her. "Trust you to be involved in all this rubbish," she spat at the man at the door. "You were always a sneaky little shit. I never liked you or your idiot mother!"

"Get inside!" the blond said. "Not her!"

Tomasz stepped in. Magda grasped Daniel's arm. "They won't help you, Daniel. They just want to use you. Come home with me."

He did not have it in him to push her away. But he looked straight at her and said, "No, Magda. No."

She released her grip. "Life is not a story. It is real and so is death."

Daniel crossed the threshold. Before the door closed, he knew she was still there. But he did not turn back.

"What the fuck was that, Dabrowski?"

"No problem, Karol. No problem. It won't happen again. Come on, it's me, eh? Come on."

"You didn't tell me the old witch was coming."

"Hang on," said Daniel in English.

The man turned to him.

"You want to find your mother?"

"Yes, I do, but..."

"Shut up and follow me then."

Daniel glanced at Tomasz, who frowned yet nodded. They climbed a bleak staircase to the fifth floor. No words, only the sound of their breathing growing heavier.

The man stopped before a door and pulled a key from his back pocket.

Inside was a bare studio flat, with four hard chairs, a lamp and a tall bottle of vodka on the floor. A meeting place, not a home. The man gestured for them to sit. He passed the vodka round. Daniel took a sip. The man watched him.

He said, "Nothing like that will happen again. Do you understand?"

"Of course," said Tomasz.

"I want to hear it from him."

"Yes," said Daniel.

Tomasz said, "This is Karol. I know him from before the war. Karol works with the Polish Underground. The Polish Government-in-Exile is based in London. It keeps in touch with home through the Underground. Operatives come from Poland all the time, delivering news to the government and carrying back information to help the resistance. Karol is one of these operatives."

"Do you know someone who can look for my mother?" said Daniel. "I have a photograph. Look." He took it from his pocket. He always had it there now.

Karol shook his head. "Impossible. The Underground cannot spend its time on personal matters. But, there is a way you could look for your mother yourself. If you choose to become an operative."

"What exactly is an operative?"

"A spy. Karol wants you to be a spy for the Polish Underground."

"What would I have to do?"

Karol said, "We can use you. You speak English and Polish fluently. You could teach English to our operatives. You're young, unmarried. You can travel easily, live anywhere. No reprisals on loved ones, because you have none in Poland."

"Apart from my mother."

"If she lives."

"How would I get there?"

"Across the Baltic, via Sweden."

"When would I go?"

"In a few months. Training first. Weapons. That kind of thing."

"Would the...would your organisation be able to help me? To look for my mother?"

"Let's make this clear. If we accept you, your contacts in Warsaw might help you. But if it compromised your Underground work, you'd be expelled. Maybe worse."

They would kill me, thought Daniel. He looked down at his mother's photograph. Was he in her belly when it was taken? He put it away in his pocket.

Tomasz said, "You have two roads to follow, Daniel. One stays here in England. Perhaps things will change, you might be called up later. Your newspaper might take you abroad, who knows? It would be a worthy choice, full of possibility. The other road leads to Poland. No guarantees and danger ahead. There's a lot to think about. You don't have to decide tonight. Why don't you talk it over with Magda?"

Karol laughed.

"I'll do it," said Daniel. "What happens now?"

Tomasz cleared his throat and said, "Are you sure, Daniel?"

"Yes. It's what I want."

"Good man," said Karol. "First you have to take an oath of loyalty to the Polish Underground. 'Karol' is not my birth name. It is my code name. We have one for you. It needs to be short and easy to recall, as it may well be used by radio operators. Your new name is 'Anglik'. Now for the oath. It's a Catholic one. All right?"

"Yes."

"We don't have a Jewish one."

"I don't care."

"All right. Stand up. Repeat after me: 'Before God Almighty and Mary the Blessed Virgin, Queen of the Polish Crown, I pledge allegiance to my Motherland, the Republic of Poland. I pledge to steadfastly guard Her honour, and to fight for Her liberation with all my strength, even to the extent of sacrificing my own life if that is needed. I pledge unconditional obedience to the President of Poland, the Commander-in-Chief of the Republic of Poland, and the Home Army Commander whom be appointed. I pledge to resolutely keep secret whatever may happen to me. So help me God!'"

Daniel repeated it, one sentence at a time.

"Do not tell anyone of what has passed here tonight. Do not tell anyone of your plans. We will be in touch. Welcome to the *Union for Armed Struggle*."

Tomasz and Karol lifted their right hands in the two-fingered Polish salute. Daniel copied them. As he raised his arm, he drew air deep into his lungs, felt the oxygen feed every fibre within, believing he had been waiting for this moment since the stone embrace of that Warsaw doorstep a lifetime ago.

CHAPTER FOUR

Reading back over my other diary entries, I can't believe how naïve I sounded. Such a mixture of feelings I had about the ghetto. There was even optimism. Now, after months here, I can testify that it is nearer to hell on earth than any human soul could imagine.

It is winter in the ghetto. There are now half a million people here, within an area of a little more than a square mile. Only a handful of the population is allowed to cross into the Aryan side to work. For the rest of us, the other side of the wall is becoming a foggy memory. Did we have another life? It seems like a childish dream, that once we were free citizens, free to walk, to board a train, to sit in a café and eat apple cake. Now we exist in a heap of human misery, racked by overcrowding, starvation, disease and death.

Since the boundaries of the ghetto have been stable for a while, our little world is settling into a new landscape, with its own unwritten laws. There is what is called the large ghetto and then there is the small ghetto, connected in only one place, from the corner of Zelazna Street and over Chlodna Street. Lucky for us, we live in the small ghetto. This is not as crowded, and is largely occupied by the intelligentsia and richer middle class, who take more precautions over lice and disease. We feel safer here. But in order to access some facilities, to get particular items of food or ration cards, or visit a doctor or a client, we have to walk up to the large ghetto. This must be the most terrible place in the world. It is a warren of narrow stinking streets, infested with lice, full of crazy traders who have no money and have to earn their food on the streets. Karmelicka Street is the worst, swarming with crowds of people who shuffle along in a kind of blank terror. A heaving mass of humanity fills every crack and corner of the street, people tugging at your sleeve constantly, a cloying and hideous intimacy.

Negotiating the crowds is a horrible fact of daily life, and drives one to long for solitude and silence. Even at home, there are times when I cannot bear the closeness of Isak if he puts his arms around me. I'm ashamed to say I have pushed him away, desperate to feel air around my skin. Ilsa clings to me and it is all I can manage to stop myself doing the same to her, but I will not inflict rejection upon my child. She would not understand. Isak must learn to. He does not feel the same, I believe, as he barely leaves the apartment and does not suffer the nauseating nearness of others. He works on the business, such as it is, and uses this as his reason for allowing his wife and daughter the risky task of tramping the streets each day to find food. I have attempted to leave Ilsa behind but she cries if I try to and begs me to take her along. I think this is more to do with her fear of losing me, than it is of a desire to be outside, as she well knows the streets are full of nightmares. But at least her mother is with her. I have talked to Isak about how he is turning into a hermit and have explained to him with patience the dangers present in the streets, but he does not seem to hear me. He talks little now and just sews faster as I speak. I will give up asking Isak how he feels. One might imagine that the quiet I find at home is strangely comforting, after the boiling noise of the streets. But I fear for Isak's sanity. What is happening inside him? Perhaps his soul is screaming. As we sit in silence, Ilsa's hot little body clutching mine, I can almost hear the shrieks of his imprisoned mind. Going for a walk is a relief.

Most people walk as the trams are far too expensive, yet the richer Jews take advantage of them to avoid the closeness with the common hoard. This constant walking from place to place, negotiating the ins and outs of the seventy-odd streets of the ghetto, has turned us ghetto-dwellers into topographers, constantly reassessing our space in terms of danger points and opportunities. When we leave the apartment, I keep Ilsa close by my side and walk as briskly as I can through the streets, dodging the beggars and corpses and keeping my eyes at middle distance; look down and you'll see death and misery, and it is imperative to look forward in order to spot any problems well ahead. As we walk, the stream of people chorus a bubbling river of questions: any blockades today? Any raids further on? Is Chlodna St. open? Thus, most pedestrians trade warnings, and if there is danger sensed ahead, for example, a Gestapo car or a couple of German soldiers taking a sinister stroll, then the crowd can shift and split in a moment, rippling with hidden meaning like a muddled shoal of filthy fish. If only our medium were water, then we couldn't smell the stink of the ghetto, a mix of unwashed bodies, unhealed wounds and the sickly-sweet stench of starvation.

It is curious how, despite the horrors of the streets, everyday life continues. It has its own complex movement. There is a constantly evolving stability which rests for a while, until the situation alters again, due to new German decrees. If we could live without food, we would walk about in the ghetto as little as possible, because of the risk of catching disease or being lynched in the street, or other forms of casual German torture and murder. It is safer to stay indoors. Because of the intense overcrowding in the ghetto streets, it is difficult to let the Germans go by unmolested, as there is simply no room. And the Germans certainly hate to get too close to us filthy Jews, terrified they will catch diseases imaginary and all too real. When news spreads in the street that

Germans are approaching, the streets empty. But unlucky Jews still manage to attract attention only by virtue of being alive. The beatings and cruel games continue, and now kidnapping and shooting in the street are so common that I have become accustomed to the screams of the terrorised and the sound of gunshots. Anyone can be taken at any time. One of the most fearsome sights in the ghetto is the black limousine that belongs to the Gestapo. This cruises the streets and stops, whereupon some unlucky Jew is grabbed and bundled in. We hear that the Gestapo regularly search for random Jews in a destroyed building on Dzielna St. and then, whatever they find or do not find, they shoot them. After street shootings, the perpetrators ring the nearest doorbell and order the concierge to stack up the dead bodies and wash the blood from the road.

Thus the streets are full of the dead, from shootings and starvation and disease. It is Ilsa's recurrent nightmare that wakes her up screaming, that she is walking through the streets of the ghetto at night and is forced to stumble over thousands of corpses. The truth is not far from this image. Yet, believe it or not, there is also humour in the face of death. People do not say 'to die' but 'to hand in your ration card'. There is a popular ghetto song, which goes like this: "Oh, those coupons, I won't give up my coupons, / 'Cause Pinkert is on call / That bastard takes them all / Oh, those ration coupons." Pinkert is the name of the ghetto undertaker. He makes good money for himself by arranging elaborate funerals for those who can pay, and who can afford luxuries nowadays? Mostly, families of the recently dead are forced to leave the corpses in the street and Pinkert's carts pick them up the next day. These corpses are naked, as clothes are too valuable a commodity to be left for the dead. They are covered in a sheet of paper, which flaps in the wind showing the waxy white flesh beneath. Yet more often than not, the paper is stolen too. Nothing is wasted in the ghetto.

A lot of these deaths are from disease. There is typhus everywhere in the ghetto. It is one of the chief topics of conversation. It is widely known that Dr. Weigel's vaccine can help protect you from typhus, but it is hugely expensive – several thousand zloty for one phial for one dose – an impossible price for most. We must be vigilant about the typhus-spreading lice, which are everywhere and in everything. They fall from the ceilings in every building and nestle in your clothes. The ghetto authorities do their best to help prevent the disease, but it is a poor battle: there are quarantines for new arrivals, and 'steambaths' can be provided for infected apartments, houses and even entire buildings from mobile sanitation units. But the only way to avoid it is to take personal precautions on every trip, to find the lice one by one and kill them. So, every time we have been out and then return to the house, I make Ilsa or Isak stand at the front door and I go over every inch of them and myself with a pair of pincers and a bowl of spirits, and I drown the little bastards. We all know the signs of typhus: the high fever, the headaches and weakness and then, three days later, the deadly rash appears. The early symptoms are everywhere in the ghetto and we are in constant fear that one day we will find the rash on ourselves or our loved ones, and then we will know we are doomed. And there are other choices of death in the ghetto - the tuberculosis epidemic - and thousands are dying of this because they have no fat, no milk and no sugar to eat to keep them healthy.

As for us, we do our best to find food and remain a family. Our business has waned, as people who cannot afford enough food are not concerned about their clothes or even their armbands any more. We eke out a living doing repairs for tiny amounts of money, so that people can continue to wear bundles of rags held together by our careful threads. And this economic uncertainty is the same for everyone. As time has gone on, the whole population of the ghetto is heading towards destitution. People who at first worked and managed might at any moment find themselves among those who are barely existing. Yet even these are better off than most. Around you there are always the countless hordes of the nearly dead to remind you how alive you remain.

Amongst these nameless thousands, the ghetto has its characters who have achieved a kind of morbid fame amongst us: Rubinstein, the crazy beggar, ragged and dishevelled, carries a stick, hops and jumps and hums and mumbles, joking about ghetto life to make people laugh. He is the king of the Warsaw beggars, and is also known as *"Alle glajch"*, Yiddish for 'everyone's equal'. Even the Melody Palace put on a cabaret about him, played by the actor Edmund Minowicz. There are other famous personalities in the streets. The madman who only sings *"Jestem glodny"* ("I'm hungry") in a variety of melodies. More tuneful and less tragic are the numerous street performers - the singer with a pince-nez, the skinny violinists – who bring a little life and hope into the squalor. They even make money from their music; it is strange but people would rather give a few groszy for a pretty tune than an inch of bread to save a starving man. Melodies are more attractive than starvation.

Starvation is everywhere. Food and hunger are everyone's first priority. The official rations are suitable only for starvation. Thousands a month are dying from lack of food. And because of this, disease spreads more easily: if you have no money for food, there is certainly no money for soap. Buying food has become a hateful experience. In our rations, for example, they give three kilograms of beets for one ration card. But the beets disintegrate in your hands as soon as you hold them. They have been frozen and thawed countless times before you receive them. There is only vinegar and ice in them. Those of us who can afford these delicacies are the lucky ones. All around us are the poor souls who die in the streets from lack of food. In our rations, Jews receive the same amount of goodness from their food as perhaps eating one slice of bread per day at most. And by this, I mean the good bread we used to eat before the ghetto. Now all we can find is this sawdust bread and a minute monthly ration of sugar.

Other items like potatoes or jam we receive infrequently in tiny quantities. As I write, ration prices are fixed for bread at 30 groszy per kg in shops using the ration card. But if your ration cards have run out, as everyone's do within days, it will cost you 8½ zloty on the black market, over 20 times more. Ration cards are bought and sold like precious gems and we have heard that dead bodies are hidden by families in order to keep claiming their rations. We are lucky that our business still exists. We can at least work and be paid a little for it. Together Isak and I earn about ten to fifteen zlotys a day. Many earn nothing like this or nothing at all. And from this we have to pay rent, taxes, light and gas (whether or not it is available), materials for the business, our own clothes and shoes, and any visits to the doctor and other unforeseen expenses. Food alone costs about five zlotys a day per person and that is being frugal. We are scraping by, though we are always hungry.

Yet I am ashamed to use the word 'hungry', now that I see what true hunger is. It is starvation. In the ghetto, there is a small group of elite people who have enough to eat; these are largely the Jews who were rich before the war and have not yet run out of money or things to sell. Then there is a large group in the middle, the 'ordinary' people who more or less manage, who still look human, who are still clean and dressed without the tell-tale swollen stomachs. At the bottom are the hundreds of thousands of paupers who are struggling to fend off death. You have to learn to eat your own food without thinking of them, as it will drive you to despair if you do. I have learnt a horrible truth, as I look about me in the streets, that starvation reduces humans to animals. There is something wild and primitive about those who are starving. Despite the horror of their situation, starving people won't kill themselves, just as animals don't. They keep fighting for food until their last breath. Starvation is like a disease of the mind as well as that of the body, a life reduced to indifference to everything but food. They die running to get hold of bread, from the effort of it. I saw one dead man lying in the street, who had actually died with a piece of bread still in his mouth, no energy left to consume it.

Food has become the number one commodity. Street selling is commonplace, with most items exchanged for food and sold either in the ghetto or, at a better price, on the Aryan side through smuggling. The art of smuggling has become big business in the ghetto. Along the miles of walls, at intervals there are gaps in the wall at ground level, where water flows from the Aryan roads into the Jewish gutters. This is where children wriggle through to smuggle goods. At other quiet points along the walls, away from the guarded exits, I often hear a whistle or other agreed signal and see the bags and packets come sailing over the wall to be caught by shadows emerging from the buildings who scuttle away with their booty. There is even a regular smuggling trade run by those rich merchants Kon and Heller, who have bribed the police and have whole columns of carts coming through the ghetto gates daily, packed with fine foods and alcohol, and even fancy goods for rich Jews. But for most, smuggling is a fraught affair, committed out of dire need. And the punishments for the smuggler if caught are horrific. Just last week I saw a man catch a loaf of bread thrown over the wall to him, and two German gendarmes strolled round the corner and spotted him, and they set about stabbing him in the head with their bayonets. I did not stay to see if he survived, yet I doubt it. His screams rang through the streets as I ran on home. Murdered for a loaf of bread. Such is the price of life in the ghetto.

I see these sights every time I leave my door. And there is nothing I can do to change it. Beggars swarm the streets and claw at your clothes. There is a particular type of beggar we call the 'grabber', who will take any packet or bag you don't have a firm hold on, and grab it to see if it has anything to eat inside. Then they stuff any food in their mouth before you have a chance to take it back. People are beating beggars for stealing or being too pushy. But the worst ones, the ones who really break your heart into pieces, are the children. The starving children who cannot walk or talk. There are two children who have become quite well known, who always sing a strange song about a bad father whose children suggest ways he can kill himself. Some cry out for hours on end without stopping, "Have mercy on us!" or "Have pity!" Some you can't tell if they are a boy or a girl, their red legs covered in blisters, their cheeks yellow and swollen, their eyes hollow.

As a mother, I find myself cruelly split between two extremes: I look at the starving children in the streets and I want to take them all home with me and make them a good broth. That's what I want. But I know I cannot afford to, and if I did, I would put my own family in jeopardy, my own child. Isak and I still give most of our food ration to Ilsa and there are days we go completely hungry, in order that our daughter receives enough food for her bones to grow straight. And if you give even the smallest piece of bread to a begging child, they scratch at your arm and scream at you every time you go past and frighten Ilsa to death. I cannot have her scared like that every day. I want her mind to grow straight, too. Isak says, "The ghetto freezes you." And he does not mean only the cold weather.

Oh, I have to look away, I simply have to! I cannot help them, I have to feed my own family, I have to feed myself.

Thank heavens, it is now spring. Conditions are no better now than when I last wrote. In fact, the ghetto worsens weekly. The arrival of spring has a sad side too. No season is truly friendly in the ghetto: spring can bring painful memories of freedom, summer will bring unbearable heat in the overcrowded streets, autumn's cold encourages illness and winter brings the most deaths. Yet there is primal hope which dwells in the coming of the new season and few of us are immune. As I hoped, from the window of the highest apartments near the wall, the sight of blossom on the trees of Aryan Warsaw is visible, and in the sweeter air up there, up above the stew of humanity in the streets, one can just about smell the scent of the flowers. Our apartment is not quite high enough for this, yet Vladka's place is, and I find myself taking Ilsa there more and more, to remind her that there is life and beauty beyond these walls.

Even Isak has improved with the coming of spring. I think he was in a kind of drawn-out shock that lasted for the first few months of ghetto life. Now that the weather is brighter, the days longer, his face itself has lightened and his heart too. He talks to us more and even plays a little with Ilsa. Yet the most dramatic change has been that he actually wants to go outside, after his self-imposed exile. He undertakes the daily search for food, whilst Ilsa and I can work at home, she helping me in her little way with the sewing. And just recently, Isak and I are beginning to touch each other again. I have now ceased to menstruate, I think because of my diet and the stressful life we are leading. I am surely far too young for it to be the change. It is a relief, as there is no need to find wadding for the blood, and, if Isak and I ever wanted to make love again, which may happen one day, there would be no need to worry about pregnancy. Although, a baby does remind you awfully of life.

Thus, our little family is healing itself. We even go out as a family and have made new friends, particularly with our neighbours in our apartment building and in a café we visit. Vladka's Samuel has secured a job in the kitchens of the Sztuka Café in Leszno Street. It is the biggest café in the ghetto, and has a marvellous atmosphere due to its clientele of artists and musicians. There are regular performances in its concert room, of poets and comedians and musicians. Isak, Ilsa and I have been there a few times, when we can scrape together enough zlotys to buy one drink apiece and a meal between us, and Samuel has been kind enough to give us a little free food at times, when he can hoodwink the boss into not noticing our unpaid bill. We sit and chat with Vladka, who spends most of her time there. Vladka has not been able to continue her work as a portrait painter, of course, as you'd imagine that few have the spare cash or self-pride to commission a painting of their disappearing selves. Yet, she does continue to sketch, and we often see her drawing with a stubby pencil on second-hand paper, the backs of menus or official notices. It is her way of recording life in the ghetto, just as this diary is mine.

Vladka has become dearer to me than ever. When we meet, in her apartment or in the café, we embrace like long-lost sisters, thrilled to see that each of us has survived another few days, not lost in the street shootings or succumbed to the ever-presence of typhus. We kiss each other on the cheeks and can find ourselves weeping, just to say hello. It reminds me of the rocky emotions of pregnancy, when the smallest worry becomes a terrifying anxiety, and the simplest joy, like feeling your growing baby kick inside, becomes the greatest of joys. Swings of emotion are common in the ghetto. Everything is intensified to a sharper focus. People make friends more easily in the ghetto. Because there is less time for development of friendships, this means that relationships become powerful very swiftly. This reminds me of when I was a child at the summer camps and you met other children you knew you would only share a few weeks with, you developed intense friendships very quickly, more intense than the lazy time-wasting of ordinary life. The ghetto friendships are like that, but not because the end of the summer is coming, but because our deaths await us at the end of every street.

Yes, the ghetto is coming to life, in some ways, for some of us. 'Normal' life continues somehow: we eat, we sleep, we work, people make love, they are unfaithful, they argue, they laugh, they experience completely ordinary tragedies. Otherwise we will all go mad. It's also a defence of some kind of inner freedom, despite the walls that surround us. A demonstration of one's own normality is a kind of resistance. And there are even some forms of entertainment developing in the ghetto. It is not socially acceptable to enjoy yourself too obviously, as this is seen as poor taste. Yet some joyful occasions have taken place, like the Carnival Dance in the Melody Palace, where they held a competition for the girl with the best legs. There is a pathological sense of humour seen amongst us ghetto dwellers. After a particularly bad day neighbours gather in courtyards and literally scream with laughter. It's a necessary release. As long as it doesn't happen too often or too loudly.

Even Ilsa has come out of her shell now and plays with the other children from our apartment building. They play one very poignant game: 'Table, lay yourself', where they think up wonderful dishes of food which appear in a moment on an imaginary table and they all wolf it down. I try to tell her how lucky she is to have food, unlike those we look away from in the streets. But all she understands is the ache in her belly. I cannot tell her she is wrong about that.

I try to teach my daughter my own versions of right and wrong. Yet, education does not hold the same importance in the ghetto as it once did. Now practical skills are more crucial; in the face of death, various kinds of these skills, which offer a chance of getting a job, earning money, actual survival, take on a greater pragmatic value. Vocational courses, which offer exactly these skills, are very popular in the ghetto. I myself am teaching several young girls now to sew and repair clothes. I may be doing myself out of future business, but we have no concept of future here, remember. And I earn a little from teaching these children anyhow. And it does me good to see children learn. But children are changing. Children are not children. They now earn a living for their families and take awful risks in activities like smuggling, for which their size makes them the most suited. Children now play an active part in family decision making. Ilsa is becoming independent and growing up fast, spending more and more time with other kids, streetwise and savvy. I mourn the passing of her innocence. Whatever I try to teach her, she is learning too much from the streets.

There is talk of resistance against the Germans. But I think active resistance is almost impossible. We have the particular terror that there is no 'acceptable subservience' to save us Jews, as it has done in the past, when Jews have been persecuted throughout history. For example, qualities of hard work, compliance, or even conversion to Christianity would save a Jew from the harshest master. But the Germans do not hold with these practices. I believe they simply want us to evaporate. And what if we attacked them, weak as we are in body yet ferocious in spirit? There is the added horror of frequent reprisals for resistance. In a place where heroism, such as killing a German, means a thousand Jews will be randomly murdered in reprisals, who can live with all those deaths on his hands? So, we must find other kinds of resistance. There is a Yiddish verb I hear a lot in the streets and courtyards – it is *uberleben,* which means 'to live through'. Survival is our greatest weapon.

Despite the continued miseries of ghetto life, I often feel in those around me that the mood is optimistic. The war will be over soon, surely, people say. The Russians will come. (Most Jews love the idea of the Russians, though the Aryan Poles despise them. But we are not in the same war, are we?) There are prophecies made by clairvoyants predicting the imminent end of the war. People like to believe in these. Powerful rumours spread through the streets. They are the only good news that we hear. Only bad news comes from the Germans or even our own authorities, the Judenrat, such as our rations being reduced.

The most worrying news recently is that all Jewish men born between 1881 and 1926 need to register with the Judenrat and undergo a medical test. This includes Isak, who was born in 1889. He will have to register soon. I am fearful of what this will mean. Even the process to register is full of danger and corruption. Isak has seen the queues to register on his daily walk, and says they are chaotic: vendors selling places in line as well as bread, pretzels, sweets, cigarettes and hot coffee at exorbitant prices. The Jewish police try to control the crowd and beat those who step out of line. And we are still not sure what the meaning of this medical test is. The word on the streets is that you should try to fail it if possible, but nobody knows why or where this rumour has come from. Surely, you'd be more useful if you pass your medical test, but nobody knows to what purpose this information will be put by the Germans. And we have heard that the Judenrat officials and the medical commission profit hugely, particularly from those attempting to fail the test. This is because you can ask to be referred to a specialist, who may pronounce you unfit, if you are rich enough to pay: apparently, referrals to a specialist cost around ten zlotys at least. And everyone is told they have to have two photos, officially stamped, which also costs a lot. Making money from others' problems. And added to this worry about the extra costs and danger involved, we are still very uncertain as to what these registrations mean. There is gossip going around that the purpose of all this is to place all Jewish men in labour camps, that there will be mass deportations of men. If so, then perhaps it would be better to fail the medical test. But what happens to those who do? Will they simply be allowed to stay here with their families, or something else? What does a farmer do with an old horse, unable to work the land? Sell it to the glue factory, that's what. What will happen to Isak?

I worry about the future, though I know I shouldn't, as what can I do to change it? I often think of the past, though I know I shouldn't, as it only leads to self-pity. Most of us ghetto-dwellers live in the present. Time is almost non-existent in the ghetto, as death walks beside us. But I have my secret weapon. My diary. Writing helps me to keep a hold on time. I can impose structure in my diary, assign meaning to the lawless mess of ghetto life. Many people in the ghetto are writing diaries, or poetry, drawing and painting or composing music. They want to record and pass on to others their own experience. We are aware that we are taking part in something unique, something uniquely unspeakable. This makes me think about my own writing. It is not merely a record for my own sanity. I would like it to be a record to be read one day. And with that in mind, I feel I need to record more detail, what people say to me and the colours and shapes of things. Just as Vladka draws the details of the ghetto world, I would like to convey more than mere facts. I will try to write more as an artist as I go on, to entertain a future reader. Does that sound ridiculous, in a place and time such as this? Maybe it does. Although I feel unable to share my diary with anyone right now, just as Vladka hides her drawings, I am aware that it may be of use to others, after I am gone (and who knows how soon that will be?). I want to warn people, to protect humanity from a repetition of anything like this again in the future. Though I know that even a thousand pages from me will mean very little in the epic dramas of this war, that one person's diary can only ever be a pitiful fragment of the complexity of being alive. And not only that, but one person's voice cannot dare speak for all those who have had no opportunity to speak, to have their voice heard, on paper or otherwise – those naked corpses wrapped in paper in the streets of the ghetto. Where are their words? No-one can speak for all those who never wrote or whose writings have been lost.

But I continue to write. To bear witness is a defence of the human dignity and individuality that the Germans are denying us all.

My writing may not win prizes, but it is better than silence.

CHAPTER FIVE

Darkness. Heat. Nausea. Aching bones. The odour of grease and sweat. The sound of clattering saucepans, spitting oil and Swedish babble. The wallowing swell of the ship on the Baltic Sea. Daniel had been shown to his hiding place that morning. He had not been visited yet and not eaten yet. He'd drunk a lot from his water bottle and used his emergency toilet facilities: a jug. He held his foot against it, so that if the boat lurched, at least it would only splash his boots and not soak the coat on which he sat.

He felt inside the bag on his lap, found his torch. He knew he should not waste the batteries. He turned it on. He saw his piss slosh in the jug. How many hours now? Dad's wristwatch told him eight hours had gone. It was ten times that to come. The cook had said almost ninety hours' journey to Gdynia. He shone the torch round the confines of his cubby hole. It was perhaps four foot by three, maybe a bit longer. He could not stretch out his legs. If that blasted jug weren't there he might have manoeuvred onto his back, legs up the wall. It would feel like lying down. He was lucky he wasn't a tall man. He'd cursed this when he was younger, but he was glad of it now, here. He turned off the torch and put it back in the bag, then rifled round for something to eat. Magda's salty crackers. They would make him thirsty, but he didn't care.

He had little to do but think: of the months since he joined the Underground back in London, saying goodbye to Tomasz, who left soon after to be stationed in a middle-of-nowhere place called Swinderby, annoyed to leave the south-east and his trips to London, sad to go before Daniel left. He told him, "I wish I had something wise to say. But I'm only a pilot, not a poet."

Then the promised training that never materialised, only a couple of sessions with Karol in that same bare flat, where he was shown how to aim and fire a pistol, theoretically.

"You won't need much else," Karol had said. "Not sabotage or espionage training. They'll use you as an English teacher. You'll teach other members of the Underground, to improve their English for roles as couriers coming over here. Don't look disappointed! You want to stay safe, don't you? So you can find your mother?" But it was thrilling to hold a gun. To imagine shooting a Nazi, even killing one.

One week before Daniel left, Karol told him what to bring:

Valid British identity card, passport and press pass, for passage to Sweden.

Lighter.

Matchbox.

Wristwatch – he took Dad's.

Large penknife.

Thermal underwear.

Woollen vest, pants and socks.

Two shirts, scarf and two pairs of trousers.

Woollen gloves.

Handkerchief.

Boots.

Enamel cup and spoon.

Small notepad and pencil.

Toilet equipment including razors, shaving brush and soap, toothpaste and toothbrush, toilet paper, small towel, comb.

Torch and two sets of batteries.

A few lightweight rations; a water bottle and small flask filled with brandy ("to keep you warm", Magda said); pouches of tobacco and cigarette papers (about which Karol noted, "Everybody smokes. It would seem out of place if you didn't.")

All of this packed economically into a lightweight backpack. Daniel carried his life with him.

A day before, Karol gave him:

A map of Poland (scale 1: 100,000).

10000 Polish zloty, 1000 Swedish kroner and 1000 German marks.

Suicide tablet (issued to all Polish Underground operatives).

Microfilm hidden in a pen, containing key instructions for a contact in Warsaw. He was told the microfilm was undeveloped and if danger of discovery presented itself, he could unscrew the pen and expose the film to the light. The contents would be destroyed. He was told to guard it with his life. He was not to be told what the microfilm contained, as then he could not reveal anything if tortured. If the microfilm fell into the wrong hands, several good people's lives would be worthless.

A Colt .45 and two reserve magazines of ammunition. Karol said to secure it in his baggage until he reached Warsaw – the Underground was always in need of weapons – but he must not let it be loose in his bag before he reached Poland. Karol said the best way was to wrap the gun and spare ammo in a cloth backed by card and sew them into the lining of his backpack. If he was searched the packet would feel like the bottom of the bag. Magda did it for him. Daniel had watched her needle and thread at work, the same hands that had sewn up his trouser cuffs since childhood.

The last thing Karol handed him was a list of all the code names, addresses and passwords he was to use with his contacts in Sweden and Poland. He had one night to memorise and destroy them. There were names of people and streets, in Swedish and Polish. The passwords for his contacts consisted of sets of questions he had to ask them when they met and answers they must reply, or vice versa. It seemed impossible. Magda said, "Make a little story about them in your head." Daniel spent that final sleepless night telling himself inventive tales of lust between oddly-named Swedish girls and Polish men. He would not forget that.

The next morning, he had walked all the way to Euston Station with Magda. In the months between his decision and that day, she had refused to talk to him. But only for one night. After that, she peppered their daily conversations with assurances that he would change his mind. Later, her tactics changed to guilt: poor Mr Summerskill turning in his grave. The fool's errand of his mission, the untrustworthy Karol and his retarded mother who went with any peddler in Warsaw. Her concluding plan was herself. Poor Magda, a mother to him all those years, a woman alone in dangerous London. The bombing had petered out somewhat by the time he left at the end of August, but Magda still insisted she could die any day and he would never know, off who knows where in darkest Poland. She even tried Helena. "You might not like her, you know. She might be dull. Or a drinker." But nothing worked. He was not called back to the Drill Hall, he had no urgent missive to serve Great Britain. His father was dead. Magda was safe financially, surrounded by friends. Poland called to him. Helena haunted him.

Magda knew this. She gave up. She began to polish his Polish, correcting usage and teaching him titbits of Warsaw slang, hauling it up from her memories of two decades before. She pulled out an old Warsaw street map and talked him through it, street by street, building by building. They talked of newspapers and customs, sayings and curses. Daniel knew her knowledge would be hopelessly out-of-date but he loved her for it. She promised she would lie to the *Chronicle* for him, tell them he had been called abroad to be with his uncle, his only living relative. She sewed and ironed and sorted and packed and repacked and fussed. Everything a mother would do.

On the platform at Euston, she gave him a gold ring. "I knew a wealthy man when I was a young woman. He gave me that ring and a hatful of promises, but then married an heiress. I kept the ring as a memory of my hopes. You should take it. Hide it. Sell it when you need to. Gold will be worth more than paper on the streets of Warsaw now." She sobbed at goodbye. The last thing she said was, "Bring her here, Daniel. When you find her, bring her home."

His train took him to Glasgow and then he caught a local train over to a small town near the coast called Cupar. From here, he had been instructed to take a taxi to a military airfield, where a small passenger plane was waiting for him, two other journalists from Scottish newspapers and a diplomat from Edinburgh. The plane was pokey and the trip turbulent. From a tiny window, he looked at the stars and knew only a thin layer of metal stood between himself and the night sky. His co-travellers talked little. He was asked by one of the Scottish journalists why he was going to Sweden and used a story about an article on neutral countries for the *Chronicle*, feigned exhaustion and pretended to doze off. He was too excited to sleep.

They landed at a small airport just outside the city of Stockholm. Once off the plane, a smartly-dressed man appeared next to him and asked in English: "Are you staying at the Paris Hotel?"

"Yes, thank you for meeting me."

He motioned for Daniel to follow. The password had worked. There was no conversation. They took a taxi to an impressive building, which the man called the Polish Legation. Deep inside was an office where they met an official with whom they talked for an hour. Daniel was quizzed about his mission and experience and family background. They spoke in Polish and listened carefully to everything he had to say. Afterwards, they left the room for a few minutes. They came back and shook his hand. It seemed he had passed a test, though he wasn't sure how.

The official gave him a fake identity document, an ID card of a workman at the Gdynia port in Poland, which would let him make his way through the port in case he was stopped. He also showed him a tiny hand-drawn map of the route from Gdynia port to the safe house nearby. He was told he had to memorise it there and then. Feeling the sweat build up on his neck, he sat and stared at the map, walking through the streets in his mind, using Magda's methods to remember the landmarks. He hoped the story would stick, because to get lost in Gdynia could be fatal. After a few minutes, the official asked if he had the route memorised and he confirmed this. He shook hands and they wished him luck. His contact took him to a hotel on the same street, booked him in at the desk and told him he would come by for him at seven the next morning.

Before he left, he told him to be extra careful in the streets of Stockholm. Sweden might be neutral, but its neighbours, Norway and Denmark, were occupied. Swedes were vigilant of any threat to this precarious stability. Daniel had a quick dinner at the hotel bar (roast pork – the first decent meat he'd had in over a year) and stayed in his hotel room all evening.

In the morning he was taken down to the port and introduced to his new contact on the dock next to the boat, after which his smart-suited colleague took his leave. His new contact grabbed his hand and shook it roughly. Again, no names were mentioned. This was the ship's cook – a robust, middle-aged man with a bushy silver beard. He spoke to him in English, saying he was Norwegian and had no qualms about involvement in anything that "messed things up" for the Nazis. They walked on board and the cook said nothing further until they reached the ship's galley. He said that Swedish ships brought iron ore from the Baltic coast and returned with coal. He said quite a few Poles escaped from Poland this way, and it had become a route for Polish Underground couriers to travel between England and Poland carrying information. The Gestapo were certainly aware of the possibility of stowaways on these boats and regularly searched them with dogs. He showed him the hiding place. It was in a secret compartment behind a cupboard, with a board placed across it as a false back to the real cupboard in front. He said he should go straight in and get settled, because the boat would leave in an hour and soon the Swedish crew would begin to turn up and they were not as keen on engaging in anti-Nazi activities as he was. He squeezed inside. The cook said, "Good job you are a short-arse!" and shut him in.

That was hours ago. The sounds of the kitchen dwindled. Plates and cutlery were put away, talking receded. The sleepless sea surged beneath him. Daniel retched. There was a knock on the panel. The cook's big face appeared, the kitchen dim behind him. Daniel stretched his legs, went to a real toilet and had a glorious shit. The cook gave him bread, sausage and cheese. He took the jug and replaced it with a wide-necked corked bottle, said sorry he couldn't find it earlier, that this was better for toilet business. The cook refilled his water too and then sent Daniel back into the cupboard.

The next two days passed in the same way. Daniel marked off the hours in his notebook. He turned on his torch to look at Helena's photograph, the red ribbon. He thought about Dad and Magda, then tried to imagine what Poland would be like. He realised the boat was slowing down. It stopped. Was it over? A scrabbling sound. Claws on the kitchen floor. Dogs. A yelp. Sniffing. German voices, loud and close. His first contact with the enemy. They were badgering the cook, demanding answers. Then laughing, more scraping from the claws, but further away. Another yelp. Movement. Silence. An hour later, the cook released him.

"What happened?" said Daniel.

"Gestapo. But dogs want meat they smell everywhere in

kitchen. Cannot smell you or anything else. Just meat. We are here. Gdynia."

The cook gave Daniel a pair of dirty overalls and a cap so he could pass inconspicuously through the docks to get to the safe house. They disembarked. It was mid-afternoon, cloudy and grey. His first breath of Polish air. All he could smell was brackish water and fish. The Norwegian cook did not say good-bye. He turned and wandered away in the opposite direction. For a moment, Daniel wanted to follow him, his only friend in this land. Men were everywhere, hurrying to and fro, all talking in Polish. A whole country speaking Polish. As a child, he'd had dreams about being in a room, full of people he vaguely knew, all good friends with each other, all ignoring him. He would wake overcome with loneliness, intense as sickness. He felt it now. Alone, not in a room, but in a vast foreign land. But there was no time for reflection. He made his mind picture the route he'd memorised in Stockholm. He wanted to walk purposefully, but it was hard, as he had to keep looking up for landmarks. He went down one street and saw nothing from the map he had learnt. He was lost. Two men outside a bar watched him. He turned around and went back to the last place he knew. He stared at his shoes as he walked and forced his brain to make the image of the map there on the dirty road before him. Three German soldiers came around a corner, talking away in their own language. Their faces looked like British Tommies, just a different uniform. They didn't notice him, in his scruffy dock clothes. For once he was happy to be ignored. He looked up and saw the name of the right street. He had found it.

Halfway along the street was the house. He knocked on the front door. A woman about Magda's age opened it, smiled, spoke in Polish.

"Come in. How is your cousin?"

Daniel answered, "His leg has mended very well."

Once the door shut, his hands began to shake. The woman saw this and beckoned him to follow. She sat him down at a table in the kitchen and poured him a glass of milk. No words, just cold milk. His hands steadied. She sat opposite him.

"They call you 'Anglik'."

He nodded.

"Polish for Englishman. Not very original, is it?"

He gave a little laugh, relaxed a bit. She passed him a plate of meat sandwiches and watched him eat.

"I'm Wanda. It's your first mission, isn't it?"

"Yes."

"You'll get used to it. Come with me."

She showed him to a small room at the back of the house.

"Leave those old clothes here. I'll wake you. Good night."

It was only five o'clock, but Daniel slept all night and woke with a start. Wanda gave him cheese, bread and apples for breakfast. Again, there was no small-talk. This was the mode with operatives. She told him to get his things together and handed him his documents.

"This is a fake Polish identity card. And this is an *Ausweis* – a German work card, which protects you against arrest and deportation to forced labour elsewhere in the Reich. These are for your use anywhere in Poland. This is the return portion of a permit which allows you to travel from Gdynia to Warsaw, for the purpose of 'visiting your family' in Gdynia, as one needs permission from the Germans to travel more than a hundred miles in Poland. Leave your British identity documents here. Your new false documents are under the Polish name of Stanislaw Getka. In a minute, we'll walk to the bus stop nearby. You must ask for a ticket to Gdansk railway station. From there, you must find the train to Warsaw East. Someone will meet you. You may be stopped at any time and asked to show your documents. Don't forget your name. *Stanislaw Getka*."

Another new identity. First Magda named him Feliks. Then Henry gave him Daniel Summerskill. Karol called him Anglik.

Now his papers read Stanislaw Getka. Had Helena given him a name, before leaving him on that doorstep?

Wanda walked him to a bus stop nearby and waited. She didn't speak. When the right bus came, she nodded for him to get on, said, "Goodbye, son," and left. He wanted to say thank you, for the milk, for her courage. But it was not the Underground way.

From the bus, safely through the clouded glass, he had his first look at Nazi officers. Back home, they seemed a legend dreamt up by the Ministry for Information, unreal creatures of evil created for the cinema. Here, they were real men in their uniforms, not shiny and new as on film, but unkempt and slovenly; not arrogant and sneering, but young and awkward, old and tired. Not myths, just men.

From Gdansk railway station, Daniel quickly found the train for Warsaw. On the train, he was only asked for ID once, by a Polish guard, who briefly scanned his card and permit. He did not even speak to Daniel. When Daniel arrived in Warsaw, he was met at the station by a young woman. She was not pretty. She looked him up and down then looked away. She seemed disappointed. Not the dashing Englishman, he thought, just a boy pretending to be a man: small stature, dun hair, no one special.

She said, "Are you here for the Brushmakers' Convention?"

"Yes, I'm sorry I was delayed."

She led the way to a tram, which sailed through the streets of Warsaw. Busy roads bristled with cars and trams and bicycles as scores of Varsovians made their way in all directions along the crowded pavements. Preoccupied with their daily tasks, it was easy to imagine that there was no foreign occupation, no war even. The tram went by a beautiful park, approached a bridge. He saw that part of its name was Dabrowski – the same as Tomasz. Where was he now? Safe in rural Lincolnshire or killed? It seemed impossible that a life that had blazed bright in his memory could have been snuffed out. The tram crossed the River Vistula, slate-grey water snaking away north through this city of his birth, joined other rivers, surged to the Baltic Sea, merged with the North Sea, mingled with the English Channel, to which flowed the Thames.

They alighted soon after and walked down side streets where there were fewer people and less noise, and Daniel grew more aware of the silence between him and this woman. She stopped at a large grey stone apartment block. His rooms were on the top floor. She let them in, handed him the key.

"You can call me Lidia. They call you Anglik?"

"Yes."

"There's enough food in the kitchen cupboards for one week. You must not leave the flat. I'll be back in a few days with another member of the Underground, Warsaw chapter, and he will initiate you. I will knock five times on the door, and you should check through the spy hole."

She left, without a goodbye. He looked about the flat. A little bedroom, flowery wallpaper. A narrow kitchen, food in the cupboards, as she said. A living room, with a comfortable couch and one chair and heavy pink curtains. A bathroom with long dark hairs in the plugholes and a creaky floorboard that shifted as he stood on it. He knelt down and saw it could be moved. Underneath was a perfect cubby hole. He unpicked Magda's stitches at the base of his bag and retrieved the gun and ammunition. He gathered his other valuables: the microfilm, documents, his money and Magda's ring. He stashed them all under the floorboard.

He kept his mother's picture and ribbon in his pocket. He cooked a frugal meal from the supplies, boiled potatoes and cabbage, stale bread and tasteless cheese, and a pear for dessert. He stared down at Warsaw, the narrow view of it offered from the sitting-room window. An ordinary street in an ordinary European capital city. His place of birth. And it occurred to him how very far he was from home. From London, from Blake's tomb in St. Paul's; the moorhens in Regent's Park; the little garden in Tavistock Square; Dad's armchair in the flat; his blue-striped egg cup in the kitchen cupboard; Magda's hands. And that he may never see anymore of them more. He might die here.

He stayed in the apartment for four days, thinking he'd been forgotten. At midday, there were five knocks on the door and he looked through the spy hole. It was Lidia, with a man beside her. He opened the door and grinned at them, relieved to see someone, anyone.

The new contact was a lanky man with grey eyes and grey flashes in his black hair. He did not smile. These operatives certainly took life seriously. But what was he thinking? Of course they did. This was no adventure for them. It was life and death. As it was for him too, now. Perhaps he had nothing to smile about.

The new operative made no attempt at conversation. The first thing he said after shaking hands was, "Give me the microfilm, the gun and the ammo."

He retrieved them from his bathroom hiding place and handed them over. The man pocketed the microfilm and ammunition, and put the gun into his trousers at the back. He began a lecture on Daniel's new role in the Polish Underground.

"Don't ask questions. Do as you're told. It is dangerous to know too much. Do not ever trust intuition when dealing with people. You may think you know human nature, but it's never enough. Only rely on passwords, recognition signs and code names. Never reveal your real name. Don't say more than you have been charged with. This is not a social club.

"Initially, you will be watched without your knowledge by members of the Underground, who will follow your movements. This is because we do not know you well enough and have to keep a check on your ability to be trustworthy. If you betray us, you will be found and shot.

"You must be constantly vigilant – I cannot stress this enough – you must never allow yourself to rest from being on full alert, wherever you are, even shut up here at home. Mind who you talk to, who you look at, where you go, even how you walk. At any moment, you could be noticed by an undercover Gestapo agent, or a Polish informant, caught and interrogated, most likely tortured for information. Yet you have the advantage of belonging to a widespread and powerful organisation, which in return for your allegiance will help to protect you, provide you with documents and money when needed, as well as a relatively safe place to stay and a good cause to work for. You are one of the lucky ones."

All of this was spoken in a cool voice, as if it had little to do with him personally. Daniel made a mental note to try to take the same tone when addressing other members of the Underground. He didn't want to reveal himself as nervous or untrustworthy. He decided to practise his poker face in the mirror that evening.

The man handed him forged ration cards for use in Warsaw and told him that he would be able to use his new identity papers and this safe house for a limited time only, as Underground members moved around and changed their fake ID frequently to avoid detection by the Gestapo. He would be told when and where to move. The man said he'd be back soon to give Daniel his first mission. Until then, he was permitted to leave the flat, but only for short trips to purchase food or other essentials.

The man asked him if he had any questions.

"I've come here to find my mother. Did they tell you about this?"

"We heard about it."

"I was told that I'd be given help, and in return I'd act for the Polish Underground in any way I can."

The man and Lidia exchanged unreadable glances. He replied, "What information do you have concerning your mother's whereabouts?"

Daniel said none, really. Only a photograph with the address of the photographer on the back. He took it out of his pocket and handed it over. They stared at it.

"This is her?" said Lidia.

"Yes. They found it in my blankets, at an orphanage in Warsaw."

"So young," she said. The man said, "It's not that far from here, north-west. You are given permission to look for this photographer's shop. If you find him, you can talk to him, see if he remembers taking this photo of your mother. But you must ensure that you reveal nothing of your true situation. Tell him only that you need to find this woman as she is a relative of yours. He should believe you. Your accent is good, very good in fact. You do sound like a Varsovian, not an Englishman."

Daniel told him he'd been taught by a local woman.

"She taught you well, Anglik. In the meantime, we will make contact with our friends in the Jewish Resistance. Perhaps they may agree to help you. We can arrange a meeting."

"Thank you! Thank you very much."

The man held out his hand. "You can call me Jerzy," he said.

Then they left.

That afternoon, Daniel ventured out. He began at a grocer's nearby, to buy supplies and find out the way to the photographer's place. He asked the woman in the shop for directions to the address on the back of the photograph. He had memorised the street name, as he didn't want to show just anyone the photo, especially this close to his safe house. Being a young man looking for a Jewish-looking woman was risky enough. The woman was helpful, explaining how to get there on foot. It was a walk of perhaps a half-hour, she said, or he could ride two trams. He thanked her and left. He decided not to take the tram. He wanted to see his city on foot.

He walked through Warsaw. His impression was that it was a fine city, with beautiful architecture, or rather, it had been once.

Scores of buildings were either damaged or destroyed, just like London. Every corner Daniel turned, he imagined that his mother may have walked this pavement, that he himself might have been carried along it by her, inside her womb or even in her arms before she gave him up. How strange to have been born in a place, to have breathed its air and seen its sights and heard its sounds, and yet retain no memory of it. Magda was born here too, grew up here, tired of it, jumped at the chance of leaving. Dad worked here, rode the trams, wrote down his thoughts, took a baby home.

His walk was dominated by churches, passing four and spotting spires for several more. Then, he came across a tall brick wall, which curiously traversed a street called Bonifraterska, right across the centre of it. It was the ghetto. Inside, countless Jews were caged. Perhaps his mother was there, perhaps other family or friends of hers. Of his. He wanted to walk up to it and touch the bricks, to feel contact with his fellow Jews inside. Remembering Jerzy's advice, that he should even watch the way he walked down a street, he hurried on. It would not do to be seen patting the walls of the Jewish Ghetto.

Further on, he saw graffiti which intrigued him, splashed in red across a wall, which looked like a letter P with its base turned into a kind of anchor. He stopped across the street to get a better look at it. Two women walked towards him and were glancing at the graffiti too. One of them whispered to the other and he just caught her comment: "Polska Walczy", she said. Poland Fights. He realised the emblem was a P and a W. It was heartening to see blatant resistance on the part of the Polish people. It made him proud to be born there.

He reached the correct road. It was mostly a few boarded-up shops and dingy street vendors. Then he spotted it, a narrow shop front with a name above the door. It was the same as that on the back of his mother's picture: Michal Taborski. Next to the door was a display window. Inside, there was a tiny room, more like an alcove than a shop, with a desk behind which sat a little old man with pure white hair. He was looking through a magnifier at negatives on his desk. He looked up.

"Good morning, sir."

"Are you Michal Taborksi, the photographer?"

"I am."

"I'm wondering if you can help me."

"I'll try. If you want me to take a photograph, it'll be ready tomorrow morning."

"I just have a question for you." The photographer's eyebrows arched with interest. "I'm looking for a distant cousin of mine, who used to live in Warsaw. She had her photo taken by you when she was a young woman, about twenty years ago. If I show you the photograph, maybe you might remember her and perhaps know where she lives. Perhaps you sent an invoice to her address. Or you might even have known her. It was a long time ago. But you never know."

He handed him his mother's picture. Taborski peered at it and said nothing for over a minute.

Daniel said, "Did you take this photograph?"

"It has my name on the back, so I must have." He continued to stare at it. "When did you say it was taken?"

"About twenty years ago."

"That's a very long time ago, young man," he said indignantly. He looked again at the photo and rubbed the corner of his mouth, infuriatingly slowly.

"Do you remember her?"

"This is one of a thousand faces that have floated before me. And such a long while ago too."

Daniel felt the weight of disappointment on his shoulders. He knew going there that it was improbable, almost pointless. But there was a part of him that hoped, all the same.

"Never mind," he said and went to take the photograph.

"One minute, my boy," he said, turning the photo over. "Give me time to think."

Daniel waited, sweating.

Taborksi looked at him curiously.

"And she is your aunt, you say?"

"Yes," he answered. "No! I mean, she is my cousin. A distant cousin." The phrase sounded like the lie it was. He was furious with himself. To have fallen clumsily at the first hurdle. What a blithering idiot. Taborski's eyes held the hint of a smile. Was he suspicious? Was he an informant? Daniel felt his face burn.

The photographer passed the photo back to him and spoke.

"Listen, son. I don't know who you are or what you are really doing here. Or why you are looking for this woman. But I like your face. And I don't believe there is any malice in it. You don't have to worry, I won't tell anyone of this."

Daniel stared at him and didn't attempt to speak. He knew whatever he said would ring falsely. Jerzy's warning: "Do not ever trust intuition when dealing with people." But he felt he could trust this man. He didn't know why, and he knew that in itself was hazardous. Yet he did believe there was no harm in him.

Taborski said, "I do remember her."

"You do?"

"Yes. I wrote her name on the back."

"So it's your handwriting."

Daniel was disappointed. He wanted it to be hers.

"Yes. The man said her name was Helena. I wrote it on the back."

"What man?"

"She came with a man. They were, you know, kissing and cuddling. She was a young girl. They never came back."

"What did the man look like?"

"I can't remember. Older than her. But I do recall one thing about him. It stuck in my mind because it was quite interesting. He said he was a poet."

"A poet, are you sure?"

"I think so. He said she had such a lovely face, one day he

would write a poem about her. It's not every day you hear something like that."

"And you never saw them again, the man or the girl?"

"No, never. No one came for the photo. I liked it, I liked her face. He was right, it was a lovely face. I put it in my window. One day, I was in the back room when I heard the bell ring. But no one was there. The photo had gone. Someone had stolen it. I don't know who – maybe it was him, maybe it was her, maybe it was a stranger who just liked the look of it. Who knows? Maybe it was you, young man!"

But Daniel knew who had taken it. It must have been her. How else would it have been wrapped in his swaddling clothes? She went to that trouble for him. Yes, she abandoned him. But she also took the risk of stealing her own photograph from a shop, probably as she had no money to pay for it. She bequeathed her image to him, to tell him, her baby, who she was.

He thanked Taborski, who said, "I'm glad I could help you. Oh, there's something else. I do know that this photo was taken in 1920, during the war."

Which war, Daniel thought? But he couldn't ask that. His lack of knowledge would be suspicious. "How do you know?"

"I remember that the poet was full of talk about Russian defeat. Said he'd write a poem about that too."

Taborski said this last with a glint in his eye, mocking the poet and his big ideas.

"Anything else you can remember?"

"I don't think so."

Daniel slipped the photo carefully into his inside pocket.

"One more thing," said Taborski. He was looking at Daniel's pocket. What did he want? "Wait here," he said and went through to the back room. Steady footsteps going upstairs. Did he have a phone up there, to ring the Gestapo? A window, to signal someone? A hot prickle flared in Daniel's cheeks and down his neck, across his chest and into his stomach. If he ran, it would look suspect. But if he stayed, was he waiting like a fool for his own capture? Christ, he thought, I'm a lousy spy. The stairs creaked again.

"Here," Taborski said and handed him a copy of Helena's photograph, a pristine version of the same image he had been carrying around in his pocket for months. Clean and new, it was as if Helena had stepped forward from her girlhood and stood between them in the shop. Her black eyes were blacker than ever, her shyness glimmering from the shiny paper.

Taborski said, "That photo you brought is old and tatty, like me! I keep copies of all my pictures. You should have it."

Daniel offered to pay him, but he shook his head. "This woman obviously belongs to you. I don't know how and I don't want to know. But I won't take your money. She is yours."

Real news of Helena. Many-coloured threads to weave into the fabric of her story. A shy young girl with dark eyes walks into a Warsaw photographer's studio in 1920 with an older man, her lover. He is a poet and talks of the war with Russia. He calls her Helena. She has her photograph taken and never collects it. Later that photo is stolen and in June 1923, it appears in a baby boy's blankets outside a Jewish orphanage.

Who was this man? Was he Daniel's father? What happened to him? Maybe he was killed. There was a war on, after all. Young girl and older poet fall in love, he marches off to war and dies, she is left with a baby and no one to turn to. Yes, that could be true. That would be tragic. But the date. Taborski said the photo was taken in 1920. And Daniel wasn't born until 1923. He was not inside his mother when that photo was taken. He came three years later. Magda didn't mention anything about a war being on when she found him. And Dad was reporting on poverty, not the war. It must have been over before 1923. Where was his father? Had he deserted her? Daniel began to hate the man who was with her, this older man, this foolish poet full of talk of war. Where was he when Helena left her baby on that step? The bastard.

Questions and doubts, supposition and invention. As he walked back to the flat, he tried to silence tales patched from second-hand half-known shreds. The fact was he was no nearer to finding her. But at least he felt closer to her. He could picture her and her lover, kissing in the shop, talking of poetry and war. They had thanked the photographer and left, walking away down that shabby Warsaw street. Where did they go?

Three days later, Jerzy arrived early with a suit, coat and hat for Daniel to wear.

"We have a fake job for you. It's a credible reason for leaving the flat every morning and it'll give you somewhere to go. You'll be masquerading as an insurance broker, working from an office not far from here. In fact, in a back room, there is a listening post. These are dotted all over the city to monitor radio broadcasts from London and elsewhere, as well as news reports on what else is happening in Poland itself. Gestapo vans drive around trying to locate these radio signals and if found, the wireless operators almost certainly face death. You'll go to this office daily. That's where you'll receive your instructions. Get changed first. Then come with me. I'll show you the way."

Before they left, Daniel asked, "Is the office where I'll meet my pupils?"

"What pupils?"

"My English pupils."

"What are you talking about?"

"Karol, I mean, my contact in London, told me I would be an English teacher."

"Did he now?"

"Yes."

"Well, we do have some teachers. Trying to stop our children becoming dunces, as the Germans have shut the schools."

"I'm supposed to be teaching your couriers."

"Look, Anglik. I don't know what rubbish they told you. But you won't be pissing away this war on verbs and adverbs. We need men for actions."

"What kind of 'actions'?"

"Didn't they tell you anything? This month we lost two men when we hijacked a German lorry and it crashed. Last month, three died setting a bomb to blow up a key bridge on the supply railway line to Warsaw. Also, two of our men carried out murders of one SS man and one Gestapo man. But the reprisals by Germans were terrible. They took a hundred into a public square and shot them. So, the latest directive from the Underground leadership is that assassinations should still continue, yet in a way to remove suspicion from the Varsovians. We now need operatives to follow Germans when they go on leave and kill them outside of Warsaw. We lose men all the time, some die, some go on missions, some never come back. We need new blood. That is why you're here. Come on."

It was a short walk to the office. On the way, Daniel thought about Karol and decided the blond operative had lied to him. He'd made it sound less perilous, sitting in rooms repeating days of the week, months of the year. Or perhaps Karol was simply ignorant of what was really going on in Warsaw. Only now, walking beside Jerzy to begin his first day at work for the Underground, Daniel was hit with the realisation of what he had signed up to: danger and death. Boyish notions like adventure and missions, spies and intrigue all rang hollow. What on earth was he doing?

The office was on the third floor of a corner building. A main room with a large table and chairs, filing cabinets and a calendar on the wall, pot plant on the window sill. A door in the corner opened to a small dark room, and there sat the two radio operators with their equipment, a man and a woman, young, serious. They nodded to Jerzy and did not speak to Daniel.

The woman said, "Today."

"All right," said Jerzy. "Anglik, it's time for your first action."

They took a series of buses west across the city with three changes. All this time, Jerzy did not speak to him. Where were they going? What were they going to do? His mind picked over the possibilities. Hijack, bombs, murder. Operatives die or disappear. He saw a road block, where trams passed through a street bordered on each side by the walls of the ghetto. Aware of having to appear normal, he had to suppress his urge to crane his neck and stare, yet he did manage to see two huge groups of ragged people, one on each side of the street, waiting to cross. They were guarded by gaggles of German soldiers, one of whom waved a rifle erratically towards them. He assumed these must be Jews crossing from one part of the ghetto to the other. How long they had to wait there was anyone's guess, and what bored German soldiers did when surrounded by large groups of captive Jews he didn't want to think about. He wondered if his mother stood among them. If he were going to find her, he would need Jerzy. If he deserted to go off to find Helena, no one in the Underground would help him. They might even kill him. He knew that every time they asked him to risk his life, he feared not only for himself, but if he got himself killed, he would never find Helena and get her out of there. Yet he had no choice but to do their bidding.

Jerzy got up to leave the bus and Daniel followed. They walked along three blocks before arriving at a private house in a back street. Jerzy rapped seven times in a rhythmic pattern on the door and they were let in. An older woman with square spectacles nodded in recognition at Jerzy and gave Daniel a wary look.

Jerzy said, "I vouch for him."

The woman simply turned and fetched clothes from a cupboard behind her. Two postal workers' uniforms, complete with bags. Yet inside were no letters, only a can each of gasoline, a clump of rags and boxes of matches, as well as a pair of thick gloves. Following Jerzy's lead, he swapped his suit for the uniform. It was too big for him and he had to fold the trousers over at the waist. Only then did Jerzy stop and talk to him.

"We have planned an arson attack on an SS barracks. It must be today, as a huge consignment of supplies has arrived and there is a full cohort of officers there stuffing their faces as we speak. Behind this house is an alleyway, which backs onto the barracks, a converted school. We'll go over the wall and we'll be behind the kitchens. The cooks are friends of the Underground. They've finished for the day and have left the back door open for us. We'll set the fire there, by soaking the rags in gasoline and stuffing them around the ovens. Then straight out the back door, and over the wall, down the alleyway and back into this house. Do you understand?"

Daniel nodded and followed Jerzy through the house and out into the back yard. From there, they went out through a gate and into the alleyway. They walked along it to a dustbin snug against the wall. Jerzy hopped onto this and was over the wall in seconds. Daniel clambered onto the bin and heaved himself up. There was a bit of a drop and his knees jarred. A door nearby was surrounded by more dustbins filled with stinking food remains. They entered and were in the barracks' kitchens. There was not a soul there, yet in a distant room he could hear the sounds of men carousing. It must have been the SS officers eating and drinking their fine foods and wines, while Warsaw had to manage on crumbs. Hearing the sound of SS officers close by was exhilarating and terrifying. They worked quickly. He followed Jerzy's example of putting on the gloves, soaking the rags in gasoline and stuffing them in any gaps they could find around the ovens and hobs in the kitchen. They retreated to the door and their last act was to use the matches to set light to their little trail of ruin. They stayed only a few seconds, long enough to see the fire catch and flare, before they bolted out the door and ran back to the wall. Daniel had never jumped so high and so quickly in his life.

They reached the house and went through to the front room.

"Fucking hell!" Daniel said and fell into an armchair and laughed and laughed and laughed.

Jerzy walked over and said, "Anglik, look at me." He reached out and slapped him hard across the face. Daniel held his cheek and stared open-mouthed at Jerzy.

The woman came in with their suits and said, "Uniforms, bags and gloves."

They took off the postal uniforms, put the gloves in the bags and gave them to the woman. She stuffed them into a sack and left through the back door.

Once alone, Jerzy said, "You were in shock."

"I know. I'm sorry. Ridiculous."

"It's all right. You're young. You're new to this. It's normal."

"I'll get used to it."

"Yes. One day you'll be a cold fish like me."

Daniel did not want to be him. He did not like Jerzy. But he admired him, his bleak resolve and grim courage, his knowledge gained through acts, not books. He liked his precision of speech and clarity of purpose, and that he put Poland first, not himself.

The next morning he put on his new suit and walked to the office.

Jerzy was there, with Lidia.

"News of yesterday," Jerzy told him. "The fire was tremendous, gutting the building and destroying SS supplies, including uniforms and bedding and weapons. And piles of gourmet consumables imported from France. Most importantly, two SS officers were burned and several hospitalised for smoke inhalation. No one was killed. Unfortunately."

"And we have news for you," Lidia said. "Soon, you'll be able to meet with representatives of the Jewish Resistance organisation. We have contacted them to see if they can help you find your mother. They have agreed to meet with you at this office in a few weeks."

The Jewish Resistance. The words flushed his cheeks, like first love. At last, a step towards the ghetto.

Jerzy said, "Look, Anglik. You did well yesterday. Especially for a first action."

"Thank you."

"We have another job for you today. By doing it, you will prove your allegiance to the Underground. You will truly become one of us. Are you up to it?"

He wanted to be one of them. He wanted to believe in their cause. He even wanted the buzz of danger. He had the surety of youth that he would not die yet. Most of all, he wanted that meeting with the Jewish Resistance, and if he continued to serve the Underground, he believed he would get it.

"Yes, I am," he said.

Jerzy nodded at Lidia and she left.

"Anglik, not all of our operatives are as loyal as you. We have discovered one to be an informant. He has a girlfriend who's sleeping with a Gestapo officer. In return for money and black market produce, this man has been supplying the Gestapo with information about Underground activities. Today, he will be brought before a kind of Underground court. We have our own judicial system, with secret sessions convened, qualified magistrates and judges, alongside witnesses and all proper procedure. We publish our rulings in the Underground press. We employ punishment squads to carry out retribution. Defendants include informers, blackmailers and other types of collaborators, as well as common criminals whose actions are directed against the Polish population and are therefore seen as against the war effort. Punishments include beatings or head-shaving, or even executions for serious offences. It is said that enemies of the Secret State now walk in fear. What do you think about this? About Poles punishing Poles?"

"If they betray their own people, then they deserve it."

"Good. Come with me."

They caught a tram to another office, another back room. Inside, a hearing was taking place. They arrived as it was ending. There were three magistrate types and the defendant. No one else was there. The man stood with his arms tied before him and bruises on his face. He offered no defence for his actions and admitted his crimes. This man looked worried, but not scared. Daniel wondered what would happen to him. Once the questioning was over, the magistrates conferred in whispers, nodded agreement. The chief judge passed sentence. One word: "Execution."

Jerzy stepped forward and took the man's arm and shoved him out of the door, saying, "Come on, Anglik." Daniel followed as Jerzy forced this man to walk quickly down the stairs and into a damp basement room, a slit of a window. The man stumbled on his way, because his hands were still tied. He was beginning to shake all over as Jerzy ordered him to stand up against the wall. Daniel watched Jerzy as he drew from his pocket a gun, the same Colt .45 Magda had sewn into Daniel's backpack.

Daniel watched Jerzy pull the hammer back half cocked, open a little gate at the back of the revolver, drop in bullets, one, two, three. Then ease the hammer back full cock with his thumb.

"Ever fired a gun?" Jerzy said.

"No."

"Have you been shown how to fire a gun?"

He remembered his brief training with Karol, back in that flat in London. It had seemed exciting at the time. What a child he was then.

"Yes," he said, "but…"

"Here." Jerzy held out the revolver. "This man has betrayed the Underground, and is responsible for the torture and death of several operatives. He has been fairly tried by legal means and now his sentence has been passed. He must be executed. Will you carry it out?"

Daniel glared at Jerzy. He could not bear to look at the man, who by now was whimpering. He wanted to say 'no'. No, he did not wish to carry it out. He did not bloody wish to shoot this man. No, he did not want to murder him. No. But Jerzy didn't budge and stood there, his hand held out, absolutely still, his face a mask. A phrase in Daniel's head, over and over: *this is wrong, this is wrong.*

But was it wrong, to kill this man? He was a traitor, he was responsible for others' deaths, to satisfy his own greed. Daniel had set a fire, knew people would be hurt in it, maybe die. How was this different? But it was. They were Germans, SS officers. Daniel was a Pole. And this man was a Pole too, standing before him, crying like a little girl. But what if Daniel refused? Would he be thrown out of the Underground? Worse?

"Anglik?" Jerzy said, his arm a rod of iron, the gun still as sculpture, the air leaden. "Will you do your duty?"

Daniel felt his hand move and take the gun. Jerzy stood to the side and folded his arms, waiting.

He lifted the gun, as Karol had shown him. He was about ten feet from the man, who was now crying. He did not beg to be saved. He looked straight at Daniel, weeping with abandon. Daniel wanted to close his eyes. But he had to take aim. He had to stare right at him. He tried to aim at his chest, but his hand was shaking. He held up his left arm and supported his right hand on it. The gun was steady. He took one last look at the man's face, distorted with terror and smeared with mucus and tears. He pulled the trigger and a tremendous noise assaulted him. The explosion of the gun and the scream of the man. He didn't know if he began to scream before the bullet left the gun, when it was in the air hurtling towards him, or when it had hit him. It was all one moment. He saw the man go down. He had shot him in the stomach and he was crumpled in torment, groaning, sobbing. Jerzy stepped over and took a look at the man's injuries.

"Have mercy," groaned the man. "Have mercy."

"Again," said Jerzy, "this time in his chest. Come closer."

This was too much. He had done it. He had shot the man.

Surely he would die of his injuries. Perhaps Jerzy just wanted to make sure. Or perhaps he did not sanction a slow painful death, even for a man like this. Daniel's arm was limp. Jerzy grasped his hand and the gun in it, aimed it at the man's chest.

"There," he said. "Finish your task."

Daniel shot again and the man's head smacked the wall behind him. He had hit the right spot. Jerzy checked his jugular for a pulse, though it was only a formality. The blood, the dark syrup seeping through his suit, pooling on the floor. Dead.

Jerzy took the gun and tucked it away. He gave Daniel a handkerchief to wipe his hands. Two men came in and went over to the dead man, to deal with the body. Jerzy took Daniel upstairs. He showed him into a toilet with a washbasin and shut the door. He vomited once, again, again, everything down to the bile. His insides convulsed with disgust. He grasped the washbasin and pulled his body upright, then washed his face and hands. There was no mirror to see himself.

Jerzy opened the door and said, "Are you recovered?" He had no idea what to say to that. Jerzy reached over and placed a firm hand on his shoulder.

"Well done. You are now a fully-fledged member of the Underground. Death is not desirable. But we are a free state occupied by a ruthless foreign force. We have no choice but to answer death with death. Germans in our country are first in line. But Poles who betray us run a close second. Perhaps their crime is worst of all. You have dispensed justice today."

Jerzy accompanied him back to his flat.

Before he left, Jerzy said, "You were a stranger to us, come from England, your intentions unclear. We had to know if you could be totally loyal. We have tested you. You have passed. From now on, your duties will be less…dramatic. At least for the time being."

Daniel said nothing.

"Do you have anything you want to say to me, Anglik?"

"What was his name?"

"I don't know that," said Jerzy, and patted him on the arm. "And it doesn't matter."

With that, he went. It doesn't matter, he'd said. It doesn't matter.

It snowed that morning, silent and soft. Women wore fur collars and men fur hats. It was November in Warsaw. An eastern cold Daniel had never felt, chilled to the marrow. Tramping through the muffled streets, blinking at the white world, he tried to shake off that same dream of that same man and his black blood. The coldness outside gripped his body, yet inside too there was a splinter of ice, placed there by what he'd done. He had killed a man. The only way to live with it was to drain it of feeling, to freeze it, to freeze his own heart. Now he felt he understood why Jerzy had no softness about him, his character showing only the sharp angles of icicles. It was the way to survive.

Since the killing, he had been assigned new duties. He was a runner again, just like at the *Chronicle*, though riskier. Traversing the city, he picked up bundles of Underground news-sheets, hand-pressed in cellars, and delivered them to shopkeepers who wrapped purchases in pages from German newspapers with the secret Polish news-sheet hidden inside. Once he was asked to mail a copy directly to Gestapo HQ, the delight of a Polish jab in the eye for the German overseers as he let it drop in the post box. He carried copies of communiques from the radio operators at his office, news gathered from the BBC or WCBX in New York. Once he was allowed to stay and listen, and when he heard J.B. Priestley's earnest tones asking the British people to stay strong, quiet tears ran over his English cheeks and conjured Dad's chocolate-brown wireless and the beefy waft of Bovril.

He stamped the snow from his boots and closed the external

door, climbed the stairs to the office, backpack straps cutting into his shoulders. Stuffed inside were:

10 tins each of ham, beans and condensed milk.

10 vials of morphine and 20 sterilised wound dressings.

10 balls of string and 5 needlework sets.

A week before, Lidia had given him a note from her contact in the Jewish Resistance. It read:

If you wish us to help you find your mother, we require proof of your intentions to help us in return. We will come to your office in one week and ask you to bring the following items to be handed to our representative at the meeting. Success in this regard will assure you of our attention.

Lidia had said, "Jerzy gives you permission to find these items. Here are extra forged ration cards to use. But don't make any promises to these Jews, Anglik. Your work is with us. The Warsaw Jews are in a desperate situation, we know that. But there is hardly anything we can actively do for them. The sooner we win this war against the Germans, the better it will be for the Jews, for all of us and all of Poland. That's the only way."

"All right," he had said. He could see her point. It was the only way an army could operate, even a covert one. He reminded himself of his oath to the Polish Underground, to unconditional obedience. He knew all that.

Two men sat at the table. One man was old and looked shattered. The other was about Daniel's age, keyed up, eyes darting, impatient and fidgety. They didn't give any names. They did not smell good. Their jackets were crumpled, worn at the elbows.

The older man spoke first: "Why are we here? What do you want, young man?" The way he spoke was utterly distinct from the clipped, professional Underground tone to which Daniel was accustomed. It was the dry remnant of a voice, splintered and hollow.

Daniel sat down and took from his pocket Helena's photograph, the dog-eared one. He explained everything: Dad, the Blitz,

Magda, Tomasz, Karol, the boat, the photographer, the Underground. They listened and inspected the photo carefully, glancing up at him as they did so, as if it were proof of his good intentions.

When Daniel had finished, the old man sighed, put down the photograph and looked up. His eyes were lit with a crazed melancholy.

"You are very, very fortunate that you were taken away from this country when you were a baby. You were fortunate to have been brought up never knowing you were a Jew. What are you doing here? Your mother is most likely dead, if she were ever here at all. The Aryan Poles of the Underground are the lucky ones. They are free to defend their nation. But we Jews, we have no nation, no country, no government. We are systematically being murdered, by starvation, disease and quicker, more deliberate killings. But all are to the same purpose, to wipe out the Jews."

Daniel said, "Look. My mother is a Jew. That makes me one too. I want to find her. And I want to help you, if I can. We are all Jews here in this room."

The old man almost spat at him with derision. "What really joins you to us? Nothing. We are not joined ourselves. We are rats drowning in a barrel. Our situation is the only thing we have in common. Other than that, we will all trample our neighbour to keep our heads above the water. This is what the Germans have reduced us to. What can you do for us?"

The younger man spoke up.

"This 'Anglik' has a lot of courage. He could've stayed safe in England. But he didn't. He risked his life to come here. He risks his life every day working for our country's Underground. I still love Poland, despite the Poles. And I know you feel the same way too."

With this, the old man's eyes filled and he had to turn away to prevent himself from weeping. Daniel had never seen such despair. It frightened him.

"We can use you," said the young man. "If you can help us, we need you. We want someone friendly in the Polish Underground. They haven't lifted a finger to help us yet."

Daniel said, "We're all on the same side."

The old man shook his head and the young man uttered a humourless laugh, saying, "Sure, we both hate the Nazis. But that's where it ends. When we got here today, your friends on the radio in the back room, they came through and stared at us like rare birds. They couldn't believe Jews were still alive in Warsaw. We won't be around for long. And that's just the way the Aryans want it. With the Nazis spending all their hatred on the Jews, they don't have as much time for killing Poles. But what happens when there are no more Jews to exterminate, eh? The Poles will be next. So, they don't mind the Nazis torturing the Jews, but they don't want us to die out altogether, not yet. They give us bits of help every now and again, just to keep us going."

Lidia had made it clear, the Underground's aims, the subordinate role of the Jews to that greater Polish purpose. Yet although Daniel had risked his life for his Underground comrades, set fires for them and killed for them, he looked at this broken old man, this fervent youth, and he knew he would defy the whole of the Union for Armed Struggle to help them. After all, the Jewish Resistance and the Polish Underground were fighting on the same side, so it wasn't really betrayal. Perhaps these Jews would give him a much better chance of finding Helena, but it went beyond that. He felt akin to these two in a way he never had with Lidia and Jerzy. He saw his journey from London to this moment as a series of steps not only closer to his mother but now, he realised, closer to his true self.

"What can I do for you?"

The young man went on: "We've had hardly any help from the Polish Underground in getting weapons, which is what we need most of all. If you're prepared to work with us, in smuggling weapons and other supplies into the ghetto, we'll do what we can to begin a search for your mother. Her name's Helena, right? This is a problem, as it's a very common name. If only we had her surname. But anyway, we have her picture and that'll help. We have the possibility that she's a seamstress, and that'll help too. I'm not saying it is likely to be successful, but I promise you we'll do what we can. Did you get the stuff?"

Daniel put his bag on the table and emptied the contents. The old man pawed at the tins, the medical supplies, as if to check they were extant. It was a curious brew. And not enough to help a whole ghetto. But Daniel was proud he'd got everything on the list. Did they really need those particular items, or was it a kind of test?

"Well done!" said the young man.

The old man said, "I'm surprised you got a bean from those Polish bastards."

"That's enough!" said the other. It seemed a power shift was happening. The old man shrugged. The young man turned to him, his face resolute.

"My name is Natan. What's yours?"

Daniel was touched he had chosen to share his name. He didn't know if the Jewish Resistance had the same rules as the Polish Underground, if it was really his own name or an alias. But he was glad to know it anyway. As for his own name, which should he choose?

"I have several names now!" he laughed. "But I suppose you should call me Anglik. That's what I go by round here."

They shook hands.

"So, Anglik. Thank you for agreeing to help us," said Natan.

"I'm glad to. And I hope perhaps you can help me too, in trying to find my mother. I've come a long way to get here."

Natan looked thoughtfully at him for a moment. The old man was gazing out of the window. He had lost all interest in the conversation.

"How strange it must be for you, Anglik. I was born and brought up in Warsaw. I've never known any other home. You could say the same thing about your London in England. And here you are. Thousands of miles away fighting a different cause in a different country, just because your mother happened to push you out into the world here."

Was he mocking him?

Perhaps Natan sensed this, because he went on, "But I admire it. If only more of our fellow Poles were like that, Jewish or not. Maybe we wouldn't be in a mess now. But most people are too damned selfish. That's the truth."

"I'm selfish too. I want to find my mother. That's why I came here. For myself. For her too, but mostly for myself."

If he'd been really honest, he'd have told him the whole truth: that it had all once seemed a great adventure, an escape from the frustration of life as a journalists' dogsbody. But that was all long ago, as if it had happened to another person, to some boy who used to bike around London.

"Yes," Natan said, "but I believe you're really sold on this cause. The Poles and the Jews, and all this resistance business. Don't get me wrong, I am too, otherwise I wouldn't be here now, risking my neck every time I cross the wall. But what about going into the ghetto? I'm not sure you'll cope with it. You're too starry-eyed, I think."

Daniel had heard little about the ghetto, as Jerzy and Lidia wouldn't talk about it. Yes, they were locked in by those walls. And everyone knew the Germans treated Jews worse than the Poles. But how bad could it be? He had seen things in London, in that cellar in Warsaw. Such things he'd never imagined. He was not that boy on the bike anymore.

"I'm ready for it. I promise you that."

"But life here, in Aryan Warsaw. It's heaven. Yes, it's under occupation, there are arrests, beatings and shootings. But people are living like humans. In the ghetto, Anglik, it is...not human. I can't even explain..."

The old man placed his hand on Natan's arm.

Daniel said, "I've hardened up a lot since I came here. I've had to."

Natan considered him, shook his head.

"Never mind. You'll see. How about this evening?"

"For what?"

"To come into the ghetto."

"Really?"

"We've got business to do today, but I can meet you here at five. Bring the goods and we'll take them over the wall. You can stay with me tonight. What do you say?"

He had no Underground duties that night or the next morning. He had nowhere else in the world he would rather be. The ghetto.

"Yes!"

"Good man!"

"How do we get in?"

"There's an alleyway which runs alongside the ghetto wall called Parysowski Place. It's a prime location for smuggling. There's a thriving Aryan black market operation going on there, where Poles go into the ghetto to buy stuff from Jews at very low prices or go to loot houses. The guards make a good living bribing smugglers, Jewish and Aryan. That's where we'll go over. Do you have cash? We'll need 75 zloty to get in."

"Yes, I'll bring it."

"Good. Try to prepare yourself, Anglik. The ghetto is hell. You will probably be sick. Don't eat lunch."

By 5.30, Daniel and Natan were stepping off a tram in the north-west of Warsaw, a couple of streets from the ghetto wall. They shared the goods between them, in Daniel's backpack and Natan's bulging shoulder bag. The old man was not there, he was visiting a friend this side of the wall. Daniel had asked, why didn't he stay out for good? Why live in the ghetto at all, if you can get out? Natan had stared at him, laughed.

"You really are green, aren't you!"

Two streets from the tram stop, Daniel saw a winding lane with no lamps. There were few people about. Natan took a piece of cloth from his pocket. He pulled it up his arm, the Star of David facing outward. He gave Daniel a handkerchief from his other pocket.

"This'll do for you."

Daniel tied it round his arm.

"Listen, people are used to smugglers round here. We probably won't even be noticed. But there could always be a patrol there or a random German on a killing spree at the moment we go over. Keep your wits about you. Have you got the money? Let me have it."

Further down the alleyway, Natan pointed out a man hanging around in the shadows, cap pulled low over his eyes, like a movie villain. He nodded at them and waited. Natan handed the smuggling fee to the man. He got a ladder from a doorway and put it up against the wall.

Natan grasped Daniel's arm. "You'll have to jump down. On the other side, stay close. Do as I do. Ready?"

Daniel nodded.

Natan first, up and over, gone.

Daniel climbed the ladder. At the top, he looked down. The thin moon cast no light on the blue-black ghetto street. A memory came to him, of reading myths as a boy, the young hero on his journey, crossing the threshold to the land of the dead.

CHAPTER SIX

Tonight Isak has not come home. He went out this afternoon to find bread and fat, and he has not returned. It is now approaching midnight and well past curfew, and I cannot go out to look for him. Besides, where would I begin? And I can't leave Ilsa. As I put her to bed, she asked and asked where her Daddy was and I had to be very careful to appear untroubled. I told her he was staying with a friend on the other side of the ghetto. Since it is a Friday evening, he wanted to take a little holiday and see his friend for the night. She asked me why he would do that, why couldn't he see his friend during the day, why wouldn't he come home? I said it was quite a way to his friend's house and he would be tired. He will sleep there tonight and come home in the morning. I think she believed me. She is growing up quickly, it is harder to fool her with stories. I wonder what I will say to her when she wakes in a few hours. Meanwhile, I keep my lonely vigil. I have walked to the window and back a thousand times, though I know he won't be able to turn up now, not until curfew lifts in the morning. Where could he be? I am trying not to imagine the worst possibility. I am thinking of all the reasons why he could be somewhere that is not here, and be there alive and well. Maybe there were round-ups in the streets and he dodged into a friend's house. Yes, perhaps he is sleeping safely on Vladka and Samuel's floor right now. That sounds plausible, yes. I suppose I must try to rest now. Tiredness and this weak candle I write by are making my eyes ache. I will write again in the daytime, when Isak will be back by my side, I am sure.

It is now Saturday night. I went to Vladka's very early with Ilsa and neither Vladka nor Samuel has seen Isak. I left Ilsa with them and went out into Sienna St., unsure of where to go next. I decided to be realistic and think of possible bad things that may have happened to him. The best place to start was the hospitals. I have spent the best part of the day tramping between the four of them, from the ones on Berson-Sliska and Berson-Leszno/Zelazna, to the one on Leszno and all the way up to the other one on Stawki. I had to negotiate my way through the filthiest part of the large ghetto to reach the last hospital. I haven't been through those areas for a long time, as it is Isak who does most of the food-hunting now. It is worse than ever there. I feel sick even thinking of it. I can't bring myself to write about it tonight.

Isak wasn't to be found at any of the hospitals. Another day has passed with no news of my husband. I wanted to be more honest with Ilsa tonight. But when it came to bedtime, she again asked, where is Daddy? I wanted to confide in her, tell her my worries, my fears. But she is still a child, however she has grown up in this past year in the ghetto. I still endeavour to protect her, though she is surrounded by the glare of evil every day. I told her he was enjoying his friend's company and decided to stay another day. I also lied to her about where I'd been, saying I'd had business all over the ghetto, to earn us money to buy more food. Mention food and Ilsa forgets most other things. I think she still believes me, though she gave me one of her sidelong glances when I said goodnight, that same funny look she used to have as a baby, when I'd give her something new she wasn't sure she liked – like her very first spoon of porridge – that look which says, I'm not sure if I really trust you, Mama, though I love you very much.

She's sleeping soundly now, awaiting her father's return from his 'friend's house' tomorrow, and I have another sleepless night wondering where on earth I am going to start looking for Isak tomorrow. When I find him, I'm going to kill him for making me worry so. I am going to find him, you know. Tomorrow I will. Sunday. A good day for a walk.

I found Isak. He is dead. His body was lying on Ciepla St., minutes from our home. He was naked. Someone had taken all of his clothes, even his underwear, which I mended myself. I had spent the morning wandering the streets of the large ghetto and was on my way home. I decided to visit the market on the corner of Ciepla and Grzybowska to find something for Ilsa's lunch. That's the only reason I found him, because I walked down Ciepla St. I never really look at the corpses. They are commonplace. But it was his hair I saw. I suppose his image was filling my mind, as I have spent two days scanning every man in the street looking for him. And I saw his wiry brown hair flapping in the breeze. But it was attached to this naked corpse in the street. I was confused. How could Isak's hair be attached to this naked corpse? I actually walked past him, glancing back only to wonder again why his hair would be there, as if someone had stolen it and glued it to the head of that dead body. Then I stopped and walked back. I stared at the face on the corpse. It was a waxwork of Isak. It frowned and sagged. His chest was a mess of congealed black blood. I stood and stared at his body for a long time.

A man came up to me and touched my arm. I looked up at him but I couldn't speak. He was quite an old man. He had a kind face. He told me there was a round-up in this street a couple of days ago. They took some away in a truck. Some they just shot in the street. I looked at Isak's chest.

"That one they shot, I suppose," said the old man. He asked if it was someone close to me. I thought about speaking, but it didn't seem possible. I just nodded.

"Is it family? Your husband?" I nodded again. He said he was very sorry. He said that the funeral cart hadn't come by there for a while, but it was only a few streets away and coming this way. He said he'd go and tell them to come by here, and pick the body up. He went off. I let him go. I didn't know what to say to him anyway. And I didn't know what to do. What do I do with my husband's body, I was thinking? It's naked and dead and it's in the street. And it's heavy. Do I ask someone to help me carry him home? Do I run to Vladka's and get Samuel to help? But I couldn't move from that place. Once I'd found him, I just could not leave him. Alone and dead, in that street, the wind blowing through his hair.

What would I do with Isak once I got him home? What would Ilsa think, her Daddy's corpse stretched out on the floorboards? I knew it was impossible. I knew that the only way was to let him be taken. I had no other choice. After a while, the old man returned. He said the funeral cart was coming. He waited beside me. We didn't talk. I just stared at Isak's hair. It was the only part of him that moved. The breeze lifted it and then let it lie still. Up and down, up and down, up and down.

The cart arrived. There was a pile of other corpses in the back. There barely looked room for another. Two burly men drove the cart. They glanced at me, jumped down and picked up Isak.

"Be careful," said the old man in a strong voice. "It's her husband." I imagine if I'd not been standing there, or if the old man hadn't spoken, those men would have flung Isak onto the cart like a bag of grain. Just another sack to shift. But they did it with care. Isak's body curved backwards as it settled on the rounded heap of corpses beneath him. I thought how I'd never seen him lie like that, his head back, his arms flung out. I thought I knew everything about his body. Now I was seeing him anew. For the last time.

The cart went. I watched it go. It trundled down Ciepla St., turned the corner and was gone. I stood there and stared at the space it had just been. The old man was still there beside me. He asked me a question. I think he said, "Aren't you going to follow it?" I couldn't really understand what it all meant. I just shook my head. He told me the cart would be going to the cemetery on Okopowa St. He said I should go there and I could arrange my husband's funeral. Then I spoke. I remember this. When he said about the funeral, I realised I hardly had any money. My rational side woke up, I suppose, because I said, "I can't afford a funeral." He told me they'd arrange it. But I should hurry, or I might not see where they put his body. I understood that. I started walking. I didn't even stop to say thank you to the old man. I just walked up Ciepla and turned left onto Grzybowska, and through the small ghetto. I waited at the crossing at Chlodna for quite a while, staring across at the other side, not even noticing the guards jeer at the crowd of waiting Jews, as they always do. On and on, up through the large ghetto and the heaving crowds and finally reached the Jewish Cemetery.

I have not been there before, but I have heard stories about it. Because it is a Sunday, the cemetery was heaving with ghetto tourists. The German soldiers bring their girlfriends there at the weekends. They stroll round and look at the corpses. They take photographs. Some come to observe. Others come for sport. I've heard they make Jews do Hasidic dances around piles of the dead and they film it. Today, there were hundreds of Germans milling around, arms around their women, pointing at the dead, pointing at the mourners. Laughing at them. Like a zoo. Just like a visit to the monkey house. Look at the funny monkeys. They almost seem human, don't they?

I kept my head down. I didn't want any dealings with Germans. I couldn't see my cart. I asked a driver from another cart where the shed was. There is a shed where they keep the corpses, ready for burial. I knew about that. He showed me. I went up to the door. I didn't know where to look. Yes, there are corpses in the streets of the ghetto, everywhere, every street. But piles upon piles of the dead, limbs and torsos all twisted together, a sculpture of frozen snakes. And the smell. My God, the smell. I barely glanced in that hellish shed, before I knew I could not look for Isak there. I backed away and looked around helplessly for my cart. I could not find it. Maybe it had come before me and gone away again. I stayed at the cemetery for a few hours, waiting for it. But it never appeared. The sky was growing dark and I thought of Ilsa, waiting for me. I left that place. As I walked away down Okopowa St., I said *kaddish* for my husband.

Goodbye Isak.

I haven't written for months.

I've not had the heart for it.

Isak was not my first love. He was not Jan. He was my other love. My second love. I think if Jan had never left, I would never have found myself with Isak. I needed him after my years in the wilderness. He healed me. I loved him for that. There was none of the ardour I had with Jan. We did not share poetry, we were not young and foolish, we did not cast ourselves as romantic leads in our own melodrama. I see now that we did not really know each other. We did not see into each other's souls. As Jan and I had. But, after all, what good had that done me? Isak loved me. And I loved him in my way. I loved him most of all for making Ilsa with me. Through her, I loved the parts of him I saw in her; her serious eyes, her gentle voice, her curly hazel hair.

Ilsa does not talk about him now. The day he died, I told her that he rested in heaven. She asked me, "Does he miss us?" I said of course. She nodded and turned back to her playtime. That is the only question she has asked and the last time we spoke of him. I wonder what goes on behind those serious eyes. I worry about her. I am afraid the ghetto has turned her cold. Isak's eyes look out at me from her head. She is as mysterious to me as he was.

I miss him. I think he must miss us terribly, though he must be happy in paradise. If he is. The old certainties about God in His heaven have left me, if they were ever certain. Everything is fluid now. There is no truth. Only hard facts. And rumours.

There are rumours sweeping through the ghetto, filling the evening gossip sessions in the courtyards. The main gossip is about the round-ups. Since the new year, there have been more and more round-ups in the streets. Buildings are closed off and all the inhabitants are piled into trucks. It is on a small scale and random. But there is talk that these are a prelude. There is talk of resettlement, that Jews from this ghetto and other ghettos too are being taken away to labour camps in the east. That is what the registrations were for last year, they say. But if they registered everyone, why are the round-ups random? I think they do it just for fun. The German soldiers get bored and say, "Let's go round up some Jew bastards." I do think that the marvellous war machine of the Nazis is a dangerous mixture of order and chaos. Not everything they do has a meaning, not everything is due to German precision and planning.

But still, the round-ups are increasing. The rumours too. Some say camps in the east. Others say that all Jews rounded up are actually deported to their deaths. But few believe this. Why bother? Why not kill us all here? Unless they have shame about that too, just like the German who stole our stock of dresses but made us pretend they were gifts. The Nazis may be stealing Jews from ghettos to send to their deaths, but their shame at wholesale slaughter makes them call it by another name: "resettlement". Or perhaps they are simply guarding against mass panic. That is a colder reason. That I can imagine of them.

There is another wild rumour, so horrible I am superstitious of writing it down, in case this makes it come true. There is talk of a kind of camp near Chelmno. It is not a labour camp, for no work is done there. It is a place only of death. The inmates never unpack. They are unloaded from their transport and immediately killed. A few are kept alive to dispose of the dead. The word is that someone has escaped from there, come back to the ghetto and is telling all of what he has seen. I haven't met him. What I hear of it is third, or fourth, or fiftieth-hand. And you know how whispers change truth into fiction. Many of us have heard this. Few of us believe it. Or want to.

Not everything we hear is bad. A curious rumour has recently reached the ghetto. Jews in other parts of Poland, away towards the east they say, are escaping from ghettos and going to live in the local forests. There they are taking up arms and making trouble for the Nazis, who get lost in the woods the locals know well. And the Jews survive because of this, as well as their bravery and cunning. They live precarious lives eating only what they can find in the forest. But they are free. Free Jews. Can it possibly be true? It sounds like a fairy tale. And all fairy tales end up in the forest.

The latest news is not encouraging. Just yesterday, posters were pasted up all over the ghetto. They say that the German authorities are to cleanse the ghetto of 'undesirable elements'. It doesn't explain what this means. But I have a bad feeling about it.

I do not know when I will write again.

It has begun. They are calling it the Gross Aktion. It started this morning on July 22nd, 1942.

Ilsa and I were at home, sewing. We heard a commotion in the courtyard and rushed out to see. All talk was of a huge round-up, going on in different parts of the ghetto. Our neighbour Chaim said he was visiting a friend near Gesia St. this morning, and they watched it happen from their top-floor apartment. In the next street, Chaim and his friend heard marching feet and they looked out to see Germans, Jewish Police and foreign-looking auxiliaries never seen in the ghetto before strutting down the next street. They stopped and proceeded to set up a cordon around the next block. The Germans watched as their minions blew whistles and summoned all the Jews in every building down into the street. All were warned that those lagging behind would be shot. The Germans were firing their weapons and terrorising the people with shouting and vicious lashes of their whips. People were rushing down into the street, crying and wailing. The empty buildings were searched, whilst the inhabitants were forced to squat on their haunches in the road. Gunshots were heard in the empty buildings. Probably those who decided to hide. Police were seen pocketing goods from people's homes. Then there was a rough kind of selection. Chaim saw the Jews lined up and each one had to stand before this one particular German who looked in charge. With a flick of his whip, he sent them to the left or to the right. Chaim's friend recognised some of those on the left as being the family of a Jewish policeman. A few others joined them on the left. But most were sent to the right. All were lined up again, in these two new groups. After an hour of squatting in agony, those on the left were sent back to their homes and all the others were forced to move off at a terrifying pace. The talk is that they were going to the Umschlagplatz, the railway depot at the north end of the ghetto. Where they went after that, who knows? Another neighbour Hanna came back and added further worrying news. Apparently, some of the major institutions of the ghetto have been cleared out. The old-age homes and the hospitals. All stumbling down to the Umschlag, cripples on crutches and the elderly shoved onto pushcarts. All talk of labour camps in the east has evaporated. After all, what would labour camps do with the sick and the old?

Terror gripped the courtyard. The talk was wild. More news came, vital news. The word was that you needed a work permit. Only those with the permits would be spared deportation. Everyone was yelling: where do we get them? The answer came from a passer-by: from the ghetto factories, for a fee. I ran back to our apartment with Ilsa and told her to stay put. I thought again and couldn't bear to leave her, just in case, God forbid, she was gone when I got back. I ferreted out every last zloty I could find. I had no idea what this fee would be. Altogether, I had 132 zlotys. I decided to leave 5 zlotys hidden in the closet. I'm not sure why. A kind of vague insurance, I suppose. I also took this, my journal. Again, superstition drove me.

My plan was to go up to the Oschman place, where they launder and mend German uniforms. I sometimes do freelance work for them, sewing fine embroidery on a vain German's lapel or such nonsense. There was a chance they would give me a permit and that would mean escaping the Aktion. Before we left, I grabbed my sewing machine and put it into its carry case. I didn't know if they wanted people to start straight away. We went out into the street and the rumour was that the round-up crews were coming our way. We ducked down back streets and took a circuitous route to Oschman's. On the way, I explained to Ilsa where we were going and how important the work permit was. She listened in her solemn way and said, "I will smile at them for you, Mama. Maybe they will like my smile and give us the ticket." How sad it is, that she has to decide in advance whether to smile today or not. We hurried on.

I soon realised that hundreds had had the same idea as me, as when we got there, a queue stretched down the street and round the corner. We joined and waited. Everyone in the queue was jostling and impatient to reach the front. All talk was of the round-ups. Apparently, they had been happening all over the ghetto, blocks shut off and buildings emptied. All the while we queued, everyone was looking over their shoulders, scanning the streets for signs of police, listening intently for the sound of marching boots.

After about three hours and late into the afternoon, we reached the front of the queue. My heart gladdened as I saw pani Stagel, the woman who had hired me before for freelance work. She was now one of the officials from the factory who was taking enquiries about permits. I managed to work my way over to her table and she greeted me. It would be no problem, she said, for me to be issued with a work permit for Oschman's. She called it the 'shop'.

"All workers are required to be quartered at the shop," she said. "But only the workers, I'm afraid." She looked at Ilsa. "Not their families." I asked her what she meant. She explained that I had to live at the shop, but Ilsa couldn't.

"But that's impossible," I said. "I can't leave my daughter." Pani Stagel shook her head.

Ilsa said, "I can smile for you, madam." I watched as my daughter forced her mouth into a smile, a ghostly remnant of the natural smile she used to show me all the time when she was a baby. Oh, my darling girl, what has the ghetto done to you? But it worked.

Pani Stagel looked askance then said very quietly, "All right. When you come back to register, make sure you see me at the tables. I'll get both of you in." I was about to take her hand to kiss it, but she stopped me. Any looks of glee would be suspicious. I could understand that. I calmed down and thanked her quietly.

"Now for the fee," she said. "For both of you, it'll be 5000 zloty." I nearly screamed. What could I do? I decided to try trading further on her sympathy.

"Pani Stagel," I began. "I have always worked hard for Oschman's, for you. I have produced embroidery of excellent quality, I believe. And I asked for small recompense for such fine work."

Her face hardened. "You were lucky to be paid at all," she said.

"I know that," I countered. "And I thank you for that, pani Stagel. But now, 5000 zloty is a sum from my dreams. An impossible fee. Today I collected every zloty I have and all I can muster is 100 zlotys." I pulled out this amount and put it on the table. I had decided that against impossible odds, I may as well keep the other 27 zloty for ourselves. What did I have to lose? Pani Stagel looked down at my filthy, crumpled banknote with disdain. I prayed to whatever God I had forgotten to please help us, just this once, just now. I stared at pani Stagel as she lifted her eyes to mine.

"Oh, for heaven's sake," she whispered angrily. "What Jew in this godforsaken place could afford 5000? The whole thing is ridiculous. Here is your permit." She scribbled details down on a card and handed it to me. "Now get out of here. Come back tomorrow to register. One bag each, that's all. And you must bring that sewing machine with you, or you won't be hired. Next!" Again, I wanted to thank her, but she waved me away. She looked uncomfortable in her own skin.

What we saw as we walked back to our apartment was macabre. Streets usually bustling with traders were empty and silent. There were dozens of corpses of the freshly killed, in doorways, in the middle of the road. Puddles of black blood glistened in the gutters. I did not bother to cover Ilsa's eyes. She has seen everything.

"We shall soon be away from this," I told her. "Safe in the factory, with my new job." This was true. But for how long?

When we reached our building, we were horrified to discover that it had been cleared out. None of our neighbours were there, nobody was. As we walked up to our apartment, the staircase was littered with belongings, those the plunderers could not carry or did not want. When we went into our own place, we found that every room had been ransacked. Anything of any value had been taken. Even the 5 zloty. Only a few clothes were left hanging in the closet. Thank God I'd taken my sewing machine with me. Thank God I'd kept the 27 zlotys in my pocket. Thank God I hadn't left Ilsa at home.

Thank God. Thank God. Thank God.

I have much to thank Him for.

And much to hate Him for.

I write from the barracks at Oschman's. Our new 'home'. I brought my journal with me. I now write in even tinier letters than my usual small script. I use up as little space as I can, even though there are pages left. I am still optimistic, you see. That I will live longer than it takes to fill this notebook.

We have been here about a fortnight. The work is repetitive and tedious, sewing seams on Nazi trousers. But it is work, which carries a work permit, which means life. The little things we rely on these days, a small square of card to escape death. Ilsa is here with me. At night we share our bunk and cuddle all night for warmth and comfort. She sleeps soundly. I do not. During the day, she hides with several other illegal children staying here at the shop. We put them behind a huge bundle of old uniforms that has been left in the corner of the factory floor. Here the children can play quietly, as the noise of the sewing machines drowns out their voices. But they mustn't come out. From time to time, the German overseers come in to check on our work, or a Nazi marches through to show off his authority. Or the boss visits, to touch our shoulders and whisper in our ears. Our boss is a Volksdeutsch, a Pole who chose to become a German. Once or twice a day, he appears at random times and takes a stroll through the ranks of seamstresses, seeing which one takes his fancy that day. He leans down and pretends to show interest in their work. He has not approached me yet. I am glad.

Keeping the children hidden is not easy, especially as one of them is a baby. He is only about two years old and is boisterous. His mother often has to rush to the heap of uniforms and quieten him down. Though sympathetic, we other mothers scold her for not keeping him quiet enough. After all, he could give them all away, and what would become of our children? When someone is coming, we give the signal for the children to keep silent. Someone shouts, "More thread, more thread!" This is our signal. Ilsa tells me that when the children hear it, they have to smother the toddler to shut him up and he wriggles like a bag of worms. He thinks it's all a game. Lucky for him.

At night, one of us waits until the boss has gone and the night guard is having his customary vodka break, and we collect the children and sneak them into the barracks. How long we can keep this up before we get found out, I cannot tell. The most dangerous times are when we have to sneak them food, especially as we are only given soup. We drink a little of our own then take the cans to our children to finish the majority. We just have to hope that no one sees us do it, that no one ever looks behind that pile of clothes. Or searches the barracks at night. I am amazed that no one has bothered to do that yet. I suppose they think a bunch of women with their sewing machines do not pose a threat to the

German army. And they'd be right. But rules are rules, and if they find our children, who knows what they will do?

There is a strange kind of calm here amongst us women. We know that this is only a temporary home, a hiatus in the doom all around us. But all of us live quietly with the knowledge that we have escaped death by being here. We don't know how long this will last. But we are thankful to have snatched a few more months, or weeks, or days of life. We know we are lucky. But all of us are acutely aware that our days of safety are running out. How long will they keep a few raggedy factories going in a ghetto which is emptying fast? The latest rumours talk of the eventual destruction of the ghetto. We seamstresses and other workers in other shops have been kept here only to squeeze a few last banknotes out of the Jews before we are all exterminated. I tend to believe this is true.

Now we must be sensible and plan. I have managed this long to keep myself and Ilsa alive. And I won't give up now. Only those who have renounced life refuse to think of the future. The talk is of staying in the ghetto or escaping. Those who decide to stay do this: they sneak away from their shop, and find an empty building in the ghetto. There they build shelters with supplies in, to last them through the next deportations. Once the Germans think all the Jews have been cleared out, these hiders plan to escape from the ghetto and disappear into Warsaw. But how long can they live like that, with little chance of finding fresh food or fresh water? And there is much talk that the clearance of the ghetto is a prelude to its destruction, that the Germans' fear of any remnants of Jewish filth and disease would cause them to level it. What if the dismantling of the ghetto turns into a slow death? Those Jews still hiding could be holed up in those bunkers for months or even years, with no work permit and dwindling supplies. They would live with the constant fear of being found by one of the 'hunting' parties, German soldiers or errant Poles who come through the ghetto looking for stray Jews or booty from the empty apartments.

The only other alternative is to go over the wall. Go and live as a non-Jew in Aryan Warsaw. But one needs money and Aryan friends in order to survive there. And one false move could mean death. I have heard of Jews caught on the Aryan side brought back to the ghetto and shot on their own doorstep. It is difficult enough to escape. But once over the wall, what do you do then? If you have Aryan friends from the time before this war, perhaps one of them would hide you. But a few months ago, a decree was issued that the punishment for helping Jews is death. What kind of Aryan acquaintance would risk his life for me? The alternative is to pretend to be an Aryan, to live a lie on the streets of Warsaw. It is possible, I suppose. But again, one would need money and contacts to set yourself up and keep alive. You'd need a place to live, a job, false papers. Where on earth do you find it all?

Here is the cruel dilemma. Stay or go? There is one other possibility. To escape the ghetto, but then to go on, to leave Warsaw altogether. Find a safer place. But where could that be? Where do the Nazi claws not dig in? Now, during my wakeful nights feeling Ilsa's chest rise and fall against my own, I think of faraway places. I think of my family. Are they alive? How has the war treated my old home? Would Hitler bother with my home town or are all Jews fair game, not just the ones in the big cities? Is my mother dead? My father? Is my brother Jakub still roaming the woods like he did in his wild boyhood, hunting, with twigs in his hair? Does my family think of me now, if they are still alive? Would they welcome me back, after my disgrace? Or would all that be forgotten, now that the disaster of war has overtaken our past?

What a thing it would be, to take my daughter and leave this condemned place, to get over the ghetto wall, to dodge the thieves and murderers all around and get out of Warsaw, to travel across occupied Poland, away from the cities, away and away to the quiet countryside in the east, to the vast forests, the forests where those legendary free Jews are said to live, the forests near my home, the dense and lovely forests surrounding Novogrodek, the forests of my youth. I can almost smell the woody scent of the pine trees.

It is a beautiful dream.

A foolish one.

We are planning to leave the ghetto. I cannot quite believe it myself, but it is true. A chance has come to us. Through good fortune and friendship, we are going to try to escape from this hell.

And it has come at just the right time. Last week, I heard that they deported the orphanage. The famous one where Janusz Korczak the writer tends his flock. People talked of a little procession of them down the ghetto streets, Korczak leading them in song as they trotted towards their deaths. I thought, if the Nazis can murder these doves, there is no hope for any of us. I have to get out and take Ilsa with me. But I had no hope. Until last night.

My good friend Vladka contacted me. I had not heard from her or Samuel since the day of the Gross Aktion. I wondered if they had been deported but had no way of finding out. They have managed to get work in the Toebbens factory. Yesterday, I received a message through a mutual friend that Vladka was coming to the barracks that evening to talk to me. Apparently, someone bribed the guard to turn the other way. It sounds like Vladka has powerful friends. I couldn't believe it would really happen, but last night there she was, strolling into the barracks like she lived there.

We wept and wept to meet each other again. To see a dear friend in this place is a precious gift. Ilsa cried a little too. It's the first time I've seen her show any real emotion in weeks. Though it was tears, I was glad to see my girl come back to life, for a moment at least. Vladka soon got down to business and we went to sit in a quiet corner of the barracks where we would not be overheard. I asked her what was this urgent that she risked her life to come and see us here.

"I have a way to get you two out of here, out of the ghetto." I was shocked. I sat open-mouthed. She asked, "Do you want to get out?" It was not as silly a question as it sounds. Some have resigned themselves to life here or even to deportation, trusting in God's will to help them. I am not one of those.

"Yes, I do," I said and she proceeded to tell me the most extraordinary things.

This is what she said: apparently, there is an organised Jewish resistance group. I had no idea. It engages in all sorts of activities, including helping Jews escape from the ghetto by providing routes out, papers and contacts in Aryan Warsaw and even help with finding a hiding place on the other side. They call this hiding place a '*melina*'. Well, Vladka revealed that she has two cousins who now work for this Jewish Resistance, young brave men who smuggle in guns. With their help, Vladka has arranged her own passage with Samuel out of the ghetto and into a safe *melina*. She said she can do the same for us.

She said, "Guess who I heard from the other day? You remember Krystyna? She used to buy your dresses and eat at Samuel's place. She was a bit of a snob, wasn't she? But she was all right." I did remember her, an Aryan woman of around my age, a widow whom I'd felt a little sorry for. Vladka told me that Krystyna was willing to provide a *melina* for Ilsa and me, at a price. It seems some Aryan Poles have contacts with the Polish Underground and through them, the Jewish group. They put their names forward to earn extra money. But I knew this was our downfall, as we are penniless. I told Vladka we have virtually no money. She said the Resistance would help with that too, giving me enough to settle us and keep us going for a little while, until we began to make our own way on the other side. I couldn't believe it. It was as if an angel were before me, holding her hand out to lift us on great wings, up and away from the underworld. I clutched onto Vladka's shoulders and cried and cried. The others in the barracks began to stare and Vladka had to calm me down, patting my back and shushing me. Ilsa was staring. I told her that Mama was all right, just happy. She actually smiled. A little smile and all too brief, but a real, true Ilsa-smile nonetheless.

Vladka went on, bombarding us with information. I had questions. This is everything I can remember of what she told me. I asked her how on earth Jews were able to contact people beyond the ghetto walls. Apparently, to talk to people on the Aryan side, there is a telephone available at the courthouse in Leszno St. Guards can be bribed and hundreds of Jews have made contacts with Aryans this way. Vladka said she talked with Krystyna on the phone just the other day, and Krystyna agreed to take Ilsa and myself into her flat for a little while.

I asked Vladka about escape. I couldn't imagine how my young daughter and I could possibly do it – and get away with it.

Vladka said, "There are as many routes out of the ghetto as

there are Nazis to stop them!" I was amazed. She listed scores of them. The ones I can remember are these: an alley called Parysowski Place parallel to the ghetto wall which extends along Okopowa and Dzika, where you can get over the wall into a quiet area where no one usually spots you. Other places include Feifer's factory on Okopowa St. near Gliniana, adjoining the ghetto. People have also left the ghetto on trams posing as Aryans; in carts covered up with old clothes; using faked legal passes to get past the guards at the gates; through a back door in the law courts which opens onto an Aryan street; through Gesia St market; posing as outside labourers by tagging along with work parties; even through the sewers. Also bribery, usually of a Polish policeman to lift a plank for a Jew to skip through.

I had no idea that escape was so prolific. Apparently, hundreds of Jews negotiate their ways back and forth between the ghetto and the Aryan side every day, and have been doing this since the early days of the ghetto. I realised that Ilsa and I had been living in a depressed haze of hopelessness for a long time. There was this whole world of Jewish ingenuity that we knew nothing about. However, all of these adventures sounded terrifying when I actually contemplated myself and Ilsa trying any one of them.

"I can't imagine doing it," I told Vladka. She told me not to worry. She had found one of the safest escape routes. There is a house on Bonifraterska St., whose front door opens out onto the ghetto. However, it also has a cellar with a hatch that opens a manhole cover on the Aryan side of the street. It is a derelict house and is used regularly by the Jewish resistance for smuggling things in and out of the ghetto. But it's not well known by the general ghetto population and thus is quiet and often deserted. Vladka said this is where Ilsa and I would go through.

. . .

I asked Vladka what we would do once we left the house on Bonifraterska St. This is what she told me: "You should be able to get over to Krystyna's place all right and after that, to live openly as an Aryan in Warsaw." This was news. I'd imagined we'd be hiding at Krystyna's place.

"Oh no," said Vladka. "That's just for very Jewish Jews, ones who can't pass. It's more trouble to be hidden. People have to keep you quiet and bring you food and all that. Aryans don't like it. It's better to try and pass as an Aryan. The Resistance will get fake papers for you and Ilsa and you can live as legitimate citizens, find a job and live out the war in the open. It's the best way, really."

By now, my head was swimming with information and Ilsa had gone to sleep on my lap. I needed to know basic facts. I asked Vladka about our fake identities. She told me the best ID was an authentic birth or baptism certificate of someone who'd died. They couldn't get this for me, but were planning a new identity with a new name. She said I'd have to invent my own new biography: "Fake siblings, fake place of birth, fake mother's maiden name. All Polish. You'll have to learn it off by heart. And teach it to Ilsa too, just the parts she'd be likely to know, if it were her real life."

Vladka asked me for a Polish sounding surname I'd like to use for myself and she'd pass it on to the forger, who would make our false papers. I didn't have to think for a second.

"Kucharski," I said immediately. Jan's name. My old love.

"It's a good Polish name," said Vladka. She doesn't know about Jan, or about little Janek. I never told her. I never told anyone. "That'll do. And for a first name? Choose something very Polish sounding too." I thought of a Polish teacher I'd known as a child, a good woman who I'd admired for her knowledge of Polish poetry.

"Franciszka," I said and Vladka replied, "Perfect. Good and Catholic. As for Ilsa, it's best that she keep her own name. Children often give the game away when they are forced to adopt a new name. They forget easily. Ilsa is not an overly Jewish name. It should pass all right. I'll let the forger know."

I thought of something crucial and my face went hot as I thought of how it could be our undoing: "What about photographs for the ID? I don't have any. Our apartment was wrecked before we came. They even stole our photo album. I don't have any photos, Vladka. What shall we do?" Vladka calmed me down.

"No need to panic, Helena. I had photos of you that I took from before the war, on days out with Samuel and Isak. Happy days. There is one I took where you had just looked round at me, you were not smiling, thinking about something or someone far away, I imagine. You look serious and it's a close-up. I have given it to the forger and he says it will do. You still look the same, you know, just as lovely. Though your eyes are sadder now." But what about Ilsa? Vladka reassured me that children did not require a photo on ID, as their appearance changes quickly. I was very relieved. How clever Vladka is. She thinks of everything.

With that, we were done. The two hours she was there had flown by. We hugged farewell and Vladka promised to return again in a little while with my papers and money, as well as final instructions on the escape plan. We will be leaving the ghetto within two weeks. And she was gone, into the ghetto night. I cannot believe how our lives have changed suddenly once more. Yesterday morning, there was nothing for us, only pointless dreams. Now there is a plan. Now there is hope.

The edge of disaster. This morning, one of the German overseers marched into our sewing room and shouted an order. He wanted one of us to take a batch of embroidery samples over to a supplier in the northern part of the ghetto. Knowing the danger on the streets everyone bowed their heads and focused resolutely on their work. This angered the jumped-up little German.

"Who will do it? Who will do it?" he barked. But no one spoke up. He said he'd choose. He stormed through the ranks and turned in my direction. Without thinking, I ducked my head. This was a big mistake. But I couldn't help it. If someone comes at you, you react on instinct. This just made him angrier. I think he was mostly mad about being short. He cuffed me round the head twice and told me to get up. He pushed me out of the room and into the corridor, where he handed me a box tied round with string. It felt very lightweight but I did not question it. He ordered me to take it to a house on Muranowska St. and sent me on my way.

I was let out of the gate and found myself in short sleeves and worn-out shoes walking through the streets of the ghetto. No ID on me, no money, nothing. I thought of Ilsa back in the factory behind the pile of uniforms, without me. I just hoped that I could get through the ghetto without incident. I did not want her to worry. I walked as quickly as I could. Running would have drawn attention to myself. The ghetto was utterly godforsaken. There were so few people, it seemed the middle of the night instead of a hot August afternoon. Those I saw hurried past, afraid to be out, afraid to acknowledge another living soul, afraid of their shadows. Almost every building I passed looked empty, devoid of colour or life. Doors and windows stood open as if their occupants had just left. I felt the weight of death all around. I prayed to a God I don't quite believe in. I asked that God help me get back to the shop, that's all. That is how I pray nowadays. Just the next step. To get through this moment or that. Small miracles.

I heard a commotion a couple of streets away. I could hear German shouting and Jewish screaming, the only music in the ghetto now. I froze, unable to decide whether I should go on or go back. But I could not risk the overseer's wrath. I had to deliver this cursed package. And I was only a few minutes from Muranowska. I saw a gang of soldiers appear at the end of the street.

Immediately, they spotted me and one of them ran up to me and grabbed my arm.

"Come on, Jewess. Come for a walk with me. We are going on a train ride." He was no more than a boy, very young, perhaps eighteen. Around my Janek's age. He had downy hair on his cheeks, like a baby. I tried to talk to him as his hand clutched my arm.

I tried to explain: "Please, sir. I am delivering a very important package for my German boss at Oschman's factory. I have a work permit for there. I have to deliver this package." The soldier grabbed the package from me and ripped off the string. He tore it open to reveal nothing. It was completely empty.

"What's this? An empty box? Looks very important to me! Come on!" and he threw the box down and kicked it away. He yanked me down the street and I glanced back at the empty box, crumpled in the gutter. I kept on talking and talking.

"I don't know why the box was empty, sir, but I assure you that it came from Oschman's. I come from Oschman's. If you would just come with me to Oschman's, they will vouch for me. At Oschman's. I work for Oschman's." I repeated the name like a charm, wishing it would transport me out of this boy's grasp. But he did not listen. He held onto my arm hard yet with glee as if I were a slippery fish he'd just caught from a summer stream. There were other soldiers there, and other Jews, most head down and hurrying along. No one else was talking but me. Perhaps all their chances had run out long ago. But I am a worker, I have a work permit, I am legitimate. I would not give up. I said it to him again – Oschman's, Oschman's, Oschman's.

"Oh, shut your mouth. I don't care if you work for the Führer, you stupid Jewish bitch!" And they all laughed at that. I could see we were heading for the Umschlagplatz. I was being led down a labyrinthine series of alleyways towards it. The smell was apparent from hundreds of yards away. It stank of shit and death. And the sound. A wave of human misery, crying and shouting and moaning, all punctuated by staccato gunshots or German commands, growing louder and louder. My whole being filled with terror at the thought of it. The Umschlag. They were taking me to the Umschlag. It was all over for me. I was dead already.

We came around the corner of a high brick wall and the sight hit me like a German fist. Thousands of Jews were crammed into the oval space, surrounded by buildings and fences and other alleyways coming off. Heaving with people, the Umschlag breathed like a great dirty beast. Where had they all come from? The only explanation I could fathom was that these were the last of the deportations before they began on the factories, and those desperate souls looked as if they had been there for hours or even days, so ragged and exhausted they were. As I scanned the crowd I began to see that there were corpses everywhere, strewn amongst the living, the dead having fallen where they stood. Beyond stood the railway sidings, empty for now. Who knew when the trains would come?

In desperation, I turned again to my boy German to beg him to reconsider, but in my shock I had not realised he had already gone. I was alone now in the Umschlag. I did not know why I was there or how long I would be there or what I was supposed to do. But nobody did. I had no choice but to sit down on the ground where I was. Soon a group of foreign auxiliaries made their way through the crowd, pulling out corpses and loading them onto carts. I saw that some of the dead were not quite dead, they groaned as they were moved. But the Ukranians or whoever they were did not care and loaded the moaning ones with the stiff ones. They would all be dead soon. I must have sat there for an hour or two. Time ran dry. All I could think of was Ilsa. What would she do without me? Who would take care of her? Perhaps someone would get a message to Vladka. Yes. Vladka would come and take care of Ilsa. I felt relieved when I thought of this. But how I missed Ilsa. Her solemn face. Her small hands. I would never see her again. Never hold her again. My head sank down and I wept there, I wept and wept and wept, adding my tears to the millions shed there before mine. As I looked around that Godless yard, I knew for sure that 'resettlement' was a great lie. We were all going to our certain deaths.

I heard a new noise, rumbling below the Umschlag cacophony. Then a screeching of metal against metal. The trains were arriving.

"Three days," I could hear people saying. "We've been waiting for three days." A surge of panic swelled the crowd, away from the trains and towards them, as if the horde could not decide: death here sooner or death there later? I stood up and was crushed on all sides. I could see up ahead that the Germans were organising those nearest the trains, separating them into two groups. Every Jew knew what the two groups meant. The one with the fewest people was the one you wanted. Though why the Germans bothered to temporarily save a few wretched Jews was beyond me. A voice screamed in my head, why not just get it all over with and kill us all, right here and now? But a smaller voice whispered in my mind to keep living, keep hoping. For Ilsa. The crowd was moving me forward towards the trains. I had no control over my limbs, let alone my destiny. After an age, I found myself near to the front of the queue, watching the Germans sort the soon-to-be-dead from the temporarily-alive. I had come up with no ingenious plan. My mind is not made that way. I thought only I would repeat about Oschman's, Oschman's. Though I knew it would do no good.

I was in front of a German soldier. He was in charge of the selection, whilst around him were gaggles of other soldiers, standing around and smoking, talking and laughing, ignoring the small matters of life and death enacted around them. This one was middle-aged, bored and irritable. He did not even speak, just motioned with his coiled whip to the left, to the right, to the left, the left, the left, to the right. I stepped up and spoke.

"Please, sir. I work for Oschman's. I sew German uniforms. I am an essential worker. I sew for Oschman's. I have a work permit for Oschman's. Oschman's factory. Oschman's." The German looked at me vacantly. I found the last of my courage and went on, "Maybe I've sewn the very uniform you are wearing. I am a good seamstress and I work for Oschman's."

"Who works for Oschman's?" said a voice. And someone turned round. Someone within those gangs of lounging soldiers turned around. And I saw his face. It was my boss, my sinister Volksdeutsch boss who puts his hands on all the women. There he was, smoking a cigar with the soldiers. I was never as happy to see such a scoundrel.

"That's my boss!" I blurted out. "Please, sir. He will tell you. I work for Oschman's." My boss came towards us and stood next to the German in charge.

"Does it work for you?" said the German in a voice of extreme boredom. The boss eyed me up. I wondered if he was deciding, do I like this one enough? I tried to smile. I must have looked a state, but I raised my dark eyes wide and becoming to him and smiled again. He smiled back.

"Yes, yes," he said and offered the Germans a packet of cigars from his inside pocket. "An excellent seamstress, yes. Can't really do without her. Must have been a mistake."

Yet the German was past caring and had already waved me away. My boss held out his arm and took me from that place. We walked in silence through one gate and another, into the maze of pathways and out onto Zamenhof St. The hellish sounds of the

Umschlag receded to nothing as we walked. The silence, the space, the freedom of the street. Like spring water after sewage.

There he stopped and offered me a cigar.

"No thank you," I said and tried to smile again, but I was beginning to weep from relief and tried to stop myself. He patted my shoulder.

"There, there," he said quietly. "It's all right now." I was uncertain what I should say. Every Jew's dilemma when he is faced with kindness from Aryans. What do they want from me? I looked up at him. He puffed on his cigar thoughtfully, a slight frown on his face. What was he thinking? He spoke again.

"What were you doing out in the street anyway? You know it is forbidden to leave the shop." I explained my errand and the empty box and he smiled. "I see. You were the subject of a bet, my dear." I didn't understand. "The overseers at Oschman's, they have devised some new fun. Pick a Jewess from the floor and send her out on a pointless mission. Bet on whether or not she ever comes back. You will lose a lot of people a lot of money, I wager, eh?" And he laughed and laughed. I found myself laughing too, but there was a kind of madness in it. We walked on, towards the shop. All my mind said was Ilsa, Ilsa, again and again. I will see my Ilsa again, touch her, hold her. Ilsa.

He talked easily with me on the way, telling me of the pressures on him as a Volksdeutsch, how he knew he had to make his way in this German world, how he often hung around with the Germans offering them fine cigars, chocolates, cheeses, wine, or anything else he could bribe them with. "The Germans are winning this war, and what will become of us all afterwards? The smart people do as I do, butter them up. That's the best way, my dear. Realise who your bosses are and make them your friends." I listened but said nothing. There was nothing to say. Jews were left out of these equations. Their only role was to die.

We had reached an empty street around the corner from our shop. I could almost feel the softness of my baby's hair beneath my hand. He stopped, and his arm came around my waist and he pulled me to him.

"Are you grateful? Are you grateful to me, my dear?" he whispered, his cheek against mine.

"Yes," I said. "Thank you, sir." And he put his tongue in my ear. I stood very still and let him do it. He whispered obscene things to me. I won't write them down. He said he lived nearby, we'd go there. I was trying to think straight, to think what would happen next, what I must do for the best. How to get back to Ilsa and keep her safe. I tasted cigar smoke and garlic as he kissed me. I felt I would vomit. My body cried out for Ilsa.

"I'm bleeding," I said.

"What?"

"I'm bleeding, woman's blood. If you don't mind. I just thought I'd warn you." He looked away and puffed on his cigar.

"Oh," he said and wiped his mouth. He looked unsure. I was terrified he would ask me to prove it. I had not bled there for months.

"It will be over soon, within a day or two. If it bothers you. We can...postpone." I smiled again, mustering up whatever female wiles I used to possess, in my other life, a thousand years ago.

"All right, all right," he said. It was the best thing I could have said. He looked disgusted. I know some men feel that way. Others do not care. He was obviously one of the fussy ones. Well, he had plenty of others to choose from on the factory floor, after all. He turned and walked ahead of me towards the shop and motioned me through the gate. I went back to the sewing room alone. I broke all the rules and rushed to my child in her hiding place. I held her so tightly and so long. Child of my body. I am here.

Tomorrow we will leave the ghetto. A message arrived from Vladka soon after we saw her that we would have to wait a while for the forged ID, as their regular forger had been shot. Poor brave man, whoever he was. Tonight, Vladka appeared again in the barracks. It was wonderful to see her. The time since she last came has seemed like an age. There was my near deportation to cope with and the worry that my boss would try it with me again. But he has not. Perhaps the thought of my menstruation put him off. Thank the stars.

The fear that Vladka would never return was also consuming me. Being close to death there in the Umschlag has made me more determined than ever to survive. And yet I knew she was my only chance. But here she was, this evening, a returning angel. We went into the corner of the barracks again, Ilsa beside me. This time Vladka seemed more secretive, often peering over my shoulder to check none of the other women were listening. She said she didn't have much time. She began by handing over all the different documents I would need for Ilsa and myself. It was odd to see my photograph next to this concocted name: Franciszka Kucharski. I thought about Jan. How strange it is that two decades after I lost him, I now have his name. Not in the way I'd hoped I would, all those years ago, when I wanted to be his wife. But his Polish name may save me now. And Ilsa, my child. My second child. Isak's child now has the name of my first lover. But my little boy Janek does not. Never will, of course. I wonder what his name is now. I wonder if he lives. Thank heavens he left Warsaw before this inferno. I hope he never came back.

Vladka talked me through each document, saying what it was

needed for. We each have a *Kennkarte,* which is the general identity document. A fingerprint was needed for both of us and Vladka produced a tiny case with a black ink pad inside. Ilsa and I printed our fingerprints on the cards. Ilsa thought this great fun, like finger painting.

But Vladka warned us: "Go and wash your hands immediately. Ink stains for both of you might raise questions." When we came back, Vladka explained that the underground had placed a false record of my new identity at the registry, to back up my *Kennkarte*. It meant that if my *Kennkarte* was seen by police or other officials, there would be corresponding paperwork in case they did a background check. Vladka also gave me a ghetto pass, which I'd need if we got stopped on our way from the shop to the escape house. The next document was a work permit, a bulky thing of several pages.

Vladka explained: "This is your work certificate, the *Bescheinigung*. This is your evidence that you are a working Aryan Pole. There are street round-ups every day to check for this. If you don't have one of these, you can be taken for forced labour or simply shot. As you can see, you have to sign it and state that you are an Aryan. Sign it now. Also, there is confirmation by your building manager that you live where you say you do. We have bribed the manager at Krystyna's residence to sign this for you. He seems reliable. But watch out for him. He now knows you are an unregistered person. He doesn't know you are a Jew, but he does know that something is not quite right with you. There are unregistered people in Warsaw who aren't Jews, those in hiding from the authorities, underground agents, unregistered officers of the Polish army, the unemployed hiding from the Labour Office. Being unregistered is not unusual in itself. But you don't want him snooping. Just avoid him is my advice."

"What could he do?" I asked.

"We don't know. But he doesn't have any love for the Germans, that's for sure. Don't worry about him." I tried not to think about this. But this man's knowledge frightens me. Next I wanted to know more about my new career.

"Where am I to be working?"

"Nowhere. It's a fake job. We have created one for you at a clothing factory in Warsaw. Your employer doesn't know anything about you, but we have a man in their offices who plants fake records. There is what is called an *Arbeitskarte*, or work card, for Franciszka Kucharski at this factory. If the authorities check up on you, they'll find your name in their records. It's a huge factory and the employers can't possibly know every employee. Remember that you are supposed to be working there. You'll need to have an excuse for why you're not at work, if you're ever stopped in the street. Of course, eventually you'll need to make your own living. Your dressmaking skills will get you by, I'm sure."

She talked about the escape. She had with her a small leather holdall in which she'd kept the fake documents. She gave me these instructions: "Tonight you must pack this bag with a few possessions, clothes for both of you, essential items only. Tomorrow morning, you must leave Ilsa in the barracks. Don't be alarmed. One of the Polish guards is secretly working for the Underground. There are others like him who have infiltrated the shops and are helping Jews escape. His name is Witold Romer. He will keep an eye out for Ilsa, and he'll make sure no one goes in there and finds her. Then before lunch he will call you out to run an errand. He will let you into the barracks to collect Ilsa and your bag, then will see you out of the gate. From there, you must walk quickly to Bonifraterska. If anyone stops you on the ghetto streets, show your ID together with your ghetto pass. If you're asked your business in the ghetto, say you've been visiting a friend at Oschman's. Give Romer's name. He can vouch for you. Once you arrive at the house on Bonifraterska Street, ring the doorbell.

Someone will be there to meet you. You'll be taken downstairs to the cellar and shown where the manhole cover is. Before you go through, you must remember to take your Jewish armbands off. After that, you will go upwards and onto the Aryan side of the street. And then you must get to this apartment."

Vladka handed me a slip of paper with Krystyna's address on it. Her place is on Wilcza Street, near the junction with Marszalkowska. There were instructions written down about the tram ride I would need to take to get there. There was also information about the cost of a tram ticket in Aryan Warsaw, because of course a Jew does not know such things, having been holed up behind these walls for years. They had thought of everything.

Vladka warned me: "Memorise this tonight and then destroy it. People who know where they live do not carry around their address and directions on them. When you get there, Krystyna will be looking out for you and come down to meet you. She will greet you in the street as an old family member. You are to masquerade as her cousin, who lives with her. Just in case anyone is watching. This is to convince the locals that you are her family. But when you are making your way across town to her apartment, your papers indicate that you are a normal resident of Aryan Warsaw. You must act as if you have been living there for years. Helena, try to recall that only a few years ago you were a free Varsovian. You must wear the face of that person tomorrow."

So much to remember. So many lies. My face ached from the frown of concentration.

"And one more thing," Vladka continued. "Well, there are a hundred things I could tell you about escaping the ghetto, about passing on the other side. But I don't have the time. One thing is vital though and you must remember it. Helena, you've lived in the ghetto for a long time. Your daughter is growing up here. You've lost your husband here. As horrible as it is, you've become accustomed to it. It is your world, as much as you hate it. Out there, on the Aryan side, everything is different. I've been out myself a few times, smuggling with my cousins. The Aryan world is like a memory of how our lives used to be. It will shock you, I promise. You will find yourself wanting to wander around with your mouth wide open, with tears running down your cheeks. And that is what will kill you. Every Jew who escapes from the ghetto has this potential of being caught, merely by the look on his face. Amazement and surprise at seeing the old Warsaw again. And those sad, sad Jewish eyes of yours. In all Jewish faces that have known such loss. Poles particularly recognise these looks. Maybe someone will come up to you, say you're a Jew, he wants money. He's a blackmailer, extortionist – *szmalcownik* is the common name – a man like him will look for those sad eyes, he will prey on them. That is your first lesson. You must put on an Aryan face. You'll have to practise it tonight, both of you."

I had not thought of this at all. I wondered how I could stop my eyes looking sad, when I hadn't even realised they were. I thought of Ilsa, her quiet blankness, unlike a normal Aryan child skipping along the street.

"How on earth will we manage it?" I asked Vladka.

"You will, because you'll have to. The blackmailers hang around on streets near the ghetto walls, looking for escapees like you. And that reminds me. You must try to dress as smartly as possible. Tonight find the best dresses and shoes for yourself and Ilsa that you can and make sure they're mended and neat. It's easy to spot a scruffy Jew. You must not look like one. Do your best. You're lucky it's summer. In winter, it's a sure sign that a Jew has escaped when they don't wear a fur collar. At least you can wear a summer dress, Ilsa too. If a *szmalcownik* approaches you, you must bluff it out, pretend you're appalled by the suggestion. You have ID which will get you by. And remember that what they are trying to do is illegal, the Germans frown on it because they want the Jews caught not blackmailed, so the punishments are severe. Stay in public and they'll probably leave you alone. Swear in Polish, say

'Mother of God!' or 'Jesus, Mary!' Say, 'I'm not a Jew, how dare you!' Things like this. Don't let them see your sad eyes."

She looked carefully around the barracks, as if checking who was watching us.

"We can trust the other women," I whispered. "We are all in this together." Vladka just shook her head.

"Don't be naïve, Helena. And don't tell anyone here of your plans for tomorrow. Just get on with it as I've told you. Here, take this and hide it now." She slipped a roll of cash from her hand into mine. I pushed it up my sleeve. I had not seen this much money in years. "It's to last you as long as possible. I know you'll use it wisely. Listen, one last thing. Samuel and I are going next week, staying at another *melina* in Warsaw. Once you're safely out and at Krystyna's, we'll come and find you. You won't be alone, I promise."

She stood up and held her arms out to me. We hugged and I knew she was going.

"That is everything," she said loudly, so the other women could hear. "It was good to see you both safe and well. Perhaps I will visit you again soon." She hugged Ilsa too, who had listened silently to all we'd discussed. Ilsa held on to Vladka for a long time. Vladka let her. It brought tears to my eyes. Vladka hugged me again and whispered, "Be safe, my friend." She turned and left us.

It is late now. Everyone is asleep but me. I write by moonlight. This evening, I have prepared Ilsa as best I can for tomorrow's events. I have shown her the fake documents again, explained to her where we are going and what we are doing. It was not easy, as I had to whisper everything to avoid being overheard, though I'm sure the other women were listening. No one has said anything. I have also tried to spruce up our best dresses. I did have the foresight to bring a nice one for myself and one for Ilsa when we came here, just in case we needed to impress. I didn't know at the time why I'd done it; it was a case again of acting on instinct. I'm learning that is what will help you survive, as well as your friends, if you are lucky enough to have any still alive.

The hardest part was teaching Ilsa about sad eyes. I tried to explain this, but she did not understand. I told her she must pretend to be happy. But she asked me an impossible question, a question that broke my heart to hear my child ask. She said, "How does it feel to be happy, Mama?" She has forgotten, as surely as she forgot the colour of grass. Yet there was one way to help her remember, the one thing all Jews live with day in and day out these days.

"Imagine you have just eaten a huge plate of potato dumplings." Ilsa thought for a moment. She smiled. And what a smile! But it disappeared so quickly. I think she remembered how hungry she was. I felt a terrible guilt for reminding her of pleasures, when I could not possibly give them to her. Perhaps tonight she will dream of potato dumplings. Better that than the horrors she has seen.

I have to decide whether I should leave this diary behind. There are plenty of blank pages left, as I have been using a tiny script for a long time now, a flea's hand. But it is written in plain Polish. Anyone could read it and find out everything about me. It is foolish to take it. I could hide it and hope that one day someone will find it in a free Warsaw. I know it's the last thing I should be worrying about. It's only words, after all. Is it worth the risk? But there is a part of me that needs it. Needs it to be with me. This journal has become the voice of my soul. It is my confidante, my sanity, my friend. It is the only one I can rely on. I used to feel that way about God.

Tomorrow we go. I pray that we will leave the shop safely. I pray that we will not be stopped in the street on the way. I pray that someone will be there to let us in at the house on Bonifraterska Street. I pray that we can get out of the manhole cover without being seen. I pray that we can find our way to Krystyna's apartment without being accosted by a *szmalcownik* or worse. I pray that Krystyna has not changed her mind. I pray that I don't die in my sleep tonight.

So much to pray for.

Is God listening?

I will take my diary with me.

CHAPTER SEVEN

Her name was Marysia.

At first glance, Daniel thought she was a boy. Slight, with bobbed hair tucked behind her ears. Then she turned around and he saw her full mouth and long eyelashes.

"Be careful, Anglik," said Natan. "She's dynamite. But I don't think she's interested in boys."

"Oh no!" he said. "Not one of those!" He was thinking of the women he'd heard of in bohemian circles in London.

"No, no, no. She goes with men, not girls. But she's too busy for all that these days. Obsessed with her politics. We're old friends. But we don't agree. Every time I see her we end up arguing. And she never backs down, ever. She's so stubborn, it drives me mad. You'd do well not to get tangled up with that viper, Anglik."

"She sounds wonderful."

He laughed at him. "Well, we might all die tomorrow. Good luck to you. I bet she's a good fuck!"

They had just arrived. It was the big Resistance meeting, planned for weeks. The language in the room a dissonance of Polish, Yiddish and Hebrew.

Natan pointed out a young man at the edge of the crowd, standing silently, waiting. Slim and dark, an expressive mouth.

"That's Mordechai Anielewicz, our leader."

"He looks young," said Daniel.

"Only twenty-three. He was in my youth group before the war. He actually escaped from Warsaw when the Germans invaded, but came back to fight."

Daniel was impressed, awed even. To have escaped this hell and to return, to defend his territory, to fight the Germans? It was the stuff of heroes.

Natan pointed out other people he knew or names he had heard, labelled each one according to their political leanings. A muddle of groups with names like ancient cities: *Akiba, Dror, Gordonia.*

"Why are there different groups? We're all Jews, aren't we?"

Natan shook his head. "It goes back years. Old arguments."

Daniel was watching Marysia.

"Who's she talking to?"

"That's Zygmunt, a big shot in the ZZW. She's his courier. She lives outside the ghetto and takes messages and goods in and out for him."

"She's in a different group from us?"

"Yes and if you want to get her into bed, you don't have a hope. You know they hate our guts."

Daniel knew about this. When he began his work with Natan, he had joined a network of youth groups, with leaders of the Jewish Resistance handing down orders. He'd spent the last months smuggling goods. The ghetto was changing. Deportations increased and the population thinned. Arguments stormed about where the trains were going. A few weeks before, new orders came from above: avoid the deportations at all cost and escape from the trains if you can. Natan and Daniel distributed leaflets all over the ghetto warning that the deportations led to death camps, gave them news that free Jews were fighting in forests all over Poland, that the ghetto meant death, but escape could mean life. Hopefully, this had saved lives. Otherwise, some who had gone into hiding or fled would have said yes, thank you, to the bread and jam on offer at the railway yard and boarded the trains, their final journey. Did his mother see one of those leaflets?

Dodging deportations was not enough. In July there was a meeting where the Resistance formed a proper coalition of Jewish fighters against the Nazis. They called it the ZOB, or *Zydowska Organizacja Bojowa*: the Jewish Fighting Organisation. But discord raged, a split occurred. Two main factions emerged. The ZOB was one, and the other was the ZZW (*Zydowski Zwiazek Wojskowy*), or Jewish Fighting Union. The two groups would fight together in spirit but separate in body. The word on the wind was that, despite their common aims, the two groups despised each other.

Anielewicz was asking people to sit down. He waited until everyone was still.

"The time is for action, not words. The time is for attack, not co-operation. Our first objective should be to organise, train and acquire arms. Our second, to eliminate traitors and collaborators."

People began to murmur, laugh, shake or nod their heads.

"We propose the creation of a new political group, the *Zydowski Komitet Narodowy* or ZKN. It will be a non-partisan group. It can bring us all together, offering joint political representation for all the different factions of our Jewish Resistance. Brothers and sisters, we must set aside our political differences and join together to face the Nazi aggressor. The final wave of deportations will come soon. We will amalgamate all forces and organise military training for armed resistance to these. We ask you to discuss this now, thrash it out, then later we will vote."

The room fell into debate. Daniel stepped through the throng, tapping shoulders, showing his mother's photograph.

"Do you know this woman? Her name's Helena. Have you seen her? She's older now, in her thirties. She's a seamstress. Helena. Do you know her?"

Nothing. As every other time he had done this, for months now, he was met with blank faces and shaking heads. At first, he was keen, looked into people's eyes. By that night, he barely glanced at them, but asked, asked and asked again. If he didn't ask, he'd never know.

He looked around. Who hadn't he asked?

He saw Marysia, watching him. She looked away, sitting with a group of young people on the floor. He made his way over, casually.

"The only way to deal with the Nazi scum is to actively resist, to take up arms against them. What else? Die like a farm animal, slaughtered like stupid sheep?"

Her colour was up, her eyes shining.

One boy said, "My parents died like that. They weren't stupid."

Marysia put her hand on his arm. "My parents were deported too. We know what happened to them. We mustn't ignore the truth. It's our duty to get revenge. We get every gun or bomb or dagger or stick we can find and murder those bastards. Yes, we'll probably die trying. But we're all going to die anyway. This way our deaths mean something."

The youths fell quiet. They were thinking of the lost ones.

Daniel said, "Can I talk with you?"

Marysia looked at him, stood up. They moved to the wall. Her face was a focused frown.

"I'm a friend of Natan's. I'm Anglik."

"I know who you are."

"Do you?"

"Yes, we've all heard about the English one. Not found your mother yet?"

"No, not yet."

"You know she's probably dead, don't you?"

Blimey, that was a bit harsh, he thought. She had light brown eyes, almost green. Clear, honest, radiant. As pretty as they were, he felt a chill akin to that he'd always had from Jerzy. But those eyes...Surely eyes so lovely couldn't belong to a girl with no feelings.

"I don't know that about my mother."

"Probably best to forget her. Fight instead."

"I can do both."

"Up to you."

Her eyes wandered across the room. It was going badly. He had hoped to tell her his story. He thought she'd be impressed. A young man come all the way from London to rescue his mother. He was sure it would be a winner. He decided to change tack.

"Natan says you're dynamite."

"What?"

"He says you always give him a hard time."

"He deserves it."

"Why?"

"I'm in the ZZW and Natan's in the ZOB. So are you. What else is there to say?"

"We're all on the same side."

He realised he'd said that before, months ago, at his first meeting with Natan. He still wanted to believe it.

"Yes, we are. But we disagree about the important things. You know before the war, Natan and I were in these youth groups? His was called *Hashomer Hatzair* and mine was *Betar*. His was Socialist, mine was Revisionist."

Daniel tried to follow. He had talked with Dad about politics, knew the difference between the main wings. It sounded like Natan was left wing, Marysia was right wing. Beyond that, he knew he'd make a bloody fool of himself if he tried to fake it any further. But she went on.

"We trained for life in the new homeland. We learnt about relying on yourself and the land. Not being a damn merchant but a farmer or a worker. We all agreed on that and we all agreed on our aim: Zionism."

Daniel had heard the word but couldn't remember what it meant. He was watching her mouth, wanted to stop it talking, wanted to kiss her.

"But we disagreed on everything else. How it should be done, what we'd do about the Arabs. Natan's lot believe in equal rights for them. We want more land too. Natan's lot are weak, trying to be nice about it. But this is our right. Our destiny. What's your position on the Palestine question?"

He thought about all the nonsense he could string together, to persuade her he was a politically active intellectual who had thought deeply on these matters.

But he found he could not lie to her, could not string her a line, could not pretend. He just wanted to be himself.

"I didn't even know I was a Jew until two years ago. I'm very ignorant about Jewish matters. I'm learning more all the time. I'd like it if you helped me. To learn what it means to be a Jew. If that's all right with you."

She smiled. It was the first time he'd seen her smile.

"Show me her photo then."

Daniel handed it over. She looked for a long time.

"I don't know her. I'm sorry."

"It's all right."

"I'll ask around."

"Thank you."

They looked at each other. The room was busy with the machinery of human noise. Daniel and Marysia stood in the midst of it. Still, quiet, secluded.

Natan led Daniel through the ghetto night to a bombed out hospital to meet an old Jew called Steiner. A week after the meeting they were on a ZOB mission, its official name 'expropriation'. They needed cash to buy weapons. The rates for arms were skyrocketing. More money had to be raised from 'donations', that is, expropriations from wealthy Jews. They called them 'exes'. A rich Jew would be informed by letter that a sum of money would be collected at a date, time and place. There was no room for refusal. The Resistance was becoming almost as unpopular as the Nazis. They arrived at nine and waited for a tedious half hour.

"Fuck this," said Natan. "Let's go to his house. Give him hell."

But there Steiner was, shambling along, impeded by his big belly. Natan had told Daniel that Steiner had always been wealthy and then he'd made a fortune in the ghetto, dealing in black market goods and selling to the *Judenrat* and Jewish Police. That was why he'd been spared in the deportations so far. To the Resistance, he was guilty of collaboration and profiting from the Nazi system. He was lucky to be walking, as others on the blacklists were not. The sight of this man, his obesity in the midst of so much hunger, sickened Daniel. He grimaced at him, felt his fists clench and his chest tighten. The moon was bright and Daniel could see Steiner's face clearly. When Steiner caught sight of them, his eyes betrayed fear yet old-school defiance, as if to say, 'There was a time when you would call me sir.' Steiner stopped and eyed them again.

He began to speak in Yiddish, but Daniel interrupted: "Speak in Polish," he said.

"Why?"

He remembered something Magda always said to him as a child.

"Because I say so." He didn't want to admit to the man that he knew no Yiddish. He wanted to be a proper Jew, to fight for the

Jews, to represent them. Daniel didn't want this traitor to think he was more Jewish than him.

But Steiner went on, albeit in Polish: "I don't see why I should be ordered around, in my own ghetto, by a couple of youths."

"Just give us the money, old man," said Natan.

"I don't see why I should. You bring me here after curfew, risking my life. You demand money of me. And for what? A pathetic resistance movement that's doomed to failure? What do you think a few pistols are going to achieve against the German army? You are imbeciles, all of you!"

A terrible rage swept over Daniel. He had never hated like this before. It overwhelmed him, but there was a grim thrill in it too. He imagined his mother shoved onto a train, while this old git was haggling over his ill-gotten cash. He grabbed Steiner by the throat.

"Give us the money, you fat bastard!" he spat, choking him.

There were rolls of flab around his neck. Steiner fumbled around in his inside pocket, gasping. Daniel saw his hand draw out a bundle of notes, which Natan pinched and said, "All there." He let Steiner go and the old man dropped to the ground, reaching for his throat, coughing and moaning.

"You little shits!" he croaked.

Daniel went to kick him, but Natan held him back.

"Let's go," he said and pulled him by the arm. They had to get away before the ten o'clock patrol passed by. As they hurried off, Daniel heard Steiner retching. He hoped he would cough himself to death.

Two days later at Natan's ghetto hideout on the fourth floor of an empty building on Muranowska Street, Daniel wrapped up four revolvers and ammo. They'd been bought from an Underground contact at an inflated cost but less than the usual street price. None of the revolvers he'd bought were in working order, but they would take them to Leon. He was an old friend of Natan's, a weapons repairer for the Resistance, a gunsmith before the war. He lived with his wife and child in a bunker where illegal Jews had been staying since the big July Aktion. They were illegal because they had no official job in the factories. Instead, home was a hole in the ground.

Natan led the way. Daniel watched his friend walk before him, picking his way along a street where every house had been bombed and left in piles of broken masonry. Not so very long ago, the war was just an idea on the horizon and Natan had been a boy growing up in Warsaw, his home, his future spread before him like an intricate quilt, comforting, optimistic. Natan's good humour, his quick wit and his insight into others, all those parts of his character would have revolved around getting girls, studying books and defying his parents, most probably. Now it was twisted into gun-running and extortion. Daniel thought of himself outside his own bombed home, his father dead, seeing that little boy collect shrapnel. They were all boys once and war had slapped their faces and snatched their futures away. Now, they were stumbling through the ruins of a new future. At least he had his friend Natan to face it with and the rest of their group, all the Jewish groups, despite their squabbling.

They clambered over some rubble and went round to the back of what had once been a building. Natan found a door in the ground, once a beer cellar. He knocked in a rhythmic pattern. A faint tapping came in reply. From down the cellar stairs came the strong odour of humanity. The stench of people too close for too long. A memory came of his disgust at the stinking crowd sheltering in the London tube. What a bloody little snob he'd been.

A woman came with a candle and lit them through to the main

room where he saw a dozen worried yet curious faces in the flickering light. A man embraced Natan and he was introduced to him, Leon. A kind face, not suited to war.

A child's profile loomed out of the darkness and asked, "Is it food?"

It was awful to say no. Daniel thought, why hadn't they brought food? What did resistance matter when a child was hungry? He was about to say to Leon that next time he'd bring supplies with him. But he didn't. He couldn't promise him anything. Should he risk his neck again for these particular Jews? He did what he could. But he'd met these people face to face now and that made all the difference.

Daniel saw Leon watching him as he glanced around the crowded room.

"We are lucky," said Leon with a rueful smile. "Some of these bunkers house twenty or thirty. We're only thirteen 'wild' Jews here. And I get money from you lot. We do all right."

But they looked thin. Every few seconds someone coughed in that room, not the polite coughs of concert intervals, but hacking coughs that smacked of lung disease. The child who'd asked for food came and sat on Leon's lap. Daniel guessed it was his daughter. She looked mournful in the candlelight.

Beyond them, others murmured or slept. Two men played cards, squinting. Two bodies writhed together by a wall, making love. How accustomed they were to communal living. Perhaps they bickered over rations, but he saw no evidence of it that night. Just a quiet knowledge that they were surviving together, helping each other to live a little longer. Daniel still resided alone in his Underground flat, the same one since he first arrived in Warsaw. He was told then he'd be moved frequently. Nobody ever got round to it. He was glad, as it was a kind of home to him. He was out much of the time on missions with Natan, so he wasn't there much. But despite the dangers here, he thought how good it must feel to be surrounded by friends and allies at all times, sharing, discussing, even simply playing cards. He'd never been to boarding school, he'd never had siblings. He was so lonely in his little flat at night. He glanced at the humping couple in the corner. He thought of Marysia. Every time he'd seen her recently had been at a meeting, politics and business all around them, not a moment to really talk to her, to tell her how he liked her. And none of the peacetime ways to arrange a date or take steps towards getting a girl alone. He'd never been with a girl before the war and this was a hell of a time to learn how. But maybe the danger in the air could help him, could speed up the usual pleasantries. He daydreamed that if he ever got up the nerve to actually ask her, perhaps one night Marysia might be lying beside him in his cold bed.

Leon reached for the revolvers, inspected them one at a time with his spare hand, his daughter still on his lap. She closed her eyes and fell asleep on him as they talked.

"Any more coming soon?" Leon asked.

"Not likely," said Natan.

Daniel said, "Jews are charged three times the price as Poles for the same arms."

"How much?"

"This lot? To a Pole about 3000 per gun. Maybe 3 or 4 zloty for ammo. We paid 10,000 for each revolver and 80 zloty for the ammo."

Leon sighed. "It's a sellers' market. Always the same in wartime."

"It's not the same for everyone," said Natan. "The ZZW are getting stacks of weapons, German and Italian stuff. They've got contacts with the People's Guard, and those guys like the Jews. Anglik's contacts are with the Polish Workers' Party, and they hate us."

Daniel considered defending them, Jerzy, Lidia, his other contacts who worked selflessly to rid Poland of the Nazis. But he knew Natan was right. The last time he'd seen Jerzy, they'd argued and fallen out badly.

Jerzy had said, "The Home Army have their own plans for a Polish uprising. The ghetto must not get ahead of itself and start a rebellion against the Germans too early."

"But the Jews can't wait!" Daniel had cried. "They're out of time!"

"Still, they must wait. What's good for Poland is good for the ghetto."

The harsh ignorance of it. Jerzy was blind to the chasm between Aryans and Jews. Daniel saw it stark and clear, his first days in the ghetto, that a brick wall could divide paradise from purgatory. He hated those outside for their indifference. Inside, he had assumed Jews would walk the same ground. But he found seams of ancient mistrust beneath. All Poles, all Jews, separate as atoms. Why did it have to bloody well be that way?

"I still don't understand why the ZZW won't share their weapons with us," Daniel said.

"It's politics," said Leon, keeping his voice low so his daughter could sleep. "People are looking forward to the end of the war, preparing for power shifts they think might be useful one day."

"But to a Jew, this is nonsense, isn't it?" said Daniel. "We might not survive to next week, let alone years ahead. If only we could..."

Natan interrupted: "No, no. It's about Palestine. Look, the Germans want us all to die. But if, God willing, they don't get their way, and some of us survive, what do we do then? My youth group was planning our future before this war. Why should we give up now?"

Daniel answered, "Who cares about Palestine when you might die in Poland tomorrow?"

Natan was shaking his head. "You don't understand. We grew

up with this. It's part of us. It doesn't make sense to you because you...well, you know, you're an outsider."

Daniel glanced at Leon, who looked down and kissed his daughter's hair. Natan stared at the floor.

Of course. Who was he to have an opinion? Only a new Jew. What he said didn't count.

Leon hugged his daughter. Daniel envied him. With all the danger and privation of Leon's existence, he envied him. But how long would it be like this? The ghetto was emptying. These few Jews hiding in a warm hole, they looked cosy. A fragile moment. Too many flowers in too little water. They would not last long.

"Would you lads like dinner?" A woman stood beside them, placed her hand on the child's head. Leon's wife. "I've made some potato peel pancakes."

They said thank you, but no. They could not take food from those poor souls. Daniel showed the photo around before leaving. No luck.

Outside, Natan said, "Poor bastards."

Walking home, taciturn, they passed rows of vacant houses staring through glassless windows. Behind doors, below ground, Jews hid. Beyond the walls, the enemy prepared to smoke out this filthy hive. This prison, this haven.

In January, Daniel stood beside Natan in a cellar with other operatives making Molotov cocktails. A Home Army leaflet told them how to do it, a small Polish favour. Working far into the night, they slept late at Natan's digs and were woken by gunfire outside. They both sat bolt upright and stared at each other a moment, before scrambling to the window, and peering from behind the curtain. Below, a unit of German soldiers was marching, before them a cluster of Jews. Some prisoners were shot indiscriminately, their bodies stepped on by those who came behind. More shots came from the streets beyond. An explosion. Another. In their street, the German unit stopped marching and their commander looked into the air, as did the Jews they had rounded up. One of the Germans lifted his rifle and swung around randomly, aiming at butterflies.

Then an extraordinary thing happened. From a house, an unseen Jewish hand lobbed a grenade into the middle of that German unit. The enemy was blown to pieces right there in the street below them.

"Fuck!" Daniel said in English.

Most of the unit were killed, with a few Germans left staggering about. Jews were killed too, but most scattered and escaped. For the first time in their war, Daniel and Natan were watching Germans in fear, crawling along the ground, crying out, hugging the walls as they tried to creep away from the devastation.

Natan said, "Jews killing Germans!"

It could only mean one thing.

"The uprising's started!" said Daniel and the two friends looked at each other. Natan gave a short bark of a laugh. In shock, they stood for a moment, then Daniel gave him a quick embrace and Natan clapped him on the back.

"Let's go!" They grabbed their revolvers, both weapons having been assigned to them only a few days before. Daniel opened their window wide and they lifted their guns.

"I'll take the left, you the right," he said.

Daniel picked out a German survivor who was sitting on his arse, rubbing his eyes. He raised his gun and went through everything he'd learnt about taking aim at faraway targets. He believed he had him. Fired a shot. Missed. But the German jumped a mile and scrambled along the dirty road. Natan took a shot, missed too.

A German shouted, "The Jews are shooting!"

The astonishment he heard in that soldier's voice. The despicable Jews had guns, the despicable Jews were fighting back!

Over the next few days, Daniel and Natan dodged in and out of buildings, on forays for food and weapons. They met other fighters, Daniel showed his photo and shared stories. Nothing on Helena. Details heard like brushstrokes gave them a portrait of the uprising. Around twenty enemy were killed by Jews and at least forty wounded. An astonishing result. Despite Daniel's pride in their success, the numbers of their dead made miserable hearing. Over a thousand Jews had been killed and thousands more deported.

"It's because we never had enough weapons," he said to Natan. "Not enough to be a proper fighting force."

"It was only because we were all so fucking brave and skilful at street fighting that more Jews weren't killed."

"Absolutely. The Polish forces did nothing. If Poles and Jews had fought together, there'd be a lot more German dead out there."

In the days following the start of the uprising, Daniel and Natan received orders that all combat groups must live in barracks under strict military discipline. Daniel was to leave his flat in Aryan Warsaw, move to a house on Bonifraterska Street and bunk with Natan and the rest of his combat group. Bonifraterska Street was in the Central Ghetto. The ghetto was now small, only three defined areas, all within a few blocks of each other: the Central Ghetto, the Brushworks Area (named after a workshop there) and the Factories Area. This web of streets was the homeland to defend come the final battle.

It felt good to leave his Aryan flat. It reminded him what the Polish Underground could have done for the Jews, but chose not to. He felt his contacts with them were almost broken now. Only a major turnaround in their attitude towards Jewish resistance to the Nazis would change his mind. He had little hope of this, but a little hope was better than none. Perhaps the success of the Jewish fighters would spur on the Aryan Poles to support them. They certainly surprised them. He chose not to tell Jerzy or Lidia that he was leaving. He hoped the little flat would stay empty, wait for him, in case he needed it one day. Who knew what would happen in the weeks to come?

He was not a fool. They all knew the Germans would return with retribution. This strengthened their resistance. It was not about beating the Germans. That would never happen. It was about choice. How to live and how to die. The ZOB slogan said: *All are ready to die as human beings.* Was he ready to die? He didn't want to. He wanted to fight and kill more Germans. He wanted to find his mother. He wanted to see Marysia and lose his virginity.

Before he moved to Bonifraterska, Daniel went to see Marysia at her new lodgings with her combat group in Muranowska Street. She looked surprised but pleased. She gave him a friendly hug. The warmth of her body was electric to him. He wanted to never let go but didn't want to blow it. He stepped back.

"Good to see you alive, Anglik."

"You too."

"Here on ZOB business?"

"No. I came to see you."

She looked away. Eyes averted, she launched into a lengthy report on the ZZW's actions in the January uprising. All fought bravely, with massive losses. He realised she was nervous. Maybe she'd never been with a boy in that way.

They were in the communal room with other men and women milling around. When she finished speaking, he took her hand and led her into a corner. He thought of those people he saw in the bunker that night, making love against a wall. He kissed her. He did not want to hear about all that combat stuff. He just wanted to kiss her.

"Anglik, the others can see us."

"Call me Daniel," he whispered in her ear.

"Daniel," she said and nuzzled his cheek. He wanted to say how mad it was that they could not be together. They were in different combat groups, but it was worse than that. He was in the ZOB and she was in the ZZW. They may as well have been Montagues and Capulets. But he didn't say anything. He knew how she felt about her cause. He felt it too, but it was different for her. Her combat group were her gang, her family now. He didn't have that. He couldn't give that to her.

"I want to be with you. Alone with you," he said.

He knew nothing about making love to a woman. But in that crowded room, he felt he could take her and make her love him. He wanted to tell her. He could feel the heat of her and the softness of her hair and he loved her. He wanted to say it. She wasn't resisting. She wasn't pulling away.

"I've been thinking of you, all the time. I want you, Marysia. I want you."

He pushed her warm body up against the wall and felt her mould into him. He kissed her and felt their tongues meet, a deep pit inside him flooding with a shimmering warmth. For a moment he was lost. But there were people everywhere, fighters all around them, talking about losses and ammunition, battle plans and weapons training. Two women laughing. Were they laughing at him? His body was sure of itself, pressed into hers, but his nerve was gone and he pulled back, his hands shaking. He could kill a man, but this girl was making him tremble?

"I have to go now," he said. He stepped away. He looked beyond her and saw that nobody was watching them, immersed in their own lives. What a fool. He'd broken the spell and for nothing. He looked at her and saw those hazel eyes look kindly on him. He didn't want her pity, her understanding, only her desire. He wanted to kick the wall in frustration.

"Daniel," she said. It was good to hear his name from her lips. His real name. She held his hand and her touch inflamed him again. Perhaps he could kiss her again, but she was standing stiffly now, keeping him at arm's length. "These are complicated times."

"I know, I know," he said, brushing it off, looking away from her. "Don't be so damned grown-up." She laughed at this. "I'll come and see you again when I can. If you want me to."

"Of course I do," she said softly. "Listen, I've been asking around. Nobody knows a seamstress called Helena. I'll keep asking."

"Thank you."

A man coughed nearby. She stiffened.

"Good luck with your combat group," she said, suddenly formal. "Train well. Be prepared."

Her face had changed swiftly. She was back in battle mode. She looked older, so much older than the girl he kissed. He almost saluted her.

Daniel was living with Natan and their combat group on Bonifraterska Street. There were twenty of them, all young men.

Pawel
Michal
Stephan
Bernard
Celek
Yanek
Azriel
Alexander
Tuvia
Wladyslaw
Stefan
Eliyahu
Maniek
David
Leon
Moses
Benjamin
Bronislaw

Pawel was their group leader. He was twenty-four years old, and had trained in weapons before the war. He was quiet and thoughtful, kept apart from the others. He spent time cleaning his gun and reorganising his kit, scribbling notes and drawings on scraps of paper. He was not stand-offish, not rude or ungracious. But Daniel felt the younger lads needed someone with a bit more fire. Maybe Pawel would change when the time came.

It was so good to live with people again. Natan was friends with several before the war. There was loads of banter and mucking about. The group did everything together. They followed a daily routine of keeping watch and weapons training. They talked through attack scenarios. Pawel showed them his papers and it turned out they were battle plans. They were trying to be ready for anything. Peppered with dirty jokes and schoolboy pranks, Daniel wondered if they were playing at soldiers. Yet every one of them had lost family to the Nazis. A number were the last left, with mothers, fathers, brothers, sisters, uncles, aunts, cousins and grandparents all murdered. Natan had only one relative left in the eastern ghetto, his dead mother's cousin. The youngest of their group at seventeen – Eliyahu and Maniek – were child smugglers from the earliest days of the ghetto. They still looked like children, skinny from malnourishment. Both had lost all family, from disease, street shootings and deportations. Let them throw socks at each other. Why not? They could laugh before they died.

Daniel knew his mission had changed. It was shared now, not solo. To fight the Germans, to die fighting. He knew it must be. He could escape, leave Warsaw and get back to London somehow. There was no sign of Helena. His purpose in coming here had failed. Magda awaited him in London, with marmalade sandwiches and a cup of hot tea. Why not leave? He had not painted himself into a corner. He could step out. But he knew he wouldn't. He didn't want to. He'd never had a gang. He never was a joiner. Educated at home, he was a reader, a thinker, a witness. He never roamed around London with a bunch of mates, never traded marbles or threw stones at cars. At the *Chronicle* too, watching the journalists ease into fellowship, lubricated by confidence and alcohol. Here, for the first time, he was one of the lads. Yet it was more than a boys' club. It had the most serious purpose. News had come that the ghetto was to be liquidated within weeks. The factory owners told their lies that all would be sent to well-maintained labour camps. Nobody was listening. Bunkers were built all over the ghetto. The Resistance prepared for the final battle. He was one of them. A moving part in a righteous human machine.

One morning, he was on watch with Natan. They were bored and frozen, sitting on the roof, the weather unseasonably cold. Around two o'clock, Michal called up and said he was going on a food run with Yanek. Michal and he had been squabbling, because he'd nicked Daniel's underpants and lied about it. The night before, he saw him wearing them and they had a ruckus while he tried unsuccessfully to get them off. They were his best pair, with only one small hole. His other pair was falling to pieces. Michal had said he'd have to wait till he was dead in the street before he'd get his underpants back.

That day Michal said, "When you see me leave the building, don't shoot me!"

Daniel hurled back English expletives for him. (They liked it when he cursed in English. They thought it sounded dirtier.) They watched as Michal and Yanek went out across the road to a house on the opposite side of Bonifraterska. A contact lived there who traded with the Aryan side and got them food.

Men were shouting. Two Germans came running down the street and, before they could take aim, had caught up with their lads and grabbed hold of them. Yanek managed to struggle free and tore off down the road. He knew better than to go back up, as he'd give their position away. Michal was less lucky – the two men had him in their clutches and were shouting at him in German about bunkers and Jews. As they watched, they were both aiming their pistols and trying to take courage to fire. But they were terrified of shooting Michal by mistake. Despite training, they were both bad shots. Pawel burst onto the roof and said, "Shoot, you stupid bastards!"

"We might hit Michal," said Natan.

Daniel was aiming again, sure he was on target, but his hand was shaking. He didn't want Michal's prophecy to come true. He didn't want his underpants back that way. But Pawel was swearing his head off and about to shoot down there himself, when Daniel pulled the trigger. A German fell backwards. He'd killed him with one shot. The other German looked up, aghast. Natan took a shot and that bastard's face turned inside out and he dropped down, a bloody mess. Michal was free.

He looked up and shouted, "You missed me, Anglik!"

Yanek appeared, running up the street, grabbed Michal and both ran inside. They celebrated by getting drunk on a raw moonshine the Poles made called *bimber*, which could make an old penny gleam.

Pawel came to Daniel later and said, "Good shot, Anglik." Not effusive. But it meant a lot to him.

That night, the lads talked of better days past and to come. They spoke of a place where Jews weren't killed, don't wear armbands or get kicked in the street, or even looked at, or even noticed. A place to blend in, to be yourself, to not be a type, a label, a pigeon in a pigeonhole. He'd never had to imagine freedom, because he'd had it. He told the lads about his childhood in London. He told them he didn't know he was a Jew then. They all said he'd done the right thing, that Warsaw was where his family was, his roots, his self. Pawel listened and rarely joined in. But that night he spoke up.

Daniel was telling everyone about Helena and Pawel said, "So you never knew your mother. Lucky you. We knew our mothers and they were murdered. You had better stop talking about your mother, Anglik."

They were all quiet.

Family. Home. Taken, yet never lost.

Even here, ready to die for them, he was the outsider again.

A month of training passed. He couldn't get away to see Marysia and he ached for her. Late one evening, she came to his barracks at Bonifraterska. He saw her speak to Pawel, saying she needed to talk to Daniel on official ZZW business. They went and sat on the stairs, for privacy. He had to stop himself from throwing himself at her, but the feel of her presence, so close to him, was almost more than he could bear. He leant over to kiss her, but she turned away.

"What's wrong?"

"You know my parents are long dead."

He thought, *I don't want to talk about death. I want to push you back on these steps and have you.*

"Of course."

"I only have one person left in my family. My cousin. She lives in the ghetto, in a bunker. Today, she was on the street looking for food, and a man came to her, made her go into his bunker. He demanded money. If she didn't pay, he threatened to rape her."

"That's awful!"

"He took her money. Then he beat her. She's in a bad state."

All desire left his body in an instant. Instead, ice lodged there, the cold anger he'd felt before.

"We'll get the bastard, don't you worry. Where's his bunker?"

"The man said he was collecting funds for the ZOB. He mentioned your combat group."

"What?"

"That's what he said."

Daniel felt sick. But then he thought of his comrades. Brave boys all, living and training and sleeping all together, around the clock.

"It's impossible. Nobody here would ever do that."

"I want you to ask them. Find out who did it."

"I told you, it isn't possible. We've all been together all day today. And why would he have his own bunker, if he was in my combat group?"

Marysia narrowed her eyes, nodded.

"I thought you'd do this."

"Do what?"

"Take their side. She's the only family I have left in the world. And you'd rather protect your mates."

"Hey, that's not fair. I know you're wrong about this, that's all."

Marysia stood up, began to march up the stairs. "I'll see for myself."

"No, you won't!" he called and caught up with her, took her arm.

"Let go of me!" Her voice was getting louder. Three of his group appeared at the top of the stairs, seeing what all the fuss was about.

Daniel said to her, "You're not going in there."

"How dare you give me orders!" she shouted. "I know it was the ZOB. Why would he lie?"

"Why would he lie? Why the hell not? He was probably one of yours. You lot make me sick. The ZZW and the ZOB and the Z this and the Z that. If we hated the Nazis as much as we hate each other, we'd win the war!"

Natan stood at the top of the stairs, laughing.

Daniel was not in the mood. "Fuck off, Natan!"

Marysia pulled her arm away and went off down the stairs.

"Let her go. Silly bitch."

"I told you to fuck off!"

He saw Natan shake his head and go back in with the others.

His friend laughing at him. His girl screaming at him. Were

they even his, that man, that woman? Why was he here? What the hell was he doing? Who was he to think he was Polish anyway, or even a Jew? He thought of Magda. London. His father's Bloomsbury grave, unvisited, untended by his only son. His adopted son. Marysia said, her only family left in the world. He thought, where is my family? Where do I belong? Nowhere. To nobody.

He was certain Marysia was wrong. He was angry with her. But he wanted her. He wanted her for himself, something for him, someone for him alone. He bolted down the stairs, flung open the door and ran to the end of the street towards her digs. A tap on his shoulder. He spun round expecting trouble. It was Marysia.

"I knew you'd come after me," she said.

"Let me kiss you," he said.

"All right."

He kissed her hard on the mouth, then on the neck, biting gently.

"Will you come with me?" she whispered, holding on to him.

"Anywhere." He reached up and touched her breast. He wanted her to sigh with pleasure, he imagined she might, but instead she said, "Come with me and find this man. I need your back-up. I'm going to kill him."

"What?"

He let go of her.

"He beat up my cousin, robbed her, threatened to rape her. And if what you say is true, he lies about the Resistance, gives it a bad name. He must die. Surely you see that. And I need your help. Help me, Anglik."

"For Christ's sake!" he said in English.

"What's that?" Marysia frowned, hearing the strange language. His language. He thought she'd kissed him for himself alone, not to persuade him to act as an accomplice to murder.

"I'm sure the ZZW has plenty of strong young men who would

be only too happy to assist a pretty little thing like you. Good night."

He gave her a ridiculous salute and walked away, back towards his barracks. But she came after him. He strode on as she talked, yet she kept pace.

"I know what you're thinking. That I don't care about you. But I do. I always have, since I first met you, that first night, when you asked me to teach you about being a Jew. It was a sweet thing to say. I've never met a man like you. You are very courageous, coming all that way from England on a boat to save your mother. I wanted to tell you that night. I liked you. But I didn't know how to show it. I am shy."

"Shy!" he laughed. "That's a joke."

"No, it's true. I can talk like a whirlwind when it comes to politics. But I've never talked about love. I don't know how. My parents. They didn't have time to teach me. I was only fifteen when they went. They didn't have time, Anglik."

He stopped and looked at her. So young. So old.

"Don't call me Anglik," he said. "Call me Daniel."

They went to the man's bunker. It was the one room left of a burnt-out office building, empty, except for a pile of rubbish in the corner. It moved. It was a man, turning in his sleep. The pillow under his head was a ball of dirty clothes. He was very thin with a filthy beard.

"Is this him?"

"My cousin showed me the building. She said he had a beard."

Daniel put his foot on the man's chest and pushed. Harder.

The man sprang up, wiped his eyes, his beard.

"What? What is it? Who are you?"

"You know why we're here," said Daniel.

"No, I don't. No, I don't."

His eyes flitted between them, the door, his bag of rags on the floor.

"You beat a woman and took her money," said Marysia.

"I didn't. I didn't."

"Yes, you did. You said you'd rape her, you bastard. You said you were in the ZOB."

"No, no, no, no, no."

Daniel turned to Marysia. Under his breath, "This man's crazy."

"So what? He attacked my cousin!"

"How do you know it's him? Look at him. He's nearly starved to death. He's lost his mind."

The man bolted, leapt around them and made for the door. But Daniel was stronger and quicker, grabbed him, pushed him down to the floor and held him there. It was easy.

"No, no! Don't hurt me, don't hurt me!"

"Shut up!" said Daniel as he tried to subdue the wriggling thing beneath. The man was screaming, mouth wide and black, white eyes goggling. Daniel punched him hard in the face, again, again. The man's arms flailed and slapped.

He called out, "Have mercy on me. Have mercy on me!"

Daniel stopped and stared at the man.

"Come on!" said Marysia. "Kill him!"

Daniel did not move.

Marysia kicked the man in the side. He cried out and scrambled away, holding his stomach.

"This is all wrong," said Daniel, his hands empty, the man groaning in the corner. "All wrong."

"He'll do it again," said Marysia. "He'll rape next time."

"Look at him."

The man was squirming on the ground, weeping. "Have mercy, have mercy," he said, over and over.

Daniel marched over to him. "Listen to me. You don't go near that woman you beat. You don't talk to her, even look at her. Understand? Understand, you piece of shit?"

"Yes, yes, yes."

"I know you now. I'll find you. I'll kill you, understand?"

"Yes, yes, I'm sorry, I'm sorry."

The man hid his face in his hands, cried like a child.

Daniel turned away and took Marysia's hand. He had to yank her out of there.

"What are you doing?" she said in the half-bombed hallway. Two walls stood, the other two jagged from damage, the street peering through the gaps. "Finish the job."

"Do it yourself."

"Do it for me," she grasped at his collar.

He felt her body against him, hot in the chill night air. He held her tightly, kissed her hard, pressed her against the wall. They were grasping and pushing and teeth clashing, like fighters not lovers. He pulled her down to the floor, lay on her, crushed her. Slower now, they kissed deeply. She stroked his hair.

She whispered, "I can't bring a baby into this world."

He stopped. He didn't want to think of their world, he didn't want to think at all. Everything in him urged him to carry on, except his conscience, and the cold hard centre that he now carried within him always.

"I know."

He kissed her lips gently and put a hand on the floor, and stood. He held out his hand to help her up. They were striped with white dust.

A sound behind them and they turned. The man was in his doorway, watching them. Shifting from foot to foot, hugging himself.

"Take her home," said the man.

They went through Bonifraterska to the Aryan side. They hid in shadows to reach his flat. They crept up the staircase, he took the key from under the doormat and unlocked the door silently.

Inside, he led her to his bed. Beneath the musty sheet and blanket, they warmed each other. It was too cold to undress. They held each other so close, faces buried in each other's hair. He pulled away as he wanted to see her eyes but it was too dark.

She pulled him closer and whispered, "We'll probably both be dead before a baby comes."

They lost the last of their innocence that night. Afterwards, sleep came tenderly and drugged them till dawn.

CHAPTER EIGHT

This is what happened.

This morning, I did everything just as Vladka instructed. I left Ilsa in the barracks and there waiting outside near the door was a guard who gave me a special look. I knew he was Witold Romer. I nodded to him and he came and stood near the barracks. I knew he would look after Ilsa and I went to work with a lighter heart. A couple of hours passed interminably, then before lunch, Romer appeared and called me out on an errand. Everyone stopped sewing and watched me go. I caught a few of my fellow seamstresses' eyes as I left, and each one gave me a complicated smile, as if to say, I am envious of you, sister, but I am glad for you. Romer led me back to the barracks. There I called Ilsa who brought our bag and we followed Romer to the gate. He saw us out and turned away. He never spoke to us or even looked at us again after that first knowing glance. I wanted to thank him, but I understood that it would be dangerous to do so. Maybe I will meet him one day after this madness is over and I will kiss him.

We walked quickly and silently to Bonifraterska St. and found the house. We saw not a soul on the way. It appears that the ghetto is truly gutted now. Only a few working Jews remain. We are leaving at the last moment before the final purge, it seems. Lucky for us. We knocked and waited. After an age, a young man opened the door.

"Hello there!" he said loudly and grinned. "Come in, come in!" he added, as if he were my oldest friend. We followed him and as soon as the door was closed, his face turned to stone. His voice too. "Give me your armbands," he ordered. We did this and he spoke instructions swiftly, pointing out where we should go. He left us, bounding upstairs from where drifted the muffled sounds of men talking. I felt a bit at a loss. I knew what to do, as the young man had told me. But I suppose I wanted someone to be there with us. I got the impression that we were a little unwelcome, that this was a house for the Resistance and we were only pesky civilians.

We went along the corridor and through a door to the cellar. We found the ladder in the corner which led to the manhole cover. This was it. I crouched down to my Ilsa and talked to her. I told her that this was the most important moment of our lives. This was the moment when she must do everything I say and not question me or misbehave in any way. As I said those words I knew it was nonsense, as Ilsa was insular, far away from me and the world, stuck inside herself, that she had no notion of childish naughtiness. I have often wished in the past years that she would break out of her shell and disobey me, show defiance and anger at her situation. Her listless obedience is clear evidence of her stunted upbringing in the ghetto. But at that moment in the cellar I was glad of it, thankful I did not have an unruly toddler to deal with who could ruin everything. Ilsa just nodded calmly. I knew she would be all right.

Up the ladder and, with fear eating a hole in my stomach, I pushed gingerly at the manhole cover above. It was stiff and I had to shove with all my strength. The thing went shooting off and clanged on the road overhead. I was terrified to stick my head out, convinced a whole street of Aryan Poles would have stopped in their tracks and be staring at us. But as I peeked out, I saw we were in the far corner of a twist in the street, where no businesses were evident. No one came and went. Thank the stars. We got out quickly and replaced the cover. There we were, on the other side of the ghetto walls. In an Aryan street in Warsaw. My heart leapt as I looked up at the buildings around us. Aryan Warsaw. The gate to our cage had been opened and we had flown. I wanted to sing. Then I remembered Vladka's warning. I brushed myself and Ilsa down and neatened us up. We were ordinary Poles in an ordinary street in Warsaw. Now we must walk with a quiet confidence to find our tram stop. We came round the bend in the street and there were people crossing over here and there, and beyond, a busy Warsaw stretched away, full of Poles coming and going through an ordinary day in their own war. I thought hard about my face. No sad eyes. I looked at Ilsa and she stared at me, expressionless. Did her eyes look sad? I didn't have time to answer that question, because someone tapped me on the shoulder.

There was a man standing in front of me.

He said, "Do you have something for me?" I didn't know what to say. Was he working for the Resistance? No, no. I did not know who he was. A horrible word floated before my eyes: *szmalcownik*. Blackmailer. I knew I must put on the act, right away.

"What are you talking about?" I said and tried to sound annoyed and inconvenienced, not terrified.

"You know," he said.

"I don't know, and I don't know you. Now if you'll excuse me." I stepped around him and walked swiftly away with Ilsa, but I tried not to walk too quickly, not to look like I was running, afraid. But he followed. I could hear him just a step behind us. He began mewing like a cat. A horrible sound right behind my ear. He was saying things like "I can follow you all day, little kitten" and "There's no escape from me, pussy" and other threats. Now I was walking blindly. I did not even see what street I was on. The tram stop we were supposed to take was long gone and I just ploughed on, my hand a vice around Ilsa's. Why us, my mind screamed? How did he know? We were neat and tidy, we hadn't wept with joy in the street. How did he know? It must have been our sad eyes. I cursed my eyes.

After a while, I decided that I could not walk all day and perhaps a tram might be a good place. At least it was public. I headed for the nearest tram stop and queued. I stood resolutely and stared into the street, willing the tram to come. The *szmalcownik* stood nearby, waiting. When the tram came, I gave the correct money and sat down. He did the same and found a seat at the other end of the tram. But he could see us and stared at us the whole time. I tried not to look but every now and again could not help but glance at him. Each time he smiled horribly and nodded. What could I do now?

I thought of taking a series of trams, one after the other. We might get lost in the crowd and elude him. Once the tram was particularly busy, I got off amidst a group of people and hurried across the street to an approaching tram going in the opposite direction. But once we were on it and sat down, there he was, right behind us. I resolved to try the same trick again, and I did, three times. By this time, about two hours had passed, travelling up and down and up and down the Warsaw streets, always our tormenter nearby, smiling and nodding. All this time Ilsa had said nothing, just followed my directions and held my hand. She whispered in my ear: "Mama, I'm hungry." My poor darling. I was too, my stomach groaning. If I got off the tram and went to a shop, I'd have to talk to a shopkeeper, hand over money. I hadn't prepared myself for dealing with anyone else but tram conductors. I was frightened my words or the look in my eyes would give us away. But I could see that this endless tram riding was getting us nowhere. I resolved to get off at the next stop and find a shop to buy food for Ilsa. But it would have to be on a main street, somewhere the *szmalcownik* couldn't get us alone. I waited for the tram to turn onto a busy road and we got off. He followed us as we walked on, as I was trying to look, without appearing to look, for a shop to buy something to eat.

He sidled up beside me as I walked. I ignored him. He went on and on, his voice in my ear: "Come on, little cat. I know what you are. Just give me money and I'll leave you alone. You can go on your way, back to your little den. I won't follow you, I promise. Just hand it over. Give me 3000 zloty or I'll march you off to *Aleja Szucha*. You probably don't know what's there, do you? It's Gestapo Headquarters, pussycat. Yes, that's where we'll go, eh? But you don't want to go there, do you? Give me the money." Fear swelled inside me.

I spotted a grocery store, with fruit and vegetables outside in boxes. I went up and felt the fruit like I was fussy, deciding which was choicest when I couldn't care less. I was hungry enough to have eaten grass. I took two apples and went inside. There were no other customers. I picked up bread rolls and cheese. Such food we hadn't eaten for weeks. Only the watery soup we were given as pay at the factory. Ilsa's eyes were wide with wonder at the rows of cans and other goodies in the simple grocer's. All food except soup was luxury to a ghetto Jew. I knew this could give us away. I hurried to the counter. The shopkeeper was an old man with lively eyes. He looked at Ilsa with a smile, then more interest. Her amazement was obvious, it shone from her face.

"Mama," she said, "all this food!" I was mortified, looking at the shopkeeper to see his reaction. He was frowning. He knew, he knew. And there in the doorway waited our *szmalcownik,* pretending to inspect potatoes. We were trapped.

I looked into the shopkeeper's eyes. A little voice inside me spoke. Trust him, it said. Trust him.

"Help us," I said quietly. "That man there is trying to blackmail us." Now I'd done it. In one moment, I'd find out if it was the worst mistake I'd ever made. The shopkeeper looked at the *szmalcownik,* looked back at me and Ilsa.

"Hey!" he shouted, so loudly I jumped. "Hey, you!" He was pointing at the *szmalcownik*. "Get away from here. Go on, get away. We don't want your sort here. Get lost!" Our tormenter was shocked rigid and just stood there. "Are you deaf?" yelled the shopkeeper. "I said get lost, you blackmailing bastard!" With that, the *szmalcownik* turned and ran away down the street. He actually ran. It was a wonderful sight.

"Thank you," I said and held out my hand to the shopkeeper. He shook it briefly and waved me away when I tried to pay for our purchases.

"You better be on your way," he said and didn't look at us again. We left. Alongside Witold Romer, here is another person I plan to find after the war, and kiss him with thanks. Why he helped us, I don't know. What makes one Pole a blackmailer of Jews and another a rescuer is beyond me. I don't even know what I would do in their position. In this war, I think there are a few heroes, a few bastards, and thousands of ordinary people in between who just want to get on with their lives.

After that, I had to walk before I could get my bearings. It has been years since I was in my city, and everything looked different. Eventually, I recognised buildings and knew which direction I had to go to reach Krystyna's. We took a tram and sat there eating our bread, cheese and apples. I had to warn Ilsa to eat slowly. I must have sounded like a mother chiding her daughter's bad table manners, but really I was a fugitive teaching her not to look like a starving Jew.

We reached our destination in the late afternoon. True to Vladka's word, I saw Krystyna watching for us from her third floor window, a pale face. She disappeared and soon came to answer the door. I was so relieved to see her, I had to stop myself from crying in the street. Vladka was right about being a free Jew. You had to force yourself not to weep, at the clean streets, the plentiful food, the smiling people, the giddy joy at being free of the walls. And there we were standing outside a safe house, our *melina*.

Krystyna smiled broadly and said, "Franciszka, my cousin! How good to see you!" I greeted her with a hug. I was choked, I could not speak. Krystyna turned to Ilsa and said, "And my little Ilsa, how tall you've grown! Come in, cousins. Come in." And with that, we left our act on the Warsaw street and crossed the threshold to safety. Up three flights of stairs and into Krystyna's place. When she shut the door, I collapsed on the floor and wept. Ilsa held my hands and wiped the tears from my eyes. I could not see Krystyna through my tears, but I know she said nothing. When I had stopped crying, I looked up and saw she was standing with her arms folded, waiting.

"Get up," she said without smiling. "That's the last time you'll make a noise like that here. I only hope the neighbours didn't hear. Come on." And she showed us to our room.

And here I am, writing. I know it sounds cruel, the way Krystyna spoke to us. But she was right. I have to remember that she is risking her life to shelter us here. Later this evening, she did cook us a wonderful meal and talked more kindly. Ilsa was asleep across my lap, unwilling to be apart, even to go to bed. Krystyna was less terse, but still business-like in our conversation. She told me that we can stay for a few weeks, but we will need to find another place. I'll have to think about that tomorrow.

Krystyna went on to give me a series of warnings about how to behave. I realised she was doing it for her own good, to protect herself from suspicion. But I appreciated the advice anyway. This is what she told me: "You have to learn to be an Aryan. It won't be too hard for you. You were always that sort of cosmopolitan Jew, not interested in religion, mixing with Jews and Aryan Poles alike before the war. And your face will pass."

I asked, "What do you mean, 'pass'?"

Krystyna explained it to me: "I mean you have a 'good' appearance. You don't look too Jewish. Neither does Ilsa. You can pass. You are dark but you have a good nose. Ilsa's got your husband's light brown hair, your fine features. You can both pass. If you have a good appearance and can speak Polish well, as you two do, you should be all right. But only if you learn the rules of how to be a good Catholic Pole."

I asked what these were and she listed a frightening array of imperatives about how to pass on the Aryan side: "You are a Catholic Pole now. You must be able to say a Catholic prayer or two. The Polish police check this sometimes. I can teach you the 'Our Father', the 'Hail Mary' and the Rosary. And you must know your patron saint's day, and Ilsa's too, of course. Also, you have to talk like an Aryan. Don't say anything that sounds like a quirky Jewish saying. But most importantly, don't talk to anyone you knew before the war. Cross the street to avoid them. If someone says they know you, blank them. But show no fear, no doubt in your eyes. Laugh. Poles are better than Germans at spotting Jews in the street, so it's everyone you need to be suspicious of, not just the Nazis. But you mustn't look like you're suspicious. Yes, you're going to become a Pole living in occupied Warsaw, which is bad enough. But you will not be one of the cursed, not a Jew. You mustn't have the look of one, the down-trodden hopelessness, the bowed shoulders carrying the burden of being a Jew. You're a Pole and proud to be one. You're just waiting for these Nazi pigs to move on. You're not defiant but you're not miserable either. You're quiet and confident of your place in the world. Don't be nervous or fidgety, never fearful. It's a look, a way of holding yourself, of looking others straight in the eye. Something that Jews have forgotten. It has to be learnt. Do it in the mirror."

It was good advice. I know Ilsa and I really will have to practise in the mirror, as absurd as it sounds. I am sure it was our sad eyes that got us in trouble this morning. After our talk, Krystyna did give me a quick hug goodnight.

"Sleep well," she said and left us. That was nice. I do understand her position. We were never friends as such before the war. She's a young widow, and she needs the money the Resistance have paid for sheltering us. It's a dangerous way to earn a living. She must be desperate. It's a business arrangement, all of this. And it all depends on Ilsa and me, on our ability to be Polish. And never, ever let our guard down, or do something foolish, or say the wrong thing, or walk the wrong way, or look sad. I hope we do not fail.

But there will be no sadness tonight. I end this entry with a smile. The day I escaped with my daughter from the Jewish Ghetto of Warsaw. And survived. Ilsa is fast asleep in our proper bed with a soft mattress and a pillow of goose feathers. I write by candlelight from Aryan Warsaw, the other side of the wall, safe in our safe house, our *melina*. And I do feel we are safe here. Safe for the moment. I am learning this is enough. The moment is enough.

Warsaw used to be mine. I came here with Jan when I was fifteen. A girl from a small town, I knew nothing of city life. But I soon learnt. I walked these streets. Building my business alone, I went all over the city to find customers, trade with suppliers, make deals. By the time I met Isak, I felt a true Varsovian, almost like him. But my city was taken from me. I was locked inside it, but I might as well have been on the moon. Now I am back, but it is not my home. My city is populated with potential enemies. On the streets, we see Gestapo men with their yellow coats and swastikas on their arms. They are garish and poisonous, like wasps. They own Warsaw now. Yet Vladka and Krystyna were right; there is a look in the eyes of the Poles who pass by, a way of holding their heads up. A kind of quiet knowledge of their own Polish destiny. I know I don't have it. I try to study them without looking like I'm looking. I try not to look down either, to look downtrodden. Ilsa and I sail through the streets of Warsaw as Aryan swans. Beneath the surface, our Jewish feet paddle like crazy to keep us running smoothly.

I try hard to look like the woman I used to be. But too much has happened in between. Too much has been lost. I am half eaten away. And I have to appear whole.

Krystyna has given us more warnings about our behaviour and how to avoid blackmailers. She told me of a notorious *szmalcownik* in the area who rapes Jewish women. She told me what he looks like and reminded me to stay in busy areas and put up a front if anyone ever tries to blackmail us in the street. Apparently, the going rate for extortion these days is kindly negotiated with the victim. After all, a successful blackmailer has to avoid complications, and cannot be too greedy. There is no point demanding millions of zlotys if the Jew has nothing. The current market price you pay for not being denounced is around 3000 zlotys. That is exactly what the *szmalcownik* was going to charge us on the day of our escape. Good to know he was quoting a fair price.

Krystyna also said that far more sinister than your street-dwelling *szmalcownik* are blackmailers working for the police, the Polish *kripo*. These are the Blue police who are allied with the German Criminal Police, responsible for searching out Jews. These Poles make a good living from bribes given by ghetto smugglers and from Jews in hiding. Krystyna says they might arrest you, take a bribe, but denounce you anyway. They can come to your house, because they have the connections to research you and find your address. Apparently victims have been cleaned out of everything they possess by the *kripo*, and have returned to the ghetto or turned themselves in or even killed themselves after this. A *kripo* might come to the apartment, if someone reports us. He might say they have received a report that a Jewess is living here and ask to see our papers. If so, we have to act appalled and all of that. The thought of these *kripo* types makes me sick. Dangers, all around us. If you thought about each one of them, every day, you wouldn't breathe for fear of denunciation.

At least we have a safe home, for the time being. Since we arrived, Krystyna has taught us three Catholic prayers. Ilsa and I recite them countless times a day, babbling the words like mumbo-jumbo. Perhaps a Catholic God is listening. Does he know we don't mean any of it? We have also been busy inventing our autobiographies. We have come up with fake siblings for myself, fake places of birth, fake maiden name. Ilsa thinks it mostly good fun, an exercise in storytelling. I often have to remind her how crucial it is. A clever interrogator may ask her, what was your name before this one? I tell her she must never think of her old name again. There never was an Ilsa Dedek, I say, nor Helena Dedek. And certainly not an Isak Dedek. There was a fake Aryan husband and father, conveniently dead and buried before the war away in eastern Poland. But his name was not Isak. I have chosen the name Jan for him. I have told Ilsa to forget her Papa. I teach her to invent the ghost of a new father. Our past must be dead to us now. There is only Franciszka and Ilsa Kucharski. Kucharski, Kucharski, Kucharski, I tell her. She chants it like a prayer.

We have some money left from the wad given us by Vladka, but it will not last long. Krystyna requires 500 zlotys per week for room and board. For everyone in Warsaw, the cost of living is high. She is not being unreasonable. She is only on a widow's pension, after all. I must start working soon. I know that we have been warned not to make any contact with pre-war acquaintances, but I do have a plan to find pan Bradecki. I can sell the furniture and other items he has been holding for us, in order to provide us with more money. I wonder what kind of reception I'll receive? He was always a good man though.

So far, we have not ventured outside often. Already, I can feel Krystyna tires of our constant company. There is something about us that irks her. I have a feeling it is our closeness. Ilsa is very clingy and we sit wrapped around each other. Krystyna watches us. I wonder if she is jealous. I try to talk with her, about her life before the war, her experiences in recent times. I hope this might ease her envy, and we could become friends, she could be like an aunt to my Ilsa. But she is a shop with the shutters down. There is inequity of power between us. I give her money. She takes it. I am fake. She is legitimate. I am Jewish. She is not. A lot of reasons for her to lord it over me. Yet there is one element that could topple her: she is hiding us. She could be shot for that. She relies on me to prevent that. And she may suspect I am only nice to her so that she won't throw us out on the street.

We are flies caught in the same sticky web.

I found Bradecki. He has moved several times since I last saw him in 1940. He is wealthier than he was. I tracked him down through visiting old addresses and asking questions. I went alone, as I felt Ilsa would be safer back at the apartment. When his maid answered his door, she looked down at me from the lofty position of being a rich man's drudge. I was shown into the hallway and no further. He came out almost immediately. He looked worried.

"Helena," he said and enfolded my hand in both of his. "So good to see you are safe. How are Isak and little Ilsa?" I told him of Isak's death and our current situation. He shook his head. "I'm sorry to hear that, pani Dedek. But you must know how dangerous it is for me to have you here. You must leave, my dear, immediately."

I replied, "I apologise, pan Bradecki. I'm sorry to put you in this position. But you did help us before the war. And now I have need of my possessions. I have come to retrieve them, or else ask you to sell them for me." Bradecki looked away and scratched his beard.

"My dear, I'm afraid everything has been sold. There is nothing left."

"What do you mean?" I asked.

"You must understand. It has been difficult for all Poles in this war, Jewish or not. The occupation has brought hard times for us all. And reports about the ghetto led us all to believe that there was little good news about the Jews. We assumed, you know. We all believed, in good faith."

"Believed what?" He could not look at me.

"That you were dead. So many of you are. We couldn't imagine you'd ever come back. Of course, I'm very glad to see you are alive and well. But there is nothing for you here." It was strange, conversing with a man who stared pointedly at the wall, waiting for me to go. But I was not finished with him.

"Then I need recompense," I said. "You must pay me the worth of the items you sold."

Bradecki looked at me. "Oh my dear, that will never happen."

I felt my blood boiling. "But they were mine. You have no right."

"I am afraid you are the one who has no rights. You should leave now and if you ever come back, I will open that window over there and shout into the street, 'Fetch the police! There's a filthy Jewess here!'" He stood there with his dead eyes. He waited for me to do the ladylike thing and go quietly. As I stared at him, my cheeks burned. I wanted to strike him to the floor, kick him in the ribs. Over his shoulder, I saw a picture on the wall. It was a beach scene in charcoal, a lone couple walking along a blustery seashore, tiny against nature. Isak gave me that picture for our first wedding anniversary.

"That belongs to me," I said and pointed at the picture. Bradecki glanced briefly and folded his arms.

"Not any more. Get out now." I had no arguments left. Only the pointless anger of the doomed.

"Shame on you," I said and left.

I did good business with that man before the war. We would sit and chat over coffee when he brought new swatches of buttons for me to look at. He was a cultured man, who liked reading and music. We would have brief philosophical discussions about the latest book on this or that subject, or the violin concert we had attended. Who could imagine that one day he would stand before me with my dead husband's gift on his wall, calling me a filthy Jewess?

This was a few days ago. Since then, I have been taking steps to begin earning as a seamstress again. Krystyna knows of a woman who does this. She has good customers and earns a high wage for a seamstress in these times. She makes about 40 zlotys a day. I know what this means. Even if I were to make contacts and find work, despite my illegitimate status, I would still have a shortfall of nearly 1000 zlotys a month. Honestly, I don't know what to do next. There is no news from Vladka. She said she would come and visit us once we were here, but she has not. I do hope she is safe. "*You won't be alone,*" Vladka said to us. "*I promise.*" I hope she was right. I feel very alone now.

Since returning from Bradecki's with nothing, tensions with Krystyna have worsened. She comments about the danger she's in, about being found out, denounced for hiding Jews, taken or shot in the street.

"I don't know," she sighs. "The risks I take for you two." There is nothing I can say to her at these moments. She is right. This morning, she told me she would have to put the rent up, to 3000 zlotys a month. I was not too proud to beg. But she said, "Well then, if you can't pay the extra, you need to start looking for a new place to live. I can't keep taking this awful risk for so little money. I have to live, you know."

I assured her I would pay the new rent.

But I was lying. And she knew it. It is all impossible. We have come through serious situations before, but this time I have no ideas.

I went out this afternoon to look for signs in shop windows requiring seamstresses. I found nothing. I saw two Polish policemen grab a man in the street and drag him into a doorway. Before I forced myself to look away, I saw them pull his trousers down. I heard them laugh and one said, "That little snip is your death sentence, my friend."

Lucky for me that I'm a woman.

Vladka, my friend. Where are you?

We are not staying at Krystyna's. We had to go.

We had to leave this morning. Around midnight Krystyna shook us awake, telling us to get up and pack quickly. She was in a terrible state. She kept saying, "It's burnt. It's burnt," and as we dressed I begged her to explain.

"We are discovered! A neighbour has come round just now and told me the building manager has sold us to a blackmailer. This *szmalcownik* is coming round in minutes to get his first payment. You must get out. If you go now, he'll have nothing on me. Hurry up, hurry up!" Ilsa was slow with sleep and stumbled as I tried to dress her. Krystyna came at Ilsa with a bag and raised it over her head, as if to smash Ilsa's skull in. I leapt before Ilsa and slapped that woman in the face. Krystyna was screaming, "How dare you! How dare you, you, you..."

"You what? You filthy Jewess? Don't worry, we're going. We wouldn't stay here if *you* paid *us* 3000 zlotys a month." I heard myself spit out these proud words, but I knew I was a fool. What on earth were we to do, two Jews in Aryan Warsaw after midnight? We couldn't go out there now. But if we stayed, the blackmailer would find us.

Once we were packed up, I stopped and told Ilsa to sit down.

"What are you doing?" yelled Krystyna. "Get out of here!"

"Listen to me. If you throw us out now, we will not survive the night. You know this. We will be caught by the police for sure. And if we are, the first thing I'll do is give them your name, Krystyna."

Her face was aghast. "You can't! You wouldn't!"

"I will do it. Be assured of that. So, here we are. It's not in either of our interests for us to be wandering the streets of Warsaw tonight. We will go to the basement of this building. You'll help us get down there safely by checking the stairways are clear and distracting the building manager if you see him. We will wait there till morning. Before dawn, you will come down and give us a list of people you know in Warsaw who might be able to help us find a place to stay. I know you have contacts with the Underground. And we're not leaving this building until you give me that list. Once we have it and curfew has lifted in the morning, we'll leave and we won't trouble you, even if we're caught, I'll never repeat your name or what you have done for us."

I waited for Krystyna to make up her mind. Luckily, she saw sense.

"All right, all right, I'll do it. You Jews are too clever by half." With that, she was gone, out of the apartment and down the stairs. We waited in silence, Ilsa too scared to speak. She held on to me tightly and I stroked her hair. I had to force my hand to stop trembling. Before long, we heard footsteps coming up the stairs.

We did not know if it was Krystyna, or a new enemy. All we could do was wait. Krystyna appeared alone in the doorway and beckoned us to come.

We sat awake in the basement, watching through a tiny window the night sky turn to day. Krystyna came to us just after dawn. She said nothing, just stuck her hand out with a scrap of paper in it. I took it and she turned to leave.

"Wait," I said. I looked at the paper carefully. It was a list of a few names with addresses all over Warsaw. I did not know whether they were inventions or real, yet I had no choice but to take it in good faith.

"Did the blackmailer come?" I asked. She shook her head. I wondered if he ever existed. "Thank you," I said. I meant it. Krystyna had saved us once, after all. She was just scared, like the rest of us. She said nothing. Her face twisted into an exhausted sneer and her hand rubbed her eye involuntarily. Then she went. Once we heard people up and about in the building and on the streets, we crept out of there and walked away down the road.

I had five names on the list. I chose the nearest one. I had no idea if these were real names and addresses, if we were going to a new haven or on to hell. We had to get the tram there. Once on board, we sat down and Ilsa fell asleep on me. I glanced around the carriage and saw a woman I'd known before the war, a friend of a friend of Isak's. A Jewess. I couldn't remember her name. But I knew her face. She had with her a little boy. He was small, perhaps three years old. He must have been born during this war. She looked up and saw me. A shock of recognition crackled between us. I know who you are, our eyes spoke to one another. But we said nothing. An unwritten rule bound us to stay silent. A Jew recognises a Jew, but if he acknowledges this, he endangers that Jew. Who knows how 'wild' that Jew is, with or without papers, chased by police or blackmailers, about to be denounced? No one can be trusted. We looked away. We rode the tram together, two Jews ignoring one another. But our knowledge burnt like a bright fire between us.

I heard someone shout, "That woman's a Jew!" Ilsa woke with a start. I looked up in horror. A man stood above me, but was pointing away from us. The other Jew.

"I know her. I knew her before the war. She's a Jewess." He was talking loudly, to no one in particular. Everyone else in the tram was looking round, looking for the Jew. But no one else got up or did anything.

One man said, "Oh sit down, will you?"

Someone else said, "Shut up, loud mouth." Other people started murmuring, a Jewess, a Jewess. She said nothing. She stared at the man, Jewish eyes wide with fear. She did not try to defend herself, she did not act the indignant Aryan. The tram came to a stop and the man went for the woman. He grabbed her arm and she pulled back. I had to stop myself from leaping up. I had to protect Ilsa and myself. The man pulled her off the tram, her boy clinging to her. The tram was stationary as several people got on and off. The man had hold of her arm and a yellow coat came into view. A Gestapo man, flanked by a Polish policeman. Everyone in the tram was looking now, watching the little drama unfold beyond the greasy windows. We could not hear the conversation. Not until she began shouting. Her voice was high and piercing.

"Take me, take me!" she begged. "Spare my son." The boy was crying now. The Gestapo man gave the Polish policeman an order. The policeman looked away and shook his head. The Gestapo man pushed the woman against the wall of a building and her son was wailing. I pulled Ilsa to me and buried her head in my chest. She struggled to free herself but I was stronger. She was not going to see this, not this.

"Shoot me!" the woman yelled. "Not my son!" The Gestapo man reached out and grabbed the boy's arm. He raised his gun and shot the boy in the head. The woman's scream was excruciating to hear. She fell on her dead baby. The Gestapo man shot her. Soon after, the tram went on. No one said anything. People were reading their newspapers.

My head was heavy with heat and sickness and fear. I clenched my lips and my teeth behind them. I must not vomit, I told myself, I must not vomit in front of all these people. Ilsa was buried in my chest. She had not moved since the shots. I had lost all track of space and time and realised the tram may have taken us past our stop. I looked around and saw we were nearly there. I nuzzled my mouth into Ilsa's ear.

I whispered as quietly as I could, "We are going to stand up now. You have to be strong. You have to pretend you are not upset. Do you understand, my darling? Nod your head if you understand." She did so. I made myself stand, my legs like iron, my head whirling. Ilsa stood too and held onto me. She did not cry. Her face was blank. The old ghetto ice had returned to her. I managed to get us off the tram and down the street. I looked again at the list of addresses and checked the street names. We were not far.

After a while, Ilsa said, "Was that lady like us?"

"No," I said. "We are far more careful than her. We are luckier than her." I knew it was a pathetic response. Ilsa thought about this for a few steps.

"How do you know? Why are we luckier? Does God like us more?"

"Hush now, Ilsa. Let me find this place. Keep quiet now." We walked on in silence. But I knew my daughter's mind was full of questions for which her mother had no answers.

When we got there, I checked the name on the door with that on my paper. Stefan Lipski. I rang the bell and thought in the moments before it was answered what on earth I was going to say to the person who lived there. A man's voice said, "Yes?"

I replied, "Hello, this is Franciszka. I'm Krystyna's cousin. We've come for breakfast. Can you let us in?" I had no idea what I was doing. I stood in that street talking nonsense into that microphone, my daughter staring at me, trusting that I would save her again. A woman came out of the doorway beside me and gave me a darting look. I was sure she was suspicious. I waited and could hear the voice from the apartment breathing. The buzzer went and I knew the door was opened for us. We went in quickly and found the apartment. The door was already open when we got up the stairs and standing in the doorway was Vladka.

My knees went under me and I collapsed. I had fainted. The next thing I remember was waking up on a sofa in an apartment, Ilsa holding my hand tightly, her little face wracked with worry. I smiled at her and she kissed me violently. She used to do that when she was a baby, before she knew how to kiss. I told her I was all right. I saw Vladka again. For a moment, I wondered if it were a vision, a beautiful dream.

"Hello, my friend," she said and I knew her voice was real, that Ilsa's hot little hand squeezing mine was real. Vladka gave me a drink of tea and vodka. I saw Samuel, her husband, standing behind her, and beside him another man with an amiable smile. Before long, I was recovered and we were all sitting around a table eating a simple yet delicious meal of potato dumplings stuffed with plums.

"Look, Mama!" said Ilsa. "Potato dumplings!" And I remembered what I'd said to her in the ghetto a lifetime ago, telling her to think of potato dumplings to make her smile. I was happy to see my daughter wolf down those potato dumplings. They were the best potato dumplings ever eaten on this earth.

Everything was explained to me during that meal. Vladka and Samuel had only just managed to get out of the ghetto, two days before today. When they went to their designated *melina*, their hider turned them away, saying the *melina* was burnt, that is, discovered by the enemy. (So, that's what Krystyna meant.) They had to try several other places but were turned away from all of them with similar stories. They were desperate. That day, the man who owns this apartment, Stefan, was in a café with friends and recognised a contact of his from the Underground, who was looking worried. He asked him what was wrong and was told that he had two Jewish friends who needed a place to stay. When he asked their names, it turned out that Stefan was an old artist friend of Vladka's from before the war. He gladly took them in. Stefan is one of the Aryan contacts used by the Underground to hide Jews, and that is why his name was on Krystyna's list, yet she did not know Vladka was staying here as it had only just happened. I cannot believe the miraculous string of coincidences that led to us all meeting here tonight. I am just glad they did. During dinner, I told everyone the story of Krystyna and what led us here. But I did not tell them about the woman and her son.

Stefan showed me where to put Ilsa to sleep, a double bed in his spare room to be shared with me. Vladka and Samuel had been sleeping there. I said we would not turn anyone out of their bed and would make do on the sofa together, but Vladka insisted.

She said, "I would never take a bed from a child, especially yours," and added that she and Samuel would sleep beside us on the floor, all old friends together. My poor darling girl was exhausted and fell asleep immediately. I watched her breathing change as she slipped into her dreams. They were happy dreams, for she slept soundly. I wished I could keep her there forever. I wished she would never wake up into this world. For a moment, I wished she were dead. Then I wept silently. I did not want to wake her.

Vladka appeared at the door. She beckoned to me and I went to her. Sinking into the arms of a friend was better even than potato dumplings.

"You are safe now, both of you," said Vladka. We sat down on a comfortable sofa. Samuel and Stefan were playing chess across the room and drinking vodka. Vladka poured us a little. She watched me drink. She said nothing.

"Something else happened today. Something terrible."

Vladka waited. It was the silence of someone who had heard terrible stories.

"A woman and her boy, in the street."

"Denounced?"

I nodded.

"Shot?"

"The boy first. She begged and begged. But he shot the boy first. He shot the boy first. So she would see."

I cried again, while Vladka held me. Quietly, though. Quietly. I must not wake Ilsa. Stefan and Samuel continued playing their game. Once I calmed down, I could hear the intermittent tap of a chess piece being moved, closer and closer to its destination.

"We can't stay here," I said.

"You are safe in this place," said Vladka.

"I know, I know. And I am thankful for that. But I mean Warsaw. Poland, even. I have to get Ilsa out. Out of this. I haven't thought any of this through, but I think I'm going to just walk, walk us out of Warsaw, out into the countryside, where nobody knows us, and keep walking until we reach somewhere, somewhere safe. If I don't try, it's only a matter of time, before..." I knew it was all gibberish. Where is safe now? Nowhere, nowhere for a Jew. I waited for Vladka to talk me out of it.

But she said, "You're right. Samuel and I have been planning the same thing, for a while now."

"Planning what?" I couldn't believe she was taking me seriously. I had in my mind an image of myself growing wings and flying Ilsa out of Warsaw to a fairy grotto in the woods of my childhood. That's what I was thinking. What could Vladka possibly have in mind?

"You're right about Warsaw. It's a death trap now for all Jews. Samuel has two cousins in the ghetto who are with the Jewish Resistance. They tell us there's going to be a final revolt there soon. Once that's put down, as we all know it will be, we think the Germans will destroy the ghetto, brick by brick. There'll be nothing left. And once the Jews have gone, the Germans will turn more attention to the Poles of Warsaw. And that means more street hunting, more denunciations, more babies shot in the head. We have to get out. We're going to Hungary. Samuel has relatives there. My family are all dead, before the war. I was an only child. But Samuel has family in Budapest. We are only waiting for Samuel's cousins to leave the ghetto and, if they survive the uprising, then we will all go together. It will be a dangerous trip. It's very risky to try to leave the country. But we feel we must go to our own. I suggest you do the same, Helena. You are not from Warsaw, are you? I remember you mentioning this, ages ago. Where are your family? Where are you from?"

I was shocked by Vladka's revelation. Again, she has come to me in a dark hour and struck a match. Recently, I had only thought of another *melina*, another, and another, dodging blackmailers and the police until we were caught and shot in the street like mad dogs. But to escape from Warsaw, to go home? I had imagined it once before, in the ghetto one desperate night. But it was all a fantasy.

"I come from Novogrodek. In the east. It was Russian for a while. Byelorussian too. Then Polish. It's in German hands now though. No good going there."

"Novogrodek, you say? Wait a minute. Stefan, where was that partisan group from? The one you were telling us about last night?"

Stefan said, "Novogrodek. Why?"

"Helena is from Novogrodek," said Vladka.

"Really?" added Samuel and came over.

"Ah, Novogrodek," said Stefan, nodding. "All sorts happening there."

"What? What about Novogrodek?" I sounded exasperated. How could my obscure little town arouse undeserved interest?

"You still have relatives there?" asked Stefan.

"Yes. Well, I don't know. Aren't the Germans there?"

"Have you not tried to contact your family?" asked Samuel.

Too many questions. Stefan, Samuel and Vladka all staring at me. I wanted to push them all away. I did not want to talk about my family and certainly did not wish to explain my reasons for losing touch with them. I was not about to reveal my shame to these fine people.

"I left home when I was very young. I never went back. I had my reasons." All three looked concerned. I wondered if they thought my family were bad people, that I had escaped from bad treatment. I couldn't leave them thinking that. I owed my family that much, at least.

"It was not my parents' fault. It had nothing to do with them. Or my brother Jakub. It was my choice." All three nodded and looked away. I wondered what questions they held in their heads. But they still had not answered mine.

"But why? What is happening in Novogrodek?"

Stefan said, "There are unconfirmed reports filtering in from eastern Poland that there is a very brave group of partisans in the forests around and about Novogrodek, led by a group called the Bielski brothers, from Stankevich. There have been massacres in Novogrodek and a ghetto constructed. But these brothers and others have been living in the forests and coming into the ghetto to rescue friends and relatives. They've also been carrying out various other partisan activities, sabotage and so forth. Novogrodek is becoming quite famous in Underground circles. It's giving everyone hope, that Jews can indeed fight back and even win!"

A memory came to me from months ago, a rumour of free Jews living in the forests out east. Could it be them? From my home town? I thought of my family, my parents, my little brother Jakub. Massacres in Novogrodek, Stefan had said, and a ghetto. I know my father; he would never make trouble. When we were children, I remember he would never complain about anything like a bad waiter or a rude clerk in public. He would always smile and say it was all fine, and moan about it afterwards when we got home. I knew if there were Germans ordering people around in Novogrodek, telling them to line up on streets and get onto trucks, he would do it without question. And Mama always followed him. I think they must be dead, killed in those massacres. My Mama and Papa, shot in the head. But my brother. Oh, little Jakub! What a terror you were! If he is still alive, I'm sure he is just the type to get involved in partisan activities. He was never bookish like me; he was always fighting and driving our parents to distraction with his pranks. Yet it was me who brought disgrace to our family. Nobody expected that. Perhaps Jakub is sitting under a pine tree right now, cleaning his gun. A free Jew in a forest.

"I have heard of this," I said. "But I couldn't believe it were true. Are they really from Novogrodek?"

"Around there," said Stefan. "And it's only oral reports so far, but they are from pretty reliable sources. I'd say it's true, yes. Did you know the Bielskis?"

Twenty years stretched behind me, as I tried to picture Novogrodek and its buildings, its synagogues and shops, its homes. I thought of that village Stankevich. I don't think I ever went there. The Bielskis, the Bielskis. The Bielskis from Stankevich. I shook my head.

"It's such a long time ago. I don't know."

Vladka said, "It's no matter. But there is hope there. Listen, Helena. You know I love you and Ilsa. You know you are welcome to come to Hungary with us." But I saw a slight movement from Samuel, the tiniest twitch of his head, as if to suggest that this had certainly not been discussed with him. In that moment, I could see how Ilsa and I would be trouble for them. A child in these times is an awful liability.

"I would not think of it," I said. "You two have your own plans. We will make ours. It will be better for all of us." Vladka, for a moment, looked torn: half relieved, half disappointed. How I wanted to take refuge in Vladka and her solid husband and her Underground friends. But I decided there and then not to look for help in that direction. I loved Vladka too. And I wouldn't endanger her. She had helped us too much already.

"All right," said Vladka. "So what about Novogrodek? We have decided that the risks of finding our way to Hungary match the risks of hiding out in Warsaw. Perhaps your situation is the same.

Stay here and live with the constant fear of denunciation or get on the road to the east and find that partisan group? It sounds crazy, but we know that a Jew in Warsaw would have to be mad to stay. What do you think?"

Tonight I sleep on this thought.

It is decided. Stefan has given me a map of Poland, and Vladka, Samuel and I have worked out the best route across the country to Novogrodek. Through his Underground contacts, Stefan knows of friendly people we could call upon along the way, if we need to rest up for a while. We decided the best way is to get a fake travel pass and if questioned, say we are visiting relatives in Novogrodek. Aryan Poles are allowed to travel, but only with a travel pass. Stefan went out today to organise one for us in our Aryan name of Kucharski, and managed to get one this afternoon. I was shocked it was this quick. And a little disappointed too. I had counted on this taking a few days and we could hide here and rest for a while longer. Now we have the correct documents, there is really no excuse to stay for long. We will get the city train to Bialystok, then a local train to Grodno. From there, we are not sure what the transport will be like. We will probably walk to Novogrodek.

Once there, we are all unclear on what will be the best course of action. I have to find the partisans. But where do I start? Stefan suggested we book into a boarding house in town and make gentle enquiries into recent events, see if I can find any old friends I can trust or someone who has heard of the Bielskis and take it from there. Also, I did once know the local forests well. I used to walk for miles and find a soft place amongst the trees and read my poetry books. And I went to those places with Jan too. Not to read. I could go into the forests and look for the partisans myself. But will I remember the way after all these years? And how long will we have to walk before we find any partisan camp? Hours, days, months? Well, the whole enterprise sounds ridiculous, doesn't it? But what is the alternative? That woman yesterday, seeing her son's brains on the pavement. So, that is that. We are not staying here.

I think we may go the day after tomorrow. I don't know yet. I need more money and Vladka says she will get it for us by then. Stefan will also give us warm clothes and supplies for the journey, as well as buy our train tickets to Bialystok. Such kindness. I don't know how I will ever repay it all.

I do not know what this journey will be like. I do not know what we will do if we get there. But I do know that death waits for us on every Warsaw corner. I would rather Ilsa and I die with woodland air in our lungs than stay in this damned city another day.

Today, I explained our plan to Ilsa. I just said we were going on a journey to get away from the city. It would be nicer there, I said. There would be lots of trees and grass and birds. She was most excited about travelling on the railways.

"A real train?" she asked. Later, she said, "Where are we going again, Mama?" I told her, Novogrodek. "But why there?" she asked.

"Because it's where I grew up. I lived there when I was a little girl. When I was seven, as you are now, I used to go to school in Novogrodek and walk home along the streets with all my friends. We used to play hide and seek amongst the trees in the forest in the summer. I was very happy there." It was true. I was happy there. Why did I leave? Ilsa listened carefully to all of this.

She said, "But are there any bad men there?"

I wanted to lie, but didn't have the heart. "There are bad men there, Ilsa. I'm sorry. But I think we will be safer there. I think we can look for a safe place to hide until the bad men go away." Ilsa thought about this for a while. As I watched her sitting there, the weight of my choices on her shoulders, it dawned on me that she looked like a little woman, not a little girl. Not the little girl I remembered as my seven year-old self, skipping along a dusty road. I didn't have any bad men in my childhood. Not at that age anyhow. Ilsa has never been allowed to be that carefree. I decided she ought to be an equal part in our decisions. She has earned the right by giving up her childhood. I asked her, "Is it all right with you, if we go to this place?"

She considered this, then said, "I think it will be safe because it is your home."

Tonight we sleep in a safe *melina* with friends by our sides. I thank the stars for this night, though its quiet shelter will not last. Soon, a long journey will begin. But strangely, I am not afraid. I see the walls of Warsaw fall and my way leads to the forests. Tonight, as I write, I hear the soft hush of my daughter's breathing. Beneath it sighs the pine-fragranced breeze of my home.

CHAPTER NINE

"As you know, this morning at 6 a.m., Polish police surrounded the ghetto walls. Our intelligence sources tell us there is to be a large German operation starting tomorrow. These are the orders from our leader, Anielewicz. If you have arms, you must fight. Our first phase of fighting should exploit the element of surprise and kill and injure as many Germans as we can. The ZOB has twenty-two combat groups, totalling around seven hundred men and women, placed all over the Central Ghetto, Brushworks and Factories Areas. Here in the Central Ghetto, the leader of all eight combat groups is Israel Kanal.

"Our combat group has the same number of weapons as the other units, that is, for each of you a revolver or pistol and ten to fifteen rounds, four grenades and five Molotov cocktails. Some fighters have rifles. The ZOB also has one submachine-gun and one light machine-gun, but not much ammo. Because the Germans have superior firepower, the second stage of the fighting should move to partisan warfare. You must attack from windows and roofs, twenty-four hours a day. In this way, we can defend ourselves and stay alive long enough to do real damage to the enemy.

"Those without weapons are to go into bunkers and, whenever they can, escape to Aryan Warsaw and head for the woods, preferably during the first fighting. There are other fighters, not affiliated to us or the ZZW, the so-called 'wild groups'. Civilians who wanted to fight, but couldn't join a combat group because they had no weapons. Group leaders, including myself, have told them they might be called upon in days to come to relieve exhausted fighters.

"This is it, boys. The final battle is upon us. On this night, our comrades have posted notices on walls throughout the ghetto to encourage all Jews to die with honour. There is also a bold streamer tied near the ghetto wall calling on Poles to rise up against the Germans. Tomorrow, when Germans will die by Jewish hands, Poland will wake up. Fight bravely, help your comrades and kill as many of the bastards as you can. The world is watching."

Pawel ordered his group to check and clean their weapons, go over their battle strategy, rest. Once their tasks were done, Daniel and the others stretched out, but nobody slept. Whispering, playing cards, writing. Pawel lay away from them. His back was to Daniel, so he could not see if Pawel was asleep. He was breathing heavily. Daniel tapped him on the shoulder.

"What is it, Anglik?"

"At the big meeting today. Did you hear anything about the ZZW?"

Pawel turned over and sighed, rested his cheek on his upturned palm.

"News of your girlfriend, you mean."

"Yes."

"They say the ZZW are a smaller fighting group than us, but

have a better weapons array. Their main force is centred around Muranowska Street. Zygmunt will be there. Your girlfriend too. Right in the thick of it."

"I wish she weren't. I wish she were a thousand miles from here."

"I know. Get some sleep, Anglik."

They were up and ready by 4.30 a.m. At 5, a powerful loudspeaker proclaimed in Polish that all Jews must report willingly for resettlement. They could hear vehicles driving through the ghetto. Pawel ordered Moses and David to find the source of the traffic. They returned with white faces.

"It's massive," said Moses. "Tanks and armoured cars, lorries packed with infantry and support vehicles."

David said, "They looked like they're facing the entire Allied army, not a few raggedy Jews with home-made bombs!"

Moses said to Pawel, "What are we going to do?"

"This is good. It means the Germans think we're more heavily armoured than we are."

Some nodded, some stared at the windows, their feet, each other.

Natan whispered to Daniel, "We're fucked."

Daniel gave him a grim smile and they considered each other for a moment, friends born from war, comrades, brothers in arms. Natan nodded at Daniel and Daniel shook his hand, grasped it tight. There were no words that could say more.

Stationed at windows and roof spots in their building and the next, awaiting their first sight of the enemy, they heard singing. German voices singing. Boots marching. Machine-gun fire. Fighting in other parts of the ghetto, gunfire and explosions, vehicles reversing, men shouting. Daniel and Natan awaited instructions. A few of the others wanted to get out there and join in, but Pawel ordered them to stay put.

"The action will come to you soon enough," he warned.

At midday, their lookout spotted Germans at the end of Bonifraterska Street. They were to attack as soon as the enemy came within range. Daniel was at a window on the next floor down with Natan. They had a pistol and twelve bullets each, grenades and Molotovs. Natan whispered a prayer. Daniel closed his eyes and pictured his mother's face. He opened his mouth and imagined the touch of Marysia's lips. That was his prayer.

Germans below them, creeping like pantomime villains. He shot three times and Natan twice. They both hit a German – the same one at the same time. He staggered about and dropped. The other Germans were firing wildly upwards, heading for doorways, shrieking at each other. He felt a power over them, perched up there in the gods, raining down his small measure of death. He might perish soon, but he made those Germans feel fear, made them suffer in pain, made them die. He heard his comrades shooting and other Germans were hit and wounded, two killed. The fighting lasted half an hour. Germans left their street. His combat group met upstairs, laughing and shouting. They had collected weaponry and uniform from German dead that other soldiers had not dragged away.

In the afternoon, there was more fighting on their street with the little ammo they had left, and later they moved via roofs to a house on Franciszkanska, where they used two grenades to disable an armoured car. By the end of the day they were back at base, none dead, a few Molotovs and grenades left, some bullets. It was quiet from seven o'clock. They sat around, worn out, sharing stories.

At eight-thirty, a lad came in to their barracks.

"Can we help you, brother?" said Pawel.

"I'm Aaron. I'm just using your house to get through to the Brushworks. I'm with the ZZW."

Daniel stood up. "Do you know Marysia? Zygmunt's courier?"

"Yes, yes, she's all right. There's been great fighting at Muranowska Square. I was there for a while. Saw her lob Molotovs and kill Germans."

Daniel was proud. He wished she'd bloody leave the ghetto though. But he knew she wouldn't.

"Any news of the ZOB?" asked Pawel.

"Yes. ZOB command fought really well in Mila Street. Attacked two tanks. I think one blown up and the other hit with Germans regrouping behind it. Quite a few dead and wounded enemy."

Cries of *yes, yes*!

"Loads of fighting from Jews at Nalewki Street, who went on all day till the bastards set their house on fire."

Another cheer.

"And a weird story that the Home Army tried to blow a hole in the ghetto wall to help the Jews escape, but screwed it up."

The group booed, cursed. Daniel thought, so that was the only Polish help. Perhaps there was more, and they hadn't heard about it yet. Perhaps not.

"But listen," Aaron went on. "Bad news. Someone told me about mobile German units in the ghetto with flamethrowers. Got to go now. Got to get to the Brushworks."

Pawel sent Stephan and Stefan to find out more. A number of Germans dead. Some dead fighters, but all reports suggested no fighters had been captured. A few hundred civilians were taken.

The Germans withdrew from the ghetto at eight p.m., scared of the night-time when they could be picked off like moths to hungry bats. The Germans had run away. Great news all round. But there was one sickening report which, knowing the enemy, they did believe: that the SS broke into the hospital at Gesia Street, threw the sick and nurses into the fire, smashed new-born babies' heads against walls and disembowelled the pregnant mothers.

Pawel said, "This is why we must fight on."

That evening, the ghetto regrouped. Comrades flitted from building to building, telling tales and showing war wounds. Natan and Daniel went with Michal and Yanek to a house in Walowa Street, where Michal's uncle was staying in a bunker and reportedly had booze going spare. When they arrived, an event was taking place. All the bunker inhabitants sat at a table laid with wine glasses and plates with titbits of food. A single candle lit the scene.

Natan stopped and clapped his hand to his cheek.

"I forgot," he whispered. "Tonight is *seder*."

Before Daniel could ask what this meant, Natan shushed him and they sat in a corner to watch the ceremony. One man dressed in a white shirt spoke in Hebrew, reading from a book, periodically answering questions from individuals seated around him. Now and again, they would take a small bite of the portions on the plate and a sip from their glasses and say prayers together. A young girl sang a lovely song. Daniel had no idea what she was singing about, but a fount of sadness brimmed inside him. He thought of his mother, heaven knows where in Warsaw, or maybe dead, long dead or recently dead. The song opened up a gate inside him and out flooded loss. He listened to the falling strains and willed himself not to cry. That would be unforgiveable, a fighting man weeping like a child. But he felt like a child and he wanted to find his mother. He missed Magda and thought how she must be worrying dreadfully about him. Why had he abandoned her? Was it worth it? Before leaving, he showed his photo of Helena around and asked the same old questions. No luck.

They moved on to find Michal's uncle who shared grog with them, while the others told him of that day's battles. But he only stayed long enough to take a few gulps and let it warm his throat and bring a little fog to his weary head. And he showed the photo around again, of course. Nothing. Now he was keen to get away and visit Marysia. He found her celebrating with a bunch of fighters at her ZZW base, smoking and shouting in Yiddish. When she saw him, she threw her arms around him. They kissed passionately at which her comrades whooped and jeered, but he didn't give a damn.

Coming up for air, Marysia said, "Sit with me a while and talk." They went to a corner and sat beside each other, legs and hands entwined. They related their adventures of the day. He asked her about the *seder* meal.

"It was beautiful, but I don't know what it meant."

"Tonight is the first night of the Passover. It's our festival of liberty. The man in white was a Rabbi who was telling the story of the Exodus of the Israelites from slavery. The story is called the *Haggadah*. It reminds us of the Promised Land. That we're directly related to the Jews who came out of Egypt."

Daniel saw pictures in his mind from childhood stories, Egyptians whipping slaves building the pyramids stone by stone. Was that it? Dad the atheist gave no religious education. Magda bought him a secret children's illustrated bible, took it out when Dad was busy in his study, but it bored him. He never imagined it would be useful.

"One day," Marysia said triumphantly, "we will be led in

freedom to Zion with a joyful shout, next year in Jerusalem rebuilt!"

"What exactly does that mean?"

"Going to Palestine, of course! It's been talked about at Passover forever. It must happen now! It will happen! At the beginning of the *Haggadah,* it says, 'This year we are here; next year – in the Land of Israel! This year we are slaves; next year – free men!' Now we're facing our worst trial yet. Europe is murdering all the Jews. Now is the time to go. Whoever makes it through this mess will be on the first boat to Palestine. There we will build Zion and the rest of the world can go and hang itself!"

At this, a number of the ZZW fighters rallied.

Daniel thought of home. "Not everybody in Europe hates the Jews."

Marysia's face twisted in disbelief, that any one could be as great an imbecile as Daniel.

"Listen, Europe has hated us as long as we've been here. There have always been massacres of Jews. Don't you know anything? Christians have spread lies about us for hundreds of years, like at Passover, that Jews kidnap Christian children and sacrifice them, mixing their blood with the Passover bread. That's only one of their excuses for hating Jews, putting them in ghettos like this one, murdering them. The Nazis are nothing new. They've just raked up old hate. It's bigger now. They can kill more of us more quickly. We must go. We must have our own land, where no one will ever be able to do this again. I'm telling you, this war is it. Whatever happens, the Jews will have their own land in the end. And no *goyim* allowed."

"Who are the *goyim?*" he asked.

"The gentiles. Non-Jews. Oh, you may find one who pretends to be tolerant. But give them a chance and most of the world would get rid of a Jew from their street if they could. In our daily prayers, we thank the Lord for not making us *goyim.* We hate them and they hate us."

He didn't know what to say to that. His father, Magda. Both *goyim*. Did they hate the Jews deep down? Before he knew about himself, did he? He couldn't think straight about it. He changed the subject. He wanted to talk about her, about him, about them. He beckoned Marysia closer and spoke into her ear.

"I want to spend the night with you. I know I can't but I want to anyway."

Marysia smiled and touched his face. "You're right, you can't."

"Do you want me to?"

"But you can't, Daniel. It doesn't matter what I want."

Her zealous commitment to her cause. He admired it. It irked him too.

"You can still want things, can't you? Even though you can't have them. It's important to know what you want. To dream. I think about you all the time. I imagine us together, after the war, free. It keeps me going."

But Marysia shook her head crossly. "No, no. I never think like that. I never think beyond today. We might die tomorrow."

"You think about Palestine."

"That's different. That's a Jewish dream, an ancient dream. It's part of a Jew's mind and never goes away. It's part of our souls. Romance is nothing in comparison. It passes away. Passion is a short-lived thing, a sad thing. Like a moth."

He looked at her. She had such beautiful eyes. She said such beautiful things. He took hold of her, kissed her tenderly.

He whispered, "I don't care what you say. You're not as tough as you make out. I know you want me."

She held on to him. He felt her warm tears at his throat.

She whispered, "What is the point? What is the point of loving when we are probably going to die tomorrow?"

He pulled away and looked at her face, her usually clear eyes blurred.

"That is the best time to love," he said and kissed her wet cheek, wiped away a tear with his thumb. She pulled him to her and they fumbled about down below, shoving off tiresome clothing yet trying to stay small and unnoticed in the corner. Daniel knew others might be muttering behind them, watching, but all propriety was gone now, an unlamented casualty of the extraordinary days through which they lived.

"I love you," he whispered in her ear. "I love you, Marysia."

She said his name and clung more tightly to him. He kissed and kissed her, hoping she'd say it too, willing her to, but then he realised she was crying. He stopped and said, "I'm sorry, I'm sorry," but he did not know what for. They lay still, their hold just as tight, their breathing slower, lengthening, matching each other breath to breath.

They lay like that, wrapped around each other, for a long time. They did not sleep. Despite his desire to, he knew his hours were numbered and soon he'd be asked to leave, to go back to his combat group. This was war, not summer camp.

They roused themselves from their embrace and pulled their clothes back on. His back to the room, he didn't want to look round and see if the others were watching. He looked at her only. She was frowning intensely, as if working out an inextricable problem in her mind. When he was ready, he stood up and held out his hand to her, which she took and stood up. She clutched him and whispered urgently in his ear, "I do love you, I do, Daniel. Please be careful. Please don't die tomorrow."

A ZZW fighter tapped him on the shoulder.

"Time to go, son," he said and flicked his thumb towards the door. Marysia abruptly let go and turned from him, wiped her face and ran her hands through her cropped hair. She walked away a few steps, towards her combat group. She was gone again, back to them. He was grinning from ear to ear, buoyed by what she'd whispered to him, but he still wanted one last loving look before he left for the night. But she couldn't give that to him, he didn't know why. Instead, she turned and saluted him goodbye, her smile all too cheerful.

He said, "I'll see you very soon, I promise."

But it was an empty promise, he knew that. Who knew what would happen tomorrow? Making his way back to his digs, he was warmed by his girl's words of love and his comrades' successes that day. Tonight they all had cause for celebration. But Marysia's words had also left a bitter taste. That day was a great victory for the Jews. And he fought with them as a Jew. He didn't believe in any God, Jewish, Catholic or otherwise. What was being a Jew to him? When he saw the *seder*, he was moved. But did he hear ancestral voices calling him? It seemed quaint, picturesque, exotic and he couldn't deny the emotion that had welled up in him. But he had no belief in any of it. Perhaps he was not a religious Jew then. But what was it to be a secular Jew? Not a question of race, certainly, even though the Nazis would have one think it. To be a Jew was a way to live, think and believe. It was flimsy, this Jewish thing. Yet steadfast as bedrock. His mother was a Jew, therefore he was a Jew. If he survived, would he ask Marysia to go back with him to London, Magda and his old life? Would she ever do it, even for him? Or would he go with her and the other Jews to Palestine, a hot dusty country on the other side of the world? Where would his home be?

All these questions were worse than useless. More fighting tomorrow. Marysia with her group, he with his. They both may be dead by lunchtime.

Pawel ordered everyone up. Blinking away sleep, scrabbling to stand.

"The enemy is setting up a gun site at the end of our street. Looks like they're going to start shelling houses. We've bullets left and grenades, but we've nothing to repel that kind of assault."

An explosion. Daniel's cheek hit the floor. He saw Dad's white face. He opened his eyes and got to his feet.

"Abandon base!" yelled Pawel. Some grabbed weapons and all sprinted downstairs and through the back exits along Bonifraterska, ending up near Krasinski Square. Germans were shelling there. On to Walowa Street, they found a corner building with views and running water. Pawel organised them into positions and they sat down to await the next assault. Breathing fast, some held their heads, others itched to fight. Daniel and Natan stared at each other. Natan laughed loudly then stopped and his face fell, a picture of dread.

"It's all right," Daniel said in a low voice. He patted his comrade's arm. "We're in it together."

"Yes," said Natan in a kind of dry gasp, then stronger, pulling himself together. "Yes, my friend. We are."

Hours later, they watched from windows, hundreds of enemy soldiers marching up Walowa Street towards the main gate leading to the Aryan side.

Pawel said, "There's a mine buried there."

A Jew somewhere pushed a lever. There was a mighty boom and cheers came from Jews near and far. Body parts flew graceful arcs down Walowa. Germans lurched and scrambled.

More Germans came in single file up Walowa, embracing walls. Daniel's group threw grenades and Molotovs and killed one. All afternoon, modest groups of Germans appeared here and there, greeted with Molotovs. Pawel sent out Celek and Azriel to gather intelligence. The news was that the Germans had sent three officers with white rosettes on their lapels, shouting in the street that they were proposing a fifteen minute truce in order to collect their dead and wounded and were kindly offering peaceful transit to labour camps nearby. This was answered by Jewish fighters with bullets and bombs.

At six o'clock, Germans appeared near their house with flamethrowers and sent colossal swathes of fire across their windows. Daniel and Natan threw themselves away and managed to get down the stairs before the room they were in was engulfed. They saw Pawel on the landing shouting at everyone to retreat to Bonifraterska. They escaped with others and got back to their digs, still standing. Pawel was about to do a head count, when Moses staggered in, black-faced and hair frazzled.

"Four dead. Caught in the fire. Bernard, Alexander, Benjamin and Bronislaw dead."

Eliyahu gave him water. There were sixteen of them now. Daniel saw the others group together. Pawel began to speak, a prayer. Natan looked to Daniel, gave him a desperate kind of smile and motioned him to join them. He stood beside his friend, listened to Pawel's words. Not a word about the dead, about death itself or mourning, simply praise for their God. At points, Pawel said, "and say", and the rest intoned, "Amen." Daniel said it too. When Pawel finished, Azriel stepped forward. He began to sing. A strange language unfurled its prayer for their dead in that small ghetto room.

The Germans retreated for the night. Tuvia and Wladyslaw went on a recce and found food. There was news of losses and victories all over the ghetto, in Mila, Leszno and Smozca.

Aaron came. The first thing he said was, "She's still alive, comrade!"

Daniel knew he meant Marysia and shook his hand, laughing riotously with relief, which descended into a coughing fit. Aaron clapped him on the back and talked to him while he recovered.

"The ZZW fought an incredible battle in Muranowska Square. The SS advanced down Muranowska and were hit by ZZW machine-guns. Some SS were killed and the rest retreated. Later on, they came with anti-aircraft guns and shelled the houses. Hundreds of SS stormed into the ruins and captured about a hundred fighters. Lots of ours were wounded but walked away with the Germans, showing no fear. But Marysia had already escaped, along with me and others, and the leaders too. The last time I saw her she was in Zamenhof 16, but I don't know how long she's staying there."

Daniel went to Pawel and requested to visit her. Pawel nodded, then Daniel asked if he had a scrap of paper and a pencil. Pawel still carried them around in his pocket, scribbling down the odd bit of information now and again. He tore off a strip for Daniel and said, "I want the pencil back." Daniel wrote something down in tiny writing then handed back the pencil and left. He found the Zamenhof house. One of the ZZW fighters let him in, recognised from before. A crowded room, some wounded with makeshift bandages and bloody faces. He saw Marysia by a wall, asleep on the floor, on her back, mouth open, limbs splayed out. Her chest rising the only sign of life. He knelt beside her and watched her.

She stirred and he leant down, whispered, "Marysia, my love."

She opened her eyes and said his name drowsily. She reached out. He curled into her. He did not look out at the others in the room. He did not see them or hear them. Only her.

Too exhausted to make love, they fell asleep together. They didn't wake till dawn. At five, he knew he had to get back to his base. So spent of all energy, they had wasted their night in sleep (yet what beautiful, tangled sleep it was.) But they had not spoken of anything, had not discussed their love, the battle, the future. Nothing. Now, they were out of time. He propped himself on an elbow and looked down at her. She was sleepy and her hair was messy and she was lovely.

"Listen," he said to her and sat upright, held her hand tight. "This is important. When all is lost you must go, get out of the ghetto."

"I will," she said sleepily, smiling.

"I know you," he said, more urgently. "I know you'll want to stay with your group. But it's the end soon. It'll be every man for himself. And you must get out. We should arrange a place and time to meet, after the battle."

Her face was serious now. She sat up and stared at him, glanced around at her comrades.

"All right. Where? When?"

"You tell me. Choose a place in Warsaw and we'll meet there, exactly a week from now, and if we don't manage it that day, again exactly a week later and again the following week. We'll give each other three chances to come."

"All right. We'll meet where Chopin's statue used to be. The Germans blew it up, the bastards, but everyone knows where it was."

"I'll find it," said Daniel. "One week from today. Twelve noon. Agreed?"

"Agreed."

He felt in his pocket and pulled out the tiny scrap of paper. "Here, it was all I could find to write on. It is my home address in London. If we cannot meet here, for whatever reason, if you need to get away, if you can make it out of here and you want to find me, this is my home. Well," he paused and shook his head, "it was my childhood home. There will be a woman there called Magda. She will take care of you, if I'm not...around."

Marysia took the little scrap and stared at it, folded it so gently and placed it very carefully inside her pocket.

They looked at each other in shock, unable to speak.

Finally, he said, "I don't want to say goodbye."

"Then don't. Say, see you tomorrow."

Her mouth smiled but her eyes frowned. Such a complicated face. He wanted years to study it.

"See you tomorrow," he said.

"Goodbye," she said.

By midday, the ghetto was in flames. The Germans began shelling from outside the walls. Daniel and his group had not expected this. Any amount of partisan fighting was nothing against this firepower. And no one knew when the moment would come that a bomb would land on your house and blow you to pieces.

There was little action in Bonifraterska, but Daniel's group ventured out to take shots at stray Germans. They killed two with a Molotov. But they had so few bullets left that their actions were minor. The ghetto was shrinking. As Germans searched for Jews to round up, missiles came from Jewish fighters. But the Germans would shell those houses or use their flamethrowers to burn down apartment blocks, building by building. Some Jews managed to flee through labyrinthine routes, but others were trapped in bunkers. There were reports of Jews jumping from burning buildings. Despite this, the Germans still had to fight for access to each house, as the Jews had barricaded entrances and hurled missiles from windows. Anyone rounded up was taken to the Umschlagplatz for deportation. From above, Daniel and Natan had watched long lines of Jews being marched past all day.

By evening, they were in a house on Franciszkanska and Pawel ordered them home.

When they got back, Pawel went off with Celek to get information from the leaders. Aaron turned up. He was on his way to the Brushworks Area again.

"Marysia is back at Muranowska."

"Thank you!" cried Daniel, a wave of emotion almost flooring him, so tired he was from the fight and lack of food. Then he looked at Aaron and asked, "Why do you take such risks coming through here?"

"My sister's in a bunker over there. She's all I've got. I had seventeen cousins. They're all dead now."

He went off quickly, but soon returned. He looked ill. He told them that the whole of the Brushworks Area was on fire. He had no idea where his sister was. They offered him a little *bimber* but he refused. He just sat and stared at the floor. Pawel and Celek came back. They brought with them a communiqué from ZOB command.

Pawel read it out: "Our fighters are fighting magnificently. The morale in the fighting units is excellent. Our losses in men are relatively small. We are short of ammunition. We shall fight on as long as we are alive."

They received this with silence. Nobody cheered at the end. Aaron got up and left.

They had lost no lads that day, miraculously. Their house had not burnt down. They had a little food left. But they were quiet that night. Nobody talked of victories. Just before bed, they heard Wladyslaw ask Pawel what the plans were for tomorrow. Pawel shrugged.

All of the following day, fires engulfed the ghetto, from Franciszkanska to Wolowa, Nalewki to Zamenhof Streets. Thousands of Jews had been burnt alive. Hundreds had jumped from houses and lay in the streets begging the Germans to shoot them to end their pain. The enemy always refused. Jews had been using the sewers to try to escape, but the Germans poured creosote and gas grenades down the manholes. There had been German casualties, including prominent SS, yet these had been answered with swift reprisals, hundreds of Jews shot in the street.

It was not all disaster. There had been battles fought throughout the ghetto, with Jewish fighters resisting admirably. Partisan tactics had been very successful, like setting fire to warehouses full of German supplies, as well as killing from roofs and windows all over the ghetto. Daniel's combat group had continued to fight, moving from their base to other streets and back, taking a shot or lobbing a Molotov. They were pesky and slippery, making trouble for the Germans, even if they had killed few in recent days. At least they were still alive.

But the ghetto was dying.

Daniel stood at a window of their Bonifraterska base, watched the empty street, heard gunshots, smelt the burning ghetto. He looked round at his combat group, sitting on the floor, dozing, hungry, exhausted, out of ammo and missiles. Natan was sitting with his back against the wall, staring into space.

Daniel came to sit beside Natan and quietly asked, "Time to go?"

Natan frowned. "Go where?"

Daniel glanced at Pawel, the others. They didn't seem to be listening. "To get out of here."

Natan looked confused. "But, we haven't had orders yet. See what tomorrow brings."

Daniel could not believe his friend still had such optimism. "I want to get Marysia and get the hell out of here. Will you come with us?"

Natan looked confused. "Come where?"

"Out of the ghetto, of course."

"Abandon our post?"

Daniel was exasperated by his friend's thick-headedness. "There is no post, there is no battle, Natan. There's only death. It's time…to go."

Natan shook his head. "You are my good friend, Anglik. My combat partner, my comrade. You've brought me hope and friendship. But all my other friends are here, my family is here – dead or alive – my home is here. I'm going to fight for it, till the end. I'm not going anywhere, my friend, not even with you."

Natan was smiling, a kind of peaceful understanding in his eyes. Daniel wanted to shake him, but he envied him his certainty too.

Daniel went to Pawel. He said, "I want to go for my girlfriend. I want to get her out of the ghetto."

Pawel shook his head. "It's too dangerous, Anglik. To get to Muranowska, you'd need to go street level. You know what it's like out there. Either you'll be picked up and deported. Or shot. Or caught in the fires."

"We're finished. You know that, don't you? It's time to go."

Pawel folded his arms. "We have had no such order from our leaders. Until we do, we must fight on. Your girlfriend and her leaders would say the same. We must wait for orders. The only missions I can allow are food runs through the houses. Which reminds me, you two, Yanek and Natan. Your turn for a food run. Go now."

Yanek and Natan were gone for a half hour or so, while Daniel sat on the floor, brooding over his friend's decision and Pawel's edict. He had lost almost all heart with this uprising and saw only doom as their end, all of them. He could not see any point in sacrificing these last few brave lives – and for what? Surely survival was the best revenge. And besides, if he died with his comrades, as Natan was suggesting, what about his mother? If by any slim chance she was still alive, then he was choosing the cause over her, and if so, what had he come all this way for? He was building himself up to go over to Pawel and tell him, politely as possible, to go to hell. Then he heard a clattering of feet on the stairs. Natan rushed back in, shouting "Anglik, Anglik!"

Daniel leapt up.

"They say Muranowska is on fire! Marysia's bunker!"

Daniel leapt over comrades, through the door, down the stairs, straight out into the street. He did not look back. He heard Natan calling him. He ran on. Down Bonifraterska, along Franciszkanska, into Nalewki and up to Muranowska. His breath rasped in his throat, his chest hurt, his feet stumbled over rubble and bodies, but he did not stop, he did not slow. He felt the heat of the inferno before he saw it, heard the crackle and spit, the crash of falling beams. His feet clung to the ground. He glanced down. The street was melting. The heat from the fires was dissolving the road.

Gunfire nearby. He bolted to a doorway, peered into the street. He crept round corners to look into Muranowska Square. The heat beat him back, but he stayed long enough, his arms covering his face, eyes peering through, to see the ZZW base drowning in flame. Screams upon screams. His feet sank into the road.

More gunshot nearby. He turned and ran, found an alleyway on Nalewki. He heard an enemy unit pass in a truck, firing into the houses, shouting in German and laughing. Once gone, he ran back the way he'd come, his soles sticking to the tacky road. Explosions. Shelling nearby. Roofs toppling, slates smashing into the street. He threw himself into an open door on Franciszkanska, to the back of the building and into an alley to the rear of Bonifraterska.

A powerful blast blew him off his feet. He hit his head on the alley wall and blacked out. When he came to, it was quiet. His whole body ached. He was able to stand. No broken bones. Blood on his neck. But no gashes. He was all right. He looked around him, recalled where he was. At the back of Bonifraterska. His base was a few houses down. But half the street had gone. He could see, over the alley wall, half a house: rooms with no walls, naked and surprised, like an open doll's house. He found an exit to the street and walked down, staring at the rubble where his base used to be.

Legs and arms. A hand. Another hand. Someone's hair, forehead. Another. Three shoes. No faces yet. It could be anyone. Poor bastards in a bunker. Maybe his combat group had abandoned base. Escaped. They'd done it before. He moved a brick. Saw a crushed face. It was Yanek. Shifted more. Celek. Azriel. Michal. Eliyahu.

Natan.

He didn't know why he was alive.

He didn't know where to go or what to do.

He hid in a house still standing on Bonifraterska. He sat all evening at a window, staring into the street, looking for survivors. His girl and his friend were dead. Darkness came.

By midnight, he made a decision.

He was going out to look for a bunker. He didn't want to wait for death alone.

He had no idea where he was going. He wandered through the ghetto. Heaps of corpses. Some still moving, their eyes dead but their bodies lingering. Everything burnt out. He wanted to find a bunker full of people, life and chatter and food and water. He didn't know where to look. He heard a noise at the end of a street. He saw a head appear through a gap in the rubble, disappear again. He headed towards it. He stood where he'd seen it and waited. No one came. So he spoke.

He said, "My name is Anglik. I am a fighter with the ZOB. I have a gun but no bullets. My combat group was commanded by Pawel. My combat partner was Natan. I believe I am the only survivor from my group. I have no food or water. I need shelter. Can you let me in? I will answer any questions you have for me. You can search me. I am not an informant. Please help me."

His voice was tinny in the empty street. He felt the stones were listening, but no one else. He waited half an hour. Then came a sound: creaking wood.

A man appeared. He was bald on top, grey temples, dark rings under his eyes.

"Come in, Anglik," he said in Polish and Daniel followed him.

Did the man know him? At the side of the building a door was open. It led to a room with two walls missing. The man approached one wall left standing, piles of litter at its foot. He placed his hands on the wall and moved it. It was a false wall, made of brick and concrete, mounted on a cart. Behind it was an opening in the true wall, just above floor level, about two feet square. They squeezed through. The man showed Daniel how to secure the cart back in place, latched with heavy bars.

Inside was an extensive bunker full of people. The windows were covered with rubbish. There were five rooms: the first contained provisions, lard, flour and beans, packed in sealed containers. Three rooms were lined with cots, one with running water, with an electric light, gas and stove with a large built-in kettle. The last room had a well and a partitioned toilet. He was shown around by the man, who pointed things out silently. Most of the inhabitants were asleep. A few were sitting up in bed, watching Daniel as he passed, but no one spoke.

He wanted to know why he had been let in. Once the tour had finished, he touched the man's shoulder. He stopped and looked curiously at him.

"Do you know me?" he said.

"No. But I know about you, Anglik."

"How?"

"My wife was Natan's cousin. Second cousin."

"Natan's dead. Yesterday."

"I'm sad to hear that," he said. The man patted Daniel on the back. He was comforting him. "He visited my wife two weeks ago. He mentioned your name. Said you'd come from England. I remember that. It was the night before she died."

"I'm sorry."

"She went out to look for our son. He's dead too, months ago, but she never believed it. She used to go out and look for him. I couldn't keep her in. She was shot."

"What's your name?"

"Shmuel. Come and eat. I have cold pancakes. Taste awful but will line your stomach. A drink of water too. Come."

He slept there that night. In the morning he was given more food. He passed Helena's photo around. No response. Kind faces though. A woman asked about the outside world. They had not been out for weeks. Several had places waiting for them in Aryan Warsaw, but couldn't get in contact with anyone outside the ghetto. Beyond their conversation, he could see a man pacing, literally tearing his hair out, strands floating to the floor. Another was writing furiously.

Shmuel said, "We had four leave last week, looking for friends in bunkers in the Central Ghetto. They thought there were tunnels to the Aryan side. Others went yesterday to go through the sewers. Their plan was to tie each other together with rope."

It all sounded pointless. A few still had faith in a Polish uprising. He put them straight.

"I used to work with the Underground," he said. "They have their own battles. They won't save you."

Faces fell and he felt bad. Why tell the truth to the doomed? It couldn't help them now. Hope was kinder.

They heard shouting outside, coming from down the street. Shmuel took Daniel to the back room where you could climb a pile of broken bricks and a tiny window gave a grubby street view. Shmuel called it their peephole. They peered out. It was a bunch of Germans. They had with them two scruffy men.

Shmuel said, "Jewish stool pigeons."

They had surrounded a building at the end of the road. One of the Jews shouted in Yiddish.

Shmuel translated: "Jews, come out. The war is over!"

No one came. The Germans set up machinery and drilled through the walls of that house for four hours. They threw in poison gas and waited. People crawled out, living skeletons. Laughing, the Germans forced them to undress then beat them. The Germans were shouting about *'Juden-Bunko'* - Jewish bunkers in the area. No one gave up any information. One of the girls picked up a brick and threw it weakly towards a German. She was shot dead. They ordered them to march away.

Everyone in their bunker breathed again. Those brave Jews had not revealed their presence. A prayer was said for them. Everyone was quiet for hours. They heard someone. Shmuel went to the peephole and said he could see a Jew outside sobbing, begging to be let in. He said he was Motl's brother-in-law. A man jumped up, obviously Motl. The Jew outside was let in. His name was Moshe. Shmuel wasn't happy about it.

Moshe was sweaty and balding, tufts of black hair above his ears, unsteady eyes. He was deeply unattractive, and Daniel didn't trust him, but he was a new face, so Daniel showed him the photo.

"Do you know this woman? Her name is Helena. She might be a seamstress."

"I don't think so. I don't know. What's her name?"

"Helena. This photo was taken twenty years ago. She'd be in her thirties now."

Moshe fingered her picture. His thumb made a black smudge.

"A seamstress. Did she make armbands?"

"I don't know. Do you know her?"

He ran his hand over his moist head and bit his lip.

"Might be her. I bought an armband off someone, years ago. At the beginning of the ghetto. A woman, looked like this. There was a husband and a girl. They made armbands in their apartment. I bought one. Mine was stolen."

"Are you sure? Are you certain it was her?"

Moshe held the photo closer, as if to sniff it.

"Not certain, no. But it reminds me of her. It was a long time ago. And I only met her the once."

"Where was she? Can you remember?"

He looked up, as if picturing the street.

"Oh, where was it now? In the small ghetto. Sliska, I think. Yes, Sliska."

Sliska Street had burnt to dust. Daniel had seen it himself, days before.

"Can you tell me anything about her? Did you talk to her?"

"Not really. I just needed an armband. Someone told me they sold them at that apartment, up the stairs on Sliska. I think the name was Helena, but I can't be sure. I went up there and handed the money over. She gave it to me. It was good quality, I remember that. Lasted me a long time. Until I joined the...Well, a long time anyway. I don't know anything else. I need to talk to my brother-in-law now. Excuse me."

Moshe was turning away. Daniel held his arm.

"Hey, let go of me."

"Sorry, I'm sorry. I just want to know about her. Is there nothing else you can tell me? Where they went? What happened to them?"

"Look, I don't know anything else. I barely looked at the woman. I'm not even sure if it was her. Maybe I'm wrong."

Moshe walked away quickly, found Motl and went to a corner. They talked in low voices.

Shmuel came to Daniel.

"I don't like that Moshe."

Daniel thought, he's just in shock, like we all are. Be patient. Leave it tonight. Talk to him tomorrow.

It was the longest night, as Moshe snored and snored. Daniel stared at Helena's image, tried to clean off the greasy thumbprint. He pictured her in a flat, sewing armbands with a husband, with a child. A girl. A sister for Daniel. But was it her? It could be. It could be! What could he glean from it? Sewing armbands for the ghetto. Industrious. A survivor. Turning her craft to an essential item, clever that. Married. A child. Settled. Happy? Who knows? But alive. Yes, alive and in the ghetto. That was something. That was enough, for tonight.

Moshe slept like a baby. The next morning, Daniel waited on a chair within direct sight of his bunk. As soon as he sat up, Daniel went to him.

"Can I talk with you again?"

Motl stepped in front. "Not now. We're off out. Moshe has food in another bunker. We're off to fetch it."

Shmuel nodded and they were gone.

"Why did you let them go?" asked Daniel.

"I'm not their keeper."

Daniel paced the bunker all day. He did not talk to anyone. Hours went and no sign. At five o'clock, they heard German boots running down their street. Scraping, digging. Rustling. They could see nothing through the peephole. The smell of burning.

The Germans had set fire to their building. Moshe and Motl must have been captured. Or Moshe was a collaborator. Either way, there was no time to whine about it. Their bunker was ablaze. Shmuel and another man raced to the false wall, but push as they might, it wouldn't budge. Daniel helped, but there was no movement. Perhaps masonry had fallen in front of it. They rushed to the peephole, the tiny window Shmuel and Daniel and looked through before. It was too small to crawl through, but they decided to use it to dig through. They smashed the window and began to dig at the wall around it. The other men came to help and they used any piece of metal they could find to dig out that wall. But it was a foot thick and solid as the rock of ages. The women and children started wailing. The heat of the fire was becoming unbearable. Daniel's sweat ran into his eyes. Blinded by salt-water and dirt and ash. He dug on, unseeing. Smoke poured into the bunker and people were crowding towards them, pushing against them, coughing and shoving and shouting.

A man said, "Get back! We're digging!"

A big chunk of wall fell away and Shmuel next to him, shouted, "Anglik! Go!"

Shmuel shoved Daniel through and he clambered up into the street. He collapsed on the ground and felt others trampling his legs to get out. He dragged himself free and wiped his eyes. Dozens were coming out of the hole in the ground. Gunshots. At the end of the street, there were Germans shooting at them. Three women were shot down. Daniel jumped to his feet and ran. He didn't look back. He ran onto the next street and saw it was Swietojerska. He knew a route through one house that would take you back to Walowa; he'd done it with Natan before. He ran to that house, hearing grenades exploding in the street behind him and he ran on and on, through holes dug in basement walls and burnt out corridors and back alleys.

By that time, the Germans had withdrawn from the ghetto and it was dark, lit only by the fires in neighbouring streets. He went via Franciszkanska and saw piles of cadavers there. He saw no one alive. He felt like the last man standing. He found their ex-base on

Walowa, intact and empty but no running water. He rested there. He didn't see any more of Shmuel or the others.

He had no food or water, no company and no plan. He missed his combat group. Their camaraderie, their closeness, their routine. He sat in the corner and remembered all the banter, the play-fighting, the card games, the battle talk, the teasing and the laughing. Dead, all dead now. His friend. His lover. His Dad. He thought of Magda thousands of miles across the sea, how she had told him not to go, this foolish plan, this madness. His one contact with Helena, a sweaty traitor. Gone. Dead or captured or in league with the enemy. Daniel was alone in the wreckage of Jewish Warsaw, no family, no companions. He cried, shook his head, wiped his snot and sobbed like a child.

A sound on the stairs. He jumped up and grabbed his gun, useless without bullets but he had nothing else. He aimed it at the doorway. A face appeared.

Pawel.

"I thought you were dead!" said Daniel.

"Everyone else is."

"I know, I know. I found them."

"I came after you. When you went off to Muranowska. I ran after you, but nearly got caught by a German unit, so I had to hide for hours. When I got back, the base was gone. I waited in a house, but nobody came."

"You came after me?"

"Yes. Lucky for me. If I hadn't, I'd be dead with our lads."

Pawel and Daniel looked at each other. They embraced,

slapped backs, shook hands and laughed, tears washed their mucky faces.

They talked and talked. As far as Pawel knew, they were the only two left from their combat group. He'd heard a fleeting report from a ZZW fighter that ZOB command were all killed that day, Anielewicz too. But it was not confirmed.

"And the ZZW command," said Pawel. "He said they all died in that bunker on Muranowska."

"I know. Nobody could survive that fire."

Pawel grimaced then placed a hand on Daniel's arm. "Marysia too. I asked him. Confirmed…dead."

Daniel nodded hurriedly. "I knew that," he said, almost cheerily, though he had no clue why. "I knew she must be dead."

"I'm sorry, Anglik."

May 8th, 1943. The day the leadership of the Jewish resistance lost their lives. The day Daniel lost the love of his life. The date would be branded in his memory forever.

Pawel explained that he'd spent the last couple of days trying to escape from the ghetto. He said he had family living in Aryan Warsaw and they were waiting for him, if only he could get out of the ghetto. He'd tried the sewers and got lost and almost didn't find his way back out again. He'd tried to get over the wall and under the wall, but was repelled by enemy fire each time. He'd come back to their old Walowa base in desperation, as Daniel had. It was good to find each other.

Daniel told him about his time in the bunker, about Moshe.

"He probably joined the Jewish Police in the past. He realised he'd nearly told you, when he was talking about the armbands. Once he let that slip, he'd be thrown out of the bunker. Maybe he shopped you, so you wouldn't tell anyone."

"But I don't care about that!"

"He didn't know that though."

Daniel held his head in his hands.

"Stupid, stupid, stupid."

"It's all stupid."

The next day, they ran out of food. There was no water. They went out and scouted for supplies. Daniel found oats in a barrel and they ate them all in handfuls. Pawel found water in a bucket, a dusty film floating on top, but it smelt all right. They drank and carried it back. That night, they discussed what to do next. Clearly, they had to leave the ghetto. Pawel explained more about the sewers.

"They're very narrow in places and we'd need a guide. We might be able to find someone, if we could make contact outside the ghetto. But there are no phones and the Germans are everywhere now."

So the sewers were out. Tunnels had been dug by the ZOB and ZZW, but the only ones they knew of had been destroyed. Staying in a bunker was not an option. Even if the Germans didn't find your bunker, didn't gas you or set you on fire, there was nothing left in the ghetto to live on.

After five days of food hunting and hiding from the enemy, they were filthy and starving. That morning, a bunker down the street had been attacked. A grenade was lobbed and killed three Germans. The enemy didn't find Daniel and Pawel, but they were too scared to go out all day. Another day passed without food. They sat taking sips of fetid water, weak and out of ideas.

The sound of booming came. Very far away. Then it came closer and closer, louder and louder.

They both knew that sound. They had both lived through blitzes. Planes were bombing the city.

"The Germans are going to kill us all!" cried Daniel.

"No, it's the Russians. The Russians are bombing Warsaw!"

"Are they invading?"

"Just an air raid, I think. But they must be close."

A deafening bang. The house rocked and they fell over. They both stood up and Pawel said, "Still alive!"

They rushed to the window, as if they expected to see the Red Army marching down Walowa. They didn't see that. But what they did see was a bloody miracle. The Russian bomb had knocked a gaping hole in the wall at the end of their street. They could look clean through to the Aryan side.

Without a word, they scrambled down the stairs and out into the street, ran headlong for that gap in the wall and into Aryan Warsaw. As they rushed through, Daniel saw two Poles come out of a doorway and point at them.

"Here come the cats!" one shouted. "Miaow, miaow!"

They ran on, down the next street and the next and the next. They didn't stop running until five minutes later, when Pawel grabbed him and said, "Where are we going?"

"I don't know!" he laughed, but then it hit them. Two grubby, smelly Jews running through the streets of Aryan Warsaw after curfew. It was incredible they hadn't been stopped already. "I have an empty flat we can go to, or least I used to. It's near the river."

They looked around them and found their bearings.

"That's miles away," said Pawel. "Let's go to my cousin's. It's only a few streets from here."

So they went on, more circumspect, until they reached a block of flats near a church. It was the early hours of the morning. They had to be quiet, but also get inside quickly. Pawel rang his cousin's bell. He started singing.

Daniel grabbed him and said, "What are you doing?" But he pushed him away and carried on, singing like a drunken lout in Polish about a woman he loved once and how she was a whore and broke his heart.

"Shut your mouth!" someone shouted from a window. The door opened. A young man stood there grinning, took hold of Pawel by the scruff and yanked him in.

"He's with me," said Pawel and Daniel was told to follow. They went up the stairs and into a small flat. There were two other men there. They all flung their arms around each other, laughing and crying. They all had the same look, the same way of smiling. Family.

"This is my comrade, Anglik," said Pawel. "We were the only two survivors from our group."

The cousin who'd let them in slapped Daniel's shoulder.

"You are brave bastards, both of you!" he said. "But you also stink like pigs. Get into that bathroom now!"

It was joyous to wash. They both stripped naked and scrubbed themselves with soap and hot water, shaved and dried with clean towels. They were human again. Clean clothes, food and drink on the table. A simple meal of pancakes stuffed with the sweetest jam Daniel had ever tasted. To wash it down, tall glasses of water followed by *bimber*. The best meal.

They stayed up all night. The men were all Pawel's cousins, three brothers who were living there together. The one who let them in was called Marek, a courier who'd been living in the flat for two years, ghetto smuggling as Daniel had. The others, Henryk and Fredek, had been fighting in different ZOB combat groups and escaped the ghetto through a tunnel a week before. They spun yarns of war, spat on their enemies and drank to fallen comrades.

Daniel was free. He had survived. He thanked the Russians, for bombing his street. He thanked Pawel, for taking him to that safe house.

He had no one else to thank.

Daniel slept in. The others were up and about. He listened through half-sleep. The doorbell rang and he dreamt of Marysia touching his arm, tugging at his Star of David armband, saying wake up, wake up, Daniel, wake up, my love. He sat up and found he was crying. He heard people come into the flat in the next room, laughing, genial. He listened to them. Two visitors, a man and a woman. Her voice was high, musical. They were talking about family. About leaving Warsaw. They had a plan. Something about going to Hungary, family there.

Daniel had no family there or anywhere. Yes, he had survived the revolt in the Warsaw ghetto. But what did that matter, when you had no one to live for? He had gone to sleep the night before in the company of comrades. He had woken to find it was an illusion. Family was what counts. A man in a bunker had met his mother once, maybe. A photographer met her once too, twenty years ago. And there it ended. The shortest of trails, inches long, going nowhere.

He wiped his face and went through. There were brief introductions. The couple was related to Pawel, the husband another cousin. They shook hands with him, gracious and gentle, glad he survived, thanking him for helping Pawel. Daniel was offered tea and toast, and he sat on a low window ledge, looking down at the Aryan street as he chewed and sipped. He listened to the family at the table. Pawel was saying to his cousins they had to move within days. They had to plan a route.

Daniel thought, everyone is moving on. Jewish Warsaw was like water in cupped hands, spilt into the sea. The Underground stank of betrayal. London felt like failure. Even the thought of seeing dear Magda again depressed him. She had talked of Polish honour, yet he heard those grinning fools at the hole in the ghetto wall – "Here come the cats! Miaow, miaow!" He felt he reserved a modicum of hate for Magda, for being patriotic about Poland. How awful it was to hate, to have no one left to love.

A touch on his shoulder. The woman smiled at him. She had a nice face.

"Are you all right?" she asked.

"Of course!" he pretended. "Just very tired."

She sat down on the floor and crossed her legs. She looked comfortable. Long, fawn hair twined in a thick plait over her shoulder, greying at the crown.

"They call you Anglik. Why is that?"

"Can't you hear it in my accent?"

"Hear what?"

Still proud his Polish passed with a native. "I come from England. I came to find my mother."

The woman listened intently as he told her his story. It was gratifying to tell it again. It had been so long and he had a rapt audience. Passion for his quest in chorus with the tenor of his failure. When he finished, the woman sat frowning, leaning forward, mouth open. She looked astonished.

"What is it?" he asked.

"Helena. You are sure your mother's name is Helena."

"Yes," he said and fumbled in his pocket for his mother's photograph. It wasn't there, but he recalled he'd put it in his shoe for safe-keeping, in the other room. He rushed to get it. The men were busy with maps at the table. The woman followed him into the bedroom.

"You see. This is my mother. When she was a girl. It has her name written on the back by the photographer. *Helena*."

The woman took the photo and her hand leapt to her mouth.

"This is Helena," she whispered.

"Yes."

"I know this woman. She was my best friend."

His hand was raised in mid-air, where she'd taken the photo. His mouth was dry.

"She was? She *was* your best friend?"

"Yes! Yes, she still is. At least, she was when I last saw her. Just a couple of weeks ago. She was here, in Warsaw. With her daughter."

"Her daughter? Yes. A daughter."

Tears were running down his face. The woman reached out, brushed them away.

"It's all right. It's all right now."

He looked at her kind face. His mother's best friend.

"What's your name again?" he asked her.

"Vladka. What's your real name?"

"Daniel. That's what my father called me. My English father. He adopted me when I was a baby. I don't know what Helena called me. I don't know if she even gave me a name."

"I'm sure she did. Listen, I can tell you a lot about her. But where she is right now, I don't know. I'm sorry, but I just don't know."

"Please, tell me everything."

"I've known Helena for years. We were friends long before the war. She is a seamstress. She married a tailor called Isak and they set up their own business. They had their daughter, Ilsa. She's about eight now. They did make armbands in the ghetto. Isak was killed there. Helena and Ilsa were in a workshop for a while. I arranged a safe-house for them in Aryan Warsaw. Then we helped them leave the city, to go to her old home, the place she was born. It's a town in eastern Poland called Novogrodek."

"I know that name. I read about that place. In a leaflet, a Resistance leaflet I delivered all over the ghetto."

"I read that leaflet! Helena knew about it too. She had a plan, to look for her family. Her parents and also a brother. Your leaflet said the Bielskis were leading a group of Jewish partisans out there. If Helena couldn't find her family, her next step was to look for those fighters, because her brother might well be one of them. He was a bit of a wild one, apparently."

A wild uncle! And grandparents.

"Now, she said his name once, her brother. Oh, what was it?"

Remember, remember, he wanted to shout, as she bit her lip and thought back. Somebody's brother, from long ago, a passing name. But it was crucial to him.

"Jakub. That's it. Jakub. You have an Uncle Jakub."

"Uncle Jakub," he said.

They both laughed.

That leaflet Natan and he had packed into their bags, carried in and out of apartment buildings, shops, hospitals, cafés and bars, bringing the news of Jewish Resistance in Poland to the downtrodden Jews of Warsaw. To know it had found the right hands - of his mother's best friend, who shared it with Helena, helped her escape and set her on the road to the woods, to find her family - was wonderful. Daniel had helped his mother to escape. All those years since London, searching, hoping and doubting, had finally come good now.

"The last time I saw her she was on a train heading east. I haven't heard from her since. But don't worry about that. It's almost impossible to keep in touch with Jews in hiding. We've moved several times since then. Even if she sent a card, it may have been lost. There's every chance she's still alive."

"Do you really think so?"

"I think there's as much chance as if she'd stayed here. Maybe more. She probably has a better chance where she was going. If you go there, you might find her. Who knows?"

This was his next step. This was his plan. Novogrodek.

"Thank you for helping her. Without you, she might be..."

"Oh, nonsense. She's a strong woman, your mother. A survivor. Like you."

They hugged again.

Vladka's husband came in.

"What's going on in here?" he said cheerfully.

"A miracle!" said Vladka.

They went next door and told their story.

They celebrated the news with *bimber*. They asked Daniel a thousand questions and he talked himself hoarse, about Dad and Magda and the orphanage and the Blitz. They drank to his mother, and how good it was, knowing it was real this time, that she was a real person with a real history and a real future.

What he wanted most was to sit alone with Vladka and hear everything. His mother's character, her past, her voice, her expressions, her mannerisms, her sayings, her jokes, her sadness, her way with Ilsa, her *essence*. He wanted it put in a bottle and given to him.

"You have her eyes," said Vladka.

"I know," he said. "The photo."

It was on the table. She picked it up.

"I miss my friend."

"Tell me more about her."

"It'll all come out in a tumble. I don't know where to start."

"How did you meet?"

"I used to walk past her shop. There were always the most beautiful dresses in the window, with incredibly fine stitching on them, in intricate designs, many colours, extraordinary details, like leaves, flowers, acorns and butterflies and bees, and even a tiny wood mouse on one, I remember! I went in one day and there she was, behind the counter, pins in her mouth. I asked her, did you make those dresses? She said yes, which one was I interested in? I had to tell her I couldn't buy anything, because I was a penniless portrait painter. I said I only wanted to congratulate her. She said, what for? I told her, those dresses were strange and lovely. I knew artists who fancied themselves as great masters, and none of them had her eye for colour and design. She just smiled at me. This Mona Lisa smile. She leant beneath the desk and brought out a dress, folded up. She shook it out. A shimmering green silk dress with two little frogs on the collar. Nobody will buy it, she said. It's too strange for them, I suppose. And she gave it to me. For nothing. After that, all her unsold dresses she would give to me. She never told Isak!"

"What was he like?"

"A nice man. A good man. Quite a bit older than her. He was a bachelor, in need of a good wife. She needed him, too."

"Why?"

"I think she had a difficult time. When she was younger. I don't know a lot about her past, before she came to Warsaw. She never really talked about it. I only know that she had no contact with her family. She seemed a bit ashamed about it, as if there was bad blood. It makes more sense now, meeting you."

"The photographer told me she was with an older man. Could that have been Isak?"

"No, I don't think so. They met later, through work. Your photograph shows her as a very young girl, almost a child. That must have been at least ten years before she met Isak. I don't know who that man with her might be. Do you think he was your father?"

"Maybe. The photographer said he was a poet. I was a trainee journalist in London. Both writers."

"Ah, but Helena is a writer too. She told me she wrote poems when she was a girl. And she kept a diary in the ghetto. I never read it, but I saw it. Very detailed, tiny words, very neat, covering hundreds of pages. I should think you get your writing talent from her."

"What was she like, to talk to?"

"She didn't say much. But she was a great listener. And when she did speak, she never rambled, unlike me. She was always concise and careful. She watched people. Noticed everything."

Like me, like me, thought Daniel. We are alike, my mother and I.

"Was she a…lonely person?"

Vladka considered this. She looked carefully at Daniel.

"Yes. I never thought of it before. But yes. You're right. She didn't have many friends. She didn't find it easy to make friends. But she was confident about her business. She'd go all over the city to talk with business contacts and make deals and buy and sell things. But that was a front. She was shy when it came to friendships. It took her a long time to be really comfortable with me. I know she loved Isak. And she would die for Ilsa, in the blink of an eye. They needed her so. But I felt she was alone inside, deep down in there was Helena, alone."

Like me, like me.

"Ilsa was the same, but only after the ghetto. She was a sweet baby, always smiling and gurgling. She walked very early, and was into everything, very curious and chatty. But the ghetto changed her. Such sad, serious eyes she had when I last saw her. I hope the forests have made her smile again."

"I must go and look for them," said Daniel. "I have to go as soon as possible."

He stood up, put Helena's photo in his pocket, as if he were to leave immediately.

"Yes, yes, you must. Let's talk with Samuel about it. Let's think it through and make a plan."

Daniel, Vladka, her husband and his cousins sat with a map of Poland spread out before them on the table, amid landmarks of bread rolls and cheese crumbs. They knew about trains, they had contacts with travel permits. They would get him there. But he needed money.

"I'll go back to my old flat. I have a few things hidden there. Some cash and other things."

"It's not safe on the streets," said Marek. "The Germans are still Jew-hunting for people who got out of the ghetto. I wouldn't want Pawel out there, or Henryk or Fredek. I don't think it's safe for you."

"I could go," said Vladka.

"No," said Daniel. "You've done enough. All of you. I'll go. I need to buy new clothes too. Everything was lost in the ghetto. Can I borrow a bag?"

He wouldn't let them risk themselves for him. He had a plan now. He was fearless.

When Daniel arrived at the flat, he found the key he had secreted under the landing doormat all that time ago and let himself in.

Someone jumped him and they fell to the ground, struggled, looked at each other. It was Jerzy.

"Anglik," he said and stood up, straightened his tie.

"What are you doing here?"

"I live here now. We assumed you were dead."

Daniel pushed past him to the bathroom. He pulled up the floorboard and retrieved his property - money, papers, Magda's ring, the pristine picture of Helena – and shoved them into his bag. He heard Jerzy follow and watch him.

"If I'd known that cash was there, I'd have had it myself."

"I bet you would, you bastard."

"Listen, Anglik. We used to be comrades. It's a shame about the ghetto, but orders were clear from Home Army command. We could not risk starting a Warsaw revolt. It was the wrong time. We were not fully prepared and an early uprising would have been disastrous. You can see that, can't you? The time will come for Warsaw to fight. And you will be there to fight with us, my friend."

Daniel wanted to hit him. A shame about the ghetto? He wanted to yank him down there, show him the acres of dead, fighters against the Nazis, like him, like his organisation, yet not like him, not like his organisation. They were only Jews.

But he didn't. He had a new direction now. Jerzy was his past. To hell with him. He was about to leave without a word, but he had a sudden thought. Jerzy could be useful.

"We are still friends then," Daniel said.

"Of course. Do you want to work with us again? A fighter with your battle experience would be very useful."

Daniel had no intention of lifting a finger for the Polish Underground. But he ought to sound willing.

"Yes, absolutely. But first I need your help. A friend of mine wants to join partisans in eastern Poland. He needs information about a group in the forests out there. They're called the Bielski brothers. Do you know anything about them?"

He knew Jerzy always had his ear to the ground.

"Yes, I have heard of them. Polish fighters came to Warsaw from that region a few months ago. They reported to the Underground about these partisans, the Bielskis. A leaflet was written about it."

"Yes, I've seen it. Do you know those Polish fighters? Are they still here?"

"You seem very interested in helping this friend of yours. Who is he, another Jew?"

"Yes. A comrade from our battle days. I owe him my life."

"Ah, a debt of honour. That must be paid."

Jerzy always was a pompous ass. "Yes, I know one of them. He's still here in Warsaw, working with us now. Would you like to meet him? I can probably bring him here tomorrow."

They made the arrangement. Daniel assured Jerzy that he would soon be free to work for the Underground again. He supposed that being alive and knowing what he did, he was a kind of threat to Jerzy and his lot. If he wasn't with them, he was against them. He'd string him along until he got out of that place once and for all.

The next day, Jerzy was there, true to his word, with the fighter who knew the Bielskis. He was a wiry little man with dirty nails yet dressed in a smart suit. He looked like a soldier turned bureaucrat. Whatever he was, his information was priceless.

"Yes, yes. I know of the Bielskis. Good fighters all. Doing a good job down there. I have a contact near Novogrodek who operates a halfway house. A farming man, not a Jew, but helps their kind. Anyone wanting to find the Bielski group goes through him. Want his name and address?"

Though he looked like a rat, Daniel could have kissed him. The name of the man who ran the halfway house was Krzysztof Kossakowski. There were directions from Novogrodek to his house, which he had to remember then screw up. Before he went, he promised Jerzy he'd meet him at the old HQ the following day for new duties. It would be a lonely meeting, as Daniel would not be there. He would be on the eastbound train.

That evening, he celebrated with Pawel and his cousins, as well as Vladka and Samuel, who came to say goodbye. They were all tearful.

Pawel took him aside at one point and said, "I'm sorry about what I said that night. When I told you to shut up about your mother. I'm sorry for that."

"It doesn't matter. I owe you. I don't know what I can do to repay you."

Pawel gave him a brief hug and slapped his back.

"Live. That's your duty now."

He and Vladka talked till curfew, of Helena, Helena, only Helena. He didn't want Vladka to leave that night. Pawel's family would leave soon for Hungary, he would leave tomorrow for Novogrodek. Would they ever see each other again?

"What if I never find her? You're the only person I know who knew her."

"I know. We won't lose each other."

"But how?"

"Write down your English address for me. And Magda's last name. If we live through this mess and the war ever ends, I will write to you there. Maybe I'll come to England one day. I've always wanted to paint the London fog, as Monet did!"

They smiled. It seemed a childish hope. He wrote down his London address for Vladka. The last time he'd done this, it was for Marysia.

"I loved a girl in the ghetto. Another fighter. She died."

Vladka put her hand on his shoulder. "I'm sorry, Daniel. She abides, in you, in your memories of her. You'll never forget."

"That's true," said Daniel, quietly. There was a fragment of comfort in that.

Vladka said, "Find your mother. Tell her Vladka loves her. And loves her brave son."

He would leave Warsaw in the morning. He'd been there for almost two years. He'd worked for the Polish Underground. He'd fought with the Jewish Resistance. He'd killed men. He'd loved a woman. He'd left her body behind in the ashes of the ghetto. He was glad to leave Warsaw.

He had been making the jigsaw of his life, with pieces hidden all over the house, under carpets, in attic boxes and dark cellar corners. He had not finished it yet, but the picture was there. He was beginning to see himself.

CHAPTER TEN

It is all my fault.

The journey was easy. It passed smoothly, with no incident. We didn't even bother to stop off to see Stefan's contacts. We were not even asked for our papers until we reached Grodno. Even then, the policeman who checked us was Lithuanian and hardly looked at us. From Grodno, there were only two buses a day to Novogrodek, and we saw a rowdy group of Ukranians getting on and making a lot of noise. I decided we should walk to Novogrodek. It would take a day, I guessed, but I was sure it was safer than being in the small space of a bus, inviting scrutiny. You cannot hide on a bus like you can on a busy train. So, we set off, with Stefan's map of the country to help us and my own vague memories of the area. We still had food and drink in our pack to keep us going. But the road was long and we got lost several times on the first day. We had to stop in a village and ask the way, tempting suspicion. That first night, we slept in a wood near another village, very cold. I gave all my warm clothes to Ilsa. She has been so good, so stoic. We haven't talked on the way. She is still quiet. She still trusts me. But I got lost again the next day, and went miles out of our way and had to sleep outside again, far from anywhere. In the end, it took us five days to reach the outskirts of Novogrodek, with no food and little water left, and both exhausted. Every decision I had made was wrong. Then, it happened.

We were only a few miles from the town, coming in on a rural road with hardly any traffic. I had decided we should go into the town and find somewhere to stay. Once we had rested and bought food, we could set about planning our next move. My little girl was very tired and hungry, and I knew I had to attend to that before any idea of finding partisans. The town was close. Ilsa said, "I can smell bread baking, Mama." We heard the drone of a motorcycle come up behind us. I do not know what possessed me, but I glanced around. My eyes were met by the cold gaze of a German soldier riding up behind us. His head turned as he passed. He stared at me. Why I looked round at him, I will never know. I had told Ilsa not to look at traffic, not to ask for others to look back at us, to notice us. Immediately, I told Ilsa we had to get off the road. We were surrounded by forest. We ran into the trees and walked for a minute, until I was sure we could not be seen from the road. We sat down and waited for a while.

The sound of the motorbike returned and stopped. I heard boots walking on leaves and twigs, breaking them underfoot. The sound ebbed then came back. He was looking for us. I caught sight of him through the trees. His uniform told me he was a Nazi officer. He still wore his motorcycle goggles and helmet, like a mask. He was scanning the surroundings. I made a gesture to Ilsa to remain absolutely still and silent. The Nazi came in our direction. He kicked about in the undergrowth like a bored child. He removed his goggles and helmet. I saw his face, young and fresh, but I was sure I could not trust that face to do anything but murder. He spoke in German.

"Are you there?" He said it gently. "Are you there, little mother? Are you hungry? I have good food here for you. Sausage, cheese, fruit and wine. Don't you want some, little mother? Little girl, aren't you hungry for cheese and meat?"

His voice was that of a boy who thinks he is a man. He took out the sausage and ate. He was very close to us then and Ilsa cannot bear the smell of meat that near and not be able to eat it. She looked at me, her eyes begging, and she made a noise. She whimpered. My poor girl was hungry, she could not help herself. The Nazi whipped round and spotted us straight away. He pulled out his pistol and pointed it at my head. I held on to Ilsa tightly, I was crushing her into my bones. I was about to say, "Take me. Shoot me. Let her go." But he lowered his gun. He put it away. He stood there and smiled at us.

"You want meat, little girl?" He held it out. Ilsa looked at me, eyes wide with hunger. She did not understand his German, but she knew what his gesture meant. I could not deny her. I nodded for her to take it. I had some too. It tasted marvellous. We ate in silence as he watched. He gave us cheese and we ate that too. He offered me wine from a bottle. I declined in polite German. He looked surprised.

"Your German is excellent. Where did you learn it?" I said my father taught me, when I was a child.

"Was he a clever man, your father? A learned man?" I said he was. I didn't know where this conversation was going. I was just glad that we had eaten and that we had not been shot yet. He sat down opposite us and gave us two apples. Ilsa ate ravenously, I put mine in my pocket for later. I had to concentrate on this threat. I had noticed that the man was looking very closely at me. It seemed he was trying to judge my origins. But there was something else there too.

"Where are you from and where are you going, little mother?" he said, swigging his wine.

I gave my story, that we had come to the area from Warsaw to visit my cousins in Novogrodek. I gave the name of my old headmistress, Wyszynski, thinking she would be dead now but her family name sounded authentically Polish. The German smiled as I told him this. I got out our ID and showed him. He smiled as he looked them over.

"Very good, very good," he said, still smiling. He asked me about life in Warsaw. What was it like there, were the theatres good, the art galleries, the libraries? I told him what I could remember of the pre-war city. He listened intently and seemed to enjoy my account. I could not decide if he was testing me or genuinely interested. Then he said something surprising.

"I am envious of you." I looked away. I was unsure what this man was about. "I am stuck out here in the wilderness and here you are, all the way from the big city. I wish I'd been stationed there instead. I've always wanted to travel. I come from a place very like this in Germany, with pine forests, endless pine forests. I wanted to see the world. And here I am, back in the forests."

I did not know what to say to this. Ilsa sat beside me, very quiet. She had finished her food and was listening. I wondered what she was thinking.

He went on, "Stuck out here, dealing with these infernal partisans and those wretched Jews in the ghetto." He looked at me carefully, gauging my reaction. I did not know whether to speak or not. He went on, "Are you surprised there are Jews left? Are there any left in Warsaw?" I thought about the typical Polish reaction, that is, the one he would expect from an Aryan Pole.

"Not many, thank heavens," I said and smiled. He smiled back at me, in fact, he had had a half-smile on his face all the time we had been talking.

"Yes, of course. You Poles hate the Jews too. Well, those in the ghetto here won't last long, I shouldn't think. You won't be bothered by them, anyhow." I did not know what to say to this. Had I been too obvious? What did he want?

My questions were answered.

He turned to Ilsa and said, "Little girl, go away for a walk in the woods. Don't come back for a while. Does she understand German?" Ilsa looked at me, frightened.

"She doesn't understand. Please, we must be getting on our way. Thank you for the food. It was very kind of you. But we really must be getting on our way. Our family is waiting."

He stood up and took off his jacket. He did not look at us but said, "Tell your daughter to make herself scarce for half an hour or so."

Ilsa said, "Mama, what is he doing? What is he doing?" I held her to me and shushed her. I could not explain this one to her.

"Please, sir," I begged him now. "Please, I am a mother, this is my child. I have tried to protect her from growing up in a war that is beyond her understanding. She is innocent. You and I, we understand war, the extremes people are pushed to, but she does not. You were a child once, your mother sought to protect you from harm..." He had listened to this whilst unbuttoning his trousers, but stopped and turned on me.

He shouted, "Shut up about my mother!" I did not know why he said this, but I pushed further.

"What would she say if she saw you now?" His face was full of anger. I thought he would strike me. But he just stood there, seething. He did up his trousers. He spat at me, actually spat at me, but it missed and fell into the forest floor. Ilsa began to cry. I stroked her head.

"A bad man," she kept saying over and over into my chest. "A bad man. A bad man."

The German watched us. "What's she saying?" he said, furious.

"She says you are a bad man," I answered and looked him straight in the eye.

He pulled on his jacket and stomped about, packing up his bag. When he was ready, he turned to us and stood up straight, a military pose. He spoke formally.

"I know you are Jews. You are illegal people. I could shoot you right here and now. But I will not. I will do the correct thing and hand you in to the authorities." I felt I still had cards left to play.

"That is not true, sir. We are not Jews. You have seen our identity documents." He had been standing to attention, body rigid, face blank. He dropped his bag and put his hands to his head.

"Oh, why don't you just die? Why don't you all just die? Then it'll be over. Then we can get out of this fucking place. Why do you still run around like rats on the *Titanic*? You are not as stupid as rats. You must know you are all doomed. You're not going to survive, you are not going to live through this. You don't have a future, you will never be a little grey-haired old Jewess dying in her bed, don't you understand? Just give up, will you? Just die now. Then, it will be over. Don't you see?"

"I don't know what you mean, sir," I tried, but this annoyed him more and he dropped to the floor, his head in his hands.

Ilsa whispered, "What's wrong with him?"

He looked up, angry again. "What's she saying now?"

I told Ilsa to sit down by a tree a few feet away. She shook her head violently but I made her go. I needed to concentrate on this man. I had to manipulate this crazy person into letting us go. It would take every clever twist I knew.

"She's just a child. She doesn't understand." I sat down on the ground, not too near to be presumptuous. But close enough to talk more intimately. "She does not know what we know, about the adult world. How difficult it is, the decisions we have to make, the choices forced upon us." He was listening. I waited to see if my direction was working. Then he surprised me again.

"Do you like books?" he said. I answered yes. "What do you read?" I said not much lately, due to the shortages in Warsaw. "When you were a child, a younger woman. What did you love to read?" His face was different. He looked like a boy again. I said when I was young girl, I read Mickiewicz, the great Polish poet. I read German literature too, Goethe, Schiller. "Are you lying?" he asked. "Just to flatter me? Did you really read German literature?" It was actually true. Jan's favourite poet was Mickiewicz, that's why he'd come to Novogrodek, to visit Mickiewicz's birthplace. Of course, we all read him because we ran down the road next to the great wall of his estate every day after school. It was my father who introduced me to German literature.

"No, it's true. I had a great love for Goethe," I said. His face lit up.

"Me too! I have books back at the barracks. The other officers, they tease me about it. Say I should have stayed in a cosy library back home. To be honest, that's what I'd have preferred. I was never an outdoors sort of person. But I did want to travel, to see places. Cities, I love cities. Coffee houses and restaurants. Erudite conversation over fine wines or hot chocolate with cream. The lights glowing in the streets as night falls." He looked around him. "I hate the countryside. I hate country people. Oh God, what am I doing here?" His head in his hands again, I had an urge to run. To grab Ilsa and run. Would he chase us, would he shoot us? I stood up, very slowly. He raised his head and looked at me, his face extraordinary, no trace of the soldier, the German, the rapist. Just a boy. This was the time.

"Let us go," I said. He said nothing. He was thinking about it. I should have left it there. But I was on a roll. I said, "We won't tell anyone." His face fell. I knew it was a huge error. His face twisted.

"Damn right, you won't tell anyone. There's nothing to tell. Get up!" He pointed at Ilsa, fumbled around for his pistol. "I'm taking you in. Get away, in front of me. Walk to the road. Hurry. You're going in. Hurry up."

After that, we went back to the road and walked in front of him while he rode his bike slowly behind us. The road curved into a long hill and we puffed as we strode up it. I cursed myself. Before long, we heard the sound of a truck behind us, its engine whining as it struggled up the hill. The German must have flagged it down, as it slowed to pull in. We looked to see a truck heaving with soldiers. Before it came to a stop, our German stepped towards us and spoke very quickly, staring into the road as he did so.

"Listen, you'll be put in the ghetto. The girl will be killed because she's too young. You must say she's twelve. Say she's malnourished and that's why she's so small. Say she's twelve and has a skill. It might save her." He stood back and assumed his position of German officer. A soldier alighted from the truck and saluted him. Orders passed quickly between them, but I couldn't hear what they were. Our German looked past us and told us to get on the truck. It was too high to climb up. Two soldiers were motioning for me to pass Ilsa up, but I wouldn't do it. They pulled me up first and I pulled up Ilsa. The German soldiers weren't too bad. I think they were slightly embarrassed by the situation. They were all young and smoking. They bunched up together to give us room in the corner. I said thank you to them and turned away, holding Ilsa in front of me and looking out into the road. When we drove on, our German was fiddling with his helmet and goggles, but he looked up at us when we were about to turn a corner. Who knows what he was thinking.

The truck ride was short, just a couple of miles. The soldiers ignored us mostly. Just another pair of illegal stragglers. One of them said, "The wandering Jew," and a few laughed. But that was all. As familiar sights bumped into view, all I could think about was what our German had said: *the girl will be killed.* He said to claim she was twelve and that she had a skill. They might ask what year she was born. I made sure I knew it without thinking: 1931. As for a skill, we were lucky. She was a fine little seamstress and she would be able to prove it easily. *It might save her,* he had said. *Might.* Before long, the truck pulled up in the town and we were told to get out. This time we had no help and I had to jump down. My knees jarred and I turned back to catch Ilsa. She jumped without hesitation. She knew I would catch her. I did not have the same confidence in myself. Again, I had messed it up for us. Now we were in the direst situation.

A soldier was assigned to take us to the ghetto. First he took away my bag and we were led into an administrative building. There was an office, outside which we waited for a long time. When we finally went in, a Nazi official was sitting at a huge desk. He had lots of paperwork and looked tired. He did not speak to us for several minutes, while we stood there, staring at him, waiting to know if we were to live or die. He held up our identification documents.

"These papers of you?" he said in poor Polish. I wondered whether I should tell him I spoke German, but thought he might take it as a slur. I nodded. He took a quick flick through. He did not look at us at all. "These fake," he concluded. "You have skills? Mother?" He looked up at me. I told him I was a professional seamstress, and that my daughter was my assistant. He looked Ilsa up and down. "Assistant?" he said. I explained that she was an expert in fine embroidery, having such delicate fingers for a twelve year old. "Twelve?" he questioned, squinting at her.

"Yes," was all I said. I decided the fewer words the better.

"All right. You two go to ghetto and be useful. And this?" He moved papers on his desk and revealed my diary. He opened it and took a brief glance through. I could tell he did not want to reveal that his Polish was not good enough to read it.

"It is a novel. A love story," I said.

The official laughed. "A novel? You won't finish!"

This idea again, that the Jews are doomed. *Why don't you all just die?* our German had said. So, it is true. The Germans want to wipe us away, like a grubby smear.

"I love to write," was all I could think to say. The official looked at me quite seriously. He passed me my diary.

"Take it. Write fast."

He motioned for us to get out. He did not give me our papers. The soldier returned my bag. The clothes were still there, but later I saw all our money was gone. I thought, we will never leave this place.

So here we are. Captured and locked up in another ghetto, rife with disease. Once again I wear the Star of David. The other Jews here say this ghetto will not last long. Perhaps a month, or even a few days. I have not been able to write until tonight, as today was the first day we have been put in this hut to work as seamstresses. Before that, we were in a kind of prison: a tiny shed with no food and only a bowl of rancid water in the corner to drink. I held Ilsa and sang to her for two days, sang and sang every lullaby and folk tune and fragment of verse I could remember. I was sure we were going to die there. I wanted her to hear music in her ears when they took us out to be shot. But they did not. We were brought here, and given materials to work on. We worked all day today and our fingers ache. Ilsa is asleep. I thank the stars my mother taught me to sew and that I taught my daughter. If I had been a poet like my beloved Jan, I would have been dead long ago. A pointless profession in time of war. When I was a girl, my mother knew that being a seamstress was not a valued profession. Educated and intelligent women would not become seamstresses. Yet she always took pride in her work and taught me to do the same. Now I know that her skills have saved my life twice. But how long will I be sewing for my life? Even useful Jews will be thrown in the pits.

Was it worth it? The long journey from Warsaw, the exhaustion, the dangers? Yes, I think so. For those few days, riding the trains and walking those roads, we were free again. My daughter could breathe the air of my youth, the fresh pine forest air, not that putrid air of the Warsaw ghetto thick with sickness, or the charged air of Aryan streets alive with threat. It has cleansed us, to be here. On the way into Novogrodek, my eyes took in the scenes of my childhood. There was a bend in the road to the centre of town that I remember clearly, walking along it with my brother, going to the library, as we did often. I would go to read books, but Jakub would go to meet girls. He was only a child, but he had his first girlfriend at seven years old, I remember. What a character! I hope he is chatting away to a pretty female partisan right now. I hope he is not dead in a ditch.

But we are not dead yet. I have kept us alive at least. Ilsa even smiled today, when she finished a row of stitches she was particularly pleased with. She does not understand despair. But she knows we are in a bad situation, that her Mama could not fix this one. I do my best, I do my best. But it is not good enough. I have not protected my child. We are captive again. I used to think of ways out, of the next move, of being safe for this night and of hope for a new chance tomorrow. Tonight, I cannot do that. There is no way out of this place. We are waiting for our deaths, that is all.

Tonight, I could sleep instead of writing. Heaven knows I need the rest. But I don't know if I will die tomorrow. I have to keep telling, until they kill me.

I have news of my family. I met a man who knew them before the war. He remembers me as a little girl, but did not recognise me. He is a tinsmith who was selected to survive because of his skills. He is sharing the sleeping quarters we have here, that is, a filthy room stuffed full with twenty Jews and a million lice. This man, Yitzhak, came to me this evening and said that most nights I have been talking in my sleep. It appears that I mostly murmur names: Goldman, I have said, Goldman, Goldman. Yitzhak said that one time I called out Jakub. Yitzhak put Jakub and Goldman together and recognised my brother's name. He knew my brother quite well, as apparently Jakub thought about training to be a tinsmith in his twenties and spent time with Yitzhak observing. Yet, typical Jakub, he changed his mind and wanted to be a lumberjack. It was good to hear about Jakub grown up. He must be thirty-six now, three years my junior. However old we become, he will always be younger than me, always my little brother. Anyway, Yitzhak told me about what happened in Novogrodek after the Germans invaded.

He said the Germans entered the town in June of 1941 and brutality towards Jews began within days, helped by local Polish and Byelorussian thugs. In December, there was a massacre. Novogrodek Jews were loaded onto trucks and taken to pits near Skridlevo. They were ordered to undress, run to the pits and line up at the edge. They were shot with machine guns and fell in. A few escaped by pretending to be dead. At least one woman ran back to Novogrodek and passed on what she had witnessed. It is said that before the shootings began, Jews tried to resist and attack the Germans, whilst others attempted to escape and were shot. Yitzhak said my parents were killed in this first massacre, as well as Jakub's wife and child, a boy. He has it on good authority. They were seen climbing on board the trucks with Jakub and none of them came back. However, a local man who also escaped from the pits by feigning death as the woman did, went into the countryside and told his story to others, who brought it back to the town. This man has gone on to become a partisan. He mentioned other men who did the same as him. My brother's name was among them. Yitzhak says that all of this is hearsay. But he also says, why should the witnesses lie? He says we Jews are not in the business of propaganda, like the Germans. But I know how a whispered lie becomes a fact. I heard it in the ghetto a hundred times. Yet the idea of Jakub escaping to the forest fills me with joy. Even if he is dead by now, captured or killed in partisan action, at least he tasted freedom for a while. And it is just like him, or at least just like the boy I remember, to have been wily enough to sneak out of his own funeral. Good luck to you, my brother.

Yitzhak is a nice man, very tall and slender, with a drawn, sad face. A few years older than me, like Isak. He told me about my parents' death with a kind manner, patting my arm with his long, flat hand, awkward yet tender. Once we had talked of Jakub, he had more darkness to share with me. After that first massacre, the ghetto was established and then there was another massacre. Since then, the ghetto has dwindled further and there are only a few of us Jews left, just as our German told us. Yitzhak told me that Ilsa and I were very lucky to have been allowed in at all. The Germans have been busy trying to empty the ghetto, reducing the skeleton crew here further and further, until only this handful of craftsmen have survived. He said, "After the elderly, women and children were the first to go. I wonder why they let you in." He looked curious, as if I had done something special. Perhaps he had more worldly thoughts on his mind.

I told him, "Maybe the official who sent us here liked my face. Maybe he was feeling generous that day. Maybe he is a madman and thought I was the ghost of his mother. Who can tell?" What I was trying to explain to Yitzhak was the random luck that guides our lives in this war. One day you are saved, the next you are denounced. One German lets you go, another shoots your child in the head. If we try to look for patterns, it will drive us crazy. There is no pattern. There is no providence or power of prayer. It is all meaningless.

Here, the ghetto is as bad as it was in the worst days of Warsaw. There is little food. People are dying of starvation. Every morning corpses are taken to be buried. I have only been here for five days and already four people have died in this room alone. I do not know how long I can survive on the tiny amounts of food I give myself, as I make Ilsa eat almost everything we receive. My stomach is bloated and hurts badly. My body is dying. The only good news Yitzhak says is that every once in a while locals come to the ghetto fence to trade with us. We can give them clothes and jewellery and receive food in return. When they come, I will try to trade the few spare clothes we have left and get something nourishing for us to eat. But there is a threat no food can cure. My biggest fear is typhus. The lice are everywhere. They infect the very air. I try to pick the lice from Ilsa's hair, clothes and crevices. I do my best. But there are always more.

My parents are dead. I have not considered this properly, not until a moment ago. I thought of them when I was in Warsaw. I wondered how they were. I thought of them on their birthdays, on holy days, any days really. They were good people. They did not deserve a daughter like me. I am glad they never saw me again, never knew the truth of what I did. Mama and Papa, dead.

Shot in the back, they fell into a ditch. They are buried outside of town with hundreds of others. I wonder if my father still had that twiddly moustache. I wonder which dress my mother wore, the day she was murdered. The moment before the shots came, did they think of me?

I say Goldman in my sleep, my parents' name. I must be dreaming of them, but I do not remember my dreams when I wake. All except one. I have one dream about the forest. The ghetto is empty and I walk out of the gate with Ilsa. We walk across the fields and enter the forest. We walk and walk until all we can see are trees. All we can smell is pine. All we can hear is birdsong and the conference of breeze and branches.

A hopeless dream of escape. How stupid the mind is. Yitzhak did tell me that young men from here manage to escape periodically to join the partisans in the region. I asked him about these Bielski brothers, the ones Stefan told me about. Yitzhak has heard rumours of them, from local farmers who come to buy products made in the ghetto workshops. The Jewish police in this ghetto have taken to confiscating the boots of likely escapees at night, to encourage them to stay in their beds. But still young men do escape, boots or no boots. Good for them, but not necessarily good for us. When someone escapes, there is fierce German retribution, with others being shot in their place. Stories of escapees and partisans sound appealing enough, but other Jews here are saying they do not want to escape. Winter is coming, and who can survive the snow in these woods? I do not fear the cold, more the danger of escape. I am not a brave young man. Just a sick mother with her little girl. How could we possibly get away from this place? There are guards everywhere. Why don't they just kill us and get it over with? Because we are useful for a short while, that is all. Yitzhak says there are rumours of another massacre to come soon. Some have dug hiding places. But I have no energy left for blind hope. I hear myself echoing our German's sentiments. *Just give up, will you? Just die.*

But still, at night I dream of the forest. I dream of my brother there, the wild boy I remember, twigs in his hair and a catapult. The word *puscha* is common to Polish, Russian and Byelorussian. Dense woodland. The *puscha*. Beautiful word. I long to be in the *puscha*. But I will never see it more. I hope they bury me there.

Ilsa is ill. She has a fever and a very bad headache. I have tried to find someone who can smuggle in medicine, but there is no one. There is no help.

It may just be a bug, a virus going round. Something harmless.

But I know what fever and headache can be. I know this too well. It can be typhus. I saw it in Warsaw. It could be. It could well be. We just have to wait for the rash. If the rash comes, we will know for sure.

But for now, I must hope it is just a cold. A common cold. Yes, that is it. Ilsa has a cold. She will be all right soon.

Ilsa has the rash. She has been vomiting all night. It is typhus.

I think this may be Ilsa's last night on this earth. She seems very near death. She does not speak. She is lost to me. She still breathes, but her fever is terrible. She has the rash all over her body now. Only the palms of her small hands and the soles of her tiny feet are clear. And her face is clear. Her face is her own. Her little body is racked by a terrible cough. I hold her until it passes, but she is insensible of my touch. Or perhaps she can feel me. A mother's love is more powerful than typhus, I think. But I cannot save her.

What can I write? What can a pencil do, a sheet of paper?

My baby is dying.

My baby is dying.

My baby is dying.

I gave away a baby once. I loved him. I called him Janek, little Jan. But I was a child myself. Jan was gone and I did not know where. And there was the shame. The shame of where he came from. I could not go home. I could not lie to my family. I could not tell them the awful truth either. I was a child. I did not know what to do. I had no money, no friends. I gave up my baby. I left him on a doorstep. I thought he should never know where he came from. I thought he would be better off without me, without the truth. I thought they would give him a better life than I could. What a fool I was.

Tonight I spit in the eye of my God. I tell You, You do not exist. You never did. I do not believe in You or in anything.

There is nothing else to write.

CHAPTER ELEVEN

It was a ramshackle farmhouse with woods on one side and fields on the other. Daniel approached in twilight and knocked on the front door. A man opened it wide. He had a bald, square head.

"Who are you?"

"They call me Anglik. I was a fighter in the Warsaw Ghetto. I was given your name by a rat-faced fighter from the Polish Underground."

"I know the one," said Kossakowski. "He does look like a rat."

Daniel explained his situation. Kossakowski listened to his story about his mother. He asked lots of questions about the battle for the Warsaw Ghetto. He looked at Daniel's gun and fake IDs. Daniel told him of his plan to join the Bielski camp and look for his family there. He even told him about Dad's death in the Blitz. All this on Kossakowski's doorstep.

"No one could make up a story like that," he said and let him in. "You can stay here until Bielski partisans come by. It could be tomorrow, it could be next week. If they accept you, they'll take you to the Bielski camp. If we have any unwelcome visitors, I'll send you out to a hiding place near the house. Come into the kitchen. You must be hungry."

He had not eaten since that morning. The journey had been tiring but successful. He wasn't questioned or even suspected. His ID was solid and he was barely noticed. Just another traveller. He'd had a lot of time to think on the train. He had thought of Marysia's body, how he had touched her skin with his fingers, his mouth, how he was inside her and kissed her and how her hair brushed against his face. How her sweet soft body was burnt up and left to rot in a bunker. He imagined how it must have looked, her twisted charred limbs and her silent skull screaming. He mustn't think about it. But he did. His friend Natan too. And the others. All the others. So many he'd lost count. How many? How many should die to make a war end?

He had looked out of the window at the towns and villages passing by and wondered how many Jews used to live in each one and how many Jews were left there now. He thought how quiet the Polish countryside appeared. The fields, the forests, the rivers. All land occupied by Germany. What did the Germans have? They occupied space. They occupied freedom. The conquerors squatted over their new victims. The people endured, suffered, died or survived. But the land didn't yield to occupiers. The land persisted. It didn't know what name it was given, Polish, Russian, German or otherwise. It didn't care who claimed it, who drove tanks through it, who spilt whose blood into its earth. The land existed. It was ancient. It knew only that time would pass. The land was oblivious, mute, sublime. His train had travelled through it, blindly.

Kossakowski gave him a can of milk, some bread and a sausage. Daniel asked him about himself. He was a Byelorussian.

He had family nearby who were also farmers with wives and children, another who worked in an office in Novogrodek. He was not a Jew, but he had worked with a Jewish tailor and developed a lot of respect for the Jews. He'd even learnt Yiddish. He had known the Bielski family for years. They were the only Jews in the local area.

Daniel said, "What are they like?"

"There were lots of Bielski children, nine brothers I think, and two sisters. The ones who are running the camp are Tuvia, Asael and Zus. They are all extremely brave, courageous men. Tuvia is a born leader. He's shrewd and clever. A bit of an intellectual. Women love him, lucky dog! Men respect and honour him. I would say he's found his calling in the forest, leading those people. Like he was born to do it.

"Asael has a great sense of humour. Down to earth and honest. Loves the land. He's always calm when trouble strikes. A good dancer too! Zus is very tall, strong. Before the war, he always used to be well turned out. And he liked a good sing-song after a few drinks! More talkative than his brother Asael. Quite a temper. Often up for a fight. The farmers round here are a bit afraid of him. He had a wife and baby. They were killed in the first massacre in Novogrodek. The Bielski parents, two brothers and a sister were all killed too.

"Those boys have plenty of reasons to hate the Nazis. But you know, they're not just out to get revenge. They're doing something quite different. There are hundreds of partisans in the forests now. Lots of people are fighting the Nazis. But these lads are different. They're all about survival. Survival for the Jews, the women, the old, the children. Their aim is to keep Jews alive till the Russians come to liberate us. No one else I know is doing anything like that. We need more people like the Bielskis."

"I didn't know that. I thought they were just fighters."

"Oh, they can fight all right. They're tough boys. But their aim is not to attack. That invites trouble. They want to lay low. Keep safe. They want to protect. You know, most of those who've escaped the ghettos just want to live. They don't care about fighting the Germans. They left the ghettos and looked for the Bielskis because they saw their chance to live a little longer. The Bielski camp is in the business of survival. It has to avoid trouble, move around a lot, keep quiet. Recently they were based at Stara Huta, not far from Stankevich, the nearest village to us here. They settled there for a while. The camp became a bit like a village in the forest, with tradesmen setting up shops for locals and perimeter guards keeping watch for strangers. They all shuffled their arses and got cosy. Then a German plane flew over a couple of weeks ago and they heard German trucks nearby in the woods. They had to move on quickly. It was hard for them. They had all made a little home. But that was dangerous. To get comfortable. They went to the Jasinowo forest a few kilometres away. But I don't know exactly where. And that was the last I heard, a week ago. They may have moved on again since. The partisans will come by soon and they'll tell us where. It's not an easy life at the Bielski camp. Not heroic. It's about sneaking around and finding food and keeping stupid people quiet. Is that what you want, a young man fresh from fighting in the ghetto?"

"I just want to find my family."

Kossakowksi smiled. "Family. Yes. When it's there, you can't stand it. When it's gone, you can't stand it. A bit like a woman!"

They laughed at that. Daniel asked him how he got into helping the Jews. He said it wasn't about the Jews necessarily.

"I just hate the Nazis, that's all. I'm glad I can be useful. My house is my asset. It's far enough off the main road from Novogrodek to Lida that passing traffic can't see us. And there are no neighbours near enough to snoop. I was well placed to help. I've been a guide for fugitives and a courier of information, for all sorts of Nazi haters, not only the Jews. I was lonely before the war, no woman to warm my bed, a few friends here and there. Now I get to mix with all sorts. I like that. Also, because I have contacts all over, I can make a good business selling black market goods, all kinds of products. And making my *samogonka*."

"What's that?"

"Here, finish your milk," he said and fetched a bottle from the side, poured him a shot of clear liquid. He sipped cautiously. Fire slipped down his throat.

"*Samogonka*," he said, smiling. "Home-made vodka. Wonderful stuff, eh?"

They drank more and talked about women. Daniel stopped himself before he felt ill and went to his room to rest. He liked Kossakowski. The man made light of it, but what he was doing was very dangerous. There must be informants everywhere, a man here who wants a bit more land, a man there who doesn't mind selling out his neighbour for a cow. He wondered how long Kossakowski would survive.

Daniel was in his mother's backyard. She grew up nearby. She went to school here, played games with her brother, perhaps even met his father here, fell in love. When all of it was over, if he survived, he wanted to see his mother's house, if it still stood. He wanted to walk to her school, visit the old family graves. But maybe it was all destroyed already. Another lifetime of memories wiped out by the Nazis. He supposed none of that really mattered – buildings, streets, footsteps. It was his living mother he wanted, his sister, his uncle. He was closer to them now than ever.

Time for sleep.

Every morning he woke up hoping the partisans would come by that day. Two weeks passed, filled with farm work and talking. A different life, from the city, the ghetto, the war. Pleasant. Frustrating.

One morning at breakfast, a knock on the door sent Daniel out of the back door to the empty cowshed. He could hear Kossakowski talking to someone, laughing. A whistle. His signal that all was safe. He came back in to find a young man by the fireplace.

"This is Meyer. He's with the Bielskis."

Daniel strode across, shook his hand.

"Good to meet you. I'm Anglik."

Meyer said nothing. He was about Daniel's age. He looked tired but magnificent, a rifle slung across his body, a leather jerkin and high boots.

Meyer turned back to the farmer. "The camp was near the Neman. There was a German attack yesterday. Everyone went crazy and ran into the forest. Ten killed. The camp was all over the place. The Bielskis got most of them back near the river. They sent me to get stragglers."

"What a mess," said Kossakowski.

"What do you want?" said Meyer to Daniel, no smile, no light in his eyes.

"I'm looking for my mother. Helena. Her daughter Ilsa. I have a photo."

"Don't know them," said Meyer, before Daniel had had a chance to get it.

"There's an uncle too. Jakub."

Meyer turned to Kossakowski. "Who is this kid?"

"He's a brave little bastard who's killed Nazis in the Warsaw ghetto. He wants his family now. What do you say? Will you take him? He has a gun."

That must have swung it, because Meyer shook his hand and nodded.

"Tuvia Bielski wants to move the camp to Naliboki. Safer

there. They'll be off soon. You'll have to come with me today."

"All right," said Daniel.

"Got to sleep now."

He went to Daniel's bed and stretched out. He was asleep within seconds.

"Thank you," said Daniel to Kossakowski.

"He's a miserable shit. But a good scout. He'll get you there."

They left late afternoon. Meyer set a fast pace and Daniel hurried along behind him. He tramped through the forest as if it were his local street, spotting landmarks invisible to Daniel. As the light faded, the woods grew eerie, knowing, thick with secrets. He would not want to be lost here. Meyer seemed unaffected. He didn't say a lot, but revealed he grew up in a place called Grodno. Daniel had gone through there on his way, getting the bus from Grodno to Novogrodek. Meyer said he'd had cousins in Novogrodek, where he'd spent summer holidays as a child. They would all play in the forests together and that was how he knew them well. Other than that, he did not want to converse with Daniel. He didn't ask him anything about himself or where he'd come from. Daniel suspected from his manner of speaking that he was not highly educated. A bit rough around the edges. Perhaps he was suspicious of Daniel. Perhaps he was just tired.

After hours of walking, Meyer stopped and listened to the air. Daniel was about to ask him what was wrong. Was it the enemy? Or a wild animal? He felt like a hapless city-dweller. Meyer whistled three times. A man appeared from behind a tree. It was almost comical, like a magic trick. He was dressed similarly to Meyer, but wore a fur hat with a red star on it. Meyer and the man grinned at each other, reverted to a soldierly stance and barked something unintelligible. It sounded like Hebrew, a password. It was all an act, a forest formality, because they clearly knew each other well and embraced and laughed, chattering away in Yiddish.

Meyer turned and said in Polish, "A new one. Has a gun. Tuvia about?" The other man nodded, and Meyer motioned for Daniel to come along.

He heard the voices and bustle of people, several hundred people, spread out amongst the trees. There were partisans, some on horseback, dressed in short sheepskin coats, some with paraphernalia from German uniforms. They were armed with a range of weapons, impressive compared to the ghetto: pistols, rifles, submachine-guns and one even had a machine-gun. The rest of the camp was family groups, women and older folk, a few children. The camp was haphazard, roughly split into small clutches of people. Women cooking, men putting up tents made from clothes and branches, others cleaning weapons and couples cuddling under trees.

Daniel scanned the crowd to look for his mother. He knew it was unlikely but he couldn't help it. He tried to see her dark eyes staring out from amidst the assembly. But he saw only curiosity and suspicion from those who stared back. Meyer chatted briefly with several other men but nobody spoke to Daniel.

"Wait here," said Meyer and walked off.

It wasn't long before people started to come up to him. First, a middle-aged woman with a kindly face asked in Polish, "Where have you come from?"

He hadn't thought about what he would say to such an obvious question. It was all right to sit with a man and a glass of *samogonka* and tell him your life story, but how was he to answer this without beginning an epic? He decided on simplicity. Details could come later.

"Warsaw," he said.

"Oh," said the woman and looked disappointed.

A man asked, "Did you come through Novogrodek? Did you see the ghetto?"

"I didn't see the ghetto. Do you have family there?"

There was a general shaking of heads. He got the feeling they were desperate for news from beyond the trees.

"I can tell you about Warsaw. There was a great revolt there. Lots of Germans were killed. Jews fought bravely and some escaped. Others died with honour."

Many gasps came from those who surrounded him, rapt by his news from the wider world. But Daniel was desperate to start asking his own questions about his family. He went down on one knee in order to retrieve Helena's photo from his shoe when a young woman asked, "Tell us more about it. Did you fight?"

He was about to tell her rousing stories of Jewish heroism when the group stepped aside as one. Before him stood Meyer and two tall men. Both of them wore calf-length leather jackets and leather gloves, with knee-high military boots. Meyer motioned towards Daniel, then left. Daniel jumped back up and, not quite knowing why, saluted the men, whose glance at each other looked a little amused yet both saluted back.

"I am Tuvia Bielski," said one of the men, took off his glove and shook hands firmly.

Daniel was tongue-tied. Tuvia was an imposing figure, a wide noble face with keen, intelligent eyes and a thick moustache.

"This is my brother, Asael."

A friendly face. Daniel felt as if Asael would be your chum, but Tuvia would always be above you. Not arrogant but regal. His manner was magnanimous and welcoming, yet he had that reserve leaders must always retain, for they have to make hard decisions.

"Your name is Anglik? I hear you have an unusual history. We need to talk."

Daniel noticed that the people nearby had shifted away, as a mark of respect for their leaders and to give them privacy. They did not sit down and he felt he ought to stand like a soldier. Though the brothers' faces were friendly, he felt he had to earn his place here.

"Where have you come from?" said Asael.

He decided to start at the beginning, yet tried to be as succinct as possible. He thought how a journalist would write it. Both brothers listened seriously to his account, asking no questions.

Tuvia spoke, "And if you do not find your uncle or your mother here. What do you plan to do then?"

It was a crucial question. He had not considered it. But he knew what he wanted to say.

"I would like to stay here and fight. I have a gun and I know how to use it. There is nowhere else I want to be."

Asael nodded his head yet Tuvia remained stony-faced. He stepped back and conferred quietly with Asael a few feet away. Daniel waited and waited, sweating despite the cool evening. The brothers came back. An interrogation of seemingly random questions about his story – what was the name of his combat group leader during the uprising, where was his father born, how much was the bus fare from Grodno to Novogrodek. He answered everything swiftly. They stopped and smiled at him.

"Enemies surround us," said Tuvia. "We have to fight together against the Germans. We need people like you, young men with guns. I promise that we will make you into a good partisan. You will get the chance to fight again soon, to defend your life and the camp. And if you're fated to die here, you will die honourably in battle. My brother will induct you. For now, I must go and get ready for tomorrow's journey. Good to have you here, Anglik."

Tuvia strode away. Daniel heard several people call out to Tuvia, 'Good evening'.

Asael stood before him.

"It's all right," he said, grinning broadly. "You can stay, my friend."

He held out his hand and Daniel shook it gleefully.

"You understand why we have to ask all those questions."

"Yes, of course."

"There are spies around. The Germans send them. A few months ago we had one. We shot him. The Russian bosses will shoot a suspected spy with no evidence. We have to be careful, you know."

Asael went on to explain the set-up of the camp. There were fighters and non-fighters. Everyone had a role and this was clearer at times when the camp settled a bit, like it did at Stara Huta (the place Kossakowsky told him about). Asael hoped that the new site in the Naliboki forest would be safer and that the camp could settle, become more established and productive. The simple fact was that there existed a division between the armed and the unarmed. Asael explained that this was natural, but Tuvia in particular discouraged it.

"Everyone is equal here."

He said Daniel would be assigned in the morning to a group of partisans, and that once settled he would take part in food missions as well as patrols and other partisan activities, perhaps even actions against the Germans.

"We move at first light to the Naliboki. They will get you ammo for your gun. Sleep well tonight. The journey won't be easy."

Asael was about to turn and go, but Daniel spoke up.

"Could you tell me if you know of my mother Helena, or her daughter Ilsa, or my uncle Jakub?"

Nothing had been said about them so far. He thought the brothers were more interested in his gun than anything else. Family was all very well, but to stay here, it seemed, guns trumped all.

"Of course. Your family. Well, there are about seven hundred people here. I know many of them, but not all. But there are only a few children, so that makes it easier. I don't know any girls called Ilsa. There are quite a few Helenas. It's a common name."

Daniel stooped and removed his mother's photo from his shoe and showed it to Asael. He studied it and looked around, as if she might appear. Daniel willed him to say yes, yes, I know this woman.

"No. I don't know her. But that doesn't mean she isn't here. This is an old photo, isn't it? She may have changed a lot. People come from the ghettos in a terrible state. They soon recover but it takes its toll. This woman may look very different now. She might've changed her name. I'll ask around. There is definitely a Jakub. He's an experienced partisan, been with us a while and does come from Novogrodek. He's away from camp rounding up right now. He'll probably come back tomorrow or meet us later on the journey. He knows where we're going. When he comes back, I'll make sure I send him to you."

"Thank you."

Asael took him to a spot by a campfire, where young men were lounging and drinking. They gave him a jovial yet respectful greeting. Asael instructed them to give him a blanket and place to sleep under a shelter, as well as food and drink. The partisans were a little cool, but offered him *samogonka* first and after a few gulps they were all more relaxed. The group talked a mixture of

Yiddish and Russian, with some Polish. Their Polish was spoken with a heavy local accent unfamiliar to Daniel, very different from the smooth Warsaw tones. Thank heavens Dad taught him Russian, as well as Magda's Polish. He got by with those and his developing Yiddish. There were also words he didn't recognise. Partisan jargon. He was given bread and a lad fetched him cold potato soup. He told them a brief version of his history. He showed his photo around with greater hope than he'd had in months, but there were no takers. Some barely looked and were much more interested in his fighting tales of the ghetto. He was proud to tell them and a few of the lads shook his hand. Before long, they were putting their heads down to sleep. He was given a blanket and shown where to sleep, under a makeshift shelter with two others.

Most of the camp was asleep, except the guards and insomniacs like him. To think of the downtrodden Jews he saw stumbling around the ghetto, and to see these strong young men, their women, their children, their parents and even grandparents, all living in harmony in the forest, helping each other, sharing everything, protecting one and all. He knew he romanticised the place, but it was astonishing. And the Bielskis. Like hero brothers from a fairy tale.

He had wanted to walk into the camp and see his mother standing before him, exactly the same as she looked in the photo. He knew it was unlikely, but that scene had played over and over in his mind. Asael was right: if she were here, she may be unrecognisable. His best chance was to wait for the partisan Jakub. Until then, he would serve the Bielski brothers. He was happy there, by the flicker of a camp fire, sleeping fighters and families all around him, all Jewish. A community of free Jews living in occupied Poland. It defied belief. But he was there and he knew it was real.

They began their journey to the Naliboki forest the next morning. Around midday, a young woman came up to him as he trudged along with his new partisan group.

She said, "Are you Anglik? I was told you wanted to know when Jakub came back. He's back there, on the horse, drinking from a canteen, you see?"

He spotted a tall man with black, cropped hair, wearing a leather jacket. Could it be him, he thought? Could that be his mother's brother, or just a random bloke called Jakub? He didn't even wait to thank the young woman. He ran down the column. Walkers turned to see where he was going. He slowed to a saunter, embarrassed. He walked up beside the ambling horse.

"Are you Jakub?" he said in Polish. He felt more confident than in his fledgling Yiddish. Jakub looked down on him in every sense. An experienced and confident partisan, even atop a horse demonstrating that swagger of all powerful forest fighters.

He answered in Polish thick with the local accent: "Who are you?"

"They call me Anglik. Do you have a sister called Helena?"

Jakub's face changed.

"What's that?"

He was squinting down at Daniel, who felt a fool. What were the chances? This whole thing was absurd. He'd be a laughing stock. He was trotting beside his horse like a lackey, and Jakub even geed-up so that he had to run. After all this time, all the searching, all the hopes and losses, he'd had enough.

"Listen, stop that bastard horse for a minute, will you?" he cursed.

Jakub came to an abrupt stop.

"Are you Jakub and do you have a sister called Helena? She left home when you were very young. She never came back. Is she here?"

"Who are you? What are all these stupid questions?"

Daniel bent down and took off his boot. Standing shoeless, he reached up and handed him his mother's photograph.

"Is that your sister?"

Jakub took the photo.

"Where did you get this?"

"Is that your sister Helena?"

Daniel had to make absolutely sure. He couldn't make a false assumption now. It would be too painful if it turned out to be wrong.

"Yes, yes, yes!" he shouted. "Who the fuck are you?"

"I am Helena's son. If that is your sister, then I am your nephew. And you're my Uncle Jakub."

Jakub almost fell off his horse. He jumped down and passed the reins to another partisan. He stared at Daniel.

"Helena's son? You are Helena's son?"

He spoke as if it were the most preposterous idea ever conceived.

"Yes."

"You are. You are! I can see it in your eyes. My sister's son. My nephew. Hey, everybody! This is my nephew! My nephew, my nephew!"

He shouted with abandon at all who could hear. A few cheers went up and Jakub laughed and clapped. He laughed. They laughed together. They hugged and laughed and cried and almost collapsed from the madness of it all.

Daniel put his boot back on and they walked together. Jakub held the photo and looked at it often. They strolled along with the column and talked themselves into the ground. Daniel told him everything about his journey from London, starting with his father's death. He also told him the little he knew about Helena, gleaned from Vladka. Jakub was thrilled to hear about Ilsa, another member of his family he never knew existed. Jakub asked questions, to elicit extra details and fill in any gaps. Daniel missed bits and had to backtrack. He had told his story to others, but never to family. Telling it to Jakub was essentially different, as he had a listener with a precise interest in everything he said. Not listening politely, but desperately, gobbling each morsel like a starving man.

When he'd finished, Daniel asked, "What about you? Tell me."

"I joined the Bielski group at the end of 1941. The Nazi fuckers murdered my family. Mama and Papa - your grandparents. And my wife and my lovely boy. My baby. They took us all in trucks and shot us. One day I'll tell you about it, but not now. Not on this happy day. My family is dead. I lay in the pit, naked, beside my family, my dead family. My leg was wounded. I escaped later with a couple of others. We had heard about the Bielskis. It took us a few days to find them. We were very hungry and dressed in rags we'd stolen from peasants' houses. They took us in, fed us, clothed us, dressed my wound. They saved us. I fight for them now. I fight for revenge, for my dead family. I will not stop until they kill me or I kill every last fucking German on this earth. You understand?"

"Yes, I understand."

They went on to easier topics. Jakub told Daniel their family name was Goldman. So this was his mother's name, when she was a girl, before she met his father, or had him, or met Isak Dedek and had Ilsa: Helena Goldman. They talked about Helena as a girl, about their childhood together. He craved every word.

"I loved her, you know, in the rough way of brothers. I looked up to her, admired her. She was studious, very clever. Always reading. Always. Took a book with her everywhere. Wrote poems in little notebooks, in code so nobody could understand. I was never any good at school. I was always out in the forest, hunting any poor animal that came my way, getting in fights, smoking stolen cigarettes. My poor parents! But Helena, she was a model daughter. So good, so quiet. Never any trouble. And she was good looking, you know. Beautiful, really. Lovely eyes. You have them. A pretty girl like that, a young woman. But she never had boyfriends. Plenty of boys sniffing around, yet she brushed them all off. Like they were never good enough. Then she started having secrets. I knew she was up to something, disappearing from the house for whole afternoons. One day, she was gone. There was a note. My parents never showed it to me. They said she had run away. That's all. I asked around. Some kids who had older brothers and sisters found out the truth and told me. She'd run away with a man, a *goyish* poet from Warsaw, so they said. I told my parents. They didn't want to know. One day she was there, the next gone. And that was that."

"Nobody ever went looking for her?"

"No, no. It was a terrible shame on the family, you know. She was only fifteen years old. And he was a *goy*. I'm sorry, I know that man may be your father. But to run off with a *goy* was beyond everything. She was a disgrace, you know. I was too young. In those days, in a strict Jewish family, you didn't question your parents' actions. I accepted that I would never see my sister again. Nobody spoke about it. Her name was never mentioned. I forgot about her, the way you do when you're a kid. Like a distant relative you met once. I was a child. Now I am a man, I've had my own child and lost him. How could…"

Here he stopped. He was about to make a point, perhaps about his parents, but his voice choked and he couldn't go on. Daniel changed the subject.

"We know Helena and Ilsa came to Novogrodek a few weeks

ago. We know they never reached the Bielski partisans. Where did they go? Where could they be now?"

Jakub recovered himself and shook his head.

"Listen, Daniel. I'm a man who talks straight about things. I'm not going to lie to you. There have been massacres in Novogrodek, one in August last year, and another in February and again last month. The Nazis are clearing out the ghetto. If Helena and Ilsa reached the town, they're either in hiding - which is very difficult in a small place like Novogrodek – or they were put in the ghetto. Or worse. Helena is probably dead, Daniel. Her little girl too. There's no mercy for children. You know this, don't you?"

Daniel had to admit he was right. But that didn't mean they knew for sure.

"I know all that, but they might be alive. There is a chance."

"I agree with you. And I cannot tell you how wonderful it is to know that my dear sister, whom I lost long ago, might be a few miles down the road, right now, as we speak. And her daughter. A niece I never even knew I had! In these times, your family becomes everything, doesn't it?"

Daniel didn't need to answer.

"So what do we do next?"

"The only thing we can do is go back to Novogrodek. The first place to try is the ghetto. She was a seamstress. They might have need for her skills there. That might have kept her alive. We'll have to ask the brothers for permission to leave the camp right now. It's a difficult time. They might say no. We probably won't find our girls, Daniel. But I'm willing to try, are you?"

"Damn right!" he said and they shook on it.

He was relieved Jakub wanted to find her too. He knew there was every chance he might refuse, having his own problems to deal with here, but Daniel didn't relish wandering around Novogrodek on his own, trying to find an illegal person, that is, a

Warsaw Jew on the run without papers. For the first time in his quest, he now had a partner.

"So your English father called you Daniel?" said Jakub. "It's a good name, you know. This Anglik, it's all right for your partisan lads. But your name is Daniel. May I call you Daniel?"

He liked this. No one had called him Daniel since Marysia. It felt right.

That afternoon, Daniel and Jakub went to speak to Asael. Jakub explained their plan to him with enthusiasm. However, Asael was not keen. Daniel had the feeling he thought it was a wild goose chase. Jakub told him later Asael wanted to keep people with the group and not let them go. Not because he wanted control, but because he knew their chances were always better there than almost anywhere else. Jakub said an old woman had come with her grandchild once and had complained all the time that she couldn't stay in the forest because she had left her brassiere at home. She went on and on about this brassiere and how she couldn't live without it. She said she was going to go back. Asael just screamed at her to stay, or if not, at least leave the child. But she went and took the child with her. They heard later that the old woman was killed, along with the girl.

After some persuasion from Jakub, centred on the importance of family, Asael eventually approved their mission. He was, after all, a man who understood how it was to keep your family close, living through the war with his brothers, unlike so many others who had lost everyone.

He said, "You can't take any fighters with you. And you must try to bring back food, medication, weapons or anything else useful, then meet up in Naliboki in two weeks."

They agreed and he wished them luck. They decided to leave for Novogrodek in the morning.

That evening they ate a good meal together and drank *samogonka*.

Before he went to sleep, Jakub said to him, "If Hitler had never started this war, you and I might never have met. We've something to thank the little cunt for, eh?"

He turned over and was asleep in a minute, snoring so loudly a fighter shouted, "Shut your hole!"

Daniel thought about Jakub's wife and daughter, his mother and father. All dead. Daniel had had grandparents, an aunt, a cousin. All dead before he knew they were alive.

They set off early. Daniel slept little the night before, too excited to settle. He was shattered before they even left. Jakub was singing folk songs at 5 a.m. and pissing off the entire camp. They took only a small bag each with a few supplies and left at 5.30, moving swiftly through the forest. Jakub knew the way with hardly a glance. They reached Novogrodek by dusk. They could have laid low that night and looked the next, but they'd come that far. They'd talked of nothing but Helena and Ilsa all the way and they were eager to get on. Jakub's plan was to go to the ghetto first. They stuck to the outskirts of the town and came into the ghetto area by a back route, staying beneath the trees and out of sight of the road. They came upon the ghetto as the light was fading. They planned to break in and enter a residential hut, ask around for

Helena and Ilsa, and leave again by the same route, with or without them.

Jakub explained, "If you know how, the ghetto is easy to get in and out of. I've done it before. I've gone in with others to rescue their relatives. If only I knew that my own sister might be there!"

He told him that the way into the ghetto was to watch the guards. There were Byelorussian and Polish collaborators who walked around the perimeter every few minutes. They left sections of it unguarded for a minute at a time. There were always a few German guards at the entrance, but generally they were too lazy to make detailed checks of the perimeter and left this up to their inferiors. Jakub said the best place to get in and out was behind the toilets. Daniel's days of sneaking over the Warsaw ghetto walls came back to him. This seemed like child's play in comparison. These small town ghettos were obviously not considered as important as the Jews of Poland's capital city, a murderous snobbery.

They waited until full darkness. They approached the fence across a wide farmer's field, having left their bags at the edge in order to travel light. It was an overcast, moist night, no moon visible. Good for cover.

"A storm is best," said Jakub. "Germans can't be bothered to search in bad weather."

They'd have to make do with drizzle. They crouched by the fence behind the toilet hut as guards passed. They worked out when they were coming, and when nobody was there. They loosened fence boards and crawled through into the ghetto compound. They saw huts, small windows steamed with breath, and heard the rumble of conversation.

Jakub pointed out one.

He whispered, "I've been in there before. Inmates not guards."

They crept towards it. Jakub pushed the door and they were in. The reek of sweat and illness and death. Daniel remembered that smell from Warsaw. At first, only some noticed they had come in. Word went round and the hut was hushed to silence.

"You know me," said Jakub.

Were these people from his home town, people he'd grown up with, lived on his street?

"I'm here for my sister. Anyone know Helena Goldman? She had a daughter with her called Ilsa. Did she come here? Is she here?"

Daniel held his breath. Nobody said anything.

A middle-aged woman spoke up: "If someone escapes tonight, we'll pay for it tomorrow. You know there are always reprisals. Why should we help you?"

Jakub went up to her and touched her shoulder. "If I could, I'd take you all with me. But I can't. I just want my sister and her girl. This boy is her son. He's come from England to find her."

All eyes on Daniel.

"Help us," said Daniel. "Please tell us if you know anything, anything at all."

Silence. A murmur.

"What was that?" called Jakub, scanning the crowd.

A man stepped forward, thin and tall, curved like a longbow.

"I know Helena. She's in the next hut. But she's dying. She may be dead already. Go now, or you might be too late."

They scrambled for the door.

Jakub peered outside and nodded. They ran across to the next hut and crouched in its shadow. Jakub grasped his arm. Voices. Not Polish. Byelorussian. They waited. They had no cover, nowhere to run without being seen. Two guards strolled past, swigging from a bottle. They laughed at a joke. Gone.

Daniel reached the door. Jakub stopped him and said, "Do you want me to go in first?"

"No. I want to."

Jakub nodded. Was he afraid of what they might find? Daniel was. He opened the door and they slipped in. There were fewer people in this one. There was that same stench, only worse. Bodies lay on bunks, some dead. Others were breathing badly. In the corner, a girl sat by a bunk and looked round. She held a woman's hand. She stared at them.

They walked over to her. The woman on the bed was scarcely alive. Starved almost to death, her stomach bloated, her face drawn into her skull. He couldn't see any resemblance to his mother's photo. Maybe this was another mother and daughter. The tall man in the next hut hadn't even mentioned a daughter. Perhaps Ilsa was already dead. The woman could have been any poor starving soul. For a moment, he thought she might already be a corpse. But her chest still moved. Jakub made a sound in his throat, a bird-like cry.

The girl looked up at them.

Daniel said, "Is your name Ilsa?"

"Yes. Who are you?"

"I'm your brother. This is your uncle."

"Have you come to rescue us?"

"Yes." He knelt down beside her. "Is this your mama?"

"Yes. She's dying. Can she come too?"

"Of course she can."

He touched her cheek. Solemn, liquid eyes. He looked at his mother. A vacant shell. He turned to Jakub and whispered behind his hand, even though Ilsa could hear everything he said.

"What about Helena? We'll have to carry her. Can we get her through the fence?"

"We'll have to. Come on."

Jakub was wiping his eyes and looking down at his sister. She looked like she might crumble if they touched her. Her breathing rattled and her closed eyes sank.

"She won't make it," said Daniel. "If we try to catch up with the camp, she'll die tomorrow. We should take her to Kossakowski."

Jakub agreed. Ilsa watched all this. She said nothing. She just accepted they were her family and they had come to rescue her. Perhaps she had seen so much in this bloody war, nothing shocked her any more.

"We're going to carry your mama," Daniel told her. "Hold onto my jacket and don't let go. We're going through the fence behind the toilets. Don't make a sound. Don't talk or cry. Absolutely quiet, do you understand?"

She nodded gravely.

Jakub lifted Helena's shoulders and Daniel was about to take her feet.

"She's a feather," said Jakub and shifted round to her side. He swept her up in his arms like a sack of dead leaves. She did not wake. Her mouth fell open.

Ilsa's hand tugged Daniel's.

"The book," she said.

"Come on, Ilsa. We're going now."

"We must bring Mama's book."

She let go of his hand, reached under the bed and pulled out a battered old notebook.

Helena's diary.

"All right, give it to me," he said, put it under his arm and grabbed his sister's little hand.

Daniel and Ilsa went to the door first, Jakub carrying Helena behind. The inhabitants of the hut watched them go. Nobody had said a word. Nobody had the strength. He peered out and saw the coast was clear. It was raining quite heavily now. Good for them. They stepped lightly across the compound, looking all around. They reached the fence. Ilsa would not let go of his hand.

"Go through the fence first, Ilsa. Then we'll bring your mama through."

She shook her head violently.

"Mama first."

There was no time to argue.

"All right, Mama first. Take the book."

Jakub laid Helena down on the rough wet ground gently, so gently. He hopped through the fence and turned back, arms outstretched. Daniel stood over his mother, his sister's hand tugging at his jacket. Helena was still breathing. He lifted her. Jakub was right. She was empty. Carefully they manoeuvred her body through the gap in the fence. Her leg snagged on a fence post, but she did not stir. She was through. Then Ilsa, then Daniel. All four of them were outside the ghetto and in the field.

"Hurry," whispered Jakub and ran away with Helena flopping in his arms. Ilsa gripped Daniel's hand, their mother's journal clasped in her other arm. They followed Jakub, running together across the dark field, brother and sister. Their feet splashed crowns of raindrops from the sodden grass.

Shouts. Gunshots. Bullets whizzed overhead. The field was suddenly feverish with gunfire. They ran and ran as quick as bandits. They reached the forest and ran through the trees without a word. Jakub was fleet of foot despite his awkward burden. They stopped only once and could hear no more angry voices behind them.

Panting and wide-eyed, Jakub said, "The Germans will sweep the area looking for us, but not until morning. They'll be too lazy to bother now, especially in this rain. We have to keep moving, go straight to Kossakowski's."

It was an hour's walk at least. They had been travelling all day. It was now almost midnight. But Daniel wasn't tired. He was shot through with electricity, the charge of being alive. He squeezed Ilsa's hand and looked down at her sombre little face.

"I was ill for a long time," she said.

"Walk now and no talking."

"Now Mama is sick. But I got better. Do you think she will?"

"Yes I do. Now hush."

"No one can hear us. Only the birds and they're sleeping."

"Shh, Ilsa!"

But how he wanted to talk with her. His little sister. He loved her sad eyes, her lank curls, her hot grip. But his mother. She had not woken or even moaned since they picked her up. Jakub walked briskly, carrying her body and staring straight ahead. Daniel watched her most of the way, now and again looking down to smile at Ilsa, who never smiled back, just stared. He thought Jakub was scared to look down at his sister, scared the next time he did she would be dead.

Ilsa only spoke once more on the way.

"Do you have any food?" she said. How hungry she must have been, yet polite.

"Yes of course," he said and in the same moment realised they'd left their bags behind in their desperate flight across the field. "No, I haven't. I'm sorry. But when we reach the farm, there'll be lots of good food for you, I promise."

"Thank you," she said and walked on.

They reached the familiar fields of Kossakowski's homestead. Rain had stopped, clouds had cleared and the moon lit the farm, turning stone to silver. They were so drained, drenched, and almost out of their minds with exhaustion, they took no precaution and marched right up to Kossakowski's front door. Daniel banged on it three times and leant his head against it. He almost fell asleep standing up against that door, Ilsa still grasping his hand. The door opened and he fell forwards. Someone caught him and swore loudly in Byelorussian.

Daniel was sitting on a wooden chair. He saw Jakub take his mother's body into a room. He watched through the doorway as she was laid on a bed. Ilsa stood beside her. Jakub and Kossakowski were talking, the latter shaking his head.

"Only sips of water, mouthfuls of food. Too much too soon will kill her. I'll take care of it."

When Daniel heard that, he knew they had done it. He knew she was in the best place.

He wanted to go to Ilsa and sit with her beside their mother, watch her through the night. But his body was falling and he could not stop it. The last two years of searching had ended here. His body knew it and gave up the ghost. He got down on his knees and lay on the hard stone floor.

Daniel slept until morning. When he woke he saw grey light through the kitchen windows. His body ached horribly. He jumped up and stared at the door to his mother's room. It was closed. He walked across the hall, head drunk on sleep, mouth dry with dread. He opened the door quietly and stepped inside. There was Ilsa, asleep, still sitting in a chair, her hair splayed out across her mother's legs. And Helena's chest rose, fell, rose, fell. She was alive.

Daniel watched her sleeping. Her breathing was shallow and fast. He thought about how close she was to dying. If they'd been a day later. If he hadn't met Vladka. If the Russians hadn't bombed their street that night. If Pawel hadn't been his group leader. If he hadn't met Natan. Back and back to London. If Dad hadn't died.

Dad's death meant his mother's chance of life. So much luck, so little design. He had helped a few people in his time in Warsaw. He'd smuggled food, medication and weapons into the ghetto. That saved a few lives. He'd killed a few Germans and collaborators. That had stopped them from killing others. Quite a few people were still living because of things he'd done, and the people they might save, and the children they might go on to have. But as he stood there staring at his mother, he knew he would trade them all for this one life. It was all very well to follow a cause when you had no ties, but when it came to family there was no other cause worth fighting for. Yes, if she died that day at least she wouldn't die in the ghetto, at least she'd die a free woman, with her family around her. But Daniel wanted more. He wanted to know her. He wanted her to see him and speak to him. He wanted her to be proud of him. The fact of finding her was not enough. He wanted his Mama.

He went to the kitchen for a drink. Jakub was asleep on a couch by the fire. Kossakowski came in from feeding the animals.

Daniel asked him, "How bad is she?"

"She has symptoms of starvation."

"What can we do for her?"

"I've been giving her water with a little sugar in it. You're lucky she's here, because most Byelorussian peasants wouldn't have black market sugar. Today I'll start giving her milk diluted with water. Tomorrow whole milk. After that clear broth and then cereal, perhaps porridge."

"Will she die?"

"I don't know."

They waited.

On the table was his mother's diary. He opened it and read. Until she spoke, he had her writing.

CHAPTER TWELVE

I am alive. My daughter is alive. My son is alive. My brother is alive.

Daniel Summerskill. What a beautiful name. I told him I gave him Janek. He wants to take that name. But I said he should keep his own.

He wants to know everything. He asks me questions every day. I want to tell him. I want to tell the truth. But I do not know how. I do not know where to begin. I have said today that I will write it all down for him. Not to ask me any more questions about my past, not for the moment, please. I will write it for him tomorrow. Then I can begin at the beginning. And I hope this will help him to understand me. And not condemn me.

My son Daniel has my eyes. He is small of stature, slight yet strong, with dark brown hair and Jan's mouth. Ilsa adores him. She talks to him all the time, never leaving him alone, poor boy. I have not seen her talk so much in her life. She was like her father, quiet and thoughtful. Now it is as if her voice has been freed from a dungeon, desperate for the light of conversation. But only with Daniel, only her brother. She talks to me too, and her uncle, whom she also loves easily. But Daniel is her favourite.

My brother Jakub. My dear Jakub! He has become a fine man. He has my father's height and build, strong and powerful. A wild sapling grown into an oak. And what a heart. Every time he talks to me, his eyes water. He told me his wife and son were murdered. I grieve for them and for him. I feel lucky to have my daughter with me. When she was close to death, I was sure I would lose her. And I knew I would die soon after. Her death would kill me, as sure as a bullet. But she recovered. Some do recover from typhus. She did. But I was sure she would die. I called it a miracle. And now another miracle: my son. I said sorry to Jakub, I apologised for having my children, when he has lost so much. He said, "They are my salvation." He explained that he had been reckless these past years, taking terrible risks in his vengeful dealings with the Germans, almost desperate to die a fighter. Now, he says, "I want to live."

As for me, I am better. Apparently, I was asleep for the first few days, only waking briefly to take sustenance. It took over two weeks for me to get up from my bed. The Byelorussian Kossakowski nursed me like his child. Every day I grew a little stronger. It was the fifth day when I was sensible enough to meet my son. Before that, I knew Jakub was there. I had not seen him since he was twelve years old, over twenty years ago. But I knew him immediately. I was ill, delirious. I was not surprised to see my brother beside my bed. If a hundred angels had stood beside him, I would not have been surprised either.

But there was this young man, with such a handsome face,

dark eyes like my own, always there. Watching me. Smiling at me. One day, I asked him: "Who are you?"

He could not answer. Tears rolled down his cheeks.

I said, "Don't cry."

He said, "I am your son."

He handed me a photograph. Myself, a girl. Jan behind the camera, smiling at me. I looked at that child with her foolish dreams. I wanted to tell her what would happen to her. To make her change her path, go home. But I realised that if she had, my son would never have existed, he would never have been standing here now. And I would probably be dead in a ditch with my parents. How strange life is.

And he gave me my ribbon, made for Janek.

I looked at his face. I felt the tiny weight of his newborn body in my arms. I saw his sleeping face when I left him outside the orphanage. Even without the photograph and the ribbon, I would know it was him. My son.

I believed it all part of the dream. The dream of being safe, fed by a kind farmer, attended by my brother, my daughter laughing from another room. All of this was a dream, I was sure. A dream when dying. None of it could be real. But I got better. I sat up in my bed. The people did not go away. The ghetto walls did not return. Eventually, I knew I was alive and I was there. In that place. With my family. Another miracle.

When I was strong enough, I called Daniel to me.

I sat up and said, "Can I hold you?"

He sat down on my bed and I put my arms around him. We did not weep. We were stiff, at first.

I said, "My son."

We softened. It was then I knew him as my own. Not just as a serious young man who appeared in my room from time to time. He was my son again from that moment.

He came from England to find me. He is just a boy. Twenty years old. He was safe in unoccupied London. And he gave all that up, to travel all this way, to live in Warsaw, to fight in the ghetto, to come to the forests and find me. I am astonished that our feet beat the same earth in Warsaw and I never knew, and we never met. He read my diary when I was sick. I am relieved I wrote nothing obvious in there about his father. The time for all that will come soon, but I will write it for him, I will fashion it. No lies, but with my words I hope to win him round to a truth he will not want to hear.

I love my son. I would love my son if he were a nothing, a nobody, just a young man living a stupid life somewhere. I would love him. But to know he came all that way for me. He never gave up. I love him even more for that. But I am angry with him! He was safe in London. I took him to that orphanage, I left my baby on that step, I went away to give him a better life. That kind man took my baby to London and fed him and clothed him and loved him. He kept my picture and even my little keepsake, the embroidery I left for my son, that he would know me a little. For all those years, he told my son nothing of his past. He raised him as his own. Most importantly, Summerskill kept my baby safe from harm. And for me, my boy gave all that up, everything I had given him by giving him up. He left it all behind for me. Now he is here, in Nazi Poland, the worst place in the world for a Jew. If only I could spirit him away with his little sister, my Ilsa. Put them somewhere so safe the world would never find them. I would do it. But I am glad they are here. I am glad! I am angry they never left me. But I am happy to be alive and happy to be with my children.

I am writing from the Bielski encampment in the Naliboki *puscha*. It is the first time I have written since Ilsa's illness. I gave up writing, I thought for good. It felt too like life. But now it feels good to write again. It feels good to write leaning my journal on my knee, sitting on the forest floor. We arrived here a few days ago, welcomed by the camp as a story with a happy ending. I had heard the name Bielski whispered in the ghetto. It was a magic word to the Novogrodek ghetto dwellers. People there spoke of the Bielski camp like a fairy kingdom for Jews. But you needed contacts with those in the forest. People received letters then disappeared. And Ilsa was ill for so long, I couldn't contemplate taking her on a journey into the unknown. As she recovered, I began to ail and eventually I was too weak to do anything or go anywhere. I was waiting to die. I did not want to fight any more. I only wanted my daughter to be safe. That's the only thing that kept me alive. But I knew as my strength ebbed from me, I was less and less able to protect her. I talked to her about escape, but she would not leave my side. I told her to go to the Bielskis in the forest and look for her uncle. I hardly believed it myself at the time. And now here we are.

There are several hundred souls in this Bielski camp. It is a makeshift affair, as they have not been here long. I have not met any Bielski brothers yet, as they have been away dealing with the Russians. It is a kind of wilderness here. The Naliboki is quite different from the woods of my childhood. We are in the heart of a great forest. There are few people living hereabouts and hardly any roads. There are tales of wolves and bears nearby.

I do not know how long we will settle here. There are rumours of German manoeuvres in the area. But for the first time since the Nazis marched into Warsaw, I feel safe. I am part of a group of a few hundred free Jews. We are led by brave brothers who are determined to keep us alive. But best of all, I am with my family. I want my daughter to grow up. I want to know my son. I want my brother to meet a good girl and have more babies. I want to live.

Dear Daniel,

It is a strange thing to write a letter to your son, a son you have never known, a son who waits nearby for you to finish it. I never imagined I would be doing such a thing. But I feel I owe it to you. To tell you the truth. As I said, I am not a great speaker. But I can write. I hope to relate to you the story of my past, as well as your story, before you went to London as a baby. I want to tell the whole truth, but I warn you now: it may surprise you and disappoint you. You may even feel angry with me. I only hope that by telling it this way, in a letter written with forethought, you will come not to judge me too harshly. I hope you will come to understand me, the person I was, girl and woman, before I became your mother.

So, I should not put it off any longer. Here is an account of my youth and how you came into this world. And why I had to let you go.

I was born in 1904 here in Novogrodek. Our town had a peculiar history, as it had been part of different nations at different times. So, growing up in this place led to a curious sense of identity, perhaps no real identity at all. Some people in the world are intensely Polish, or Russian, or British. Some feel that way about being Jewish. But my family had no particular affinity to anyone, anywhere or anything. My parents were not religious Jews. My parents were strict in terms of discipline but not in a religious sense. They celebrated holy days, but generally were not interested. There was an assumption that God existed, but beyond that He did not enter into our daily thoughts.

I was the first born, followed three years later by my brother Jakub. He was the apple of my father's eye, yet I'm sure he would agree, a wormy apple. He was trouble from the first moments of his life, causing my mother terrible pain in a labour that lasted several days. As he grew, he became boisterous and unruly, wild and totally uninterested in religion, literature or anything but acting like a little savage. But he was loved. Nobody could resist loving him. He could be ruthless, but acted with humour and passion and was forgiven everything. He projected his personality outwards at all times, stamping his authority on the world. I was the opposite. I was the reader. A quiet girl, thoughtful, serious. My parents were proud of me, but I wonder if they found me harder to love than my charismatic brother. Jakub spoke every thought and feeling he had. You knew exactly where you stood with him. Even if you didn't like what he said, you could never accuse him of duplicity. My mother sometimes looked at me with narrowed eyes, as if to pry into my closed exterior and see what lay within. I gave little away. I was passionate inside. I could spend hours imagining elaborate tales with myself as heroine, usually involving a handsome hero and a deadly threat. I wrote long ballads about love and danger, but showed them to no one. I think my parents loved me. But they could not find a way to delight in me. I grew up feeling I was not very important. By the time I was a teenager, my parents had become strangers to me.

My father repaired clocks and watches and was a watchmaker

when business was good. He had a shop in town and would leave home every morning, dressed not as a craftsman or artisan, but as a businessman in smart suit and polished shoes. My mother worked from home as a seamstress, bringing in extra money for her piece work for local ladies. She began as a young woman doing general repairs, but by the time I came along she was running a healthy domestic business in fancy embroidery for women's dresses and hats. From an early age, she taught me to sew and I became very proficient at it. But I had no interest in it at all, and only worked hard at it in order to please my mother and have an excuse to sit with her. I even contributed to the family earnings this way and felt useful. I also thought that by doing this, I was helping to stave off the financial collapse I secretly believed was permanently imminent. We were reasonably well off. My father used to say to my mother that one day, when the watch making really took off, she would be able to give up her sewing work and become a lady of leisure. And my mother would smile and shake her head at this. I believe she secretly enjoyed her sewing work and had no intention of giving it up. But more seriously, she knew, as we all did, that my father was unreliable with money. Even though our life was quite comfortable when I was a girl, there were times I remember my mother taking glassware or china or even pieces of furniture and selling them in town. She would set her face in an expression of grim pride. I think it hurt her to have to sell her things. But she never complained.

My father spent a lot of money on what he called his 'library'. Our house was stuffed with books. Father constructed special wall-to-wall shelves to house them all. Wherever you sat in the house, eating your breakfast or sewing a button, there was always a row of books poking you in the back. He would dust and replace them carefully, always in the correct order only he understood. He was obsessed with Russian and German writers. He said they were the apotheosis of world literature. He had little time for Polish literature, particularly Mickiewicz, Poland's greatest poet and Novogrodek's favourite son. Father thought him completely overrated, and besides, he was Polish and my father was not a fan of the Poles. From an early age, I read Goethe and Schiller, Tolstoy and Dostoevsky, all borrowed from my father's library. Jakub went to the local Polish school, when he could be persuaded to turn up. It's true that my father disapproved of the Poles in general, but it was the best school hereabouts, and my father was even less interested in any sort of Jewish education than that of the Poles. I think my mother was secretly devout; I heard her whisper prayers. We spoke Yiddish at home, Byelorussian in town, and Polish and Russian too, when dealing with particular officials at different times. My mother taught us modern Hebrew as well. You can see how I grew up with little sense of who I was, where my home was, or my place in the world. And I was quite ignorant about the world. I was 'educated' at home, that is, told I could read any book I liked from my father's shelves. My education was haphazard and biased heavily towards rich and dramatic literature, mostly poetry and novels. Thus, my knowledge of history is patchy and my understanding of the sciences non-existent. But I could recite long passages of Faust, if ever the need arose.

It was a shame my father never appreciated the fact that his daughter was a reader like him. But he only had eyes for his son. My brother never read a book in his life. I was constantly reading or writing, but still my father's favour shone on Jakub. Thus, I spent a lot of time on my own. I was never part of a gaggle of girls. Such a thing I found terrifying. I had singular friends, always readers, always quiet like me. But I often found myself preferring my own company. I would talk to my father about literature. I wanted to ask him about the stories – how did he feel about this character, or wasn't that moment just wonderful – but he would rather quiz me about the book, asking test questions about what day of the week was this man robbed or that woman married. I soon stopped talking to him about books. My mother never read. She had the wireless on all day, every day. She gathered all her information from it and quoted to us from it, as if it were the Torah. "They said on the wireless…" and that would be that. I engaged in daily wrangles with my parents about ideas and thoughts on how the world was or how it should be, and from my mother I was given pat answers from the airwaves and from my father a quick test of the dates of wars and little else. I learnt that trying to talk to others was largely pointless. By the time I reached my teenage years I had more or less given up speaking.

Jakub was never at home, off roaming with his feral friends, but as a girl, and a bookish one, our house was my refuge and my prison. We lived in a hinterland between the rather seedy Jewish neighbourhood of Racelo Street and the more middle class area beyond it. Our street bordered the edge of the Mickiewicz estate that had once belonged to the poet. Its tall stone wall ran along the route to Jakub's school, and I would walk along it, pretending I was going to school like Jakub, running my fingers along the bumpy cold walls of the poet's grounds and think about him. I managed to get hold of Mickiewicz's writing from a friend and was addicted to his words. I secretly learned stanzas off by heart and produced tributes to him in poetic form, that is, I wrote thinly disguised copies of his poems in my own words and deceived myself they were mine. Chestnut trees from his estate would shed their fruit every year, and I would pick them up, hoarding them to eat alone later, imagining the poet eating fruit from the same trees years before. Of course, the largest part of my attraction to Mickiewicz was that my father did not like him. There never was a surer way to fuel a daughter's obsession.

Those years in which my Mickiewicz fixation took hold, political events beyond our home loomed large for my parents. In 1914, when I was ten, Germany invaded the Russian empire. They marched straight through our region on their way to Moscow. The local gentiles were appalled, of course. But it was a different matter for the Jews. The occupying Germans were actually less harsh to the Jews than the Russian despots had been. The recent pogroms and expulsions of Jews by the Romanovs had terrified Jewish communities all over the empire. The Germans actually repealed some of the anti-Jewish laws. The war itself did bring a terrible economic disaster to our region, with starvation wages and general misery. But at least the German laws were better for Jews. And remember, my father loved Germany. He held it up as the most cultured nation on earth, with literary Russia running a close second. Yet the Poles, my father held in contempt. He often talked of them as a bastard people, even claiming that one day, when his business was successful enough, we should all relocate to Berlin and make a fine life in the world's capital of culture. Then the Bolshevik Revolution happened. The Romanovs were gone, the Communists were in. When Novogrodek became part of the new Soviet Union in 1919, my parents agreed this was the best result under the circumstances. The Germans were regrettably gone, but the Bolsheviks had overthrown the old cruel order. My father had hated the Russian empire, but loved the Russia of its intellectuals. And at least the Poles weren't in charge. My parents believed that if anyone hated the Jews more than the Russian empire, it was the Poles. But before long, the Polish nation retaliated and their army marched into our area that year. They took Minsk in August 1919, and from then on, Novogrodek was Polish. My father was disgusted. I was fifteen. I did not understand and I did not care. The only thing I cared about was poetry.

One balmy September day in 1919, my mother sent me on an errand to Jakub's school, to take my brother the lunch he had left behind. I was wandering along by Mickiewicz's wall when a man's head appeared over the top of it. Then the man's foot, his leg and his whole body threw itself over the wall and he sat on top of it. Now this wall was huge, about five metres high. It was a shocking sight indeed to see a man sitting on top of it. But this man just sat there, grinning at me. I just stood there, staring at him. He was no one I knew. He did not look local. He was wearing rather scruffy clothes, but he did not look like a labourer.

"Watch out!" he said cheerfully, and leant down behind him to produce an extremely long ladder which he swung over the wall gracefully and placed beneath him. The ground this side must have been considerably lower, for when he saw how far the ladder dropped, his face fell. Yet he shrugged his shoulders, turned around and dropped his lithe body down the wall, holding on by his fingertips until his feet just touched the top rung.

"Be careful!" I said, as he tried to find his footing, the ladder threatening to slide sideways and let him fall.

"Hold it then!" he shouted and I grabbed it, watching his legs and backside descend towards me, at which point I looked away in embarrassment. Once I could see he was steady, I let go of the ladder and continued my aimless walk, this time with purpose.

"Hey!" he called, and brought up to be polite, I turned back. He was a young man. Not a boy. Not a girl, like me. A handsome young man in his twenties. "Don't you want to know what I'm doing?"

I shook my head.

"Aren't you in the least bit curious about why I'm climbing over Mickiewicz's wall?"

His accent was not local. His voice sounded like it was honed in a big city, far away from there. It sounded like cafés and trams and freedom.

"Why?" I said.

"Because the bastards wouldn't let me in! I am the world's supreme devotee of Mickiewicz. I have travelled here on foot all the way from Warsaw to see the home of the great man. I went to the front gate full of yearning to complete my quest, and the gardener turned me away like a peasant scrumping apples. I was forced to sneak in past the gate and explore the poet's grounds in secret, hidden behind chestnut trees like a common thief. When I came to leave, I found the front gate guarded by a couple of tiresome groundsmen, having a dreary contretemps about peas. I was forced to steal a ladder and heave myself over this way. It's a disgrace, I tell you, that the home of Poland's foremost literary light is not open to the public, or at least to the reading public, which is quite a different matter. Don't you agree?"

Nobody had ever spoken to me like this before. His turn of phrase, his vocabulary, his gesticulations and his voice were all as exotic as a parakeet. I could not remember the last time anyone had asked my opinion either. I had no idea what to say. But he waited for me to answer. At first, his face was serious, full of the bluster of his previous speech. But he began to smile and I smiled. And then we were laughing. We stood there in the street laughing. The sun was hot on our backs. Most people were working or at school. The place was deserted. I held my brother's lunch in my hand and at that moment, I knew he would never receive it.

"Would you like a sandwich?" I asked.

His name was Jan Kucharski. He was a poet. He lived in Warsaw and indeed, on a whim, had come on foot to Novogrodek to see his muse's house. He was a compulsive Mickiewicz devotee and had memorised everything he'd ever written. We went to a shady spot I knew, beneath an oak tree at the edge of a field running behind the cemetery. I went there to read at weekends on my own, and loved it because I never saw a soul. On a warm day it was always my chosen sanctuary. Now I'd taken the poet there and we ate Jakub's lunch and spent the afternoon swapping Mickiewicz quotations and tales of his life. Jan knew everything about the poet and told me things I'd never found out about from the books in my father's library. As I sat there with him, I knew what I was doing was wrong. I knew it would shock my parents and most of the town's elders. I knew it was utterly unlike anything I had done before. And yet, I hardly thought about it, at the moment I asked him to share Jakub's lunch, I did it as if I asked young male poets to eat with me every day of the week. But I never had. I never even spoke to boys. Jan was a beautiful young man and when I looked at him, I felt a jolt like electricity. I knew what I was doing, but I did not know. I knew what I wanted, but I did not understand it. It seemed to me more powerful than any dictum of my parents or my society. I knew it was wrong, but I did it anyway. I was already in love with him.

We spent several afternoons together in the week after we first met. It took five meetings before I would let him kiss me. Three more before I would let him touch me. The ninth meeting we made love. By this point, I had agreed to go to Warsaw with him. I was fifteen years old. He was twenty-eight. I lied to him, telling him I was eighteen. He wanted to live with me, he told me. He did not speak of marriage, but I liked this. It was romantically rebellious and fitted his poet's nature. But I did not doubt he loved me. He spoke of it often in glittering language. He loved poetry and Poland. He spoke of his great love for his country. He was a gentile and an atheist. He said he did not care if I were a Jew or an Eskimo. But he was glad I was Polish, as he called me. It did not seem to matter to him that my town had only recently become officially Polish. As far as he was concerned, I was a Pole. He said he could never love a foreigner. Poland was the greatest nation on earth, he told me. Poland had repelled every conqueror since time began - despite name changes and brutal occupations - and still came back as Poland. He said not all Poles were anti-Jewish, especially the intelligentsia, within which he included himself. He said he loved me as he loved Poland. And he spoke of practical concerns too. He told me he was about to have his first collection of poetry published in Warsaw and was expecting his career to take off very soon. He said he could look after me and we would live in style, in the bohemian quarter near to his other artist friends. He said I could become the poet I'd always wanted to be. He told me we would conquer Warsaw with our words.

What did I have to stay for? At midnight, two weeks after I'd met him, I left a note for my parents on the dining room table. It read something like this: "Dear Father and Mother. I am leaving home. I have fallen in love with a great man, a great poet. With him by my side, I am going out into the world to become a great writer. One day you will hear of me. Perhaps then you will be proud. Best regards, Helena Goldman." I took with me a few clothes, my hair-brush and ribbons, and a portable sewing kit. I liked the idea of mending Jan's clothes for him, like a little wife should. I met him near the guesthouse he'd been sleeping at, and we stole away into the night. Our plan was to walk to Warsaw, but the next day Jan said he was weary, he could not go on. He said he had been writing an epic poem for the last few days, and had not had time to eat. I used some of the money I had stolen from my mother's housekeeping tin and bought us two bus tickets to the capital.

When we arrived in Warsaw, Jan took me to his place. It was a squalid little room in a filthy tenement. Over the next few weeks, I saw there were no artists or writers living nearby. I saw there was no publication of his poetry on the horizon. I saw there were other truths he had embellished. But I was blind to it. I was blind drunk on his love. You have to understand how a woman can be drugged by desire. You live in a soporific haze. Nothing matters, only his body. You eat only after making love, only because you need it. You don't bother with conversation or even with thinking. Only him, only his body inside you, is all that matters, is all you want. I know I may shock you. I know it is not the kind of thing a mother writes to her son. But we are not conventional, you and I. And I have to make you understand. I adored Jan Kucharski.

We lived in that room with little money and scraps to eat. Jan spent his days scribbling on paper and tearing it up. He often went out and did not return for hours, saying he was going for a walk to seek inspiration. But I could smell the drink on his breath. We went on like this for a few months. We were not happy but we blamed it on the idiots who would not publish his poetry. We talked of love and a future as wealthy writers. We lived like paupers. It was not long before Jan grew restless. He would come back from his daily walks full of anger about the Russians. The Polish–Soviet war raged on. Jan was full of talk about his mighty Poland and the despicable Russians who dared to grasp at Polish land. He spoke more and more of his duty to defend his country. By February of 1920, he talked of little else. One day, he told me to dress in my nicest outfit. I thought he was taking me out for a treat. But we went straight to a photographer's, down the street from where we lived. Standing outside the shop, Jan told me that the next day he was leaving to join the Polish army. He was going to fight in the major offensive pushing into the Ukraine. He wanted a picture of me to take with him. Before I had a chance to respond, he whisked me inside and I had my picture taken. Jan stood behind the photographer and smiled at me. All I could think of was that he was leaving. He was leaving me. He was going off to fight in a war I did not care about. A stupid war about stupid nations, about who owns what.

That night, I tried my best to please him. I did everything a woman could to make her man want her, to make him stay. But in the morning he was gone. He promised me he would write. He promised me he would visit soon. I wept for a week, I think. I did not eat much. I saw my life for what it was. I had hardly any money, no prospects, no one to take care of me. I was sixteen and alone in Warsaw. I had one skill that could make money. I spent the little cash I had on dress materials and sewed samples of my work. I hawked them around the area. But everyone was poor, and I only managed to gain a couple of commissions. It was only just enough to keep me eating. Our landlady was quite fond of me. Jan had lied to her, told her we were married. She pitied me, my so-called husband away fighting as a hero in the war. But she wanted paying or I could find myself somewhere else to go, my dear. Whenever the rent was due, I did not eat that day. I waited for news of Jan. I read newspapers I found in the street, searching for news from the Ukraine. But I heard nothing of Jan. Then I got sick. I was nauseous all the time. I thought it was because I wasn't eating properly. But I had other symptoms. I had stopped menstruating. I was so stupid, so uninformed. My mother never talked of such things. After all, they never spoke about it on the wireless. I was pregnant.

Soon after, the Polish army was forced back towards Warsaw by a Russian counter-offensive. I thought this must be the time when Jan would return to me. He may be outside the city right now. There was a great victory at Warsaw for the Polish army. Everybody was celebrating. I went to a temporary barracks nearby and asked to speak to an officer. The guards laughed at me. I told them Jan's name and said I was his wife and was carrying his baby. They laughed again. I grabbed hold of one soldier's lapels.

"Please," I begged.

"Get off, you stupid whore!" he shouted. He pushed me and I fell over. The other soldier took pity on me and helped me up.

"Don't you have parents, girly?"

I said they were a long way away.

"You'd best go home to them and quick. Family will look after you. Forget about this Jan fellow. I don't think you'll be seeing him again. Besides, he might be dead. Go home, girly."

But that was the one thing I could not do. To return, pregnant by a Polish gentile, sixteen years old. My parents would never accept me. I was certain of that. The Jewish community would never forgive them. It would be a scandal from which they would never recover.

"I can't," I said. "Can you help me find Jan Kucharski?"

"Look, give me your name and address. I'll ask around. See if I can get his regiment. I'll look at the death lists too. If he went to Ukraine, he may well be dead. Lots of ours died there."

I borrowed paper and a pen from a nearby news vendor and wrote down my details for the soldier. He stowed them carefully in his pocket and said he would be in touch. I went back to the room with renewed hope. The landlady was waiting for me. Rent, she demanded. I had nothing to give her. She said she might have to let my room to somebody else, someone who could pay. I broke down. I told her everything, my condition, my age. Even where I'd come from and why I couldn't go back there.

"A Jew?" she said. I cannot forget the way she said it. I had seen anti-Jewish behaviour in Novogrodek, but I felt largely untouched by it as a child. When I moved to Warsaw, I believed Jan when he told me that the cosmopolitan type did not take up with outdated notions like Jew-hating. "A Jew?"

She told me to pack my things and get out. I went back to the barracks to see the soldier, planning to tell him I had left the address I had written for him. But he was not there. Another soldier was on guard and he would not talk to me. I went back the next day and still my soldier was not there. I returned to my old room and knocked on the front door. The landlady saw me from the front window and poked her head out – "Get away, Jew!" she shouted. I asked her, please, if anyone sends a message to this address, please keep it for me. I'll come back. But she would not listen. She shouted for me to shoo, shoo, like vermin.

I lived on the street for three days. On the third, I bent over in the street and cried out. A terrible pain came from my womb. Blood ran down my leg like leaden water. I sat in the road and bled. People passed by. My baby was leaking out of me.

I fainted. I remembered hands on me, but I was delirious. When I awoke, a middle-aged man was patting my face. I was lying on a sofa in a nice room. He told me I had had a miscarriage. He said a doctor had cleaned me up and checked me over, that I would be all right, but I must rest. He said he would look after me, that I was not to worry about a thing. The man was called Roman. He was in his fifties, very respectable looking. He lived in a small apartment, the walls lined with books. I had nowhere else to go. Roman was kind to me. He talked to me about current events and Polish history. He was an interesting man. He never asked me any questions. He never told me I had to leave. I just stayed. I recovered there. After a week, I felt a lot better. But I still had no money and nowhere to go. I told Roman that I could sew and if I could borrow a little money to buy material, I could sew samples to show people and start up my own business. I could find a place to live and leave him in peace.

"You want a little money?" he asked. "I have a way you can earn money very easily. And you don't need to do a thing."

That night, he brought a friend round. The friend took me into Roman's bedroom. I earned my little bit of money. Roman was right. I did not have to do anything. Something was done to me. I thought about my baby, who had poured out of me into the gutter. Roman's friend said I was a good girl. He wanted me again next week. The next day, Roman brought two more friends round. One started and the other waited his turn, talking to Roman in the other room about the war and food prices. Then he came in. That night, Roman gave me a lot of vodka to drink. He said it would make me feel better. I slept well, but felt awful in the morning. Roman poured more into my breakfast tea, and I felt better again. He said, "After you have a client, you should go to my bathroom and wash yourself carefully inside. Then you won't have a baby."

I lived this way for two years. I know it sounds a long time, as if I chose that life. But there was a madness in my mind. And I was still a child. I was four years younger than you are now when I met him. And Roman became like a father to me. He never molested me, he provided for me, fed me and clothed me, read to me. He bought me new sewing equipment and materials. I made dresses for myself, perfected my craft. I drank a lot. I slept a lot. I seldom left the flat. Two years can pass quicker than you think.

I saw two clients a day, weekends off. Roman kept written records of all my clients' visits and my menstruation. He kept me away from men at certain times. He made me wash myself carefully after every man. But in October 1922 I stopped bleeding again. The nausea came. I knew what it meant. I told Roman. That evening, a woman came round. She was old and had dirty fingernails. She did an internal examination of me. She hurt me inside. Roman said she would be back later with her equipment. Roman went to the toilet and I left. I just got up and left the apartment. I walked and walked. I just wanted to put miles between myself and that place. I had nothing with me, not even my sewing kit. Only my unborn child for company. You.

I begged on the streets for a few days. A nurse stopped one day to give me money and she told me about a hostel nearby that took in homeless women. I went there. It was run by an old couple with kind eyes. They said they were full, that I should come back next week. I told them I was pregnant and that I was a Jew. I don't know why I said that. Then I collapsed. I was so hungry, so tired. They let me stay there. They looked after me, but they said when the baby came I'd have to raise you somewhere else. They couldn't afford a child. They barely had enough to keep the hostel running. I said I would sort it out. But secretly, I hoped they would never have the heart to throw a girl and her baby out onto the streets. On June 1st, 1923, I gave birth to a baby boy. You, Daniel.

You were beautiful. I called you Janek. Little Jan. After the father you should have had. I did not know if Jan had left me on purpose or had died in battle. But I still loved him. I mourned the baby of his that I had lost. I looked at you and I loved you. I thought about which one of the clients might have been your father. But I knew I could never know. I spent most of those two years half-drunk on Roman's vodka. I know there were times when clients came and I was barely awake. But I knew it did not matter to me. A man, a client of a prostitute, planted his seed in me. But I grew you. I nurtured you and kept you warm and sang to you day after day for nine months. I felt you kick and rubbed my belly and talked to you of the world and its beauty night after night. I screamed for you and pushed for you and brought you into this world. I fed you from my breasts and held you and loved you for five whole days. Then my breasts dried up. I could not feed you. I offered you the breast again and again, this one then that. You cried and cried, you screamed with hunger. I tried to squeeze the milk out of me into a bottle, but nothing came. I had no milk to give you.

The couple who ran the hostel gave me a bottle of milk for you. But they said it couldn't go on like this. They couldn't afford to raise a baby. They told me about a Jewish orphanage. They said I should go. It would be best for the baby. Either that or back to my parents. But I couldn't raise the baby at the hostel. I had no more milk for you. I stole a blanket from another woman at the hostel and wrapped you in it. I made my way across town to the orphanage. On the way, I passed by a shabby little photographer's shop. In the window, I saw myself. The photo Jan had asked for, all that time ago, the day before he went off to war. There was nobody in the shop. I sneaked in and stole that picture. I saw my name written on the back. When I reached the orphanage, I stood on the other side of the street. It was a quiet side road, only one or two passers-by now and again. I stared at the building for an hour or so. You were sleeping in my arms. But soon you would wake up and you would be hungry. I watched a woman come out of the orphanage. She had an apron wrapped round her waist and a pleasant, round face. She swept the steps and stopped for a moment. She looked at the sky and squinted at the sun. She smiled. I liked the way she did that. When she had gone back inside, I placed the photograph inside your blanket, along with a little piece of embroidery I'd been doing the day you were born. I waited until the street was empty and I walked across and stood on the step. I knew if I went in there, if I talked to someone and tried to hand you across, I could never do it. I would never pass my baby to another woman. I left you on the step. I wrapped you up tightly, that you might feel as if I held you still. I touched your face and watched you sleep. I heard a noise near the door. I ran away down the street. Before I turned the corner, I had to look back. I had to make sure you were still on that step. I saw the door open and the same woman came out. She found you. She picked you up and spoke to you. I could not hear what she said, but she spoke to you lovingly.

I left you.

I cannot tell you about the days after. It was a dark time for me. I cannot write about that.

I went on living. There was no news of Jan. I sewed for money to eat. Within a year, I had started up my own business as a seamstress. I was doing quite well. I had a bit of money in my pocket, a smart outfit and a nice hat. I went to the orphanage. The woman who had found you on the step was not there. I told them who I was. I asked about the baby, I told them about the photograph, the embroidery. I said I was earning my living now. I could afford to keep you. I had a place to live and I wanted you back. They told me you had gone. A wealthy journalist from England had adopted you. They would not tell me any more details. They said that was their policy on adoptions. They were good women, running a home for abandoned Jewish babies. Good women. But their faces were like stone when I begged them for the journalist's name. I suppose they had seen too many wayward mothers swear they wanted their babies back. And too many babies left on their doorstep. They would not tell me where you were or who had adopted you. At least I knew you were safe. Better off without me, I was sure. Better off without the truth of who you were, where you came from.

After that, I just went on living. You go on. You have to live. I did think about you all the time. It hurt me inside, like a deep cut always gaping, smarting each time you bend and straighten. After a while, the cut closed over. The pain lessened. But it was still there. Any little thing could slice it open again. Hearing a baby's cry. Watching a mother kiss her son. I lived on my own for a time. I worked very hard, because I had to. Because I needed to block out the luxury of brooding over you. When I stopped working at night, I only left myself enough time to eat and sleep. I gave up reading. I gave up writing. I could not bear the thought of those ridiculous poems I used to write, about love and peril and all that infantile rubbish. I came to see fiction as dangerous lies. When I was a child, I imagined my life as if I were a character in a book.

But I learnt very young. Life is not like that. It is random and cruel. There are no happy endings. It is folly to pretend so. By the time I met Isak, my husband, I had learnt to hide my wounds. I had to conceal a lot from Isak. Ilsa came along and she helped me heal a little. But I never forgot you.

So now you know. I hope you do not hate me. I hope you can forgive me for what I did to you. I wish I could tell you who your father was. I know you wanted Jan Kucharski to be your father. I did too. His child died inside me. But when you came, I believed you were the soul of that child, returning in a new form, waiting patiently for a chance to live. I still believe that. I thought about lying to you, telling you what we both wanted to hear. But one thing this war has taught me. We may be dead in a moment. And I want you to know the truth about me, about yourself. And to know that none of it matters. Family is very important to you, I know. It may haunt you that you will never know who your blood father is. And that is my fault.

But Daniel, you know your father is that good man, Summerskill. He raised you. He loved you enough to tell you about yourself before he died. You are as much his son as you are mine, perhaps more. You are Daniel Summerskill.

If I die tomorrow, know that I was a weak, foolish girl once. I allowed terrible things to happen to me. I left you on a doorstep. But I always wanted you. I always loved you. Know that, Daniel.

Love from your mother,
Helena.

CHAPTER THIRTEEN

"Don't go, Daniel. Don't go!"

Ilsa was crying, holding onto his arm with both hands.

The thunder of the German advance in their ears, he gave her a hug and said, "I will come back to you."

The camp was on the run. They heard the enemy move in to clear the forests of partisans. Explosions in the distance. The sounds of heavy machinery moving the trees that had been left across forest paths by the partisans. The Bielskis sent the non-combatants deeper into the Naliboki forest. Some fighters would go with the family group, a hundred to stay behind to fight.

Daniel was torn. Part of him - the man who fought in the ghetto - wanted to stay behind and fight with his Jewish brothers. The other part of him - the protector - wanted nothing more than to follow the non-combatants into the forest and look after them. When the order came, Jakub was sent with them and Daniel was chosen to stay. His mother's face was wrenching. Fear, fear of losing him.

The family group left, their backs dissolved into foliage and green shadow. Russian partisans came. About two hundred, trotting through the trees, taking up positions, their commander tall with ragged grey hair. His plan was to launch a surprise attack. There was a grim excitement. Germans were approaching on foot through the trees. Three hundred partisans hushed. Waited. But someone from their group let loose a shot. Then Germans were shooting everywhere, monstrous firepower and little they could do to repel it. They fled and followed their families into the heart of the forest. He heard later the shot came from a Russian traitor. The Russians executed him.

The camp regrouped, crouched fearfully, awaiting orders. The Bielski brothers had gone to a nearby Russian unit for advice. Word came earlier from Russian scouts that the Naliboki forest was being surrounded by the Germans, who had also occupied all the surrounding villages.

A Polish partisan commander arrived and Daniel heard him say, "The Germans are only about two kilometres away. They'll probably reach you by tomorrow morning."

Groups of Russian partisans galloped past at intervals, rousing everyone to near-panic. Daniel didn't know what their next move would be. Beside him, his mother sat cradling his sister. Jakub was hanging around the camp, unable to sit still. Ilsa was not crying or fretting like some of the other children. She was silent and vigilant. His mother too. She looked at him. Since the letter, that same look. Do you forgive me?

So his mother was a prostitute. She left him on a doorstep.

He knew Helena thought he might hate her. He didn't hate her.

He hated what had happened to her. There was a tiny voice in his head that said, why did she let them do it? Why didn't she run away as soon as she saw what Roman was up to? But it was easy to throw questions at a memory. She had lost her baby. She was just a girl. He recalled himself at sixteen. He was a bloody fool in short trousers. And she came for him. Too late. But she did come back for him. How would his life have been, if those women at the orphanage had told Helena: Henry Summerskill of Tavistock Square, London? Where would they all be now? Would Dad be alive?

His real father was a man who paid to have sex with a girl. At first, he felt sick. He wanted to stab that man in the stomach and strangle him till he was dead. Was he haunted by it? That he would never know who he was. Yes. He wanted to talk to him. Who was that man? Did he have a family, a wife, other children? Did he tuck them in at night, kiss them and touch their hair, say 'Sleep tight', then go to his mate Roman's house to fuck a girl so drunk on fear and vodka she was barely awake?

He hated Jan Kucharski. Whether he had died in battle or just abandoned Helena, he still hated him for leaving her. A ruined girl alone in Warsaw, away from her family and everything she knew. How could he do it? But Daniel remembered how Dad and Magda had begged him not to enlist. He loved them all right, but he was gung-ho with the war and didn't care how they felt. He only cared about being a pilot and a hero and all that tosh. Maybe Jan was the same. But Daniel had been a young lad. Jan was a lot older, in his late twenties. He should have known better. So yes, he was a bastard, either way. Yet, do people ever grow up? They all shelter illusions, surely, even when they're old and grey. It was easier. The truth was too uncomfortable to sleep on.

Even Dad lived a lie. His father, decent and honest. He lied to Daniel about himself for years. He must have thought it better that way. Better for Daniel, or better for him? Whatever his faults, Helena was right about Dad. He was his father. He was Dad, in every way a man should be your dad. Sometimes he wished Dad had never told him the truth. He'd come all that way, found his mother, saved her life. And a fraction of him wished he were still in London with Magda, seeing out the war in pleasant ignorance, waiting for it all to blow over. Begin his life again in a free world, sad his dear old Dad was dead, but full of promise for his glittering future.

The moment he put down that letter, he felt a hundred years old.

You could know too much.

Since then he had brought his mother and sister to a haven in the forest, only to find within days they were on the run again. They came so close to capture and death and there would've been nothing he could've done to prevent that. If they'd died, would it have been his fault? You just did what you had to. You made choices, wrong or right. Sometimes you hurt people. Sometimes you killed them. He had killed. Was he a bad man? Even those clients in that seedy bedroom. What drove them to that? As for Jan Kucharski, for all they knew, he may have died on a battlefield in Ukraine, thinking of Helena and his beloved Poland. And Dad, he lied. But he did it for his own reasons, mostly to protect Daniel. Could he forgive the Germans? Well, let's not get carried away. They really were bastards.

The Bielskis returned and Tuvia made a speech.

"What we need now is quiet courage. We can survive this. We must escape at night, because the Germans won't attack then."

But people weren't listening. Shots fired from a distance.

Coming closer. Partisans at the back fled and a ripple of alarm swept across the camp and people tried to follow them.

Tuvia had to shout his lungs out: "Jews! Have mercy! Don't go mad! Listen to me."

His voice stopped them. Their trusted leader had brought them this far. All looked to him.

"I will bring you out of here alive."

The camp settled a little. As evening came, the sounds of German gunfire receded. Tuvia had been right.

Later, they saw him deep in conversation with two partisans.

"That one's Michael Mechlis," Jakub told them. "He was a forest surveyor before the war. He knows this place better than any man here." He did not know the other man.

Soon after, Tuvia addressed the camp.

"We are moving deeper into the forest. We will be crossing difficult and muddy ground. We must keep absolutely silent and obey orders."

He said everyone must take with them all the food they could carry and that was it. They must not discard things as they went along, leaving a convenient trail for the enemy. Tuvia ordered all the animals to be set free.

Ilsa said, "Why can't they save the horses?"

The camp food store was opened, with the clear order that nothing should be eaten yet, as it might have to last them a long time. Everyone took as much bread, grains and pulses as they could and stuffed their pockets or any little bag they had. Daniel's pack was bulging with handfuls of dried peas, rye and mouldy turnips.

Jakub asked around and gave them more information. The man Mechlis and the other - a peddler called Shimonovitz who had travelled those paths extensively before the war - were leading the camp through a swamp to an island called *Krasnaya Gorka*. It was about ten kilometres from there. The plan rested on the assumption that the Germans would never follow into the swamps. Daniel hoped they were right. It was their best chance.

The camp was ordered into a line, fighters at back and front and along the column keeping watch. Tuvia had told them that once into the thick of the swamp, children would have to be carried on shoulders.

Jakub said, "I'll do it,"

"I want to ride on Daniel."

But they knew Jakub was right. He was much taller than Daniel.

"Fighters, keep your firearms dry at all costs," called Tuvia.

They began their march at 8 p.m. Mechlis led them, a cohort of fighters behind him, followed by those with children. Daniel walked near his family. Helena and Ilsa strode in dismal silence, as did everyone else. Some struggled more than others, especially the older ones. Within ten minutes, the ground descended into swamp, the gluey mud pulling off shoes and the water rising and falling from waist to ankles, leaving tide marks on their legs. They took off their shoes, finding it easier to wade barefoot. The going was tough and sticky and generally a bloody pain in the arse. Daniel wanted to sprout wings and fly out of the muck. But everyone persevered. Around eight hundred people were tramping through that shit and not saying a word; there was only the sound of the squelching feet and their freed cows mooing behind them, as if to say, what about us?

After an hour, they heard Germans. Everyone stopped and cowered, but the signal came to march onwards. They could hear bullets and even the sounds of Germans shouting for them. Around midnight, the eerie sound of a loudspeaker was heard echoing in Russian through the trees, repeated in Polish.

"All partisans lay down your weapons and surrender. You know you cannot win against our tanks and cannons."

Nobody said anything. They shambled onwards. They walked all night and as light woke the forest, their leaders found them a small area of dry ground and the camp dropped to their knees. Many slept, though they were ordered to wake up anyone snoring. Jakub and Daniel made sure Helena and Ilsa had a bit of ground to sleep on.

"What about you?" asked his mother.

He pointed to a tree nearby and said he'd be there. She smiled. How lovely, to see her smile in this wretched place. He leant against the tree, Jakub too. They noticed that once the camp was settled, Tuvia and Asael along with Mechlis had left the camp and gone off back the way they came.

"Checking on German movements?" he asked Jakub, who agreed.

No sleep for their leaders. He saw Jakub close his eyes, he did too. He actually fell asleep standing up. He didn't know you could really do that, like a horse, but he supposed when you're that tired, you could sleep on a spike if you had to.

Gunfire. A mortar shell burst in a tree. Everyone went mad, yelling and crying and praying for salvation. Tuvia and co appeared and insisted everyone move. As usual, his voice worked its magic and they were off. Soon they were surrounded by very tall grasses. This was pure luck, because it completely hid them from view. They could hear a plane circling overhead and even Germans shouting nearby, trying to organise themselves. But they weren't spotted. The camp staggered on. Some were saying they could go no further, but others urged them on. All day they walked and only stopped once night came. They sat on wet ground, but there was cover to protect them and dry patches here and there. Daniel climbed into a tree, and found a thick branch to sit on. Jakub joined him and they used his rope to tie themselves to the trunk. They didn't want to fall asleep and drown face down in the marsh. But they didn't sleep, they were too wired and watchful. They sat leaning against each other, watching their women. It was good to see them sleep.

Jakub whispered, "When you watch your own baby sleep, it's the same."

Daniel thought of Jakub's dead baby in a ditch. He thought of Magda, holding him in the orphanage. Magda, always there. Always the strong one. His real mother here, sleeping on the coarse ground. She was small. Like him. She was not like Magda. Helena relied on Daniel, as Magda never did. Helena was fragile, but not weak. She had kept herself and her daughter alive. But she was damaged now. Daniel loved his role as her protector. He missed Magda's solid presence in the world.

The next day, they reached the island. It was only about a hundred metres from where they camped the night before, so after a short walk they all rested again. People were calling it 'Paradise Island'. Land, glorious land. Life felt good, despite the fact that they were several hundred fugitive Jews crouched on a tiny hillock of land in the middle of a swamp being hunted by Germans. They could still hear them, shooting in the distance, shells nearby. Tuvia warned them to keep their silence, especially not to cry out. They sat and waited.

In two days, the camp ran out of food. Daniel found raspberry bushes and mushrooms, but not enough for eight hundred people. The weak were ailing. Helena and Ilsa were all right. Jakub and he had made sure they got any food they could find. He'd seen other people getting sick around him because they hadn't eaten. But he didn't give a damn about them. He was hoarding any bit of bread he found and passing it underhand to his girls. When he gave it to Helena, she pushed his hand away.

"You have it," she said.

But he wouldn't. He was stronger than her and he could prise her fingers open. They had the same hands.

Days stretched out. Daniel was bloody tired. It had been ten days since they started the march. Some looked like they were dying. He had seen that look before. Puffy eyes. Skin peeling off. The Germans continued to rage around them. They were destroying nearby villages and left no supply lines. He pitied the poor bastards in those places. Some were eating grass and drinking swampy water. They all had the shits. People were getting desperate. They were saying, "We'll die here."

He was not going to fucking die there. He'd come from fucking England across fucking Poland and been shot at and bombed and just found his mother and his sister and his uncle and he was not going to fucking die there, in that fucking swamp with that fucking pile of hopeless Jews. Not him or his family. Death could just fuck off.

One day, it went quiet. They thought the Germans had gone. Tuvia sent his brother Zus off with a bunch of fighters to get food and do a recce. The plan was, if they didn't hear from them in two days, they should assume it was safe to move on. They were to return to the Stankevich area, not far from Novogrodek. They hoped not to see Zus for two days, because if they did, he would only be bringing bad news.

Two sunrises, two sunsets. The decision was made. They were off.

They left the island in small groups of about twenty, each one led by an experienced partisan. Daniel's was headed by his uncle and they travelled with other families with children. Ilsa made new friends who talked a lot about ponies. All along the route they saw remnants of the enemy's advance, piles of spent cartridges and old German newspapers. It looked as if the Germans had just upped and left one day. The mood was not light. Were they walking back to peril? After all, they'd been told only weeks before that they must leave there because it was too dangerous to stay.

The villages they passed through were devastated. Haunted places. The Germans had swept through like a murderous fire, killing hundreds, capturing others for slave labour, burning animals alive in their barns. Some people had escaped and a few of these stragglers walked along beside them, swapping news of recent atrocities. Abandoned farm animals tagged along too, searching for sustenance. There was food to be found. There were fruit trees and even a beehive stocked with honey. They found a field of unpicked potatoes and took as many as they could carry. They came across deserted buildings with stores of grain and vegetables. But it was a hollow thing, to take food from empty houses, knowing the ghosts of the recent residents watched them silently as they rifled through cupboards.

The camp arrived at a spot near to where they'd settled before the retreat to Naliboki. Once in Jasinowo, they heard that some of their number had a worse time of it, with one group attacked by Russian fighters. Most of the local partisans were in total disarray and picking on Jews was an easy target. The Bielskis had sworn retaliation. Recently, Zus had shot a man dead who accused him of theft. The Bielskis might have been their protectors, but they were also their avenging angels.

Their orders were to stay there a short while and move back to the Naliboki and set up a more permanent residence. They reasoned that, despite the recent German operation, the Naliboki forest was still the best place thereabouts to hide. A dense tangle of woods, very good for getting lost. It was also rampant with partisan activity. The whole area was controlled by the Russians. Big-wig Russian partisan leaders had their HQs there. The Bielski camp could set up trade with the Russians, providing services they needed and enjoying a little of their protection, or at least their proximity in case of attack.

So that was the plan. They awaited the return of all camp members, who were still arriving in dribs and drabs, some bringing animals with them that had been found still wandering in the forest. Ilsa was thrilled to see horses. Once they were all together again, it would be back to Naliboki. Those of them already there had spread themselves out under the warm August skies, with a few tent-like shelters set up and campfires burning.

Whatever might happen next, Daniel was happy for now. He liked the forest life. He liked living with his fellow Jews. He liked the idea that one day, when all this had passed, they could become a community together. He didn't know where. There was talk of

Palestine. He'd even spoken to others about coming to London. Ilsa talked of little else.

"What's London like?" she would say. "Tell me everything!"

When he did, their mother watched them, a curious expression on her face, a frowning smile. They hadn't discussed what they would do after the war. It was too early. What they had was enough for now. Daniel, his mother, his uncle and his sister. A family.

Jakub woke Daniel.

"Come on. Time for your first *bambioshka.*"

It had snowed heavily for days. They went out in a group of five in a roomy cart led by a strong horse. Jakub was their leader, as the most experienced partisan. They were heading for a farm several hours away, where the Byelorussian farmer had a large family and always had plenty of supplies to feed his big brood. One of their group, Chaim, knew the farmer before the war.

"The Byelorussians hate the Jews," Chaim said on the way. "But this one had a Jewish mistress once and thought all Jewish girls must fuck as good as her! Since then, he loves the Jews!"

"Shut up," said Jakub. "This farmer might like a pretty Jewess, but a gang of Jews taking his food is a different matter."

Chaim tutted. "Everything will be fine."

The horse trudged slowly through the deep snow. It was November in the Naliboki forest; even wrapped in layers of wool and leather,

Daniel was freezing. And weary. The work these past three months had been hard and constant. At the end of August, Tuvia had gathered together the whole group in the Jasinowo forest.

"My friends. A new dictat has come from the Russians. They want our group of around eight hundred people to be divided into two sections. One for the fighting men, and the other for the unarmed men, women and children. I'm sure you'll agree, this would be very difficult for us, to split up our families in this way, as well as losing all our defence. So we have decided to directly disobey a Russian order and leave only a cohort of a hundred fighters, whilst the rest will go with the family group to provide protection and food missions."

Luckily, both Jakub and Daniel were chosen for the family group, due to his uncle's long experience in food missions, and Jakub's insistence that he needed Daniel to help him. Seven hundred returned to the Naliboki. By November, they began to make their camp. By now they were so far into the forest that they planned a semi-permanent encampment, with solid wooden dugouts meant to last the coming winter.

To begin with, fighters scouted the locale for tools and equipment. That first day, Jakub and Daniel took a horse and cart into a local village, all burned out from the Nazi whirlwind, and found four cartwheels, sacks of grain, a cow, a sewing machine and metalworker's tools. Other useful items had been found since, from window frames and stoves, boilers to baths. Who knows what happened to their original owners?

In the camp, they built sleeping quarters. The dugouts had their own camp name, a *ziemlanka,* a lovely word which came from the term for soil. They were built to last. Foundations lined with tree trunks were wired together and the spaces in between filled with moss and then covered with boards and earth. Most of the bunker was in the ground, with only a third of its height above. The top part was formed of sticks in the shape of a pyramid. The roof was camouflaged with tree bark and leafy branches. There was an entrance door with steps down. Once inside it was dark at first, but eyes soon accustomed to the pale light which came in from a small window and the door opposite. Inside there were wooden bunks covered with straw, and in the middle was an iron stove with a pipe to the ceiling, used for warmth and communal cooking. Daniel shared his dugout with his mother, uncle, sister and thirty other people. There were smaller *ziemlankas* for the higher echelons of the camp. There was a clear hierarchy. The Bielskis were the highest, of course, and had their own private bunkers for themselves and their wives. Next in order of importance were the friends and relations of the Bielskis, the fighters after that, skilled artisans beneath them, and the lowest, the unskilled, unarmed remainder.

As well as *ziemlankas,* they constructed huts to house workshops where goods would be produced and mended to serve the local partisans. If their camp was useful, the Russians might leave them alone, and not steal their men. The Bielskis had to play a careful game, pleasing the Russians and keeping the camp safe. There was a clinic where a doctor, a dentist and nurses attended to the camp's patients. To keep everyone clean and healthy there was a bathhouse, run like a sauna with hot stones and steam. They had a small farm area, where cows were kept for milk and the horses could graze. To feed themselves and produce food to sell to the partisans, they had a mill and a bakery. They even had a sausage factory. It was said a Russian partisan would travel a few miles out of his way to buy their sausages. Their workshops housed cobblers, tanners, carpenters, milliners, watchmakers, blacksmiths and tailors. Helena had started working as a seamstress in the tailors' workshop, using the sewing machine Jakub and Daniel had found. She mended clothes and made things from the cotton found in local villages, precious items such as underwear. Ilsa ran wild with the other kids, but there was talk of a school.

It was not so much a camp as a village, recreating in miniature what had been trampled all over Europe: a Jewish community. There was little sense that they were ready to move on at any moment. They had a central square with a Main Street down the centre, *ziemlankas* and workshops laid out on either side. At the top of Main Street was the square with HQ on one side and a communal kitchen at the end with a cauldron that cooked potato soup day and night. The HQ was where the Bielskis and other commanders ran operations. Orders and work schedules were posted on a billboard next to HQ every morning, and the camp mustered in the main square to hear news from the front and other reports. Main Street looked like any avenue in any ordinary town, with people going about their business or stopping for a chat. Like any street, girls made eyes at the lads, young fighters just back from a mission with their Russian hats or German badges, trophies of their exploits.

People were not simply existing there, as Jews had done in dwindling ghettos. They were living. They worked, they socialised, they had meetings, they cooked and ate together, they went on missions, they even had fun. It felt like a life. At the back of Daniel's mind, he knew there was danger. He knew it could all come to an end. But for the first time in years, it felt as if it were worth making something good, that may last a while, that would sustain them all. They even had a camp historian recording their experiences for posterity. This was not the act one might expect from an itinerant bunch of wanderers. They were there to stay. They might have been a rag-tag bunch of Jewish refugees, living in dugouts in the middle of a wild forest, but no village with a sauna and a sausage factory could be called uncivilised.

Once the camp was built, the fighters began training. Daniel and all the fighting men had been organised into companies and taught about key elements of partisan warfare. A lot of his experience in Warsaw had been relevant there, despite the fact they were hiding behind trees and bushes rather than walls and windows. He had also been trained in how to use a rifle, a weapon unfamiliar to him.

"It's a real man's weapon," said Jakub.

Daniel had to agree. He liked the feel of it, the weight of it in his hands, the length of it across his chest. He wouldn't tell this to Helena. She hated to see him with guns. He wanted her to be proud of him, as a brave fighter. But he supposed all she saw was her boy with a gun.

Fighters were also expected to do regular food runs, known as a *bambioshka*. He had been looking forward to it but he was nervous now. Neighbouring peasants had had enough of everything, the Germans and the partisans grabbing at them for what they could get. Daniel did not expect a welcome. But it would be good to provide food for their community, a noble cause.

When Daniel told Helena about the *bambioshka*, she said, "Don't go, Daniel. They can find other work for you here. Perhaps you could help the camp historian. He needs people to write for him and interview camp members. You were a journalist. That would be wonderful for you."

Uncle Jakub overheard and butted in: "Don't be stupid, Helena. The boy's a fighter, through and through. And what do you think would happen to him in camp if he gave up his gun and took up a pen? He'd be dog meat for the other lads. Let him alone."

"And what would happen to him on one of your food runs? He'll be dog meat for some vicious Byelorussian with a cleaver, or a trigger-happy policeman, or the Germans out on a spree. I haven't found my boy to lose him like this."

Jakub took her face in his hands and kissed her cheek.

"I will be there with him, every step."

"That is what frightens me most."

Daniel felt like a child, argued over by his parents. It was a pleasant feeling he hadn't felt for years. To be wanted, to be protected. But Jakub was right. He had to do it. He was constantly juggling his roles as fighter and family man. But this one he couldn't negotiate his way out of. His camp needed him, his experience, his weapon handling, his youth. He had to go. He wanted to go, didn't he?

Daniel sat up straight in the cart and rubbed his eyes. It was dark. Food missions were always done at night, for safety. They got down and circled the front of the farm house. Jakub knocked. They all had their rifles raised. The farmer opened the door.

"What do you lot want?" he said.

He didn't seem scared, just inconvenienced.

"You know what," said Chaim. "Food for your Jewish friends. Come on, old man."

Jakub silenced Chaim with a look. He spoke to the farmer.

"You know we are partisans based in this area. We work with the Russians to secure peace for all of us. We need your help to supply our men. Show us your stores. We'll be gone quickly."

"I don't have anything. The Germans have cleaned us out."

"Don't lie to us," said Jakub. "I can smell the cowshit from here."

"All right, we've three cows left, that's all. But nothing else. And if you take our cows, we'll have nothing left, no milk, no meat."

"I was going to leave you with one cow, but because you've lied I'll take all three of them."

The farmer didn't speak, just turned and disappeared back into the house. They all looked at each other. Daniel gripped his rifle. The farmer returned.

"This way," he said and walked past them towards a barn opposite the house. He was opening the door, when something moved in the snow nearby. All of them raised their weapons. A shape sped across the snow. Someone was running away, onto the forest path towards the nearest town. Jakub took aim.

"Josef!" cried the farmer.

The shape stopped for a moment. It was a tall, slim boy. He looked back at them, his left eye catching a gleam of moonlight. He turned and ran on down the path.

Jakub shouted, "Tell him to come back."

"Come back, Josef!" yelled the farmer.

But the boy ran on. Jakub fired and the boy dropped.

The farmer screamed. He ran to the prone figure of the boy. They all walked over to where they lay in the snow.

"My son, my son." The farmer cradled the boy in his arms.

"Is he dead?" said Chaim.

"You killed him, you killed him," wept the farmer.

"What the fuck was he doing, running away like that?" yelled Jakub. "Couldn't he see we weren't Germans? What the fuck did he run for? Stupid fucking boy."

The farmer held his son close and touched his cheek. As they stood there, it began to snow. Snowflakes fell softly on the father and son, turning their hair to pepper and salt.

"Come on," said Jakub.

They followed him back to the barn. In silence, they loaded up the cart with sacks of grain, flour and vegetables. They tethered the three cows to the cart. One of their lads went to the farm house kitchen and came back with ham, butter, cheese and bread.

"Quickly," said Jakub. "He might want revenge."

They left. As they trundled away as fast as the snow and the old cart could allow, Daniel looked back. They were still there, on the ground, in the snow. Chaim saw him looking.

"He might've been running to the town, to report us. It happens. They go into town and then the Germans or the Byelorussian police turn up and we'd all be fucked."

"Perhaps he was just scared," Daniel said.

Jakub turned round with fury.

"He was a stupid fucking kid, that's all!" he shouted in his face. "You'd do well to keep your ideas to yourself, my boy."

After a couple of hours travelling, the cart stopped and two of their number jumped down and untethered a cow. One pulled out a long knife and slit the animal's throat. The other cows stood watching. Daniel wasn't expecting it, and swallowed hard as he saw its black blood pour into the white snow. They set to butchering it. They were skilful and swift. Before long, the entire animal had been hacked up into pieces and distributed evenly amongst them in sacks. They set off again. Nobody talked.

They arrived at camp early. People were up and about, and keen to see what the latest *bambioshka* had brought them. Jakub walked off to HQ as soon as they got there. Chaim and the others took their meat to their grateful families. Some would store theirs in the snow, others would cook it immediately.

Daniel took his meat to Helena. She was working in the tailor's shop. It was a busy, noisy place, full of gossip and laughter. She was bent over a piece of sewing. Her hair was tucked behind her ears, with a lock fallen across her forehead. He watched her. He had tears in his eyes, he didn't know why. When she saw him, she dropped her sewing and went to him. There were a lot of others around. They looked up to see the young man with his rifle across his chest, holding a bloody sack. There was deference in their look, a slight hush in the hubbub of the workshop. To do with the rifle, not him.

"Everything all right?" said Helena, checking his face.

"Here," he said.

Helena took the bag and looked inside. Her face lit up. She wrapped it up again and glanced around. She'd learnt a long time ago to hide good food from prying eyes. But she was smiling.

"We will have a feast tonight!" she whispered to him.

A boy's life for his mother's smile. A bad bargain, but a bargain nonetheless.

CHAPTER FOURTEEN

Life goes on. The camp is flourishing now. We had a hard winter. February was the coldest in *puscha* memory. Bitter, sightless snow. People became ill. Typhus. Some said they should be killed. But a quarantine hut was built away from the camp instead. A man took them over there in a horse-drawn cart. They would stay in the hospital for twenty-one days. Only one died. I kept my children close to me. I boiled our clothes in a big pot, adding a lump of camp soap made from ashes and animal fat. I picked off the lice. I would hang our things out in the cold. The next morning, the white snow beneath would be spotted with yellow, the lice frozen to death.

The cold and the illness made people anxious. They were despondent and looked for others to blame. Always the newcomers or the lowly ones. They are called the *malbushim*, the ones without guns or professions. You can easily pick them out. You see them on Main Street, forever traipsing about, threadbare clothes and drawn faces, nowhere to go and no one to see. They do not get the same food as the others, they are always last in the queue for soup, once all the goodness has gone from the pot and there is only greasy water left. Look at one, he might have been a professor before the war. He doesn't want to mind the cows or chop wood. Now he has no job, no role to play and no place in our little world. He was Dr. So-and-So, now he is only a *malbush*. In every dugout, at least one is labelled as a *nebich*, a word coined for the lowest *malbush*, a hanger-on who contributes nothing. We have one. He used to sell big houses to rich people. Now he is nothing. The position of the *malbushim* has never been good, but add cold weather, and everything is their fault. The thaw has helped us all. The spring brings warm afternoons and wild flowers in the forest.

Ilsa is full of life. She never stops talking! She woke me this morning with, "Hello Mama. How are you today? We're going on a walk today with Miss Czesia. It's a special kind of walk called a field trip. We are going to look for different kinds of plants that grow in the forest today. Miss Czesia says we would be amazed at how many species of mushrooms there are in this forest alone. A species means a kind of something, Mama."

"I know what species means," I said and dragged myself off my bunk. I have to tell her, "Shut up, Ilsa," and she does not listen, she just steps over it and carries on. But it is marvellous to see my quiet girl talk at last. She has never had school days before. She is catching up on her lost years.

And she adores Daniel and Jakub, of course. She mentions London a lot.

"When we live in London after the war, Mama, we shall eat tea cakes and drink Bovril." I have no idea what she is talking about. But it worries me. I cannot think about the future. In the ghettos, death was an ill-tempered landlord, padding about the hallway, banging nails into walls. You waited for the knock on your door.

Here, death seems distant, a speck in the sky. If you watch, it could grow larger, falling at great speed to squash you like an ant. But it is still a speck, very far away. If you do not look at it, you can almost forget it is there. Now and again we hear a German plane overhead or rumours of German assaults. The Red Army marches onwards. There is good news from the front. Yet I know enough never to be complacent about death. Rest easy and death will track you. To think of the future seems to tempt bad fortune. But Ilsa does not understand this. Daniel fuels it. He says, "When the war's over, Mama..." we shall do this or that, we shall live here or there. He has been close to death, of course. He has lost those close to him. But he has not had his optimism beaten from him. He still looks ahead. I am a blind pessimist. I cannot see hope because I am too grateful just to see my children alive and hear my own heart beating.

Jakub talks of the future too. He and Daniel argue about Palestine. Daniel favours London. We should all go there, he tells us. He can make a fine life for us there. He has a place to live and enough money. As if that is all you need in life. But Jakub disagrees. He says we must find a home. Not just a place to live. Palestine is the only true home for Jews now, he says. Jakub spends his free time at the watchmaker's hut. It reminds him of Father, of course. But also, it has become a ferment of political discussion. Whenever you pass, you hear a strident male voice shouting, "But the Russians won't win, and there will be no place for Jews in Europe!" or "Palestine is just a silly dream. It'll never work!" Daniel doesn't know what to think. "The place for Jews is Palestine," Jakub lectures Daniel. "And you are a Jew, my boy." My son is a Jew, yes. He lives with Jews, he fights for them. But he grew up in a different life. I see his confusion. My heart aches for him, as I see myself in his displacement. He had a life in London, then his father told him the truth and Daniel lost that life. He came to Warsaw and was let down by the Poles and their betrayals, then the Jews and their in-fighting. Now he cleaves to us, his family. And already Jakub's wild nature has disappointed Daniel, I can see that. He loves his uncle, but I think he is a little scared of him too. He loves Ilsa, but she is just a child and he tires of her at times, though he would never let her know it. As for me, I gave him a horrible truth to learn. I asked him once, "Have you forgiven me?" He was angry and said there was nothing to forgive. But I see his sad eyes. I know them well. They are the same as mine. They carry the knowledge of his past, as mine do. He cannot hide this from me. So many disappointments. I wonder if he will ever be happy. Jakub too. I think it is dangerous to look for a home. I believe we carry our homes with us, not on our backs like snails, but in our memories. Home is not a place. Home is an idea. A dangerous idea.

People here believe they have found their home. I do think that there are some who will be disappointed when the war is over! Not least Tuvia Bielski. What kind of life could live up to his life here? Here he is a kind of God to these people. Deservedly so, of course. The women love him. He has had girls. I hear them bragging about him to each other. But if the Russians liberate us, if the Germans go and we are truly free, what place is there for Tuvia Bielski? He will not be anyone's God any longer. Just a man with a horse and a gun. There are others like that. This upside-down society we have here, with working class boys lying with upper class girls, girls who would not have wasted a glance on a boy whose father was a pedlar five years ago, before the war, before this camp life. Now, most girls vie for a fighter with a gun, whatever his name or his background. It makes them feel safe. You can understand that. He is their ticket through the war. If the Germans attack, the boy with the gun by your side will not leave you or your friends. There is a name here for such a boyfriend –

they call him a *tavo* – it is a Hebrew word meaning 'come here'. That says it all. Boys with guns rule. A girl who has a *tavo* becomes his property but also acquires his powerful status. It is a deal. No money changes hands. Some girls care about their *tavo*. Others choose carefully and reject dozens before admitting a *tavo* to their bed. Some couples seem to truly love each other. But they are all deals, even so.

As for me, I am tired of all that. I am not old. Not too bad to look at. Daniel tells me I am beautiful, but he is my son. I do get the look from several men a day. One night, a man in our *ziemlanka* tried to climb into my bed, Ilsa beside me by the wall. I pushed him away yet he persevered. The next moment, the man was yanked backwards and I saw Daniel spin him round and punch him in the face so hard he landed back on his own bunk in one flat fall. The sleepers barely stirred. Daniel knelt beside me and whispered, "All right, Mama?" I nodded and touched his still clenched fist and he winced.

"Your hand," I said.

"It's fine," he replied, smiled and hopped back on his bunk.

In the morning, the man woke up with a bloody mess for a nose. Nothing was said. Daniel and I have not spoken of it, but every night now I see his eyes glitter in the dim light as I fall asleep. He watches over me, my son.

I have had no night visitors since. They do not bother me. None of that for me now. It is all folly. Besides, most of the men you see here are of a certain type. Being an outdoors man who is strong and brave are the most sought after qualities here. Men like this resent anyone capable of higher thought. If they hear a man speaking Hebrew, they say, "Don't talk like that. This is Russian territory," as if they really give a damn about the Russians. It is all pretence, all part of their new role as little partisan gods. A woman said to me the other day, "The war has cured me of all men." I felt like that long ago. The war has only amplified it.

I work hard here. I get blisters between my fingers. The nurse prescribed wheel grease smeared on thickly. It stinks but it works. We have numerous clients. The camp rule is that all services should be free of charge to camp residents. Russian partisans must pay in a useful way, with medicine, food or weapons. Thus the natural law of things dictates our trade. If someone who has paid with good food is waiting, they get served quickly. Russian parachute drops have brought us silk and we make high quality shirts and underwear for those who pay. The *malbush* who needs a new pair of coarse linen pants will not be first in line. We are not the only ones. I see the girls on Main Street showing off their new pairs of fur boots, bartered for them by their partisan boyfriends. Shoes are a priceless commodity. Many come to the camp with no shoes, and the forest's wet mud eats through leather. The shoemakers' hut constantly has a long queue of hopefuls outside it, and the cobblers always do the orders from partisans first, as they pay with food. Such is camp life. All life, I fear. Sometimes, a Bielski brother will intervene on behalf of a shirtless fellow and we all duck our eyes. And we feel ashamed.

But generally, we are happy here in our workshop. It is a lively place that reminds me of the backyard conferences we would have in the early ghetto days, before the heel of it ground us into the dirt. Here it is comfortable, useful and most importantly, it is for ourselves. The tailors are a rum crew, sitting around a long table with their scissors and needles and cotton, singing away old

Yiddish songs, telling dirty jokes, all mingled with the racket of our sewing machines, gossip and laughter.

It is new to me, to hear gaiety. There can be a heady atmosphere in the camp, where everyone seems to be laughing, horses galloping past you, men cursing and women singing. Like a fantastic circus in the forest. It can make you laugh along. But it can make you want to lie down on your bunk and weep. I cannot explain why. For the Purim holiday, the children and their teachers prepared a show, put on in the large workshop. Ilsa took part and sang a Yiddish song. I helped her learn the words. Every child was dressed in crisp white shirts and smart red ties. They looked adorable, reciting poems in Russian and doing little capers. But in the middle of one dance, a partisan from the audience stood up and cried out: "Where are my children? Revenge! Revenge!" He took out his gun and shot into the air. We all jumped at the sound of gunfire. But no one said a word. The man left, crying bitterly. Everybody sat for a long time. People got up in ones and twos and the hut emptied. I thought Ilsa might ask me about it, but she did not. She understood.

That night, we gathered around the stove in our *ziemlanka,* as we always do. But there were no songs and stories as usual. We just stared into the shimmering flames. I put Ilsa to bed and went for a walk alone around the camp. As I passed the tannery, I saw the devout Jews engaged in their evening prayers. The tannery has become a kind of makeshift synagogue. There are only a few in there. Few in the camp take religion too seriously. I listened to their voices rise and fall, rise and fall, calling their God. The night I thought Ilsa would die, I spat in the face of my God. But my daughter was saved. I live in freedom, a happy productive life, surrounded by my lost family. Who else but God could manufacture this miracle? I think I hear His voice in every chattering sound of this Little Jerusalem of the forest, I see His handiwork in every smiling Jew around me. I doubted Him. I hated Him. But I see that the enemy brought us to our dark days and we have flouted that enemy and live in our defiance. Perhaps God had nothing to do with it, the good or the bad. I do not know how I feel about my God.

I have lived a number of lives in this war. A wife, a widow. A seamstress for the Germans, a seamstress for the Jews. A mother to my daughter, a mother to my son. Now, I am free. I can come and go as I please. I do not have to stay here. And that makes it all the more sweet. In the first ghetto, in the second ghetto, I stumbled into deeper and deeper pits, trying to protect Ilsa, trying to stay alive. I could stumble no longer. I lay down to die. But angels carried me from that place. They brought me here. And here I live again, a free woman. My son and my brother are free men, my daughter skips through life like the child she is.

One of the lads is teaching her to ride a horse. A few girls and boys go out to the field every day where the horses graze. There are dozens of horses there now. Ilsa is in horse heaven. Sometimes I take a quick break from work and watch her. I see Ilsa laugh as she rides a pony bareback across a field swaying with long grass, under blue sky and spring sunshine. I see she is the happiest she has ever been in her life. When she is older, she will look back on those moments with a fierce nostalgia. I feel on the margin of it, that I was not the one who made this perfect memory for her. I feel her best memory should have been with me on a beach building castles or beside a brook catching fish in jam jars. It should have been a magical place I chose, that I took her to. Not this place. Not this war. The war has stolen her childhood from me. But I see it is no matter. It is selfish to wish to change one note of it. She sees this *puscha* village as a great adventure, the best holiday beyond anything her city-shuttered mind could imagine. And I remember how it was in the ghettos and how lucky we are to be alive and to be here, in this storybook forest.

Yes, the Germans may come yet. We may die here. But I do not believe it. Rather, I believe all of this is too good to die. It cannot be destroyed, it will not. Ridiculous, I know. But this beauty cannot fade. It is too clear and green and perfect. If the Russians come tomorrow and liberate us all from the German threat, I am half tempted to take my family and go live in that field where Ilsa rides her horse. It is my little paradise. I am afraid to live anywhere else in the world.

CHAPTER FIFTEEN

"Run as fast as you can."

"But Mama, Mama!"

"I'll find Mama."

Daniel quickly scanned the area and couldn't see the enemy. The shooting started again, so he ran with Ilsa up Main Street and pushed her off in the direction of the horse field. She looked back at him.

"Run!" he yelled and she did.

He rushed back to the dugout and grabbed his rifle. At the moment he came out, he saw a German run past their neighbour's hut and throw in a grenade. He hit the ground and the explosion rattled his bones. He could see the German about to do the same to another dugout. Daniel jumped up, took aim and shot at him. He caught his leg and the German fell, cursing. Daniel ran closer and took aim again, this time at the chest. Dead.

People were bursting out of dugouts and running into the forest, screaming. He went to Helena's workshop and found she had gone with the others. He looked about in a mist of panic, searching the backs of women running away from the camp, but she was none of them. More Germans came into the camp and he shot at them. He hid behind a dugout and took aim whenever he could. He saw some of their number run into the Germans' posse by mistake and get shot down. People he knew. A combat group of Russian partisans appeared on the scene and started shooting in all directions. Within minutes, all the attackers were dead.

Once the shooting stopped, he ran to the horse field and called Ilsa's name. She popped up out of the long grass and beamed at him.

"Where's Mama?" she called, bouncing across the field.

"I don't know. Did you see her run?"

"No, did you?"

"No."

They looked at each other. He felt sick. They went back to the camp and he said to Ilsa, "Don't look at the people over there. They're dead. I don't want you to see them."

"I've seen lots of dead people. They're not scary."

He remembered the ghettos.

"Don't look at them anyway, eh? For me."

He told her to go back to their dugout, but found it had been demolished by a grenade. They walked around the camp asking people, "Have you seen Helena?" An hour passed. Graves were being dug for their fallen at the top of the hill near the camp. Ilsa and he sat at the entrance to their burnt-out dugout and waited.

Helena came limping down Main Street. They ran to her.

"Where have you been?" he raised his voice to her. "What happened to your leg?"

Ilsa threw her arms round her Mama.

"I twisted my ankle running away. Such a fool."

They heard shouting. A woman was saying, "The Russians! The Russians are coming!"

A group of their fighters rode into the camp and everyone gathered round, calling out, what about the Russians? Where are they? Are they here? Are we free?

"The Red Army is only a few miles away!" one fighter said. "They'll be here by this afternoon."

A cheer went up and people turned to each other. Helena looked at Daniel very intensely, then Ilsa. People were laughing and clapping and hugging. Helena just stood there, very serious.

"Did you hear, Mama? The Red Army is close by."

"Not close enough," she said. "We could have been killed this morning. Me, Ilsa, you. You, my son. I could have lost you."

She was shaking. He put his hand on her arm.

"It's all right, Mother. We're all here. We're all safe. Jakub will be back soon, I'm sure. We're so close now, Mother. Don't lose hope. By tea time, we'll be free."

But Helena turned and put her hands over her eyes. Without a word, she hobbled away towards their dugout.

"Mama?" called Ilsa and went to run, but he stopped her.

"She just needs a bit of time on her own."

"But why? The Reds are coming!"

Ilsa was very excited, jumping about on the spot, doing a little victory dance. He took her hands and danced around with her, singing a silly tune. It was good to dance, to have something worth dancing for. But he was worried about Helena.

The Red Army had been approaching for weeks. At night they had heard the muffled pounding of distant battle. Russian partisans had galloped past the camp, yelling with laughter in their hunt for the retreating enemy. Daniel once saw a couple of Germans running through the forest, all mucky and sweaty and terrified. They knew their time had come. The other week, three captured

SS men were brought to the camp. When word got out, a frenzied crowd of hundreds shoved up Main Street to HQ. Tuvia made a speech. He assured them that the Germans would be judged and receive their just punishment.

"Do not disturb us in our work," he said.

But the crowd was blood hungry and wanted revenge. An SS man was led from HQ and the crowd ploughed forward. An old man found himself at the front, the oldest man in the camp, called Pupko. He shouted and rushed forward with a knife. They watched him stab that German to death. The other two were shot. It made Daniel wonder what they were all capable of, confronted by their enemy, weak and pathetic. How the mighty army had fallen, they all said. Captured Germans were pitiful creatures. They always insisted they were never a member of the Nazi party. It was the first thing they said. As if a Jew cared. Politics wasn't the issue. Any German was fair game. It was all about homeland now.

All the fighters had been desperate to get stuck in. Instead of food runs, everyone wanted to go on German runs. People came back from days out hunting Germans with gleeful expressions and tales of derring-do. Those stuck in camp for whatever reason were grumpy and itching to get out there and bag themselves a Nazi. Jakub had been going almost every day. He came back with blood on his hands, literally.

"You must come, Daniel. It's the manly thing to do."

He did talk rot. Daniel had stayed in the camp with Helena and Ilsa. It was tempting to go out and shoot those bastards. But he would not risk a thing now they were so near the end.

. . .

That afternoon, they held a short funeral on the hill for their recently fallen. Eleven camp members had been killed. Tuvia gave a eulogy.

Helena didn't come.

"I've seen too many dead."

Relatives were crying. It was horrible, to see them come so far, to lose their loved ones at the last minute. All the fighters had their guns and at Tuvia's signal, they let off a salvo as a farewell gesture. The shots rang out in the still forest air and they stood listening.

A voice shouted from the camp, "They're here!"

Daniel looked down and saw a straggly bunch of Russian soldiers walking down Main Street. People were flocking down the hill to see them. He took Ilsa's hand and rushed down, almost tripping over in their hurry. The soldiers were surrounded in seconds. They were filthy and sweaty and marvellous. They were having their hands shaken off. He managed to push through the crowd and held Ilsa up to have her Red Army handshake.

One of the soldiers was saying, "Jewish fighters. I can't believe it. Look at them."

He was shaking his head and smoking. He passed out cigarettes, whilst a fighter gave the soldiers *samogonka* in return. They stood with them for a few minutes, but soon said they had to move on.

Before they went, their commanding officer said, "The whole area has been liberated by the Red Army. You are free."

Embraces and kisses. Cheers and whoops. Some walked away with gloomy faces. Ilsa was running around with the other kids. Daniel left her and went to find Helena. She wasn't in the workshop or their ruined *ziemlanka*. He wandered round the camp. He was looking for her, but he was also saying goodbye to the camp. He went into every hut, stopped groups of people, walked up

Main Street, went to the bakery, the blacksmith, the bathhouse. The hospital, the kitchen, the mill. The soap factory, the tannery, the clinic. The stable, the school and the sausage factory. Even the slaughterhouse and the prison. He saluted every fighter he saw. He even visited the cows and sheep and saluted them too.

In the end, the last place he thought to look, he found her. She was in the horse field. She was sitting in the long grass, resting on her hands behind her, her legs outstretched. Her face was turned up to the late afternoon sun. Her eyes were closed. She looked very young. He sat down beside her. She did not move or open her eyes. He could hear her breathing, slow and regular.

"Mama, what are you thinking?"

It took her a while to answer. "I am sorry it is over." Her eyes were still closed. She hadn't moved.

"The war? You mean the war?"

"Everything. All this. I am sad."

"But we're free. We survived. We beat the Germans. We can do whatever we want now. We can live again."

She still didn't open her eyes. But tears seeped over her cheeks.

"What is it, Mama? Please tell me."

She turned to him. She had desolate eyes.

"Here, in this camp, we had a place. We lived in peace. We had food and drink, work and company, even love. But it was all...a mirage. The moment the Russians came, the dream was over. It is over and now the hardest part begins."

Her hands curved over her face, hid it from him. He put his arm around her shoulders. She leant into him and sobbed. He held her while she wept it all out. When she was quiet, he pulled away.

"I came a long way for you, Mama. I need you to be happy."

"Oh, Daniel. I am happy, with you. With Ilsa. And Jakub. I am grateful and thankful and not worthy of any of it. I am the luckiest Jew alive. But I am still a Jew. We all are."

They sat for a while. He looked at the sky, the trees, the horses grazing thoughtlessly.

He had rescued her from death. He had found her body, taken it to safety, tended it, nurtured it to health. She was alive. But within her, something had died long before he had reached her, before the ghetto, before the war even, back on that Warsaw doorstep, where he was too small to help her.

"Come on, Mama. Let's get you some soup. Lean on me."

That night, few slept. People drifted around the camp. Tuvia made a quick speech. The camp would be packed up tomorrow and they would all make the journey on foot to Novogrodek. He ordered everyone to rest. But nobody could. The men were drinking *samogonka* like water, including the Bielskis. Helena was resting, Ilsa beside her. Daniel found them a bunk in another dugout. He was to sleep under the stars, if he slept at all.

The next morning, the camp was packed up. They were ordered to take only what they could carry. They were not allowed to remove anything that belonged to the camp. Some questioned this, but Daniel heard one man say, "Do you want to go back to your town as a fighter or a looter?" A group of partisans were ordered to stay behind and destroy everything, wreck the dugouts, fill in the wells and bury anything left. This order came from Russian command.

Daniel went with his family. Jakub was in triumphant mood, but Helena was despondent. Her foot was a bit better, but she still limped so it was slow progress. Ilsa had ceaseless energy and pranced around between the travellers, singing 'London Bridge is Falling Down' over and over. People looked at her curiously as she skipped by, singing in English. She was an oddity, he supposed. But a lovely one. As for him, he didn't know what to think. He understood his mother's sadness. He could see it in other faces. Tuvia's final speech that morning summed it up. He reminded them all how they had suffered. He told them it was up to them, the survivors, to inform the world of what had happened there, what had been done to the Jews.

"We will bear witness," he said.

There was nothing uplifting about it. Only a duty they all bore. No triumph, no victory. Just a struggle to stay alive. But he wanted to tell Helena that it was good enough, it was a conquest of the murderers, that they were there, that they didn't just disappear like the enemy wanted. They had lived to see the Germans' downfall. On the journey, they passed by the rotting corpses of German soldiers. He didn't feel anything. Like Ilsa, like Helena, like all of them, he had seen a lot of dead bodies.

Days of walking. They passed through villages. People came out of their houses and huts.

"Look, Jews!"

"So many Jews!"

"They're ghosts!"

None of them would give them food. Not even a drink of water. Would anyone be happy to see surviving Jews? It wouldn't be like that in London. A more civilised place than those backwoods, surely.

By the evening, they arrived near Novogrodek.

Novogrodek, people were saying.

"Novogrodek, Novogrodek. My home town."

"I never thought I would see it again."

Helena said nothing. As they approached the outskirts, people were pointing and shaking their heads and crying.

"What is it?" he asked Helena.

They were walking past smoking ruins of houses.

"It was the old Jewish settlements," she said. "There's nothing left."

She told him that people had expected to find their old houses still standing, pristine as the day they'd left them. He supposed it was naïve, but that was what people had dreamed. Now many were finding their houses did not exist, like their families, their old lives. Vanished forever, like every rainbow. Those who had houses in town were still hopeful they might find them the next day. That night they rested in barns on a farm near the town. Daniel looked at his family. Ilsa and Helena slept. Jakub was very quiet. The long walk, the grisly sights, the unfriendly natives – it was all taking its toll on his uncle. Even his boundless enthusiasm was waning. Many around were murmuring, not about the future, but everything they had lost.

On the morning of July 16th, 1944, they all gathered in the farmyard where Tuvia made a speech. He told them all that their regiment was disbanded and they could go wherever they liked. Word was that he was directly disobeying Russian command, as their orders were to send his partisans to the Red Army for their own use. But they had done enough. When Tuvia had finished, he wandered away with his family and friends, talking quietly about their plans. The crowd drifted apart and people began to gather their things and move off. There was a kind of dishevelled exhaustion about it all. Nothing final, nothing you could say 'this is where it ended, here, now.'

Jakub suggested they go into town and find his house and their parents' house. See if they were still there and still standing. It could be a place to stay for a day or two, until they decided what to do next. Helena agreed and they walked into Novogrodek.

All the way, Ilsa was saying, "When are we going to London? When are we going to London?"

Nobody would answer her. Much of the town was derelict. Both Jakub's and their parents' houses had been burnt out. They were vacant shells with not one item left inside the walls. Helena walked through the rooms of her childhood home in silence. Jakub walked through his own home weeping.

"Not a button, not one button to say my wife ever lived here, to say she ever lived at all. I don't even have a photo of her. Nothing. All gone."

Daniel tried to hold Jakub as he crouched on the floor, his tears falling in the grey dust. But he pushed him away. Daniel took Ilsa for a wander down the street. They saw that some Jewish houses were still standing, and recognised people from the camp at the doorstep of one. There were Christians living there, standing in the doorway with their hands on the door jamb, as if to say, this is mine now.

One man said, "We thought you'd never come back."

Later, they all went with other survivors to the place outside of town where Daniel's grandparents, aunt and cousin were murdered. There was a vast expanse of common graves. Thousands were buried there. Of course, there was no way of telling where their loved ones were. Just a plain of victims. Some graves had been half dug up and he could see bones sticking out of the ground. Ghoulish locals digging for valuables. Survivors were weeping and saying prayers. Jakub dropped to his knees and said a prayer for the dead, the same Pawel had spoken for their four dead fighters that ghetto night last year. A woman fell to the ground in a faint. Daniel held Ilsa close. She did not really understand what was happening, she did not know any of these people, but she knew it was wrong, all wrong. She buried her face in his shirt and held on tight. Helena just stood there, arms folded. Her face like stone. Daniel watched her. She did not shed one tear. She looked from Jakub, to the mourners, to the desecrated graves, to the trees, to the sky. She turned and looked straight at Daniel. She did not say one word. But her face said everything.

"Look," it said. "You see now?"

That night they went to a guest house, an old friend of Jakub's, one of the few gentiles pleased to see a Jew. Earlier that evening, Jakub went to a final Bielski gathering outside town, where he received documents for all of them, certifying the war work they had done as partisans. Daniel did not go. Ilsa had begged him to stay with her. That place frightened her, he thought. Since they arrived at Novogrodek, there had been no skipping, no singing. It was as if a black pall of smoke hung over the town, thick with the ashes of the Jews. Helena had not said a word since the graves.

Over a simple meal of bread and cheese, they ate in silence.

Ilsa said, "Are we going to London tomorrow?"

Nobody answered.

Eventually Jakub said, "It's a dangerous time for us now. The Russian authorities are clamping down on partisans. They want to conscript all ex-partisans and send them to the front. We have to get away from here and fast. Tomorrow."

Daniel said, "London, then. We must go to London. We must get to a British embassy. We need to get newspapers, ask around, find out where has been liberated. Maybe north, to Lithuania. We could get to the Baltic from there. Perhaps a boat to Sweden."

Jakub shook his head violently. "No, no, no! We must go south.

That's where the Jews are going. South, through Hungary and Yugoslavia. Down to the Mediterranean and from there a boat to Palestine. That's the only way."

They argued for a while.

Ilsa saying, "London, London!" and Jakub telling her to shush.

Helena said nothing.

Daniel said, "I have a home in London, friends, contacts. I have money to keep us. There is no question it's the best place to go. If you're unsure, think of it as a staging post, somewhere to rest up for a while as we decide what to do next. Nothing is final. But we'll be welcomed there and we'll be safe. What else could you need?"

"A home!" yelled Jakub, his ears turning bright red in his anger. "England is not my home. Palestine is the only home for the Jews. Helena, say something, will you? Tell the boy he's wrong. Say something, Helena!"

Ilsa had started to cry. Daniel gave her a cuddle. Helena was sitting with her back to them, staring out of the window. They waited for her to speak.

She began quietly, her voice strengthening as she went on. "What life is there for us? What place for us in the world? We are free, yes. We are free. But where do we go? They hate us here. Europe hates us. We were supposed to die, all of us. A German told me once. That was the plan. And who tried to stop them? No one. Because the Germans were doing their dirty work. Europe heaved a sigh of relief. It had been cured of the Jewish disease. But no. There are still some of us left. Some of us have been impudent enough to survive. Wherever we go in Europe - even your beloved London, Daniel - we would be a curiosity at first, then a burden, then a thing to be hated, a thing to be got rid of. So, where do we go? To Palestine, Jakub? A land from ancient history, already populated by people who hate us more than anyone. Don't you see? There is no place for us in the world. We have to face the truth. For Jews, there is no home."

They sat in a room in a guest house in Novogrodek, eastern Poland. That was what it was called that day. Who knew tomorrow? The Russians were back in Poland.

Daniel had his family around him. Ilsa lay beside him, curled up in a ball like a kitten, as he perched on a rickety camp bed. She should have slept with her mother, but she refused. She wanted to sleep down there with Daniel. Helena and Jakub were asleep in a large double bed by the wall. They lay on their sides, facing in opposite directions.

Daniel gazed into the gentle light from the oil lamp on a table next to his bed. He knew he should turn it off and try to sleep, but he was wide awake with worry and did not want to lie in the dark. When he was a boy, he was afraid of the dark and had bad nightmares. He couldn't remember what they were about, but he would wake up screaming. Magda would come in but Dad would send her back to bed.

"What are you afraid of?" Dad would say.

"I don't know."

"Whenever you're scared, imagine the world in twenty years' time. You'll be a man. The world will be very different. Whatever you're worried about tonight will be long gone."

It used to work. The future looked shiny and bright, made of metal and glass and clean, long lines stretching into the distance. That night, it did not work. The future was clouds of black smoke billowing across a road. He walked along it with his family. They could feel the heat of the fire nearby, but they didn't know where it was burning. They caught a glimpse of the way ahead, but only through a muddy fog. If they went back or if they went forward, they might walk into the fire. Where should they go?

He was twenty-one years of age, yet he felt much older. Beside him, Ilsa stirred, opened her eyes, looked up at her brother and smiled.

"Daniel?"

"Yes, dear?"

"Mama has been so brave, hasn't she? All these years of the war."

"Yes, she has."

"When I was little, I had a doll that broke. Its face cracked all over. Mama feels like that now, doesn't she? Cracked all over?"

Daniel squeezed his sister's hand. So wise, so young.

"Yes, that's about right."

"But we can mend her, can't we?"

"I should think so," said Daniel. "Now shush and go to sleep, little one."

Ilsa snuggled down, satisfied, and closed her eyes as her brother stroked her hair. Helena turned in restless sleep across the room. Jakub began to snore loudly.

Outside, a child walked by, one of those poor orphans left wandering at the close of every war. The child glanced at the window where inside were Jakub and Helena and Ilsa and Daniel, saw the warm glow of the oil lamp make a golden square in the darkness. The child stared at it a while and yearned for it. Then someone inside turned down the lamp and the light was gone. The child trudged away, into the night, alone.

AUTHOR'S NOTE

The subject matter of this novel covers important events in history and through extensive research I've tried to render my characters' experiences in a realistic way. My research involved visiting the Reading Room of the Imperial War Museum and looking at a range of original documents from the time, as well as reading and making notes from over a hundred texts, from books to documentaries and movies, and visiting locations such as Tavistock Square. The main characters are fictional yet the details of their war are based on true events, such as the Warsaw Ghetto Revolt, the work of the Polish Underground, the Jewish village in the forest to even the pubs of literary London and so on. The details of such plot elements as Daniel's secret voyage from England to occupied Poland, the treatment of the ghetto escapees in Warsaw, the daily events of the Revolt, the swamp retreat of the Bielski villagers – all of these and more are based on accounts by participants of this war, as well as a wide variety of secondary sources. Some real people also appear in the story, such as Mordechai Anielewicz and the Bielski brothers; though many of the key events they were involved in are rendered with as much accuracy as my fiction allowed, their personalities and encounters with fictional characters are of my own invention. In writing about such an important historical topic as the Holocaust, I felt strongly that I needed to do justice to the truths of that time, yet also to avoid exploiting its horrors. That has been my aim and I leave that to readers to judge. Above all, I have striven to write an engaging story that tells of a time that must never be forgotten.

A NOTE ON THE TEXT

An editorial decision was made to use Polish names and words without their accompanying diacritics, such as accents and overdots.

This was done in order to enable a simpler reading experience.

ACKNOWLEDGMENTS

Sumaira Wilson, Nikki East and Zoé-Lee O'Farrell of SpellBound – for your vision, belief, support and brilliance in taking on this story and bringing it to readers. Eternally grateful to know you and so excited to be working with you.

Laura Macdougall and Olivia Davies of United Agents – to Laura, for a superb edit, as well as keeping the faith in this story; to Olivia for expert guidance and support always.

Early readers of this novel, from kind friends and family, to excellent professionals such as Jane Conway-Gordon, this novel has been shaped by many generous readers and I'm very grateful for their input.

Bookbloggers, reviewers, booksellers and friends on social media – particularly Facebook, Instagram and Twitter – for their continued support of my writing, as Rebecca Mascull and as Mollie Walton.

Writer friends – who have sustained me with their advice, support and kindness, especially those who take time out of their busy schedules to read my work and listen to my ramblings.

Lastly, to Poppy and to Clem and even to Tink – for all the happiness you bring.

ABOUT THE AUTHOR

Rebecca Mascull is an author of historical fiction. She also writes saga novels as Mollie Walton. *The Seamstress of Warsaw* is her eighth published work of fiction. Rebecca has worked in education, has a Masters in Writing and lives by the sea in the east of England. She is also a Fellow of the Royal Literary Fund, based at the University of Lincoln.

https://rebeccamascull.co.uk/
https://molliewalton.co.uk/

Printed in Great Britain
by Amazon

76970413R00229